HIGH PRAISE FOR SUSAN SQUIRES!

BODY ELECTRIC

"*Body Electric* is such an intriguing read that I'm still thinking about it. This is the sort of book that niggles its way inside your head and stays—so few books are as thought-provoking as this one."

—*All About Romance*

"Susan Squires has a fascinating, unique voice; is a rare talent. An absolute must-read."
—*New York Times* bestselling author Christine Feehan

"Squires's deft plotting and full-bodied characters make this whirlwind adventure worthwhile."
—*Publishers Weekly*

DANELAW

Susan Squires has an "epic style and unforgettable characters."

—Shelley Mosley

"A rousing adventure tale full of the details of life and war in the dark struggle between the Saxons and the Danes... her books are impressive in their uniqueness."
—*All About Romance*

THEY MEET

He didn't try to run. He stepped forward and took Holland by her shoulders. Silence fell inside her mind. The roar was gone. His single voice echoed in her head. *"Voices—they hear voices! I've got to find them!"* His mouth moved in sync with the words. It was a soft mouth, with a full bottom lip. His teeth were even and white. His eyes held hers. Pain. They held pain and surprise, for some reason. She could feel the warmth of his body coursing through his hands. He clutched her upper arms hard enough to leave bruises. His plaid shirt was torn over his shoulder and stiff with some dark stain. He was examining her eyes, her face, as though his life depended on it. The sound in her head seemed to have drained out through her neck and shoulders and down her arms and out into him. She couldn't even hear the crowd around her, though she realized they must be shouting. The crowd didn't matter. She was mesmerized by his eyes. Even as she looked, they cleared. His pain drained away. He examined her, shocked.

"You know, don't you?" he said, and she heard it more clearly than she had ever heard anything, inside her head and out.

No More Lies
SUSAN SQUIRES

LOVE SPELL NEW YORK CITY

LOVE SPELL®

October 2003

Published by

Dorchester Publishing Co., Inc.
200 Madison Avenue
New York, NY 10016

ISBN 0-505-52566-6

The name "Love Spell" and its logo are trademarks of Dorchester Publishing Co., Inc.

Printed in the United States of America.

Visit us on the web at www.dorchesterpub.com.

No More Lies

Chapter One

It always started with her hand, before it got the rest of her. Holland Banks could sense the dream unfolding yet again, though she could not stop it. She could never stop it. Sweat broke out over her body, soaking the thin cotton of her baby-blue sleep shirt. She opened her eyes on darkness, as she always did. Her hand lay on the white of the sheets beside her pillow. That was part of the dream. So was the feeling of evil that swirled in the room. The dim outlines of the mission oak furniture in her bedroom wavered at the edges of her vision. The ribs of the headboard and the backs of her rockers cast the shadows of a prison on the walls. The slats of the plantation shutters—meant to keep out the Los Angeles lights—weren't doing their job. Thin channels of moonlight cut across the darkness to create the shadows. Even in the canyon you couldn't escape the glow of the city. Star jasmine in the boxes along the balcony drenched the night with a scent that seemed too rich for L.A. So familiar . . . so alien. Just like her hand.

It lay on the white sheets beside her pillow, consuming her field of vision. The long tapered fingers curled softly, nails made shiny even in the dark by clear polish. The hand had a young woman's skin, smooth, the ropes of veins still softened by flesh not yet collapsed around them. The hand lay there, quiescent, somehow distant. Yet she could feel the evil pulsing in the darkness, the stench of it

1

mingling with the smell of sweat and star jasmine and the fabric softener her laundry used. The hand was alien, not human at all. What would it not do? Murder? Sabotage? Betray her, her people, her world?

As always, the panic rose in her as she realized that the evil was attached to her. How could she escape the monster when it was part of her body? The hand was about to do something terrible. What to do? Her breath came in ragged gasps. Could it kill her? Best she chop it off before it tried. With what? Chinese cleaver . . . in the kitchen? It *would* try to stop her. She sat up. The comforter duvet covered in white embroidered cotton slid to the side. Her hand, that foreign lump of evil attached to her arm, was dragged across her lap. Somewhere a cat yowled.

As though the movement wakened it, the hand sent tendrils of evil up her arm. She was too late! She clutched at the merciless wrist with her left hand, stumbling to her feet. The hand stretched its fingers wide, seeking. It wanted to touch something, something she was afraid of, and if it found what it wanted to touch, the world would be forever changed. Malevolence flowed around her elbow, searching for her heart, her brain. Fear beat at her mind. When the evil engulfed her, she would no longer be able to control what she did. Power surged inside her. It made her feel strong, whole.

She pushed herself erect, thrusting down the siren call of power. She *had* to fight it. Somewhere, someone was whimpering. She staggered toward the bedroom door. The pulsing red beat pushed up to drown her heart, her lungs. She gasped, fighting for air. A scream formed in her throat and was stifled there. Her eyes bulged. She sank to her knees. The evil roiled up her carotid artery into her brain. All that was left of Holland Banks was about to be lost and she knew that kernel of evil had always been inside her, waiting for this moment, and that the kernel wasn't human. *She* wasn't human. She never had been.

*　　*　　*

2

Holland's own shriek woke her up. She was crouched in a corner, hugging her bare knees. Her gaze darted around the darkened room, cut by channels of moonlight. Nothing. No evil—just the slats of her grandmother's mission rocker, the pristine white of the tumbled bedding, the shadowy bulk of the armoire. Her pulse beat in her ears. She sucked in the damp night air from the open window, heavy with the scent of star jasmine. Then the shaking began.

It's just the dream, she told herself, hugging her knees even tighter to stop the shaking. *You've been having it since college. Can't you get used to it?* But now it happened almost every night. And the emotion wasn't getting easier, though she often realized it was a dream even as she dreamed it. No, her nightmare was getting worse.

She listened. But all she heard was the blood humming in her ears. Tinnitus, John had called the condition when she was reduced to consulting him. The constant noise was getting on her nerves. Great. Tinnitus. Yet another thing wrong with her. John even said it often sounded like whispering. God, she couldn't believe she'd been desperate enough to tell him about the whispering. Somehow she hadn't liked to tell Dr. Grayson, old family friend that he was, at her routine check for the levels of allergen suppressant in her blood. It was easier to ask John at the hospital, maybe because he wasn't a friend of her father's. John's eyes had gone curious for a moment. No cure for it. He'd offered her Xanax and said that sometimes helped suppress the noise. But she was not yet reduced to using sedatives. The only other choice was just to get used to it. Tune it out. John might well use her weakness against her, doctor/patient confidence be damned. Why hadn't she gone to some doctor who didn't work at her own hospital? She was being stupid, and someone like her could never afford to be stupid.

She pushed the damp blonde hair out of her face. *Control yourself,* she admonished. *Your Imposter Syndrome is getting out of hand.* Everyone feels like they're in over their head once in a while. Lots of people feel like they don't deserve their position or that someone will find out they're not as smart as they're cracked up to be. People didn't think they were evil, though, or not human. That was carrying her issue to extremes.

It was hell to be a psychiatrist. Diagnosing yourself and everyone around you came a bit too easily. Holland managed a weak smile and a shake of her head as the trembling subsided. To center herself, she repeated her achievements like a mantra. Her lungs expanded and she let the air out slowly. Phi Beta Kappa, summa cum laude from Yale, premed. Second in her class in med school though she should have been first—would have been if she'd been male. Stremski's research was not nearly as original as her own project. Prestigious funded internship at the Neuro-Psychiatric Institute at UCLA. The groundbreaking studies on schizophrenia. They still called it the Banks Remission phenomenon. Rising through the ranks at several hospitals until now she was Director of Medical Services at Century Psychiatric Hospital, the most prominent private treatment and research center west of the Rockies—hell, west of the Mississippi. Head of the Schizophrenia Research Foundation. Not bad for thirty-four.

That's what the dream was about, just Imposter Syndrome. She wasn't evil. She was just an overachiever who worried that someday someone would find out that she had to work harder than anybody else to get where she was and stay there. Someday, hard work wouldn't be enough to get by, but that day was not yet. Holland suppressed the psychiatrist part which whispered that the whole thing had gone beyond a mild neurosis and that she was bordering on something she wouldn't like the name of.

She even knew the root of the problem. She had a lunch date with him tomorrow, well, today. The clock on the cak antique ice chest serving as a night table glowed three A.M.

That must be why the dream had been so virulent. Lunch with her father was always difficult.

She sighed and pushed herself up the wall. When she was sure her knees were not too wobbly to hold her, she staggered to the walk-in closet and pulled a caftan in white embroidered on white over her head. There would be no more sleep tonight. Might as well read that stack of journals sitting on the library table by the door.

In the hospital employee parking lot, Holland glanced in the rearview mirror of her Mercedes 450 at the same time as she swung into the space marked DR. BANKS. She'd chosen her spot in the corner of the flat lot rather than one in the garage because no one could park next to her. With ice plant growing on one side and the vent from the hospital's heating unit on the other, her car was not subject to the vicissitudes of careless drivers opening car doors. She'd trade isolation for a covered space any day. Besides, it was L.A. How often did it rain?

When the car had jerked to a halt, she turned off the key but left the radio running as she pulled down the visor and flipped up the vanity mirror cover. Not good news. The roar in her ears seemed worse this morning. The noise was taking its toll. She looked as though she hadn't slept. True enough, but it was the last way she wanted to look at work. The radio blared on about the latest sniper attacks. How many of these guys were there? Simultaneous events in Seattle and L.A. last night. Another four weeks of this and the whole country would be psychotic.

She took a compact out of her Dooney and Burke briefcase and layered some self-powdered foundation over cheekbones that seemed a little sharp. Not much to do about the shadows under her eyes. The blue of her irises arrested her for a moment. Patients found them unnerving. One had described them as clear turquoise, like the bottom of a swimming pool. Not comforting, on the whole. You drowned in swimming pools. An older woman had

5

said she looked as though she couldn't lie. Holland gave an almost inaudible snort. Yeah, wasn't that what Imposter Syndrome was all about—the feeling that you were living a lie? For that matter, what was psychiatry but relative truth? Not much difference between that and lying. Her father would no doubt tell her there was *no* difference at lunch today. He knew all about truth. She patted a pale strand of hair back into her chignon and adjusted a hairpin. Sleek. Professional. That was how she wanted to look.

For a moment the voices of her med school colleagues darted through her mind like random shots of a gun, just enough to wound, not to kill. She had come up behind a group of the guys one day as they talked about some woman they called a frigid ice princess. They'd laughed, right up until one of them noticed her. Their faces had frozen in horror. It was only their expressions that told Holland they were talking about her. Her surprise was closely followed by shame. The flush that filled her had turned to anger. She'd simply turned and walked away. She had never spoken to any of them again, in spite of several mumbled apologies. Didn't they know what control it took to be truly excellent at what she did, what sacrifice? Didn't they understand what price she paid to be the best of any of them?

She stared in the little mirror, examining the flawless lips, "Plum Mist" filled in for moist perfection; the big eyes, lined with subtle pencil, their naturally thick lashes enhanced with mascara; wispy fringe of bang to soften her face. Pearl earrings, the big and expensive Tahitian variety, lent their iridescent gray echo to the strand of their fellows around her neck. The gray linen dress with white piping would look crisp under her white lab coat. Professional, brittle . . . even, almost, true. That was the way psychiatrists had to look. They had to at least pretend that what they did was scientific.

She cut off the radio's hysteria with another flick of the key and slid out of her little sports car. The news these

6

days seemed calculated to fuel hysteria. Her five-foot-six turned to five-eight in her metallic gray Ferragamo pumps. She slung her briefcase strap over her shoulder, then turned back to lock the car. The susurrations in her ears got suddenly louder. It was almost like words she couldn't quite hear. She glanced around as though they had a source.

That was when she saw him. He stood on the sidewalk some five feet above the parking lot about fifty feet away, up toward Third Street. Ice plant, recently watered, covered the slope to the sidewalk. He was looking at her, she was sure of it. His hair was light brown and long. It almost touched his shoulders in the back, and brushed his chin even at the sides. It hadn't been cut in a long time—just allowed to grow. As she watched, he pushed his fingers through his hair to get it out of his face. He looked as though he hadn't thought to shave for several days. He wore a plaid shirt she would bet was flannel, even in the heat of the L.A. summer. The sleeves were rolled up on his forearms. His jeans weren't tight, but they showed his form. He was bulky through the shoulders, maybe barrel-chested, and his thighs were thick with muscle.

He was definitely staring at her. The rush of sound in her ears whined up the scale until it was almost painful. *Help me.* What? What was that? Her own thoughts given voice? Or real words in her head, hidden in the tinnitus? She shook her head but the words were gone, leaving only the roar. As she realized she had been staring back at the stranger, Holland looked away, guilty. She jerked herself around toward the back entrance to the hospital and stalked away. The sounds flooding her ears faded. But the image of the man would not be banished. Hadn't she seen him before? Her thoughts skittered over recent activities. Where? Hanging around the hospital? Or . . . was it at the gym yesterday?

God! Panic washed through her. It *had* been at the gym. He'd been walking in as she walked out. He had turned around to look at her. Jesus! He was a stalker. She picked up her pace. Where were the security guys when she needed them? She practically lunged for the door, but before she could reach it, it swung out, and a pair of huge orderlies coming off the night shift almost ran her down. They were laughing. The door banged into the wall.

"Sorry, Dr. Banks," one stuttered. "Didn't mean to nearly kill you there."

Holland laughed. Damn! It sounded just this side of panic-stricken. She took a breath and hauled her expression into what she hoped was normal range. "No problem, gentlemen. I'm just glad to see you two." Their presence gave her enough courage to turn and glance back across the parking lot. It was empty of people. An SUV pulled in at the far gate. No plaid shirt, no jeans, no long hair. The stalker had vanished. Relieved, Holland stepped through the door one massive orderly held open, refusing to meet his eyes. She didn't want to know if he was looking at her strangely.

As she stepped into the world of gleaming linoleum and pastel walls, the smell of the hospital calmed her. The vague odor of sickness—disinfectant, floor wax, starch, urine, vomit, food that all smelled the same—wafted over her. This was an environment where she knew what was expected of her. She was master of it, in spite of the dreams, in spite of the noise in her ears, in spite of the guy outside. She straightened her shoulders and clicked down the hall to the elevators. She put her professionalism on like a flak jacket. Nurses murmured greetings. Orderlies nodded as they wheeled cold breakfasts to patients in the unlocked rooms. Holland managed to return the greetings with a smile and felt herself come back into focus.

That guy wasn't stalking her. She couldn't even be sure it was the same one from the gym. Two plaid shirts—that's all she'd seen. What were the odds that the guy would be wearing the same shirt two days in a row? These dreams were making her nervous. That and the tinnitus. John hadn't been able to explain what caused it in her case. She hadn't had any blows to the head or ear infections. Weren't medical conditions supposed to be more clearcut than psychiatric ones? Maybe she just needed rest. She could prescribe herself some Ambien to help her sleep, but that was an addictive slippery slope. Dependency was not in her nature. The answer was work. She knew how to work. She pushed through the door into her office suite on the sixth floor. Time to put on the persona. Time for shrink-speak.

"Good morning, Chloe." She put her briefcase on her desk in the inner office and slipped into her lab coat.

Chloe handed her a stack of charts. "Rounds in ten minutes, Doctor."

Holland nodded. "This afternoon, I'd like to review the grant. Did Rhenquist complete the drug therapy section?"

"Turned it in last night," Chloe said. She grinned. "Just-in-time homework for that guy." The woman's lank white-blond hair and long dangly earrings were complimented by heavy black makeup around her eyes and, depending upon what she was wearing, glimpses of several tattoos from ankle bracelets to flowers over her shoulders to scroll-work at the small of her back. No one could understand why Holland put up with her. They didn't recognize the strident efficiency that balanced Chloe's mental scales. She was ruthless in her pursuit of Holland's ends, if Holland stated them clearly. What more could an over-achieving boss ask?

Holland smiled, glad for Chloe's calm assurance. "Just in time is preferable to the alternative." She clutched the stack of charts to her chest and took the porcupine set of keys from her belt. "I'll return by eleven. Let's do a calendar check."

"Patient appointments at nine-thirty," Chloe recited. "Forty-five minutes with Smith, observation with Jenkins, team consult on Raley before lunch."

Holland turned toward the door, opening a chart to glance at the case before rounds.

"Dr. Ferenghetti needs ten minutes this afternoon." Chloe dropped the bomb casually.

Holland rolled her eyes. "That man is tedious. And the subject of the meeting?"

"I'm guessing it's complaint time about the doctors' complimentary lunch buffet."

"Very well. Fit him in. And get me a copy of the menu for the next week from food service. Forewarned is forearmed." She started for the door, mumbling, "For this I went to college?" Then she realized that Chloe could hear. Not good.

"No, for this you make the big bucks. Don't expect sympathy, Doctor Banks."

Holland realized she'd let her professional demeanor slip. She smiled self-consciously as she pushed out the door of Administration. In some ways she was most herself with Chloe. That could be dangerous. She unlocked the ward door and let herself in with half-attention as she looked at the charts. Three new schizophrenics today. She glanced up to see Rhenquist hovering. "Who's first up, Rich?" she asked, still looking at the charts.

Rich Rhenquist was young and ambitious—reason enough not to trust him. He fancied himself charming. His dark good looks had always opened doors. Holland liked showing him the limitations of those credentials. He was competent. She couldn't fault him there. But in his first weeks on staff he had tried to charm her. Never try to charm Holland Banks.

"Uh, Lozano. Family checked him in yesterday. Dropped out of school last winter. Ended on the streets. Police remanded him to family custody. Now hearing voices, inattentive, personal hygiene lapses. Family insists there's no history of drug use. Precipitating event was violent act against his married sister. Scared him as much as it scared them. He checked in voluntarily." Rhenquist continued with the results of the mental-status exam.

"You've got him on Abliflu?" Holland interrupted.

"Ziprasidone. Ten milligrams every six hours."

Holland glanced up from the chart. "Forty a day? That's a fairly heavy dosage, Rich."

"It took two orderlies to subdue him."

"You said he was voluntary." Her voice was sharp. You needed a court order unless the patient admitted himself voluntarily. Breaking the rules could cost a hospital its license.

Rich backpedaled. "He was fine when he got here. He had bad dreams last night."

That she could understand. Holland glanced through the small door window that was crosshatched with metal threads. A young man sat slumped on the bed in a plaid flannel robe, staring at his hands. Plaid flannel trembled through her mind. "I'm not sure Ziprasidone would be my first choice. Too many complications."

"I got a medical history from the family." Rhenquist made it clear he was the expert on medication. "No heart problems, no other drugs. And it gives immediate results. You don't usually need Ativan to keep them calm." He drove home the final spike. "Trials up to 100 milligrams have been successful."

Holland acquiesced. "Treatment plan?"

Rich detailed his program of therapy. The drugs had made the patient docile. Was that good? What price had he paid for this calm depression in lieu of his mania? This poor soul was incarcerated because he was hearing voices. She shifted attention to the roaring in her own ears. There were no whispers of voices. But there had been. At least she thought there had been, even though she couldn't make out any words. Suddenly she longed to know exactly what that young man heard. She wanted to dart into his mind and hear what he heard and then dart safely out again.

"What do you think, Doctor?" Rhenquist was saying.

11

Holland took a breath. "Acceptable treatment plan. Keep me abreast of the results."

"Are you ready?" Her father's gruff voice came from the outer office. The door swung open, possibly from the sheer force of his personality, and he strode forward to lean both hands on her desk.

She braced herself and looked up over her charts. "Hello, Dad." It seemed so inadequate a response. But she was used to that. What could she possibly say to match her father's larger-than-life persona? His thick shock of silver-gray hair was brushed back from a high forehead with a straight hairline. His face was as bold and blunt as he was. Cheekbones poked out of flesh that had begun to sag subtly. But the stabbing gray of his eyes changed color constantly from threatening storm-cloud dark to the silver that sparkled off a steel sea in early afternoon. Someday his flesh would betray him, but never his eyes. He used the force of life that lurked there to bludgeon competitors and those who would be barriers to his goals, or those who were less intelligent than he was. That included just about everybody. The damnedest thing was Holland was pretty sure he loved her.

His suit must have cost a couple thousand. It hung off lean shoulders squared to face the world on his tall frame. How many research scientists felt the need to dress well? How many could afford to? But Leland Banks was not your average research scientist. He was more like a one-man industry. Holland reached to finger her pearls, uncomfortable. Did she get her need to project an impeccable image from her father? Why did she feel the need to wonder how much of her father had insinuated itself through genes or experience into her psyche? Maybe because knowing exactly what part genes played had become his life's obsession. Lips that habitually curved down in disapproval lifted almost imperceptibly. "Can the nuthouse spare you today?"

"Yes. The hospital can spare me." She pushed herself up from her desk and shed her lab coat. "Where are you taking me? I warn you, I'm feeling expensive."

"Matsuhisa expensive enough for you? I feel like fish." He held out an arm to open the door, careful not to touch her. He was protective without ever getting close physically.

"We'll never get in," she protested.

"I booked the private bar. Nobu is in town. He'll make us sushi personally."

"You booked the whole private bar? Well, that's expensive."

Her father caught up to her with his long strides. "Always the best for my daughter."

Chapter Two

He slowed the tan Caravan some seventy or eighty yards away from the car pulling into the parking lot ahead of him. Glancing around, he swung into a parallel spot on the street. This would do, do just fine. Fire glowed in his belly, banked against flare-ups now, but ready to go. Man on a mission, he was, certain. Ready, ready, ready to rock and roll. There she was, that cool-assed chick everyone was so fixed on. What did the old guy do to deserve such a fine-looking woman? They strolled around to the front door of the joint. Must be dough that let wrinkled old butts like that get the lookers. The science guy could dress though. Shoes? That dude knew shoes.

13

They knocked on the door. He fingered the smooth wood on the stock sitting on the seat beside him. He didn't dare lose sight of her to look at it, but he knew the fine grain, the warm caramel color of it without looking. He touched the cool smoothness of the long barrel, the fat scope sitting above it. The spider legs that braced it were folded now against the stock. It made him feel glad his skill could be useful to humanity. He mattered. He was gonna save the world, and make another hundred K in the process. The door opened and the cool-assed chick and the science dude disappeared inside. He cracked the window against the city heat and settled down to wait. The other guy was bound to show up if she was here. That guy followed her everywhere.

Sitting alone at the blond wood bar in the stark interior of Matsuhisa was intimate. Lights behind stiff paper panels of the shoji cast a soft glow over the eight-seat private sushi bar. It was cut off from the rest of the busy restaurant, an oasis of calm. The traffic of La Cienega and the heat of the L.A. summer were muted by the traditional Japanese music plunking through the sound system in asymmetrical assonance. For Holland the calm was lost in the cascading sound in her ears. She wriggled uneasily onto the high chair in the center of the bar. Her thinking felt muddied. That would never do when she was talking to her father.

In the tiny preparation area behind the bar, they watched the super-sushi chef wield his glinting knife with a sureness that must have been born in him. The fish seemed to part ahead of the blade, as though at the mere threat of that steel made sharp by skill and stone. The chef did not speak, and for a long while, neither did they, content to watch the show of gleaming fish and glistening red-orange salmon egg soaked in sake, green shiso leaf and the rich peach color of sea urchin. They were lulled by the creamy texture of hamachi in their mouths and the sour, clean taste of the plum paste. Each of Nobu's elegant creations was unique and beautiful. They did not order.

He created an experience they were meant to appreciate as an audience appreciates performance art. Her father drank sake, a tart cold blend that was costing him about thirty dollars for every small square box that nestled in crushed ice, and stole surreptitious glances at his daughter. Holland drank a Diet Coke. She couldn't help but feel that he was . . . melancholy somehow, or upset, neither of which she associated for an instant with her father.

Nobu-san created the rhythm of the meal as well. The first presentations came quickly, but as the meal waned and Holland and her father began to talk, the famous proprietor appeared behind the little bar only periodically to check on them and deliver one more of his ever more esoteric gifts.

"You're looking a little haggard," her father noted. "Did you keep your appointment with Dr. Grayson yesterday?"

"I'm fine, Dad." Her father was the last person she would tell about the tinnitus or the dreams.

"Grayson mentioned that he was a little concerned. Why don't you let him do a full workup on you, maybe an MRI?"

"Does Grayson know anything about the regulations on patient privacy?" she asked, annoyed. The disadvantage of going to a friend of her father's was only too apparent.

"I'm just worried about you, Holly. The allergen suppressant in your blood is what's keeping you alive at this point. I just want to know you're taking care of yourself."

Holland remembered back to that horrible time when she'd gotten so sick just after she got home from college. In spite of the treatment, she'd got progressively worse until she couldn't keep anything down, couldn't drink anything. She'd ended in intensive care over at Cedars, and been so sick she couldn't remember a lot of what happened. She'd given both her parents a good scare. She had to give her father credit for never leaving her side. It was her mother who'd come and gone, since she was ill herself during that time. Holland's father had been her primary attendant, and her primary support. "I gave Grayson the blood sample, Dad. He would have called if there'd been anything wrong. I take my Presentone every day. I'm doing my part. Lord, if I gave him any more blood samples, I'd begin to think he was a vampire." Her small attempt at humor fell flat, as it always did. Her father did not seem to feel that she or their relationship, or his work, or much of anything was fodder for levity.

"Are you coming tomorrow?" her father asked, as he dipped his toro sushi upside down into his tiny shallow dish of soy and wasabi. His chopsticks seemed like attenuated fingers, part of him, and not part.

Holland watched his skill, fascinated. "Coming to what?" Had she forgotten some engagement? She looked around, distracted by the sound clanking around inside her head.

"I told you. We're hosting an event to coincide with the publication of the article next week. Press will be there. You might get to talk about your precious foundation."

Her father understood publicity, and how to get it, better than anyone. That was one way he had reconciled himself to his humble beginnings. He normally just acted as though his past wasn't there. But he found it useful when it created a from-deprived-childhood-to-intellectual-king angle for his own Genomere Foundation. "I don't think so, Dad. I don't do well in groups." The truth was, she didn't want to see the Banks publicity machine at work.

Leland Banks snorted through his sake. "You're better than just about anyone I know, except me. Your grant-manufacturing plant hums along supporting the research of your little theories. I'm giving you an opportunity to get some column inches."

Holland sipped her Diet Coke without looking at him. This conflict was inevitable. "You like the father-daughter connection angle. You think it will get you a sidebar story."

He shrugged beside her. "They'd be your column inches, too."

Holland turned the conversation. "What's the announcement?"

Her father sat back in the small-backed stool and glanced sideways at her. She knew that look. He wanted a reaction from her. "If you cared enough about me to let me talk about my work, you'd know."

Holland sighed and picked at her gari, the delicate orange-pink of the pickled ginger almost transparent on her chopsticks. "If we didn't always get into a vitriolic comparison of the relative scientific rigor of your brand of science and mine, maybe I'd have the courage to talk about your work more often."

Her father humphed. "You don't lack courage, Holly. You've got enough courage to argue with me."

As if that were the height of foolhardy nerve. "Okay, Dad. What is it? What's the announcement?" The noise in her head made her even more irritable with her father than usual.

Her father's lanky frame stilled beside her. He didn't respond for a moment. She glanced over to see him staring at the little wooden platform they gave you to showcase the sushi presentation, empty at the moment, except for the pile of pink gari and the tiny grass-green heap of wasabi paste. He took a breath and his head jerked up. He smiled a crooked smile. "I've discovered a way to extend the human genome."

"What?" The human genome had been mapped for years. There could be no "extensions." "What are you talking about?"

"Extension . . . maybe a better word would be enhancement." He only seemed to muse. He was really watching for her reaction.

Holland took a breath. She hated this part. The part where he got theatrical. "I'm not the press, Dad. Just give it to me straight."

He lifted his brows in disapproval, but his tone got way less introspective and mystic. He shrugged. "We were working on something else. It always starts that way. You know about viral vectors?"

"Yes." Don't be patronizing, she thought. "They deliver new sequences to the DNA strand to correct some defect—like the gene that causes cystic fibrosis." *Take that*. "You hang the new gene sequence on the virus and infect the patient."

"But," he corrected, "the key is that in the past each virus had to be designed especially to deliver one gene sequence. I developed a vector that could express *any* gene sequence."

"That sounds profitable. You sell it to everybody, no matter what disease they're working on."

"Let's just say we weren't having trouble getting money."

"Isn't Herzog working on something like that?"

She knew she was in trouble when she saw her father's face flush.

"Herzog? That construction worker? Not an original bone in his body. I'm surprised the *Journal* let him publish that tripe." The sneer in her father's voice was unattractive.

Holland knew firsthand how competitive her father was. She should have known better than to bring up Herzog. "Granted. So you'll be revealing him for the plebian he is."

"Without doubt. *JAMA* was so impressed with my work they had to take the article even though that pedant Jackson had the gall to say that conclusions were premature."

"A delivery mechanism isn't an extension of the genome, Dad."

He shot her a withering look, but at that moment Nobusan came out from the rear, and her father clenched his teeth around his words while the master chef made them yama-imo mentai sumaki. He stacked three of the inch-long cylinders of rice, mountain potato and spicy fish roe encircled with crisp seaweed on each tiny wooden platform-plate, bowed briefly and disappeared. Holland did not take a roll. Neither did her dad.

"Herzog has expressed a single corrective gene sequence for several conditions with a single vector. I, on the other hand, can extend the genome with totally new sequences." He shook his head slowly, as if still in wonder at himself.

"This does not tell me anything. Are you going to explain this to some lowly psychiatrist, or are you just humiliating me for effect?" Holland hated how plaintive she sounded.

Her father waved his hand impatiently. "I can attach junk DNA to the human genome."

Holland frowned. "Junk DNA? What's that? Genetic garbage of some kind?"

"In a way. We all have DNA material inside our cells that isn't attached to the double helix that makes us who we are. It consists of fairly random genetic sequences that float in limbo. The scientific community always thought it was inert in a way—not functional. Now we know better."

"I never heard of this stuff." Holland felt suddenly insecure. No, she felt how much of her father's work she didn't understand. Same thing, really.

"Who in scientific circles talks much about the things we can't explain? We tend to leave the mysteries to the cable channels for elucidation. Companies have been busy taking patents on designer drugs meant to coerce some specific gene into doing what they want. There was so much to do, we just ignored the DNA left over."

"Why not just create new sections from parts already attached to the double helix? Why does it have to be this 'junk DNA'?"

"Ahhh, that's the wonderful part. We can replace a defective gene on the strand. We can insert genes from other species. But we've never been able to create whole new sections before. They just wouldn't attach. The strand always rejected them."

"So, it's like an immune system that won't accept new material, but will bond with material it recognizes, like the body's own junk DNA?"

Her father smiled kindly. "Something like that."

How that smile grated! Holland took a breath. Still, this could be big. Something in her father's posture told her it *was* big. "Are you talking about creating mutations?"

"Absolutely. But you'll never hear me call it that. I prefer 'anomaly.' If they thought we were mutating humans, the public would start building bomb shelters in their backyards and shooting 'mutants' in the streets." He smiled at something, then shook it off. "We create a kind of mutation every time we adjust a patient's gene to cure some disease. That is, a planned individual mutation affecting only the person targeted. Only if the change was expressed in the germic strands—the sexual chromosomes, could it be passed from one generation to another. That's a mutation of the species—strictly against any geneticist's rules, of course." Her father's expression was grave. He stared around the sushi bar as though he wasn't really there at all, but somewhere more puzzling.

Holland's mind raced. "So you just took some junk DNA and . . . and welded it on the string?"

"No. It was more elegant than that. We found a couple of subjects during our research who had already attached junk DNA—always the same sequence, by the way. It's a naturally occurring phenomenon but apparently not very widespread. We just took the junk DNA string from one of our 'natural' subjects, sat it on our virus carrier, and delivered it into a volunteer."

"So you've got a genetic mutation that occurs naturally, if infrequently, and you can duplicate it. What's the point? What does this string do?"

He turned to look at her as though he were memorizing her face. "That's the premature part. We're not ready to say for certain."

What he meant was, he didn't know. He always hated to admit that. "So what's your guess?" She regretted the words as soon as they were out.

"Guess?" He sat back. His shoulders were ramrod straight. "You might 'guess' in your particular brand of pseudoscience, but I deal in proven facts and truth. That

20

is the scientific way." He pushed away from the bar a little bit.

"Oh, you deal in facts, do you?" She wished she could help rising to the bait. "Seems to me your version of 'truth' is just that—a version. A version, by the way, that has to be revised every time someone discovers something that contradicts it.' "

"Our truth may not yet be complete, but we're on a true path." Her father's voice was steely, as if he had forged it into a sword to do battle. "Not like your relativistic dribble about there being many paths, each 'equally valid'." He said it as though her philosophy were a curse.

How many times had they had this argument? Now that he was revved up, he wouldn't stop. "You could be great, Holly. You could have been the best. It's all your mother's fault you went into this touchy-feely crap where you spend your time trying to talk society's misfits into feeling better about themselves. If you had more of me in you . . ." He bit back his words and she thought he was going to calm down about the whole thing, but it was not to be. "The very fact that you could *say* something like that to me is a sign of—"

Holly turned toward him and interrupted. "Dad! You know I'm not going to sit here and take this shit. That's part of our deal. We don't say these things or we don't talk." She had used the word 'shit' about five times in her entire life. It got his attention.

She saw him bite back the rest of his speech. His lips compressed into a frown. Resentment and anger burned in his gray eyes. She hadn't spoken to him for six months last year after one conversation spiraled into hurtful shouting from which neither would back down. He had tried to contact her a couple of times. But her anger would not be soothed no matter how many shrink-speeches she gave herself. If her mother hadn't gotten sick again, they might never have spoken. As it was, it was only when her mother's cancer went into remission that Holland was convinced life was too precious to waste in recrimination. Holland had called her dad.

He knew the rules now. Holland had modified his behavior by hanging up on him every time the conversation took those destructive turns of criticism or accusation. She wondered why he kept calling. It might have been her mother's influence. She grimaced to herself. Or he might have delusions that he could convert her to a true believer in the church of pure science. Worse, it might have been some need to remain connected to his only child. She could walk out of the restaurant right now. She would, if he didn't desist. But he was her father, with all the Gordian knots of connections and feelings that entailed. She turned back to the bar and picked up the delicate pink and green and white roll, swished it in the wasabi-soy mixture, and popped it in her mouth. She concentrated on the feeling of crunch in the starchy potato, the ocean taste of the spicy fish roe, and the crisp crackle of the seaweed in her mouth.

Damn him! "Okay. You have a working hypothesis?" Her voice was a monotone. Maybe "hypothesis" would sound better than "guess." Let him hit the ball if he would: it was in his court. A cylinder of sumaki was plucked from his platform by chopsticks and lifted out of her range of vision.

"The subjects show increased brain activity. The DNA addition might cause some change in the chemical balance of the brain. We're working on that. It takes a few weeks to take hold after the initial injection. Now we need to know what the string does. It probably enhances some existing capability." He cleared his throat. She got the uncomfortable feeling he was leaving out something important. "There are some problems with the subjects, however. Our ability to test them further is compromised. And we have to find new subjects." He let the words hang in the air.

Holland saw it all. Changes in chemical balance of the brain . . . problems with the subjects that made study difficult . . . "And these 'problems' with the subjects—these would be psychiatric in nature?" She watched his expression acknowledge that. "They're loons, aren't they?" she asked, amazed at his audacity. This whole lunch thing was a plot to embroil her in his research. "The ones you've found—or the ones you've made as well?" *Loons.* Not professional. She liked to think it wasn't just a lapse, that she'd said the word to annoy her father.

His nod was terse. "Both."

She had to laugh. What else could she do? It was just another way to control her—to make her more like him, less disappointing. "And so, you were thinking maybe we could link up and figure out what the scientific explanation is for the fact that they have become 'social misfits' who need to feel better about themselves before their families will allow them to undergo further experimentation? Maybe?" She pushed herself away from the bar and got up.

"Yes," he said quietly. "But it's a little more urgent than that. Two that had it naturally are dead. One suicide, one shot by the police in Seattle. She was holding some guy hostage with a scissors to his carotid. But it's much the same. She left a note saying she was going to make the police shoot her. The subjects who had the DNA expressed by my viral vector are showing signs of stress. At least they're not dead yet. We have to find out why this is happening, and what to do about it."

"Oh, well, that makes me feel much better." She paused a moment, outrage building. "So you're going to announce this discovery even when the results are horrible. How are you going to conceal what's happened to your subjects?"

He laughed, but not with his eyes. "That's the easy part. Patient confidentiality forbids disclosure of the names. The formula for the viral vector is verifiable. We have their DNA available for examination. It will clearly show the strings attached to their genome. We say the study of the effect is still in process, which is true. Nothing easier, Holly. And Herzog will be crapping in his pants."

"Well, that's really the point now, isn't it? You inserted this stuff into volunteers when you didn't even know what it did, just to prove you could do it and Herzog couldn't. I'd love to see the research subject release form those poor suckers signed. Where'd you find people that stupid? Prisons? Skid row?" Holland could hardly contain her outrage.

"No. From my lab. They're friends and colleagues who knew how important this is."

She saw him accept the responsibility for that. But somehow he still thought it was okay. "What could possibly justify this?" She answered herself. "Nothing." Her stomach turned over. She'd always known her father had a narcissistic personality disorder. He was a classic—haughty, arrogant, sensitive to criticism, had fantasies of success, entitlement and a belief in his unique worth at the expense of others. But this was getting out of hand. He was endangering people.

"It's the path to the future of mankind, Holly—the beginning of a new kind of human. I'm just accelerating the process a little. It would have happened anyway."

What could she say to him? If he was a patient she would know. But he was her father. He shook himself and continued. "The results we're getting may be caused by chemical changes in the brain. We're pursuing that avenue. But we need an immediate Band-Aid for the psychiatric consequences, just to keep the subjects together until we can figure out how to stabilize them."

"And I'm the Band-Aid. Well, that's flattering, as usual, Dad. I should have known there was a reason you wanted me at the announcement tomorrow night. Or why you bothered to try to explain to such a lax thinker the newest of your marvelous discoveries of higher truth."

"I need you, Holly. I need your expertise." Well, that was a first. He'd never, ever, asked for her help. She watched his eyes examine her. They were cold gray. That was when she knew. He was baiting her, just as he always had. Only this time he used the most alluring bait of all. He played on her need to be valued by him.

She cocked her head. The tension in her back and her neck either ramped up the noise in her head, or were a result of the increase. "Well, Dad, you're going to have to get along without me. I don't think I could stand the pressure of working in the bowels of your research machine. Give my best to Mom tomorrow night as she plays hostess."

"I'm not the only one who needs you. You may be the last defense for these people against the consequences of what's happened to them." He knew helping him might not be enough to convince her. He was going to play on her impulse to save humanity. But she'd given up saving the world a long time ago.

"What happened to them was you, Dad. Your hunger for recognition made you rush things, and now other people are paying the price. I'm not digging you out of this hole."

"You're going to abandon these people?"

He stared at her with narrowed eyes. But he knew so little about her, or maybe so much, that he apparently didn't know how else to try to persuade her. She turned toward the door. "There are thousands of shrinks in L.A. I'll grab a cab. Thanks for the expensive lunch."

Outside, the glare of the sun off the concrete and glass city sent her scrambling for her sunglasses. Her eyes burned, but she wasn't sure it was from sun or smog. The dull roar in her ears seemed to ramp up, blending with the clamor of engines and horns and the whir of a bicycle going south. It almost hurt. She didn't want to be here when her father finally figured out a way to convince her and decided to come after her. She searched the street and saw a cab stand two blocks down in front of the discrete facade of what might be condos or maybe a hotel. Two or three yellow or green cabs lined up there. She stepped over a curb above cigarettes and gum wrappers floating in the oily water of the gutter. Even Restaurant Row on La Cienega was not immune to the subtle rot of the city. Her heels sank into the asphalt, slightly soft in the heat.

Damn her father! She was going to get all sweaty walking to get the cab. And cabs never ran their air conditioning. They liked to save gas. She'd go back to work with her linen outfit looking as if she'd been washed and only partially line-dried. Already the dampness in her scalp pulled strands of hair away from their confining pins.

She crossed the street without looking back. She could feel her father following her. She hadn't really thought he'd do that. A heavier tread pounded on the asphalt behind her as she crossed on the walk signal. He was getting closer. As she reached the far curb, she spun.

"Look, Dad . . ." Her throat closed around her words. The red plaid shirt was open at the throat, sleeves still rolled over powerful forearms. Same jeans, light-brown hair hanging about his face, scruffy half-beard. The green eyes had a wild look. A small white scar snaked through his left eyebrow. God, but he looked dangerous! All she could think of was how in the world he could have followed her here. The roar in her ears made her want to shriek. She stood frozen as he stepped onto the curb, one hand pressed to his forehead. Too close by far—three feet or less! Sweat beaded on his brow. He could grab her from here.

"Dr. Banks," he began. "I want to talk to you." His voice was deep. Emotion thickened his words. She had heard the same a hundred times inside the walls of Century Psych.

She didn't give him time to say more. She whirled and dashed toward the line of cabs. He grabbed for her even as she turned. She pushed herself out of his reach, almost stumbling in her haste. She gasped and heard a little squeal she wasn't proud of, but she was running now. He would run after her and catch her and everyone would stand by and watch just as if nothing horrible were happening because they couldn't admit that kind of drama into their lives.

"Dr. Banks," she heard behind her. "Wait!"

A little snapping report popped above her head. A gun! The damn guy had a gun! Adrenaline whooshed through her, kicking up her panic another notch. She dove for the door handle of the last cab in line and jerked it open.

"Lady, get the first cab, I'm in line." The thick African accent boomed from inside the cab. She looked back. The guy wasn't running after her. He was looking around, frantic. She straightened and slid into the smell of old cigarette smoke, hot naugahyde and motor oil.

"Just drive," she commanded and pulled the door shut.

"Gonna get me a complaint, lady," the cabby muttered.

"I'll vouch for you." The cab lurched into traffic, pushing Holland into the cushions.

She craned to look out the rear window. The figure in the plaid shirt grew smaller. He ran both hands through his hair, looking wild even from here, then lunged into an alley as though his life depended on it. He was stalking her, all right. He knew her name. He'd been waiting for her. That meant he'd followed her from the hospital.

That meant he could follow her home.

Chapter Three

Holland's breath came slowly back to normal as the cab wended west through the traffic on Wilshire toward the hospital. Whatever it was that had made the thundering in her ears crescendo until she could hardly think had now subsided. Her thoughts were jumbled. She was half tempted not to go back. He had followed her even when she wasn't driving her own car. He could do it again. A hotel—she could check into a hotel and file a police report. You could get restraining orders against stalkers, couldn't you? Chloe could bring some clothes.

But that was stupid. The police never did anything about stalkers until there'd been an attempt on your life or something. She could tell them about the shot. The guy must have had a gun. But she couldn't hole up in a hotel forever and not go to work. The board of directors would love a president of the Foundation who never came to work and told crazy stories about being stalked.

Who was this guy? She was sure she had never seen him before the gym yesterday. It wasn't as if she were some movie star strangers would seek out. She was a shrink who ran a psychiatric treatment facility and directed the clinical trials and research efforts of the associated foundation. She attended fund-raisers and argued with the medical staff over the menu in the doctor's dining room. Not exactly fodder for stalking.

He wasn't her patient. She'd remember that. Had he been hospitalized? Not unlikely, since he was obviously crazy. Maybe he'd been at the hospital. Maybe he blamed her for his sickness since she was the head honcho. Maybe he just didn't like the food.

She took a breath and tried to regain control. There was no picture directory of former patients at Century Psych. The kind of money it took to stay here bought a lot of discretion. Maybe she should go to the police after all. The police had mug shots. At least she'd know who he was, if he had a criminal record, if he was even from around here. Beverly Hills drew crazies from around the country. But mug shots were a place to start. Damn! The last thing she wanted was to spend the afternoon at the Beverly Hills Police Station. She pulled out her cell phone.

"Chloe, I'll be out for a few hours. Put off Ferenghetti. He can have his ten minutes of complaining tomorrow. And leave the grant paperwork on my desk. I'll read it at home." Chloe knew better than to ask what was up. That was a good thing, with what she was about to say. "And Chloe, alert Security for a guy with longish hair—scruffy, wearing a plaid flannel shirt."

"What do you want them to do if they find him?" Chloe's tone was neutral, but Holland could hear the skepticism there, buried deep.

"Escort him off the premises. And if he makes trouble, call the police." Holland clicked the connection off. She didn't want Chloe to get up the courage to ask what the hell was going on. Chloe probably thought the guy was an ex-lover or something. If so, Chloe didn't know her very well after all. Maybe nobody did. Or worse, maybe only her father knew her.

It was still light when she returned to the hospital, but the night shift was on. She called ahead from her car for a security escort. The burly guys who patrolled the hospital were not your ordinary semi-retirees or the wimps with guns who tried out for security positions to bolster their egos. This was a psych hospital and security had to be serious. They greeted her cordially, made no reference to her orders through Chloe earlier, and got her inside.

"Just call us, Dr. Banks, when you want to leave," the big black guy said. His name was Ernie. He looked as if he had some Samoan in him somewhere, one of those harbingers of our future when everyone will have inter-bred into one delightful swirl of color and physical charms. Of course, then the world would have invented some other criteria for instant distrust and dislike.

"Thanks, Ernie, I will." She waved them off.

The afternoon had been a waste. What had she expected, going to the police? The dull roar in her ears must be wearing on her. She rubbed her forehead as if that could make the noise go away. Maybe Xanax was not so bad. Numb was sounding pretty good right now.

The police had been respectfully skeptical, sure she was mistaken about the stalking. How many times had she seen him? Only three? Was she sure it was him at the health club? Had anyone witnessed him accosting her outside Matsuhisa? Had he shouted at her or made any other threatening moves on the other occasions she had seen him? They made it seem so . . . paranoid of her. Was she sure the noise she heard had been a shot and not a backfire?

That's when she made it worse by insisting that it was a gunshot, and then remembering that the guy had run both hands through his hair. Which meant he wasn't holding a gun. Her assertion that he'd probably put it back in his waistband or something had been less than convincing.

She'd insisted on looking at mug shots, and they had taken her to a room and let her thumb through endless books of derelicts and criminals. None of them looked like her stalker. At first she had been sure of what he looked like. She had been able to place herself on that hot sidewalk and see the sweating brow. His skin had been fairly pale and fine, not only on his cheeks and forehead, but on the triangle of his throat. Not unhealthy, just a fair complexion. And the eyes, she was fairly sure they were green, but his brow slanted down so that, as he'd squinted against the sun, she couldn't be sure. His hair? Thick. It hadn't been washed, but she could tell it had some curl in it— not a lot, just waves. Even now the image of his face, the sense of strength and bulk about his body came back clearly in her mind. Yet paging through those millions of pictures, her memory had faded and morphed until she couldn't be sure what she had seen. The police had thought her a fool.

Maybe they were right. But being a fool was better than some other things she might be.

She unlocked the door to her office suite and switched on the light. Chloe was long gone, her desk a tidy landscape of blotter and dog pictures, computer and various sorting paraphernalia: in boxes, out boxes, chart racks. The cool tones of green in the patterned draperies and the upholstered waiting chairs, echoed in the detail print of Cézanne's water lily pads, were calculated to soothe. She shut the door to the hallway and pushed into her inner sanctum. Here the greens were deeper, the woods mahogany, the bookshelves filled with leather-bound texts, the only art her professional certificates and awards. The window looked out on the Santa Monica Mountains. If she craned her neck and looked to the right, she could see the houses on Laurel Canyon winding up the hill. As they got to the top, up near Mulholland Drive, they looked almost like public buildings, they were so large and blockish and, of course, expensive. Maybe she should move up the hill. She could afford more house. Then she could entertain her colleagues at home instead of always using Adriano's at the top of the hill. The thought made her uncomfortable. She'd need new furniture, of course. Decorating wasn't exactly her strong point, but her mother could help her. Mom was great at that. Holland turned to the neat stacks of binders on her desk. The grant. That was why she was here tonight. Well, part of the reason.

Part of the reason might be lurking in the parking lot even now. Better here where there were security guards than at home.

She opened the top binder. She managed to proof the table of contents and the executive summary before her thoughts strayed to the guy in the plaid shirt. Maybe she should just confront him. She could take Ernie with her when she went to her car. She knew he *would* be waiting. Well, she'd just let him approach her and tell her whatever he wanted to tell her. That might satisfy his need for attention, or whatever it was that was driving him. Or it might embolden him to try to get close to her. At least she'd have

Ernie as a witness to anything he tried. Maybe that would satisfy the damn police and she could get a restraining order.

The cone of light cast from her desk lamp on the blotter was soon an island of light in the darkening office. The windows faded to black, laced with the lights of houses in the hills. The grant presentation was professional, the study well thought out and original. They were going to use cadavers to explore the effect of truncated dendrite stems in the neurons of schizophrenic brains. That truncation might be the basis for the delusions. The neurons couldn't pass sensations adequately from one brain cell to another. She just knew they could demonstrate that schizophrenic brains, in pruning the dendrite overload of adolescence, pruned too far, causing the disease to develop in young adulthood. Then if they could find the gene that triggered the pruning . . . Well, anyone would be able to see the possibilities. She'd be surprised if they didn't get the grant. If there was one thing she understood, it was how to do a proposal. The Schizophrenia Research Foundation was living proof.

There were no more excuses to stay. Her hand hovered over the phone inset in the mahogany of her desk, reticent. *Stupid!* she admonished herself. Was she going to start sleeping on the couch over there? She punched up security.

"Ernie, I'm ready. I'll meet you at the back door."

There. She'd done it. She scooped up her briefcase and strode out into the hall. A psychiatric hospital was never dark. The gleaming hall held not a single shadow. Still, the sensation of being followed dogged her even in the light. She refused to let it show. She nodded to the night shift nurses at the station, the bored psych intern on duty.

Ernie met her at the first-floor elevators. "Dr. Banks." He turned into step with her.

She nodded in acknowledgment. "Thank you for doing this."

"You aren't a regular customer for an escort," he noted, without judgment in his voice. "This sniper stuff getting to you?"

She felt the judgment anyway. It echoed her own. She had never needed an escort to the parking lot just because the sun went down. And the fact that snipers killed three random people yesterday in a city of nine million wasn't enough to change that. It was up to about fifty murders across the nation. But L.A. had always had a dozen drive-bys a night. What had wedged itself into the psyche of the populace was the randomness of the sniper attacks. You didn't place yourself in danger by dealing drugs or being a gang member or living in the wrong part of town. These killings were really random. No one liked to be reminded of the arbitrary nature of life. Everyone wanted to believe there was some kind of plan, even if you couldn't see it.

"No, it's not that," she said finally. "A man has been following me."

"Whoa." Ernie opened the heavy metal outer door for her. "You sure?"

Her spark of resentment seemed to be ignited by the glaring floodlights hitting the three stairs down to the parking lot. "Yes, quite sure."

"He a patient?" Ernie edged in next to her protectively.

"I honestly don't know." She heard her voice from far away. Her gaze swept the parking lot for movement, looking for plaid. Shadows wavered between the harsh pools of light. Visiting hours were long over. The shrinks on staff saw their patients in the daytime. So only a few cars, their colors washed out by the light and shadow, hulked in the lot. Her stalker wasn't there. She breathed a sigh of relief. "I don't see him." She had herself in hand, but she realized just how tightly wound she'd been. This was not good. "You can go, Ernie. I'll be fine now."

"Uh-uh." Ernie shook his head firmly. "I'm gonna see you safe inside your car, Doctor. Now you just come on."

Holland didn't protest. Maybe she was glad her brave gesture was refused. Ernie took her elbow and stalked beside her to the little Mercedes in the corner. He took her security clicker and opened the door, peering carefully into the back seat.

"All clear?" she asked, smiling. What protective urges had she unleashed here?

He straightened and nodded. "You be careful, Dr. Banks. I want you locking your doors at home, you hear? You got a security system?"

She grinned. "Yes, a very good one."

"And you wouldn't be the kind that leaves it off just because it got set off once and you couldn't remember the off code and the police came and you were embarrassed. You wouldn't be that kind, would you?"

"The head of a loony-bin? If anyone's careful, I am, Ernie." She patted his beefy arm awkwardly. "But thanks."

He closed the door with a *thunk* and motioned her out of her space. She felt better knowing he watched her pull away. As a matter of fact, she felt better all over. The guy in plaid hadn't been there. She swung out onto Wilshire, refusing to turn on the radio to hear about more killings. There was little traffic at eleven P.M.: people coming back from dinner in West Hollywood or on their way to residential B.H. The show must be running late at the Wiltern Theater. As she passed the space where it was parked, she saw a car's headlights flip on. Her glance jerked to the rearview mirror. The car swung out in traffic. The glare of its lights made seeing much about it impossible. With no headlights behind it, she couldn't see the form of the driver.

But she knew it was him.

A thousand thoughts crashed through her mind. Of course he would know she'd get an escort from hospital security. He'd seen them escort her in today. Tonight he'd waited where Ernie wouldn't see him. He'd lured her into thinking she was safe. She pressed down on the accelerator. The Mercedes responded like a thoroughbred to the spur. Yet now, if she ran for sanctuary, he'd know where she lived, alone.

Her heart pounded chaotically in response to the cascade of thought. What to do? Should she not go home? Where then? Her parents' house in the Palisades? She shook her head convulsively. She couldn't let her father see her like this, afraid and begging for help. A hotel with a doorman? Abandoning the shelter of her own house seemed so . . . extreme. If she couldn't even go home, where would it end? She almost hit a car stopped at a light because her gaze was riveted on the rearview mirror, willing the driver of the car behind her to reveal himself.

A desperate feeling that she was imagining all of this, like a bad dream, drenched her. Lord knew she hadn't been feeling stable and strong lately. She *had* to know. She had to know for sure if the car was following her. It was a test of her sanity and a sounding of the dark waters rising at her knees. The rush of noise in her ears made it hard to think.

All right. The turn onto Laurel—that would tell her. Five blocks to Laurel maximum. Her breathing was so deep she was in danger of hyperventilating. She forced herself to breathe in and out more slowly. Next light. Okay. The light turned yellow ahead of her. A car blocked the right lane. But there was just enough room between the SUV and the curb for the little Mercedes. She scooted up on the right and squealed onto Laurel through the red. About two blocks in, she pulled into the driveway of a house and shut down the lights. Then she squirmed around until she was kneeling in the seat, hunched down behind the seat back and peering out the rear window. Could she even hear a car approach over the din in her ears and the thump of her heart in her throat?

Arching lights announced a car had turned right on Laurel. The lamppost at the edge of the walk across the street lit the driver clearly from the rear. Short spiky hair surrounded a pale pinched face. It looked like a girl. But girl or guy, it was not *the* guy.

Holland heaved in a breath, involuntarily. It wasn't him. She leaned her forehead against the seat and let the breath out in a gust. No one was following her. Relief filled her eyes with tears. No one was following her.

She rocked back on her knees. But here she was crouched in the driver's seat in a dark driveway, crying. What was going on here? Suddenly she saw herself as someone else might see her. Bad dreams all the time, waiting for people she thought were following her. She had even thought she heard a voice echoing inside her tinnitus saying *help me* this morning. What was that beginning to sound like?

Jesus, she had to get a hold of herself! Paranoid. She sounded paranoid. And voices? The word schizophrenic rattled around in her head. She should know. She wrote the book on it. Hysteria, so close beneath the surface, rose into her throat in a laugh she was truly glad no one else could hear. It shook her and wouldn't let her go. What happened if a shrink went crazy? White coats would show up to take the white coat away? The laughter died only slowly.

From her point of view it was all very reasonable. She had tinnitus. And this guy was stalking her for some reason. The dreams had always been there. But those inside the psychosis always thought it was reasonable. The view from inside always seemed 20/20. Maybe her best chance that she was still sane was that she thought she might be crazy. Did that rule apply if you were a shrink? Maybe shrinks could stand outside the delusion, yet grant the delusion power just the same.

Looking at herself from the outside, she saw a rumpled gray linen sheath, hair escaping its confinement and a woman who was weeping. Inside was someone who was afraid on a deep level she couldn't control. The distance she felt from herself was almost like the feeling she experienced in her dreams—the dreams where she believed, with all the certainty dreams can bring, that she wasn't human, and never had been.

Holland slid around until she was sitting in the driver's seat again, and wiped her eyes. This was getting serious. Was it time for the shrink to see a shrink again? It was required as part of training. Her colleagues still did therapy just to keep their balance so they could deal with all the crazies. But Holland's psychiatrist had retired. She'd never told him about the dreams. Somehow, she'd spent her time talking about how to live with a narcissistic personality. Now she hadn't seen a therapist in years.

She turned the key in the ignition and backed carefully out of the driveway onto Laurel. At least her house was safe. He hadn't been following her. She had some refuge left.

She wended her way up the canyon, drove across a buttressed bridge, parked in the garage and pressed the remote. The garage door hummed shut. The security seal vibrated into place. Sanctuary—from pursuers, if not from her dreams.

Busted flat today. Fumble at the one-yard line. No other word for it. First time, first time in five. He hadn't told the money guy yet. But he still had a couple of days. Best to get on with it. Dark wasn't good for his work in spite of infrared scopes. Yet he had to make up for lost time here. He cut the engine and let the Caravan roll back into a shadowy drive. The only sounds in the canyon were the crickets and the soft thunk of his opening door. He grabbed for the smooth wood stock and let the rifle slide into place under his arm. So natural, the trigger like an extension of his hand, the huge lens of the night scope like a shiny eye. Yeah. He smiled in the warm, dark night. Like he was the guy in The Evil Dead *with a chainsaw for a hand. He was the savior of the planet, man, made into a machine of death and set loose upon the unrighteous who would try to live among us before they rose up to bring us down. Not on his watch. He moved into the night as a breeze stirred in the trees around him. All he had to do was follow her.*

Holland shrieked as she fought her way up through the evil that soaked her along with her sweat. She opened her eyes, though she thought they had been open all along. She was crouching at the head of her stairs, clinging with one hand to the balustrade that edged the landing. Her other hand was at her throat, its fingers digging into the flesh of her neck. The pulse of her carotid artery pulsed through her fingers. The hand! The hand had tried to choke her, tried to thrust her down the stairs. Sputtering, she pulled her hand from her throat and held it away from her. Evil throbbed up the stairs and across the landing. What was happening here? She had crossed some threshold, broken through some barrier of sanity and separation between reality and dreaming. Sobbing shook her, and she realized she'd been sobbing for some time. Bad, this was very bad on a new level of badness. Her throat felt swollen. The raw imprint of fingernails in her neck would leave scratches. But the hand wasn't trying to kill her. It was trying to wring the last shred of goodness from her, until all that was left was evil. Worse than death. Way worse.

Beyond the open door, the view of her bedroom wavered into her consciousness. The bedclothes were strewn over the floor. The torchiere lamp had been overturned. Its stained-glass shade was shattered, bright drops of glass blood splashed across the wood floor and the white linens. The dream ebbed slowly, but the panic did not.

Not human! The alien feeling still vibrated within her. She began to shake, sweat turning clammy on her body beneath the cotton sleep shirt. As the dream receded, the noise in her ears rose. Holland blinked. That meant something, something she should know. There was a connection she should make.

"You're a shrink," she said aloud, as though her voice could break the spell of dreams that lured her to touch . . . something, something seductive that would engulf her until she wasn't even herself anymore, but another thing entirely. Something evil.

She shuddered, exhausted. The noise in her head felt like water rushing down a cataract, heedless of anything except the joy of fulfilling its destiny. She shut her eyes, alone with the sound.

You know.

The voice shocked her. It rumbled inside her, deep, in rhythm to the pounding of her heart. You know? Know what? She didn't know anything, not now. Was it her psyche, talking to herself?

She was *not* schizophrenic. Two words. She could have imagined them. Like *help me.* Imagination, simple imagination. She had wanted help to escape the guy following her. She had heard the words "help me" because she was looking for help. Two words were not the elaborate conversations true schizophrenics had with their imaginary voices. And she hadn't yet imagined that she was the King of Antarctica or abducted by aliens.

But she did have dreams that said she wasn't human.

She found herself listening to the roar in her ears, looking for whispered words.

Tears rose to her eyes as she pushed herself up to standing. Not good. She was not good. She had to get some real sleep. She'd prescribe herself some Ambien. Slippery slope or not.

Holland got up and stalked to the kitchen. Maybe a drink was what she needed to get back to sleep. She popped the wine preserver on a bottle of red wine she'd sealed earlier in the week. The air sighed out. The scent of fermented grapes accompanied the *glug* of liquid. Holland grabbed the glass and began to pace, the sound in her ears and the possibility that a voice might rise from it driving her from room to room.

The house was set in the trees of the canyon. Big oaks lighted by floodlights twisted through the decks that were built around them. In the large room that served as both living and dining room, the lights of the city glowed through their branches. She looked around the house as though it belonged to a stranger. The rooms reflected her travels—botanicals by Redouté framed in gold; and a mirror hung in neoclassical, Napoleonic splendor above the comfortable couches, themselves upholstered in Victorian-print comfort. Oriental carpets. A finely etched Southwestern pot from Acoma sat under a gaudy embroidered elephant from Chang Mai in a frame worth twenty times what the folk art inside it cost her. Temple etchings from Wat Arun in Bangkok and line drawings washed with watercolors from the St. Ives school all coexisted in a complex mash of memories. The mission furniture had belonged to her grandmother: a chest, a library table, the rockers, a dining set that was missing a leaf so she couldn't have more than six to dinner. She stalked back into the kitchen.

What matter? She invited no one here—not the professional acquaintances, not the periodic awkward dates. Her house was cluttered. It had not felt the sophisticated hand of a decorator. It was home, though. Did she want anyone to know what felt like home to her? Sometimes she thought that she lived only in the public persona she projected at the hospital. She didn't really have a coherent personality aside from the brilliant doctor mask she wore there. Her house certainly didn't reflect any clear picture of a character. It was a mishmash of unrelated stuff. Maybe what she was at the hospital—the careful professional language, the stern and organized boss just touched with human sympathy—*was* her. If so, it was time to buy a new house that reflected that.

She poured another glass of wine. She wasn't thinking straight. Who could think with this roaring in your head? A movement beyond the kitchen window caught her eye.

A surge of panic sent the wine glass crashing to the tile. Someone was out there! She snapped shut the blinds before she saw something she didn't want to see, a face, a plaid shirt—

A crash whipped her head around. The Acoma pot fell off its stand, shattering on the floor. Or shattered, and then fell off its stand? Had she done that? How?

Unreasoning fear gripped her. Something was making things happen inside her house!

She scurried to the dining room slider and pulled the wood vertical that closed the slats. And then the panic wouldn't be denied and she raced from room to room, sobbing, pulling shut the draperies or blinds even as she scanned the decks for movement. God, but she felt like she was in that old movie called *Forbidden Planet,* where the shields thunked shut around the house to keep out the horror that no one could name, lurking outside.

She checked the doors. All locked. The security system blinked green. Its seal had not been broken. She stood in the middle of the tile of the entry hall, with all views to the outside closed, and gasped against the hand pressed to her throat.

Tell me.

The words were so clear, the voice so deep. It wasn't her voice! It wasn't! Tears welled in her eyes. The roar in her ears shut her inside herself as much as locking the doors or drawing the curtains. She shook her head and sank to the floor. Dully, she noted the wet red prints on the tile, and her gaze strayed to her foot. The cataract in her head receded a bit as though a presence ebbed. She could hear herself breathe at least, through the roar. She'd cut her foot. The glass was still in there. She could see it glinting. She hadn't even felt it. She took a shuddering breath, then held herself still and gingerly pulled the red-soaked crystal triangle from the ball of her foot. She tossed it toward the door. It skittered across the tile. A throb started deep in her flesh. How had she not noticed that

41

she was running around with glass in her foot?

Her mind strayed to that movie, *Forbidden Planet*. Blinking, she remembered the end. The monster everyone was trying to shut out was just a manifestation of the sickness in the mind of the man who owned the house. The monster was the man's own evil.

She hung her head. Blond hair curtained her face. Tears dripped into the welling blood from her cut foot. She clutched her ankle with the hand she always dreamed was evil.

Chapter Four

"I don't care what you think, Doug." Leland Banks sat in his comfortable home office, but he was not relaxed in his huge burgundy leather executive chair. He hunched over the desk, earphone cord dangling from his right ear, a cigar in his left hand. "I'm publishing."

"It's not safe, Leland. You know what's at stake here. You're doing this for self-aggrandizement." The voice in his ear sounded as though Doug were standing right beside him instead of being half a continent away.

"You're as bad as my daughter." Leland brought the wet end of the cigar to his mouth and pulled against the flame. There was nothing as luxurious as the taste of a really fine cigar. "But I'm not letting Herzog think he's on the cutting edge for a single second longer."

He listened to the man's complaints, then interrupted. "You always were overcautious, Doug. You've been watching too many conspiracy theory movies."

"That's rich, Leland, very rich, after your miscalculation. You are already personally on the hook for this thing getting out of hand. If you get the public in a panic as a result of your grandstanding . . ." Doug was more than annoyed, which amazed Leland. He'd always thought guys like Doug had steely eyes and an unshakable nerve. But that was before he'd started working with them. Few acted like they were supposed to.

"Yes, yes," he said impatiently. "We're both on the hook at this point. But this announcement serves a purpose. We must prepare the public, if this thing is as big as I think it is. Better to have them get a little used to the idea than to just spring it on them in all its consequential glory. Especially if we can't keep it from spreading indiscriminately."

"Lendreaux has the leaks in hand at this point. If it goes beyond his capacity to take care of it, that's when I get involved."

Now that sounded exactly how people like Doug were supposed to: hard, implacable. It almost made Leland shiver. "Well, I've only got two left who are in any shape at all to study. So it's a good thing it *is* spreading. I'm having Lendreaux identify more. I'll count on you to bring them in."

"You know how important this is."

Doug wanted a way to stop it. How angry Doug would be if he knew that all Leland cared about was finding a way to spread it. He let a tiny bit of the melancholy he'd been feeling spill over into pain. To be shut out of the biggest development in the history of human evolution by some freakish property that made it activate only in young adults! Not fair! Not fair that some idiot like Lendreaux had it. Leland had to know what proteins the DNA told the RNA to produce, what enzymes were activated, what new organs or abilities those enzymes affected. If he couldn't get the new string inserted by the viral vector to take hold in people his age, then he'd have to figure out a way to replicate the outcome.

Forcibly, he stopped his brain from skittering down that path.

"I know how important it is, Doug," he said curtly. Then he clicked the connection closed.

The morning air sifting through the oak trees felt cleaner than usual. Too bad Holland didn't. She had opened only one set of wooden blinds. Beyond the dark gray-green mass of leaves a cluttered L.A. stretched into the distance until it disappeared into the summer haze. The scent of star jasmine still hung in the air. Birds twittered and flapped from tree to tree. These were things she had taken a simple joy in once. Now they mocked her in their very ordinariness. She turned into the house and limped through the kitchen. Shoes had been difficult over the Band-Aids she used to close the cut. She hadn't bothered to clean up the broken glass. The ruby splash of the wine had mainly dried by now. Her partial footprints were rusty brown. She found her bottle of pills on the tile counter in the kitchen and popped it open. Couldn't live without the little yellow pills that suppressed her body's virulent immune reaction to anything hanging in the air. Literally, couldn't live. No matter how bad things got, she couldn't forget her little yellow pills.

She ran her hands through her hair, loose on her shoulders. No time for perfection this morning. Just get to work. She had to get to work. An Extra-strength Vicodin left over from that time she sprained her ankle skiing, combined with the wine, had given her a kind of vacant sleep, four or five hours at least. Maybe tonight she'd try that combination again.

It was late—already after eight. When had she last been this late for work? Flats and slacks—what would the staff think? John would be in today, and he could look at her foot. It needed stitches.

In the garage, she got into the Mercedes and just sat. Her hand hovered over the remote that breached the security to allow the garage door to raise itself. What if he was out there?

But he wasn't. She wasn't quite sure how she knew. He had been there last night, but he had gone. She didn't know why, or why he stalked her. Did she really know anything?

She hit the remote.

Ernie was concerned about her limping. He took her arm. As they passed the entrance, her distracted gaze fell on the newspaper vending machine and the headlines there. "Sniper total reaches 18 in L.A." it screamed. God, it was no wonder the whole city was a little paranoid. If only that explained her own situation. She slipped in a coin and took a paper. The second lead story was about the flu epidemic sweeping the nation. Today's was a real plagues and locusts edition.

John Salvatorre herded her into the infirmary where he treated the minor physical maladies of the inmates of Century Psych for an hour or two each day, and chided her for not going to an emergency room for stitches last night. He shot up the ball of her foot with Novocain so she wouldn't feel the fourteen tidy stitches. She watched with a certain amount of detached interest. He asked about her tinnitus. She told him she was getting used to it. She refused to mention the voices this time, or the fact that they were getting clearer.

When John was done, Holland went back to her office and had Chloe send in the grant. She wouldn't review it again. When had she ever cared less about perfection? This was new.

Somehow, she saw patients, said all the psychiatric things about drug dosages, visiting privileges, and therapeutic psychobabble. She said them without shouting over the noise—at least she hoped she did. What would her colleagues say if she told them how close her own symptoms were to some of the patients she advised them about?

She ate lunch at her desk, reviewing the results of one of the clinical trials the Foundation was conducting.

But all the while, the end of the day loomed at the back of her mind like the shadows in some noir comic book. He wouldn't be in the parking lot. It wouldn't be him she saw following her with all her anxious glances. But he had gotten to her house somehow last night. He knew where she lived. He would be there again tonight.

At five the summer sun lit the Santa Monica Mountains outside her office like it was mid-afternoon. She picked up the phone and dialed the number. There would be a price for sanctuary.

"Mom?" How dared she sound like such a little girl in her own ears?

The calm voice radiated from the telephone like soothing hot chocolate. "Holly! I'm so glad you called."

"Liar." Holland smiled, relaxing. "You're busy getting ready for Dad's press conference-cum-social event tonight. Cleaners and caterers and florists are buzzing around you, even now."

"You would think it a trial, Holly, but I like it, you know."

"I know," she admitted, puzzled as always. How could her mother be so like her, and so unlike? "I'm coming." She laid it into the conversation without preamble.

Her mother showed no surprise. "Your father will be very pleased."

"That's the only bad part."

"Holly, I wish I could make it right between you two."

Holland smiled. "You'll never stop trying, even though you can't. I know you."

"I'll tell him you'll be here."

"Don't tell him I'm going to work on his study. I haven't decided about that yet." Of course if she went, he would just assume she was in and announce it. She knew that. "In fact, tell him not to announce anything or I'll have to deny it publicly."

"He needs you, Holly."

"That's a first."

"Would it hurt to take advantage of a first? Build a bridge. He won't last forever, you know."

She didn't answer her mother's guilt-inducing question. All she could think was that it was a shame her father was likely to last longer than her mother. "Mom, I'd like to spend the night, if it's okay. You know this thing will go late, and I hate to drive home from the Palisades. Maybe we can get a chance to talk." Her too-extensive explanations sounded rushed even in her own ears.

"You're always welcome, Holly. You didn't even have to call in advance." Her mother knew everything, always had—even if it didn't help her handle her ambitious only child and her difficult and distant husband. She was still the steady center around which they both gyrated, bumping each other off their trajectories at each turn. When her mother had been having chemo after the lumpectomy, she and her father had almost killed each other. Remission was a fact, but for how long? Holland hated the thought of losing her mother to some deranged cells.

"I know, Mom. I don't think I'll have time to get home before I come. I guess you're the only place I can go sans luggage without raising eyebrows."

"I'll let you borrow a nightgown, if you won't feel too old-fashioned."

Holland could hear the smile in her mother's voice. It seemed like a miracle. "I'll just be grateful, Mom." She rang off. There were several kinds of sanctuary.

Holland parked the Mercedes along the winding Palisades street that curved down to the bluff above Pacific Coast Highway. The downward slope gave her parents' Spanish-style house the view of the ocean that doubled its already-astronomical value. Yet they weren't so close to the cliff that was constantly crumbling into the sea as to make insurance impossible. Her father always bragged that they had found the ideal middle ground. Actually, it might only be her mother who had found that; she and her father surely hadn't. The ocean sparkled blue-gray with the sun still an hour and a half from setting. You couldn't hear the waves from here. Not that she could have heard them anyway. She had her own roaring breakers in her ears.

She was well aware she was not looking her best and was still limping, even with the stitches. She always went to great lengths to make sure she was dressed appropriately, whatever the occasion. Not being dressed right only made her feel more like people would know that she didn't belong. Slacks and a jacket, no matter how tailored, how sleek, didn't feel right for tonight. But it couldn't be helped. She was not going home to change.

The street was already crowded with the cars of guests too eager for the announcement to be fashionably late. The valets spirited them away to streets unknown and sprinted back for more. Several security guards from her father's Genomere Foundation were discretely strewn up and down the block and near the front door. On the lawn, camera crews fiddled with equipment labeled with various letter combinations she would know if she watched television more. She produced her driver's license for a guard and ducked under the passionflower vines dripping from a queen palm over the walk to the side door. The kitchen looked like command central of some national disaster. Uniformed people scurried everywhere importantly. The head caterer barked instructions to the servers like a general ordering troop movements. Silver trays of hors d'oeuvres covered every surface. Legions of wine bottles stood at attention on the kitchen island. The servers hurried out to the guests, shouldering their salvers, veering deftly through the chaos like starships through a video-game minefield.

No one seemed to notice her. Holland didn't look for her mother, who would be in the living room or on the spectacular deck nodding graciously and remembering small details about everyone she'd ever met. Her mother was the perfect hostess these days. How fortunate for her father that his wife had given up her own career in social work to support him and his foundation. Holland slid back to her parents' bedroom, away from the noise of the party and through to the huge bathroom. In with the sleek plum tile and graceful silver fixtures was her mother's vanity. She sat down on the upholstered stool and started opening the ranks of little drawers. There must be some hairpins in here somewhere left from before her mother cut her hair. Makeup from Shisheido in one, brushes and a dryer in another, nail polish. Holland sighed. So like her mother, who could afford Shisheido but still did her own nails every Sunday night while she watched *60 Minutes*, had been doing that for thirty years. Yes! Four hairpins scattered in the bottom of a drawer. Four—she could do it with four. She ran the brush through her hair, twisted her locks and tucked them into a chignon. Her hair was thick. But all that body meant that four pins might just hold it. She wove them into the edge of the rolled hair and shook her head from side to side carefully. Maybe.

She glanced to the mirror and quickly away. Her hands shook only a little as she fumbled in her purse for lipstick. The dark circles under her eyes weren't going to be hidden by makeup anything short of Hollywood-thick. A trowel probably wouldn't do the trick. She traced her lips with the liner and filled in with the tube. That was as good as it was going to get.

She stood and squared her shoulders. Time to face the arena. The lions waited. She twitched her jacket into place and eased out into the melee. It was just another role. She was about to play "perfect daughter" as well as "renowned psychiatrist."

"Holly!" Her father's voice boomed with paternal pride over the conversations around him. He was even better at his role than she was. Did he have to call her Holly in public? He knew she hated the diminutive, more so when he uttered it than when her mother did. Somehow with her mother, it was just a symbol of affection. Coming from her father it was something more, or maybe something less. Everyone turned from where they had gathered around him. He had picked an open area to stand—plenty of room for his audience. He had a glass of champagne in one hand and a smoked salmon canapé in the other. She knew he wasn't actually drinking the wine. He would never chance losing control of a situation he owned. He even owned her. She had agreed to play princess to his king tonight.

So she smiled and held out her hand. "Father?"

The crowd was a mixed bag. Some were exceedingly well dressed. The mayor was there. His wife wore a little black number so expensive it said her husband had used his personal fortune to fund his campaign. Scanning the faces, she saw a congressional representative and a couple of city council members. Then there were the patrons, the ones who gave big dollars to her foundation as well as to his. She smiled, warm, just right. "Mrs. Saperstein, Ralph. Fiona—how nice to see you here." She nodded as she moved through the crowd, shaking hands. She saw some slacks and sports coats in the crowd, the off-the-rack kind. Those would be the reporters.

Her father gathered her in to stand beside him. He, of course, was looking impeccable. But if he noticed the slacks or the circles under the eyes, he didn't show it. "My daughter will be joining me in the research that will result from tonight's important announcement."

"A real father-daughter team, eh, Leland?" Ralph Faber laughed.

"Better even than coaching my Little League team." Holland's smile was artificial. He'd already done it! He'd announced what she'd asked him not to. And with all the donors to her own foundation present, she couldn't make a scene. She'd have to grin and bear it until she could back out later under the pressure of "other commitments."

"Dr. Banks?" someone called.

"Which one?" Holland asked coolly. A nervous titter circled the assemblage.

"Psychiatry and genomic research?" one of the ones in the off-the-rack sports coats asked. "Just what is the connection?"

Her father held up a big, square hand. "Now, people. You know for that you have to wait."

"Wait for the cameras, you mean." The mayor chuckled.

"Holly, let me introduce you to someone very important." Her father took her arm and turned her toward a young man with painfully short hair that emphasized ears a scosh large. He didn't look important. "This is Brad Weller. He's the chief aide for Senator Lendreaux from Louisiana. You know Senator Lendreaux, Holly. He heads the Health and Human Services committee in the Senate."

Ah. Chief aide to the chief money man. Well, she could use some of that money. She mustered a smile in spite of the ramp up of the buzzing in her ears. A little toadying was all in a day's work for the head of a foundation. "Of course, Father." She nodded graciously as he shook her hand. "Mr. Weller, what are you and the Senator doing here in California?"

Holland couldn't quite hear his answer, though she saw his mouth move. The roar in her ears was building fast now, drowning out the voices. She swallowed and felt her hands go clammy. Not here! Not in front of senators' aides and donors and reporters! Not in front of her father! Her father touched her arm. She looked up as he nodded at Brad Weller. He'd said something to Holland—what? She couldn't hear! The roar was making her feel dizzy. She swayed against her father. Sound rolled through her mind. Loud, with those tantalizing susurrations at the edges. The hissing that sounded like . . .

Where?

That word was so clear she almost jumped out of her skin. She looked up at her father in horror. He was moving his mouth. But all she could hear was, *Where is she?* It was like a badly dubbed movie.

The noise inside her head became a thousand voices, not just a roar. She realized that if she could pick the roar apart, they would all be there—each voice saying something particular. She jerked around as she sensed movement at the door. The crowd crumbled. A man fell as though he had been pushed. The roar was shrieking at her, in its thousand unrecognizable voices.

I need her. She knows. The words came clearly over the roar. The voice that said them was deep, just as it had been before. It was not her own voice inside her head; she would swear to that. Of course, schizophrenics never thought the voices were theirs. She put her hand out, as though she could stop what was happening.

He stumbled through the ranks of little black dresses. His red plaid shirt made him look like a different species. His eyes were wild. Hair hung in his face. All around him people were shouting. She could see their mouths move, if she couldn't hear them. He lurched toward her. No one was stopping him. Why didn't they stop him? She felt herself scream.

You can tell me. I know you can.

The voice was in her head, over the roar. But his mouth moved as though the words were his. He was the only part of the movie that wasn't dubbed. He was shouting, shouting inside her head. She recognized that voice, deep and commanding. It had been his voice in her head all along. *Patients. Do you have patients who think they aren't human?*

She stared at him, dumbfounded. His green eyes were desperate, wild. How did he know? How did he know about her? Behind him, security guys came scrambling through the door. People scattered everywhere like bowling pins.

He didn't try to run. He stepped forward and took her by her shoulders. Silence fell inside her mind. The roar was gone. His single voice echoed in her head. *"Voices—they hear voices. I've got to find them!"* His mouth moved in sync with the words. It was a soft mouth with a full bottom lip. His teeth were even and white. His eyes held hers. Pain. They held pain and surprise, for some reason. She could feel the warmth of his body coursing through his hands. He clutched her upper arms hard enough to leave bruises. His plaid shirt was torn over his shoulder and stiff with some dark stain. He was examining her eyes, her face as though his life depended on it. The sound in her head seemed to have drained out through her neck and shoulders and down her arms and out into him. She couldn't even hear the crowd around her, though she realized they must be shouting. The crowd didn't matter. She was mesmerized by his eyes. Even as she looked, they cleared. His pain drained away. He examined her, shocked. *"You know, don't you?"* he said, and she heard it more clearly than she had ever heard anything, inside her head and outside.

Their locked gaze broke. Hands pulled him away. Noise rushed up from Holland's belly into her ears like a geyser. The man turned and decked one of the security guards.

Her father stepped out from behind her. "What did you say?" he yelled.

The man in plaid struck out and her father staggered back. Then three security guards were on him. He struggled wildly. One punched him in the belly. He doubled over. Holland saw the nightstick rise and fall and rise and fall again. The guy stumbled, going down on the rug, and then he collapsed.

Holland felt his consciousness go blank. The noise was everywhere again, inside her head and in the room, too. People were shouting. Hands helped her to a chair.

"Who is he?"

"He attacked you!"

"What did he want?"

"He's a madman!"

"Holland, do you know him?"

"He could have killed you!"

"Call the police!"

Holland blinked. Security guards cuffed the unconscious guy's hands behind his back.

"Get him out of here," her father ordered, rubbing his chin. "Call the police."

Reporters clustered around. "Do you know this man, Dr. Banks?" one asked. She turned to look up at him and shook her head.

"What made Jeff lose it like that?" another reporter said, almost to himself.

Holland turned slowly. "Do *you* know him?"

The reporter shrugged and looked at his companion, who had a microphone thrust in her face. "Yeah, we all do. Jeff McQueen. He's the investigative reporter for the *L.A. Times.*"

"I don't care who he is," her father said. "He's going to jail for this." The anger in his voice was personal, not professional. Even he couldn't keep up the act all the time.

Her mother sat beside her. "Holly, dear, are you all right?"

She nodded, tears filling her eyes. What had just happened? She couldn't think. She'd heard the stalker guy in her head. He knew about her dreams. And he was an investigative reporter. He'd publish the whole story of her delusions. Would it be discounted because it was written by a wacko? She found herself wondering whether anyone would let a loon run a loony bin.

She looked up to see a circle of mixed concern and avaricious curiosity. Ah, the power of the unexpected event to transform our mundane lives for an instant. They wanted in on it. They wanted to speculate and theorize and whisper that they had known there was something funny going on. The reporters asked questions all at once. Her father seemed stunned.

"That's enough, gentlemen!" The voice belonged to her mother. "My daughter has had quite enough. Go interview the police for your spotlight piece tonight." She took Holland's elbow. "You need to lie down."

As her mother helped Holland to the back of the house, she heard her father say to the crowd, "As soon as this excitement is over, we will still make the announcement of the most important scientific discovery in years."

Make the most of it, Dad, while you can, Holland thought. If your daughter-cum-research partner is declared certifiable, you'll get more press than you want.

Chapter Five

Holland told the police the minimum. She'd seen the guy a couple of times, thought he might be following her. Mentioned going to the BH police to file a report—they'd find out about that anyway. No idea why he was following her. Hadn't known he was a reporter before tonight, or his name. Didn't know what he meant by the things he said to her. That could be considered true in certain lights; she *didn't* know what they meant, or what it meant that he knew about her delusions. She offered her professional opinion that the guy was way around the bend. That was only too true. What that meant about her, she didn't volunteer.

Her fear that he would publish some story about her nightmares, her voices, her loosening grasp on reality, faded. No one at the very reputable *Los Angeles Times* would let a guy who lost it in front of every bigwig in town tar and feather her reputation. Her father would see to that—if it ever came up, which it wouldn't. A guy that far gone had probably been on the verge of losing his job, if he hadn't lost it already. He would have alienated family and friends. She could see he had let his personal hygiene lapse. He hadn't shaved or changed his shirt in three days that she knew of. That was a possible sign of deteriorating functionality. Self-consciously, she pushed an escaped lock of hair behind her ear. "What happens to him?" she asked the cop with hair way shorter than anyone who wasn't military or police. His navy-blue uniform brought out his eyes nicely, though.

"Going to jail for assault, disorderly conduct, trespassing, resisting arrest."

Holland frowned. Jail? "He wasn't trespassing if he's Press. Press was invited."

The cop grinned. "Okay. We'll skip the trespassing."

"I'm not sure I want to press charges." She should want to press charges. She should want to keep her stalker locked up as long as possible. But everything had changed. She needed time to think what it meant that she could hear him, that he knew her most personal delusions.

"No need, your father's taking care of that. The cop he decked will testify, too."

She could see her father in the doorway. "Maybe we should just let matters take care of themselves, Dad. That guy is obviously on 'self-destruct.' "

"Can't do that, Holly," her father said quietly. "He might not want to go out alone."

She sighed. "Yeah, maybe that's best." She'd track him down at the jail tomorrow. She now wanted a conversation with Jeff McQueen very much—but perhaps only from behind the safety of a glass partition in a visitors room.

The police finally left. She sat on the bed in the guest-room that had been commandeered for interviews with the police. Out in the living room, she could hear her father gathering the crowd to make his announcement. She wondered idly if the focus on the guy in plaid would distract everyone and let her father slide by without explaining what had happened to his test subjects. The press was elated. They got two stories for the price of one tonight. He would announce her participation, of course. She could just hear him get self-righteous about the attack on his poor daughter that made it impossible for her to join him in this historic moment. And what would her father say about the connection between genome findings and psychiatry? Not that his guinea pigs were committing suicide. That was for sure.

She looked around at pictures of her younger self with her pony, and photos from the cruise her parents took to Antarctica. Her father never went in for simple vacations. He worked too hard at being fascinating to waste time on cruises to Tahiti or the Bahamas. Masks from the Masai people flanked the mirror. She'd told her mother that the masks were external symbols among the more primitive tribes for terrifying psychological dangers within, hardly welcoming for a guest room. But her mother had just laughed. Holland shuddered. She should feel vindicated that she'd proved how dangerous her stalker was. That would teach the police not to believe her. But she felt only empty and frightened.

How did the guy know about the dreams? There was no way he could know. But he did.

And his was the voice in her head. She was sure of it. When he had touched her . . . when he touched her, the roar in her ears had calmed. It was all confusing and it all seemed real. But delusions always seemed real to the deluded. She knew that better than anyone. Jeff McQueen. The name seemed familiar, now that she had calmed down. Investigative reporter—right! She'd read his stuff in the *Times*—really gutsy pieces about racketeering, slave labor. Hadn't he gotten death threats over the article about the Mexican Mafia taking over the city council in some suburb? This was the kind of reporter Geraldo *wished* he could be: hard-hitting, not sentimental, but really perceptive about the human condition. Hell, she'd admired the guy. He was a fighter for truth and justice when there weren't too many of those left in the world.

Guess there was one less now. He was definitely wacko.

Tonight, she would sleep here, under the stony gaze of the Masai masks. Tomorrow, she had to find Jeff McQueen. Start with the Santa Monica jail, then check to see if he'd been transferred downtown.

"You okay?" her mother asked, sticking her head in through the opening door. Her cropped blonde hair made her look like a pixie. Except for the lines around her eyes, you'd swear she wasn't a day over forty.

Holland nodded. Her mother would see that nod was a lie. "Press conference over?"

Her mother slid into the room and sat on the bed. "All quiet on the Western Front."

"Where's Dad—basking?"

"On the telephone in the office. He's tireless. I think he's talking to Senator Lendreaux." Her mother's smile was looking inward for a moment, wondering. Her eyes drifted. She came to herself. "But you aren't, my dear. You're looking very tired. Have you thought of taking some time off?"

She had given up on trying to get her husband to take time off. Holland tried not to resent that her mother hadn't yet given up on her. That meant her mother didn't think she was as driven as her father. But she was. "No time, Mom." When she saw her mother's eyes blink, she softened. "Maybe this fall."

"You've been talking about Scandinavia for a while now. Better go in August. The fjords get pretty cold in the fall."

Holland smiled and shook her head. "Give it up, Mom. Besides, I'll probably have to testify against the guy from tonight. Wouldn't miss a court appearance. It's my favorite thing."

"Holly, your father wondered why that man thought you knew people who believed they weren't human."

Her father always used her mother as a go-between. "Are *you* wondering that, Mom?"

Her mother smiled, shrugged, and nodded.

"Well then, I will answer *you*." But what answer? Holland pursed her lips, then hung her head. She wasn't ready to reveal the truth because it would go right back to her father and she definitely didn't want him to know. When she looked up, she said, "I'm not sure. He seemed to be looking for patients with similar delusions." And maybe, most terrifying of all, that *was* the truth. "I know a lot of patients. He's probably connected with a patient in the hospital."

Her mother patted her leg. "Be sure to tell the police that, honey. That's a good angle."

"Yeah, Mom. I'll do that."

Two late mornings in a row. Ernie had probably called the police and reported her missing half an hour ago. She should have called Chloe, or even switched on her cell phone. But she didn't. She could hardly face having to put on her shrink act. She'd never been this late. But she had to go home and change, now that going home wasn't a danger. Appear at work wearing yesterday's clothes and the staff would start thinking she'd gotten lucky.

Last night was anything but lucky. Her stalker might be in jail but the situation had gotten even weirder. Was it her imagination that he had spoken to her in her head? Or was it something worse? This was the clearest sign yet that she was losing it. People didn't talk inside your head. No one but you talked inside your head. If you were sane, you knew that it was you, or parts of you, talking to other parts. It was only when you thought you heard other people that they needed to bring out the butterfly nets—which was looking really possible here. She'd gotten no sleep, playing the tape of what she would do to find him over and over in the wee hours of the morning as she tossed on her mother's guest bed. The only good thing about getting no sleep was that she had been able to keep the dreams at bay.

Her father had been up most of the night, too. She'd heard him come up the stairs from his office about three.

But a shower at home helped. So did clean clothes, and a suit with an actual skirt. She was looking fairly well put together by the time she got to the hospital parking lot. None of the staff had to know she still hadn't cleaned up the wine and broken glass on the kitchen floor. They didn't have to know how bad the roar in her ears was. It seemed to be getting slowly worse. Even now, if she listened, the sound seemed like a thousand whispers. If she could just separate them out . . .

God! Don't go there!

Ernie hurried over before she could get out of the car. "Dr. Banks, you okay?" He didn't wait for an answer but took her elbow in one meaty hand. "What with coming in all limping, and this guy after you. We thought . . . never mind what we thought. Let me take your briefcase."

"I'm fine, Ernie. The stalker's in jail. I was so relieved I slept through the alarm." Right. She was so relieved she was going to go find the guy. How smart was that? "I lost track of time."

"That's just what worries me, Dr. Banks. People like you never lose track of time."

They were walking slowly toward the hospital, but Holland wasn't paying attention to Ernie anymore. The sound in her ears—so sharp a moment ago that she was on the verge of picking out the voices—was getting louder, but also softening. Was it? Yes! With every step closer to the hospital door, the sounds muddied, mingled, shushed together. Like a record played at earsplitting decibels but at wrong speeds by those hip-hop DJs.

Ernie opened the door for her. He was saying something. She turned, still listening to the mushy sound inside her head. He was asking if she wanted an escort to her office. She shook her head and drifted down the gleaming tile corridor on a carpet of sound. It was getting louder still. Could she bear it? She looked around.

She knew what that meant. The realization stopped her like a brick wall.

Could it be true? Each time the sound had gotten louder in her head, Jeff McQueen had been close. Stalking at Matsuhisa, at her house the night she cut her foot, last night as he surged into her parents' living room, and now, here, in her hospital. Her gaze skittered over the gurney against the wall, the nurses station where two white-uniformed young women talked over a chart, the soft abstract wallpaper that tried to lie about this being a cage for sick animals. Her stalker, here? She put a hand to her chest to slow her shallow breathing as she glanced at the double door down the corridor just past the nurses station. The locked ward.

She sucked in a deep breath and held it for a count of five. *Steady. No hyperventilation. You wanted to find him. You were going to delegate rounds so you could call in your chits with Michaels at the county jail and see him there. Now you don't have to.*

She started toward the double doors, feeling in her briefcase for her keys. She didn't want him to be there. The fact that she knew he was there was most frightening thing of all.

Key in lock. Wave to the nurses. They were announcing something. She didn't stay to listen. Push open the doors. The mushy rolling sounds engulfed her, almost driving her back physically. It took the force of habit to make her turn and lock the door behind her. *Hook the keys to your belt with your cell phone, just like always. Turn. Walk down the corridor.* Rhenquist hovered over a chart. A mustached Hispanic man in a blue police uniform sat in a metal chair outside the door.

The sound drew her toward the door. Rhenquist looked up. His mouth was prim and smug. She had never really noticed that. Her hand rose of its own volition to ward off his greeting. It was the hand that was evil. She turned toward the window crosshatched with wire in the shut door.

He sat slumped on the bed, his arms clutched around himself, slowly rocking. The beds were metal here and bolted to the floor; the headboards carefully padded and covered with naugahyde. No pictures on the walls, no plastic flower pots, like in the unlocked rooms to make them look as if someone lived there. They never quite succeeded anyway. He wore a hospital gown of light blue, straining over his big shoulders and tied badly over his back. It left his arms almost bare. They were big, the muscles even in repose bulging under the fair skin. His thighs, too, were mostly bared by the short gown. Holland swallowed. He had a three-day growth of beard, at least. In his beard hung a string of spittle.

So, she thought, now we know why the sound is mushy. He's drugged. She managed to turn to Rhenquist, though she had to lean against the door.

"New last night," Rhenquist was saying. She could barely hear over the din in her head. He nodded to the policeman sitting impassively in the chair. "No room at the inn over in the psych wing of the jail."

The policeman touched his temple. "Don't worry. We'll post a guard twenty-four/seven."

"Is he dangerous?" Holland managed. He didn't look dangerous.

"You should have seen him last night." Rhenquist's eyes narrowed. "You okay?"

Holland managed a shrug. "I need to get off this foot." She hoped she hadn't shouted.

"Sure."

"My office." She let Rhenquist lead so he'd deal with the lock. She worked on breathing.

As they got into the elevator, the rush inside her head receded and Holland began to think again. He was here. She'd known he was here. And she knew why she knew, if not how. Now, what to do about it? Rhenquist trailed her into her office.

Chloe jumped up from her desk. "Dr. Banks!"

"Chloe, I would be indebted forever if you would get me some coffee." Since she made it a policy never to ask Chloe to get coffee for her, Chloe gulped once and jumped to the task.

Holland fell into her chair. "When did he come in?" she asked.

"About three, transferred on an involuntary from the Santa Monica District Court."

Holland almost didn't know what to ask first. "Without a hearing? At three in the morning? Did he even have an evaluation? And why isn't he in the jail ward? We're not equipped for this, and I don't like policemen sitting in my halls." Too many questions, but she couldn't help it. They just spilled out. She realized she wasn't sounding like her usual controlled, professional self.

"Don't know about the hearing. Evaluation from some guy named Dodson says he may be paranoid schizophrenic and incompetent to stand trial. Judge remanded him on a seventy-two-hour. Jail was full-up, apparently."

"Then why not to County? We don't do this kind of thing. Who's footing the bill?"

"The family had money, they're on the hook."

"They've been in touch already?"

"Oh, yeah. Our patient is the son of that TV preacher, Rev. Don McQueen. The ministry must be doing pretty well. Cashier's check was delivered this morning to cover a month."

An investigative reporter whose father was one of the most outrageous TV evangelists around? That said a lot. "He's here on a seventy-two-hour. A month is a little overkill, don't you think?" Not exactly a vote of confidence by the family.

"They probably know him. That guy was as violent as I have ever seen."

63

"What's the prescription, and how much?" She tried to make her voice flat.

Rhenquist got a little defensive. "He was fine when he first got here. Seemed distraught, but okay with being here. Kept nodding and going, 'yeah, yeah, this is good.' It was only when that stupid nurse brought up the tray with the needle on it and he saw the locked ward that he started to put up a ruckus."

"How much of what, Rich?" Enough to make him drool. Enough to blur the sound in her head. The off-key calliope sounds were still there, layered on top of her own tinnitus, though with distance the woozy noise had gotten manageable.

Rhenquist clasped his hands behind his back and began to pace. "You're going to have some workman's comp claims from two or three orderlies. He was an animal. It took all three to hold him. I was lucky to get the needle in his thigh at all." He turned to her, challenging.

She said nothing, just stared at him.

"Ten of Ativan, and three hundred of Ziprasidone." He said it like a petulant child admitting that he'd eaten all the candy bars. "The Ativan barely had any effect, so I upped the Ziprasidone. I'm injecting twenty-five every two hours."

Holland sat back. "Sedative *and* enough antipsychotic to knock out a horse, Rich? There are no trials of Ziprasidone over one hundred milligrams. And you ramp up the dose slowly unless you want to risk arrhythmia. Why not Abilify or even Haldol?" This was unconscionable.

"There have been individual cases of doses even higher with no ill effect," Rich defended.

Holland felt the anger rising in her throat. "Those were accidental overdoses, for God's sake." Chloe came in with the coffee and set it down on Holland's desk. Holland hadn't asked Rhenquist if he wanted some, and Chloe didn't offer. Holland was grateful for the break. She needed time to think. She had been about to do something hasty. She might still do something—if not hasty, at least ill-conceived. A thousand thoughts were zinging around in her head along with the noise, none of them sensible. "What's the plan?"

It was an attack. They both knew you couldn't have a treatment plan until you did an interview, and you couldn't do an interview with someone who was just shy of comatose.

"I'll reduce the Ziprasidone over the next day or so. There's time, and that would be safer." Rhenquist sounded casual.

"Rich." Something in her tone made him blink three times rapidly. "He's on a seventy-two-hour hold. We have to do an evaluation for the court in that time frame. He's got to be competent to interview."

"I can get an interview in a couple of days."

Holland took the bull by the horns. She should have confronted Rich a long time ago. "I am not going to condone that level of medication. It's not the 1950s. We don't sedate patients into vegetables. You didn't even have a medical history to assess the risk."

"He's dangerous to the staff, and to me," Rhenquist insisted. "You didn't see him."

"You know as well as I do that more than eyebrows would be raised if it became known that we medicated our patients into a stupor. Ativan and three hundred milligrams of Ziprasidone? Our reputation demands circumspection. If you are afraid of your patients, Rich, defer to another."

"You want me off the case?" He controlled his voice with difficulty.

"The question is, do *you* want you off the case?" She sighed, relenting. "No shame, Rich. You handled whatever came through the door at three A.M. Doesn't mean it has to be your cup of tea. When it comes to multiple personality disorder, you're the best. You just don't like the violent ones." She shrugged, and raised her eyebrows in question.

Rich stiffened. Maybe she shouldn't have used the word shame. "If you mean, do I like to have some control over the situation, then I would answer a resounding 'yes.' " He jerked away. "But I can't have you second-guessing me. I'll supervise until you can get somebody else."

Holland jerked in a breath and let it out. "I'll see who else is available." He didn't have to know she was going to take the case herself. He didn't realize that would be a conflict of interest, since he didn't know this guy was her stalker. And neither did anyone else at the hospital, apparently. Sooner or later, the police or the DA would come sniffing around to hear the shrink's verdict. She couldn't be the registered psychiatrist when they did. If she could get someone else to take the shrink-of-record role and testify, that person would realize what she had done. . . .

Oh, what the hell! She'd deal with that later. Right now, she needed to be the one talking to Jeff McQueen. If she could bear it. If she could hear him over the noise in her head. But the noise in her head was exactly why she had to take this terrible chance.

Chapter Six

Holland gulped her coffee as Rich Rhenquist left her office, fuming. He didn't matter. She had to get back down to the locked ward, and somehow keep the sound in her head at bay long enough to question Jeff McQueen.

She strode out the door, calling to Chloe, "I'm making rounds."

She got out of the elevator on the ground floor where the locked ward was, and the drunken reel of sound engulfed her again. This time she was prepared. The entry he had into her mind influenced the worsening tinnitus, or whatever this was that she heard so unrelentingly. Maybe he heard it too. And maybe it was what was making him crazy. That she could understand. She felt ready to scream herself.

She requested his chart from the nurses in what might be a normal voice, though she got a glance from the young black woman she had known longest. She turned quickly away. The chart said nothing of what she wanted to know. She wanted to know *why* he was crazy, and exactly what he had to do with her. The chart confirmed Rhenquist's assertions that he'd grown violent only in anticipation of being given the antipsychotic. Initially, he seemed to want to be admitted. He had asked for her. That was bad. Someone might put the story together if they read that. She snapped the chart closed and stepped toward the door.

The officer stood. "You don't mind if I do my job?" she asked.

"No, ma'am. I mean, Doctor. You just call if he gets outta hand."

She could only nod. As she opened the door, the wash of sound in her head was like the end of that track on the Sergeant Pepper album her mother liked to play—dissonant and crazy-sounding, ramping up toward painful. She blinked and walked in to stand over the slumping Jeff McQueen. His physical presence seemed amplified by the sound. She glanced to the camera in the corner of the ceiling. Best be circumspect here.

"Mr. McQueen . . ." How could anyone respond through that level of medication? But he raised his head. The green eyes, once so expressive, were dull like a dirty pond in a park, stagnant and littered with floating feathers. He blinked at her. Bubbles hung in the corners of his slack mouth. They hadn't bothered to restrain him. The medication did it for them. She wondered how many hours he'd been sitting there.

"You," he said. It echoed crazily in her head just like last night. She almost leapt backwards. His mouth worked as he tried to say something more, but nothing came out. There was no use talking to him now. Thousands of questions ate at her mind. Was what she thought was happening real? Or was it some crazed hallucination of her degrading mind? She didn't want to guess what an impartial observer would think, like Rhenquist. Or her father. She needed proof.

"It's me. Sorry about the drugs." She pressed a hand to her forehead to steady herself against the crescendo of sound and searched his face for understanding. She found only dull resistance. "You need to sleep. You'll feel better later and we can talk." The stubble obscured some of the fair skin. His lips were slack, all trace of the bitter experience and resolve she had seen in him outside Matsuhisa now gone. The courageous and perceptive reporter was not at home.

"You know." He said it as though it was his last resort, chewing the words and spitting them out with difficulty. "You hear it, too."

"Yes, yes," she agreed, so that it would sound on the tape that accompanied the camera as if she were agreeing just to keep him calm. His words reverberated, a magnified echo inside her mind. "But you rest now." She reached a hand to his shoulder to help him lie down. The shock of warmth through the thin gown, the hard ripple of muscle and sinew vibrated in her consciousness even as the cascade of sound in her ears went suddenly silent.

Silent! Her eyes widened. How long since she had heard silence? The shriek of the Sergeant Pepper orchestra vanished. She could hear the echo of an orderly's stride outside the room. McQueen's chart fell from her nerveless fingers. Papers rustled through air as it fell. This was what had happened at her father's press conference.

But even the quiet was overwhelmed by the sensation flooding her from his touch. She felt the blood throbbing in his body, his warmth gushing up over her fingers. The sense of his flesh beneath the fabric was shattering. She stared into his eyes. Dulled as they were, they widened, too. His chest expanded, straining against the ties of the thin gown. It was as if he breathed for the first time in weeks.

She knew, then. She knew he got silence too and that he had been hearing what she'd been hearing, only probably more so and maybe for longer. She would be looking just as crazy as he was if she'd been living with that din as long as he had. Her eyes flicked over his face. *You know. Tell me. Help me.* That's what he had said to her. All his pleas, all his accusations now rang true. They shared the problem, just as they shared the respite of touching.

Was she imagining this? Was this just another level of her own illness?

She wanted to test it—to pull away from him, but he brought his hand up to envelop her forearm in a callused palm. Peace washed through her. Fulfillment shot between them like souls finding souls, or like life calling to life in some amoebic, pulsing, elemental stew. That was crazy. But she had never felt the call of flesh to flesh more strongly.

"Rest now," she managed, and pushed him gently to the unforgiving mattress.

He shook his head slowly, curling up on his side. "No . . . no sleep."

She ran her hand down his body, never losing touch, and lifted his bare knees up and onto the bed. "Yes. Sleep off the drug. You'll feel better. We can talk then." The blessed silence felt like the grace of God must feel to saints. "It will take a while for the effect to wear off entirely. But tonight or tomorrow you'll feel more yourself." She was babbling.

Again he reached to her and this time drew her down to sit on the bed in the crook of his body. She could feel his belly and the soft mass of his genitals pressed into her hip. She used the corner of her lab coat to wipe the spittle from his beard.

"Don't leave me," he muttered with obvious effort. "Don't let them get me."

She blinked slowly, once. "No. I'll stay a while." How could she refuse the wonderful silence he brought her? And if he heard the same shriek of voices she did, she could understand why he might be afraid they might 'get' him. They might get her, too.

So she sat next to him and stroked his shoulder through the flimsy gown, feeling the muscles and the ligaments that made had him seem so intimidating when he was just her stalker. What was he now? Patient? Harbinger of her own insanity?

Or savior? Even as she watched, his eyes closed. The long lashes and the small, full, puckered mouth belied the strong body. As he drifted into sleep, she kept her hands on him, thankful for the godsend of silence, disturbed only by the feel of his flesh against her own flesh and the trembling awareness that it seemed to bring.

"Call off the dogs, Senator," Leland hissed into the receiver of the phone cord that hung near his mouth as he looked out across the Malibu hills. The morning sun was lighting the brown grasses and making them gold against the intense blue of the sky. "I've got the thing covered."

"Brad says the guy crashed your announcement party. Definitely one of the crazies."

"But now he's locked up where I want him. He may be just the thing I've been looking for. If his psychiatrist gets interested in his case—she may be drawn into my work, and that might help immensely. I want to know how to keep this thing from making them crazy."

"I told you. Try having them run. Running does it for me."

"But it definitely didn't do it for my last subjects. So it isn't just endorphin release." Leland's brain raced on. "That may be part of it, but it could also be behavioral."

"What do you mean, behavioral?" Lendreaux accused.

"I'm not saying you're crazy. I'm saying you have a calculating habit of mind. It may be that as much as chemicals that allows you to deal with the symptoms."

Far from insulted, the Senator's southern drawl filled with self-satisfaction. "You could be right."

"So, I want McQueen alive. Call your shooter off!"

"Will do, Doctor. Now if you think you maybe can let me go, I have a meeting with the Speaker at eleven-thirty."

Leland just grunted. The Senator wasted his time courting the wrong kind of power.

What did they want? He'd tagged four others, right on schedule. It was only this one that was the problem. He wasn't into delivering miracles. How could he do the job when he couldn't get near the damned target? The money guy had gotten damned rag-assed about the whole thing. As if he wasn't the best they had. That guy doing Iowa was nothing. Farmers. Shit, anybody could do farmers. Only witnesses might get you were pigs and chickens. And Mississippi? Bite me. Rednecks thought they knew guns. He knew guns. More than any redneck knew. Using a shotgun. That was a sissy's weapon. Only good for close range. And then you got witnesses. That Iowa guy was gonna go down in about another minute and a half. He squared his shoulders. Which meant it would be up to him. Just him between humans and . . . well, it didn't do to think much on that. He got out of the Caravan and went into the swank apartment building. He grinned to himself. The money guy hadn't been too sure about giving him cash. But how else was he gonna get the bird's-eye view he needed? The garden was his only chance.

Holland sat with her patient—who should not be her patient by any rule of psychiatric ethics—for two hours while he slept, as much for her sanity as his. After a time, she felt strong enough to think about what was happening to her, and to him. She considered what she knew. Whatever it was, she had to believe it was real. The alternative was that she was delusional, paranoid, and hearing voices. She heard him in her head—not anonymous, schizophrenic voices telling her to murder people, or that everyone was against her, or that she was the Empress of Kathmandu. She just heard his voice over the rushing sound in her ears. Was that still crazy? Maybe. Because it wasn't just his voice. She had begun to think there were other voices in the buzz. She just couldn't quite separate them.

He'd asked about patients who thought they weren't human. Her dream to a T. How scary was that? And they both heard the sounds. Maybe he heard her voice in his head, too. She had to ask him. Then there was the fact that, somehow, touching him gave her respite from the cacophony in her head. Was it because the sense of flesh, so overpowering when she touched him, drowned out her sense of hearing? She didn't know. She only knew they were suffering from the same malady. That meant Jeff McQueen was one very important patient.

One of the nurses stuck her head in the room finally and asked if she could get anything. Holland glanced up and managed a smile. "No. I think he's finally gone to sleep." Keeping her hand pressed to his shoulder, Holland got up from the bed and pulled the blankets up over his legs. Then she deliberately broke contact.

At the instant her connection with the sleeping man was abandoned, her tinnitus returned. But it wasn't the shrieking sound of a few hours ago. It was manageable. No whispers, no words, no drowning pools of sound. It was just tinnitus. She could handle that.

McQueen stirred, but Rhenquist's drug kept him under. Holland walked to the door with more composure than she had felt in some time. She realized her hair was escaping its confines on both sides of her head and pushed the wisps behind her ears. "Get me the chart, Mrs. Hernandez, would you?" She locked the door on her patient, her nemesis, her mirror image, as the young woman brought the chart.

Holland took a pen from her pocket and scribbled as she spoke. "Dr. Rhenquist has too high a patient load. I'll get someone else to take the case. We're going to ease him off the Ziprasidone. Ten milligrams twice a day. No more Ativan."

Mrs. Hernandez nodded in unmistakable relief. "I hate to see them so zonked out," the young woman said, then seemed to realize she had revealed an opinion.

"Me, too," Holland agreed. "Can you call me when he wakes up? Better leave a note for the next shift. It could be a while." She smiled. "And could you keep your eye on the monitor? I want to know if he shows any signs of distress."

"Yeah, will do." Mrs. Hernandez took the offered chart. She obviously knew his dose had been too high. She'd be on alert for signs of reaction, and maybe she would brush over Holland's unusual behavior in spending two hours sitting with a sleeping patient. "You know, you're good with patients, Dr. Banks," the nurse stuttered. "And they're good for you. You look more relaxed than you have for a while." She grinned and shrugged her apology for the compliment.

Holland nodded. "Maybe so." She walked toward the elevator. "Keep an eye on him," she threw back over her shoulder.

When she got to her office, an ugly surprise waited for her. Her father was sitting in front of Chloe's desk flipping angrily through last month's copy of *Golf* magazine.

"Holly!" he said, starting up. "How long can patient rounds take? I've been waiting . . ." Then he seemed to remember himself. "Are you okay? I mean, after last night."

Holland shot him a warning look and strode into the office. "Come in, Dad. Want a soda or coffee?" He was dressed impeccably, as always. Today it was a navy blazer, gray slacks, and Bass loafers. The tie was of the old school variety, even though he had gone to the University of Chicago and worked his way through college. Though he wanted her to be just like him, he wanted her to have the pedigree, too. That was why he'd sent her to Yale.

He waved her away and walked to the windows, staring out across the mountains. Of course, the blue shadow on his chin was a bruise from Jeff McQueen's fist, not stubble.

Holland watched him warily. What was he doing here? She didn't want him to know that her attacker was now her patient. Somehow she didn't think he would approve. "Sorry my stalker ruined your press conference last night."

He craned around to look at her. "Gave it some extra spice, that's all. I'm sorry you didn't get to hear me announce our partnership properly."

"What did you say?" she asked, curious. "That you needed a shrink because all the specimens with this extra genome stuff went crazy? Not good for contributions." Why did she always let her speech slide to colloquial when she talked to him? Why couldn't she muster her best professional demeanor with her father? Maybe because that's what he expected.

He grimaced. "You underestimate me, as always, Holly. I played it as a study of nature versus nurture, of course. We'd collaborate to study the difference in results between genetic makeup and environment."

Holland raised her brows. "Of course." Why hadn't she thought of that angle?

"But it isn't 'extra genome stuff.' " He wore his admonishing face. She'd seen it a lot over the years. "It is an

74

elongated genomic thread apparently welding free DNA on the end of the standard strand."

She shrugged. "Okay. So you're here to assess my mental state?" That was better.

He looked a little shocked. She'd only meant it as a joke. He had a hard time even noticing other people's mental state. "Yes," he said slowly. Then he narrowed his eyes as he peered at her. "You have been sounding a little wound up lately, and there are circles under your eyes. Are you feeling all right?"

"Yeah, Dad. I'm fine."

"I still think you should have a workup. Let Grayson do something more comprehensive. And it wouldn't hurt to have your blood levels checked again. I'd be glad to arrange it."

"You are way too protective, Dad." She dismissed his concerns. She wasn't going to let anyone do tests on her right now, especially someone who would run to her father with the results. Who knows what they might find, with what was going on inside her lately?

"All right, Holly. But if you won't allow me to be concerned for your health, at least let me fear for your safety. Have you been contacted by the police to testify against this madman?"

"Not yet." She shrugged.

"Yes, you have," Chloe called from the outer room.

"Chloe?" Holland said, exasperated with herself for forgetting to shut the door.

Chloe stuck her spiky blond head around the doorjamb. "You got a call about an hour ago from some lieutenant. They want to talk to you and Rhenquist after he's had a chance to make a diagnosis."

Her father rounded on her. "Well, what is the situation? Have you seen this man?" He didn't actually seem surprised to find Jeff McQueen in her hospital.

"Just to check his meds. It's odd that he was admitted here." She asked the question he should have been asking as she gently closed the door on Chloe. "How did he get an insanity disposition at three o'clock in the morning? How did family from someplace in Louisiana know to send him here? For that matter, who contacted them?"

"So, it sounds as though you saw McQueen's chart. What do you think?" Her father's eyes were a little too piercing. She knew that look.

"Confidential. Patient privilege." Her words were clipped. She sat behind her desk. It made her look more professional. She had never been able to lie to her father very well. "I can't be on the case, you know. Conflict of interest." In spades. Had she actually lied yet?

Her father leaned forward with his knuckles on her desk. "What does Rhenquist think?"

She shook her head. "Dad, leave it be! Just because the guy took a swing at you . . ." She was not going to say Rhenquist thought Jeff McQueen was so dangerous that he ought to be drugged into oblivion for the staff's safety. Maybe she could get her dad to drop the charges.

Her father stood up straight. "I want to know why he was stalking my daughter. I happen to be interested in whether it's safe to have him in the same hospital where you work."

"Okay, okay. Point taken." Not the time to bring up dropping charges. Was that the real reason he was asking about McQueen?

Her father pressed her. "So, is he crazy?"

Holland looked up at him and shook her head. What was going on here? He was keeping something from her.

Her father's form fairly vibrated with tension. "Perhaps I should talk to Rhenquist. Some of the things that criminal said, Holly . . . He's really fixated on you."

"Rhenquist wouldn't talk to you. Not if he wants to keep his license. You know that."

Her father nodded impatiently. "Yes, yes." He looked at her so strangely. "You never give in, do you Holly? Whatever I want is what you don't want. If I ask you to work with me here, even if it's because I'm concerned about you, you rebel. Everything has to be your idea."

"I might say the same, you know." She kept her voice even.

He shoved his hands in his pockets, thinking. When he raised his head, he fixed her with a stare, as though she were a specimen in a jar. "So, when can you review the two cases connected to my work? I need some answers before the newest subjects start deteriorating."

"I'm pretty busy right now, Dad."

"Holly?"

"Okay, okay." She raised both hands in surrender. "What have you got?"

"Letters, interviews with family and friends, the suicide notes."

Holland sighed. He was right. She got unreasonably rebellious when he wanted something. But whose fault was that? She felt a little guilty. But he always got his own way. Once her father got on a kick, it was only a matter of him wearing her down. He wasn't going to settle for another psychiatrist. If those people were going to get help, it was going to be from her. "Send the materials over. If I have questions, I'll call the interviewers directly."

"Their statements are in the files. But feel free to contact anyone at Genomere."

Holland nodded. "Okay, Dad. But it had better not take up too much time," she warned. "I'm on overload here, what with patients and grants and studies to supervise."

"Understood, important daughter mine." Somehow he made it sound diminutive, as though she had been self-aggrandizing. Which she had.

"Have you seen the reaction to the announcement?" he asked after a moment.

She looked up, confused. "What announcement? Oh . . . No, ah, I've been busy here."

"They're saying it may change genetic research forever." His eyes went opaque, inwardly focused. "At least they get it to that extent." He shook himself. "Small thinkers. They interviewed Herzog. He pooh-poohed the whole thing, of course. But time will tell. In the meantime I'm fending off the reporters. Let the papers speculate for a while."

"So, press conference a success." She couldn't help the accusation in her voice.

"You know, you've been looking a little . . . worn lately." Ah, he knew how to fight with fire. She looked down at her rumpled suit. God, but she was slipping into symptoms anyone but her father would recognize as indicating mental stress.

"Out!" she said sharply. "I have work to do."

He bowed in a courtly fashion and backed out of the room, smack into Chloe.

"Dr. Banks, whatever . . . ?"

He raised the shocked secretary's hand to his lips before sweeping from the room. Holland rolled her eyes and Chloe giggled. Her father could get to anyone.

Night had eased down over the city by the time Holland got a call on her direct line from the nurse's station on the locked ward. Jeff McQueen was awake.

She shot from her office like a pinball sprung from the chute at one of those old-style arcade machines. The tinnitus had been increasing all afternoon until her nerves were so frayed they might well break. On the way down, the sounds in her ears began to escalate even more. They weren't so mushy now. Ignoring the roar, Holland swept up McQueen's chart at the nurses station and glanced through it while she fumbled for her keys. "G . . . odfrey Daniels! He coded this afternoon?" she almost shouted. "Why didn't someone call me?" Damnation! "How could Rhenquist prescribe more Ziprasidone? He was just a caretaker until—"

"He's the doctor of record," the nurse stuttered. "Twenty cc's for maintenance, he said. The patient's chart said he was violent, and he sure put up a fight." The nurse was unfamiliar to Holland. Her wide eyes said she was scared. "What was I to do?"

Holland snapped the chart closed and strode to the door, the frightened nurse scurrying in her wake. Rhenquist was going to pay for this. It was an act of spite that had just about cost this patient his life. "Didn't you see the note that said I should be notified of any change?" The cop at the door stood and looked uneasy as Holland peered through the window in the door.

"Dr. Salvatorre was right here," the nurse excused. "Gave him a shot of epinephrine when his breathing got distressed, and intubated him."

"I hope to God it was norepinephrine." Of course it was. She glanced at the chart and breathed out. Epinephrine would have compounded the hypotension. They might have lost him for good.

"It was over in a second," the nurse babbled. "His blood pressure came back down, and Dr. Salvatorre took the tube out about five. He's better now . . ."

Holland grabbed the stethoscope from around the nurse's neck. At least John hadn't done a tracheotomy. She fumbled with the lock.

"I thought Dr. Salvatorre would report it . . ." The nurse trailed off.

"Bring me a blood-pressure cuff." Holland leaned into the opening door and then closed it behind her on the nurse's explanations. John should have shipped McQueen out at once. Of course, if he *had* shipped him, and the receiving hospital realized the cause, inquiries would already be in progress. John thought he was protecting Rhenquist, and of course, the hospital. Holland took a breath. Let him think that. It made a good excuse for why she had taken the case from Rhenquist.

Jeff McQueen lay on his bed, groggy but conscious.

"Hello," she said, wondering if she whispered or shouted around the noise.

He reached out a hand for her. It was shaking. He knew what to do. She glanced through the window. No peering eyes. But there was the camera in the corner that recorded everything for the courts in case of malpractice, for management action in case of employee misconduct. She didn't take his hand because that would be outside her normal behavior with patients. But she did sit beside him and let their bodies touch.

Silence settled around them. She could see his breathing ease. Her own shoulders relaxed into a more natural position. God, what sweet relief this was!

"How you doing?" She hoped he was coherent. She had fifty-four hours left before she had to declare him insane or let him go to jail, or convince her father to drop the charges. She took the stethoscope and placed it against his chest, listening for arrhythmia.

He nodded. "Clearer. Maybe better." His voice was rasping as well as deep from the tube John had inserted. "Arrhythmia gone. You've a heart like a horse." Bracing for the cascade of sound, she stepped to the door. She cracked it open and called for water. McQueen's brows drew together in pain. Sound had drenched him, too. The nurse handed Holland a pitcher, a plastic glass and the blood-pressure cuff. They should have brought him water. Rhenquist had made them afraid of him. She poured a glass and sat back down into his warmth and the silence. She felt healed, and the feeling came from more than just the silence.

McQueen laid his hand on the bed along her thigh. Nothing noticeable. He was alert enough to take her lead. But he wanted to touch her, too. She slid her hand under his head and lifted it so he could drink. The soft skin at the nape of his neck under his hair felt vulnerable.

She watched the muscles in his strong throat undulate as he gulped water. "Better?"

He nodded. "Sore throat," he rasped. She let his head down gently to the pillow.

She took a cloth that hung over the metal nightstand that sported padded edges and wiped the corners of his mouth, not only to remove the water but the dried white line around his lips, the residue of drugs and saliva. Wrapping the blood-pressure cuff around his arm, she pumped it. "Did they feed you?"

"I . . . I don't think so. Maybe."

She listened for the throb of blood, and watched the dial as it faded. "Still a little low. Could you eat?"

He searched her face. "Yeah. But I don't want food bad enough to have you go get it."

She let her lips curve just a little and leaned over him to ring the nurse's button. She heard the door open behind her. "Send in a tray. Make it a soft diet."

The door closed. "Sorry, Mr. McQueen. It's soup and Jell-O for you right now."

He swallowed and rolled his head on the pillow, casting his green eyes over her. They had come alive again. He had journeyed at least halfway back across the River Styx. "Mr. McQueen? Pretty formal for what we have together."

"And what do we have together? I've been meaning to ask you. Remember that your answer goes in your medical record." She glanced to the camera in the corner of the ceiling, trying to tell him to be discrete, though she wasn't sure he was up to it.

"We're alike, you and I, Dr. Banks."

Okay, that wasn't incriminating. Lots of patients thought they were like their doctors.

"We both have the same disease," he continued. "At first I thought you would know about others, because of what you do. But then I realized . . . I began to hear you . . ."

"I must be blunt. That's a common delusion, Mr. McQueen, for patients to assume their doctor shares their disease. You have to recognize that as part of your problem." She tried to warn him with her eyes. She tried to tell him what she really knew.

81

"But I *know* you hear it." He gripped her hand. Sweat beaded on his forehead, glistened at his throat and on his biceps as anxiety took him again. "I know you feel the silence."

The door behind them opened.

"The tray, Dr. Banks." The nurse was all business, trying to make up for her lapse.

Holland twisted and took the tray from her, swung out the metal arm of the nightstand that was meant to hold just such a tray. "You can go. I'll see that he eats."

"Can you sit up?" she asked as the door closed behind them. She scooted up with him, never losing contact, and pushed the pillows up behind his back.

"Yeah. I'm okay to eat." He reached for the soup spoon. His hands were shaking. The spoon dropped to the blankets, bounced, and skittered to the floor.

She smiled. "Looks like not. Now you get to eat your soup with a teaspoon."

He sank back into the pillows, already exhausted. He looked disgusted with himself. Sweat soaked his gown. She could feel the hot flesh of his thigh against her hip. That touch of flesh was a pentagram drawn against the dark forces of night inside their heads. She held the glass again and he drank.

"You need food and water, lots of rest," she explained, just to focus his attention. "You got quite a kick of Ativan and Ziprasidone." She scooped a spoonful of soup and held it to his lips.

He pushed his hair off his face. The gesture made his biceps bunch. He managed to suck the soup in without jarring the spoon. They worked at the food in silence. She alternated soup with Jell-O, the green kind.

"Hey, if you keep this down, tomorrow you get rice."

He managed a weak grin. "Shit, yes. That's something to live for."

"Now, we're going to set the IV in a minute. You need fluids. We don't want you to crash and try to burn again.

Think you could avoid putting anyone in the hospital when we bring in a needle?"

"Yeah. Maybe." He slurped more soup. It was beef broth with some noodle things and some green and orange pieces that might have been peas and carrots. With a hospital you could never be sure. "Maybe you could give it to me." Here was a man sure of his effect on women. And why not? She'd bet he had plenty of propositions before he started looking crazy.

"Deal." She pressed the nurse's button again, then offered more soup. He leaned back and shook his head. "Okay," she said. "You did okay." She ordered the IV and returned the tray. "So, why'd you lose it last night when you saw the syringe?"

"You mean, besides the fact that I thought they might be making me into a vegetable?" Which Rhenquist had, Holland thought guiltily—almost a dead vegetable.

McQueen continued. "Well, Doc, somebody's been trying to kill me. Just don't trust anybody right now. Not with needles, and not in the open."

Typical paranoia. "You must trust somebody sometime. I'm not out to get you."

"You might be the only one who isn't," he whispered, eyeing the syringe the nurse brought on the tray. An orderly pushed in a metal tree. The bag hanging from it was filled with a clear liquid. A plastic tube dropped from the bag. McQueen was biting his lip on the inside. Holland hooked the syringe to the clear tube, then held up the syringe and let a drop of the IV fluid shiver at its tip. He heaved a breath and held out his arm as the nurse retreated, bracing his elbow with his other hand so it wouldn't shake. It was a touching gesture of courage and trust. She only hoped she wouldn't betray it.

Holland scooted up and braced his elbow with her knee, not trusting his strength. "This is just some saline solution. No drugs. It will bring up your blood pressure so you don't feel faint," she promised. "Make a fist." She waited. "Now relax your hand." The sharp point of the silver lance dented his skin on the inside of his forearm, then slid into the blue twine of his vein. She taped the syringe to his arm. "That was easy. Lie down now. You'll feel better soon." Fear flickered in his eyes. But he slid down into the bedding.

"Stay with me . . ." he whispered.

She only nodded. "Until you sleep. No talking though." She couldn't take a chance of what he might say in front of that camera as he grew sleepy. "Tomorrow we'll have time for a nice long talk. If you're well-behaved with all the staff, we might even be able to take a turn outside in the garden. That's always a nice place for talking."

"Not out in the open!" Fear flared in his eyes. She'd forgotten the paranoia.

"It's got a nice high wall."

"Okay." He swallowed. "We need to talk. I'll be a model prisoner." His voice had already softened at the edges with fatigue.

"See that you are." She smiled. His reference reminded her that some lieutenant wanted an official opinion about his sanity. And she wouldn't be able to put him off for long.

McQueen's eyes closed, lashes thick against his cheek. A lock of chin-length hair waved across his face and she touched it gingerly to ease it back behind his ears. Smooth skin against her fingers slid sensation down her spine. Her fingers jerked away as she recognized that feeling.

God, Holland! Have you forgotten every tenet of ethics you ever had? Not only was she treating a patient with whom she had a personal involvement, but she was having feelings that were far from doctorly about him. Touching him was dangerous. She'd made it a policy never to touch her male patients. But only touch gave her and Jeff McQueen respite from their malady.

She rose and the sound washed over her. But again, it was more manageable. His eyelids fluttered but remained closed. The touching had a calming effect on both of them, she was sure of it. And without that touching, the sound cycled up to levels that could cause insanity all on their own. How could she treat him if neither of them could even think?

The answer to that was that she should not be treating him at all. It didn't have to be Rhenquist. She could rope in Petersen or Stafford. But she wouldn't. She had to know what he heard and, if he knew, *why* he heard. She turned toward the door, acutely conscious of the camera in the corner, the police officer stationed by the door.

So that was it. She was going to break every rule in every book and treat a man she could have no objectivity about. And she was going to touch him. Her sanity might depend upon it.

Chapter Seven

Holland woke on her knees in the middle of her bedroom, sobbing and gasping. She was holding her right hand in a grip that would leave bruises. The lights she'd left on all over the house seemed harsh. They hadn't banished the dream. Early light leaked through the shutters. Looking around dazedly, she saw the digital clock on her nightstand blank and dead. Its cord snaked across the oriental rug, its plug prongs bent where she'd pulled it out of the wall.

Slowly her breathing got more regular. She unwrapped her fingers from around her wrist.

Okay. The dream again. Nothing she hadn't felt before. She struggled to her feet and collapsed to sit on the edge of her disheveled bed. She wondered if Jeff McQueen had dreams.

She took a breath and raised her head. In and out. Just breathe.

The glint in the corner of the room shocked her. Even as her eyes jerked to it, she knew what she would see.

A butcher knife lay on the carpet, where she had thrown it. She must have gotten all the way to the kitchen to find it and back here to her bedroom.

Which hand had thrown it away? She was spiraling down toward a fate she couldn't see.

There was only one glimmer of hope.

She had to get to the hospital.

By the time Holland arrived at the hospital the tinnitus was out of control again. The noise was drenching. She couldn't distinguish one sound from another outside her head, and couldn't decide which ones were important. That was a clear symptom of schizophrenia, as was the fact that she was listening for voices in the cascading su-surrations.

She practically careened into the hospital parking lot at six-thirty, having dressed hastily. She'd just put her hair in a ponytail and had forgotten her lipstick all together. She didn't seem to have any in her purse, which was unthinkable. She'd have to check her briefcase. Except she'd left her briefcase at home. Come to think, she hadn't cleaned up the spilt wine or the glass in her kitchen either, and she'd left take-out containers all over the living room. Hadn't she? What was in them? Chinese food? Had she eaten at all? She couldn't think.

As she got out of the car, she looked down and realized she'd worn navy shoes with her black suit. She swallowed hard. Another sign. She was losing her sense of personal hygiene. Had she taken a shower this morning? She had. Of course she had. But her world was collapsing into chaos she couldn't control. How could you control anything with this screaming in your head? How could you trust yourself when dreams consumed you and edged into your reality? She was lucky she hadn't sawed off her hand last night. Was that lucky?

She swung open the door, waving Ernie away, and dashed inside. At least she wasn't limping so badly today. She'd almost forgotten about the cut on her foot. The roar in her ears intensified as she passed the locked ward. It took everything she had not to rush in to see McQueen.

But she couldn't do that. It wouldn't look right. She had to keep some sense of decorum as protection, or everyone would know she was insane, and they'd begin questioning her right to treat anyone. She pounded the elevator button. The nurses at the One East station were staring at her, she was sure. They had noticed that her shoes didn't match. They disapproved. Or maybe they disapproved of the fact that she sat with her male patient. Maybe they knew she touched him. Maybe everybody knew. An orderly passed. Was he staring at her? Did he know? Where was the damned elevator? She turned and rushed up the stairs.

It was too early for Chloe by hours. Holland was glad. There was no way she wanted to face those sharp eyes right now. She dropped her purse on her desk, pulled on a lab coat hanging on the back of the door, grabbed some random charts and held them against her chest as protection before she hit the stairs again.

He would be having breakfast. Nurses might be there or orderlies. She couldn't ask what she wanted to know under that camera's unforgiving eye. She'd had a plan yesterday, but now she couldn't think what to do.

She burst out of the stairwell and headed for the locked ward. Keys. Had she brought her keys? Yeah. Okay. The keys were here. Her hands shook as she fumbled with the lock. Then she was in. She wanted to ask the nurses about their observations overnight, whether he had been restless, whether he had slept. God, for all she knew, he'd been rushed to Cedars and died.

But if she asked her voice might betray her, so she raised a hand in salute and fumbled for his chart in the rack beside the station, then added it to her others. The nurse was trying to say something to her, but she brushed it off and headed for his room.

The young Hispanic cop was back. He just shook his head and pointed his thumb over his shoulder. "Can't you do something about that? He's driving me nuts." A thumping sound came dimly through the door. It was a bass rhythm to the insect whine of noises in her head.

A glance through the door showed McQueen curled against the wall at the right side of his bed, clutching his knees to his chest and rocking. He banged his head rhythmically against the padded headboard. A tray and its food were strewn across the floor. Damned nurses! They must have heard it crash. If they were afraid, why didn't they call the orderly? The patient required restraint. Or . . . maybe he needed something else.

"Jeff," she managed as the door swung shut behind her. She didn't shout, she was sure. But he didn't hear her either. The gown didn't cover him in that position. The muscles in his arms bunched as he clutched his knees. A sweep of thigh and a glimpse of buttocks startled her. But worse was the blood streaking down his left temple and the Rorschach red print against the headboard where he banged against it. Was there a screw or something sharp under the padding?

The thud reverberated along her spine. Her charts dropped to the floor. She lunged for the bed. She had to stop that horrible thudding. She stumbled, tripped over the IV stand, dragged herself up. All she could reach was his foot.

Breath hissed in through her teeth as the silence fell inside her head.

Behind her, the door banged open. Jeff's head thudded once more against the wall and stopped. She sat up, her hand on his foot concealed by her body, and turned to the opening door.

"Dr. Banks?" the orderly asked. "Are you okay?"

He was big. They all were. This one was young and white and had probably been a linebacker on his high school football team. His hair was still in a crew cut. Behind him, the police officer had risen and had a hand on the gun in his holster, his face a worried frown.

She tried to arrange her face in a smile. "Yeah," she said. "It's all right, officer."

"The station buzzed me," the orderly apologized, "but I was over on West. Dr. Stafford wanted Thompson moved." He shrugged. "He won't leave Gertrude alone. Is this one okay?"

She glanced back at McQueen. He had collapsed against the wall. Even as she watched, his face unscrewed itself. The lines between his brows and those around his mouth relaxed in some tiny incremental process. "I think so." Her voice was not quite her own. "I'll leave orders for restraints at night." She looked around at the white walls, at the camera in the corner of the ceiling. She had to get out of here. She had to get him out. "Why don't you bring a wheelchair?" She swallowed and strove for a normal tone. "Be sure it has cuffs."

The orderly's eyes opened wider. He hesitated. "Uh . . . sure, Doctor."

"Oh, and while we're out, have the facilities guy go over this room with a fine-tooth comb." She reached for the padded headboard and ran her hand over a tear in the fake leather. "Yeah, there's something sharp under here, a screw or something. And nurse, get me a bandage."

As the door closed, Holland's attention jerked back to McQueen. His eyes fluttered open. She wanted nothing more than to run her hand up his thigh, but instead she scooted up beside him and unwrapped his hands gently from around his knees. "That bad?" she asked softly. He let her unwind him, sucking in air and forcibly relaxing.

He nodded. He was about to speak, to try to explain.

"Shush," she said, trying to curve her lips up. "Save that conversation." She turned his chin to look at the side of his head. "Human flesh is fragile," she said, her voice low and calm now that she had herself back again. "You might want to be more careful with it."

His half-chuckle was shaky. "I'll try to remember that."

He had the knack of sounding sane and self-aware—when he wasn't banging his head uncontrollably, that was. She reached for the towel on the nightstand and dipped it in his drinking water. He turned his head obligingly. He had more color this morning. Blood pressure must be up. That openness reminded her of the courage he had displayed last night in the face of a needle that must have frightened him. She wiped his cheek and daubed at his temple. He'd really done a job on it. Nothing to stitch. It was a bloody pulp about the size of a quarter. "You feel up to a turn outside in the garden before we try breakfast?"

"If you're sure it's not in the open." The nurse came in and handed her a square antiseptic pad and a swab.

"It's pretty secure. How's the head? I mean, besides the headache you just gave yourself. Feeling clearer?" She tried to concentrate on his temple as she sealed the pad over the wound.

"Better now the noise is gone. You?"

She just nodded. She heard him so plainly. His voice was like ice crystals or transparent water, pure. It rumbled inside her head as well as in through her ears. She felt tuned to him. She could feel the relief he was suppressing underneath the nonchalance. And underneath that relief, the fear that clattered in the dark parts of his mind. The emotions almost had color, she could feel them so clearly. The relief was blue. The fear was boiling brown with swirling red streaks. While they waited, she unhooked the IV though she left the needle taped to his arm for future use.

The orderly brought in the wheelchair. The four leather cuffs, replete with buckles and lined with sheepskin, had metal loops sewn into them. Short chains of the kind that heavy dog collars were made of connected the loops to the arms and the leg struts of the wheelchairs. She had never noticed how much these chairs looked like something used by the Inquisition.

She lifted her brows as she saw him staring at it. "A turn in the garden?"

He swallowed. The brown and red swirls of fear boiled up. She could see them, glowing around him. It wasn't just an association of a particular set of colors with his emotion. It was an . . . aura. Holland blinked once and tried not to gasp. What was happening here? This was getting worse by the minute.

"We'll keep out of the open." The paranoia again. He thought someone was trying to kill him. It wasn't surprising with all this coverage of the snipers. Even sane people were scared.

"I promise," she managed, and took his arm above the elbow and the orderly stepped in to help. It was a great excuse to touch him. If she broke the touch, his fragile hold on sanity might break with it, and she was not far behind. His knees wouldn't hold him, but together, she and the orderly got McQueen into the wheelchair. The orderly buckled the straps around his thick wrists and bare ankles, and slid some slippers on his feet.

"You sure about this, Doctor?" the orderly asked doubtfully.

"Very sure." She tried to sound it. "Hand me a couple of lap robes." She tucked one around McQueen's hips and flapped another around his shoulders. It might be July, but the thin hospital gown did not seem enough protection against real air.

"You want me to wheel him out?"

Holland shook her head and took the handles of the chair. "I'll manage." Her hand just brushed McQueen's shoulder. She hoped the orderly or the nurses didn't catch it. As she pushed the chair out the door, the cop got up to follow.

"I'm just taking him to the garden." She found a need to justify that. "It helps start the conversation between doctor and patient."

"I'm sure it does, ma'am," the policeman said. "But when prisoners are in a regular hospital, they have to be accompanied by an officer of the law."

Holland could see she wasn't going to get out of it. "Well, to preserve patient confidentiality, perhaps you could just keep your distance?" He looked doubtful. "Patient rights are the same whether the patient is an accused criminal or not."

The cop nodded reluctantly. Holland didn't wait. She rolled McQueen down the long hall, its tile floors gleaming, toward the squares of light in the doors that meant escape. The cop trailed them. She swung McQueen around and backed against the push bars, pulling him after her.

Early morning bathed the garden in soft light. The day would be hot later, but now the air was cool and clean. Down the cement ramp they rolled and across the pebbly concrete of the patio where the staff could eat at tables under the umbrellas and smoke their cigarettes. The cop took a seat in the sun. The little garden and the patio always seemed like a miracle in the middle of Beverly Hills Adjacent. It was bigger than it looked. Winding concrete paths just wide enough for wheelchairs gave privacy. The lawns were dotted with purple trees. In spring, jacarandas littered the lawn with lavender blossoms. Now, in July, the princess flower trees and the wisteria had taken up the purple theme as they fluttered blossoms over blue lilies of the Nile and neat beds of lobelia. Blue-purple was a restful color, perfect for the garden of a loony bin.

A glint caught her eye and Holland glanced past the walls to the high-rise apartments snuggled up against the hills. The wheelchair slowed. There! There, at that open window on the nearest building. A guy in a white t-shirt disappeared into the darkness of the apartment within.

"Get under a wall," McQueen hissed. "We're sitting ducks!"

Holland didn't stop to think. McQueen's fear washing through her, she shoved the wheelchair toward a pergola at the right side of the garden. She was soon at a run, his paranoia making her adrenaline flow. They ducked under the pergola, its roof of wisteria vine sheltering them from any view. She raced down the perimeter path to a bench under the garden wall closest to the building where she had seen the glint. No one could possibly see them here. Her breath shuddered in her chest. This was ridiculous.

But she didn't push out from under the wisteria. This spot served the purpose. She had a view of the doorway and no one could hear their conversation. The cover would let McQueen relax. The cop had shifted to a spot where he could see them. She put her hand on McQueen's shoulder as she went around to sit on the bench, his chair drawn up close enough so their knees could touch. Even through the thick lap robe, his flesh called to her.

"This okay?" she asked, her asperity covering her embarrassment that she had run.

He looked up as she sat, his eyes never leaving hers. "Define okay." At least she couldn't see a halo of color around him anymore. Boy, there was a prime delusion.

"So," she said, but did not know how to go on. The professional line of questioning appropriate for a patient like this got tangled with her desperate need to know what the man knew, or thought he knew, or even what he didn't know, and nothing came out at all.

"That line about all patients thinking that the doctor shares their delusions is a bunch of crap in this case." Well, he was nothing if not blunt.

"Why do you think so?" Professional questioning to the rescue.

"Because you can hear me, just like I can hear you."

"Can you hear me? How?"

"Inside my head. You're louder. When I hear you, the others fade a little."

She wasn't going to agree with him. She just needed to know everything he knew. But the fact that what he said frightened her must have shown in her eyes.

"I know it's that way for you, too." He looked at her steadily. He seemed very sane, regardless of the wild statements he was making.

"How do you know?"

"I knew at your father's house, when I touched you."

Holland chewed her lip. "Tell me about the others. Other voices?"

"Yeah. They're getting clearer, some of them, sometimes."

"And do they tell you to do things?" Now she'd get to exactly how crazy he was—how crazy she might become.

He shook his head. "Mostly it's incoherent—screaming, chaotic thoughts, feelings of fear. Sometimes it's more like I'm just listening in on what they're thinking anyway. Gotta take a crap, want to screw that woman, this guy's lying to me . . . just whatever's in their mind. Once I heard someone thinking he'd be the most powerful person on earth. At least I think it was a he." He examined her to see how she was taking it. "How about you?"

"This isn't about me." She was determined to be the one asking questions.

"Oh, really?" He leaned forward against the restraints on his wrists. A well of red intensity rushed over her. The aura was back. She could see it glowing red around him. "Then the fact that you've violated every tenet of the psychiatric oath by taking my case and touching me when we both need touching, and even bringing me out here where no one can hear us . . . that's just coincidence, right?"

Why did he have to be an investigative reporter? She cleared her throat. "Your tendency to go on the attack is very interesting, Mr. McQueen. Now, why don't we talk about how long this has been happening to you?"

He sat back. A gray wall went up over his emotions. She could feel the red just pulsing in the background somewhere, but it was faint behind the gray. She wished the aura would disappear, but Holland refused to rub her eyes in front of him. "Have it your way. Three weeks, maybe. Steadily worse. Sound got louder, voices got clearer. Can hardly think now, except . . . well, you know when, now don't you, Doctor?"

She knew when. "Why did you stalk me?" If he wanted to be blunt, they could be blunt.

"It occurred to me, when clear thoughts were getting a little difficult to come by, that I was looking crazy." He gave a rueful chuckle. The gray wall receded a little. Holland could feel the wry sanity as healing green. "My colleagues at the paper were starting to show some concern about my well-being—you know, avoiding me in the halls, canceling dinners their wives had invited me to, that sort of thing. Maybe I *was* crazy. But, on the outside chance that something real was happening to me . . . well then, I thought maybe it might have happened to somebody else, too. In which case, people would think they were crazy. So I thought maybe I'd look for other crazy people who had my symptoms in places where crazy people hang out. Like here."

"County Hospital sounds like a better bet for research, in that case."

"Yeah, like I could find anybody getting genuine treatment in that shithole. No, I was betting that in a private hospital the staff would take time to really know what was going on with their patients. I saw your picture in the paper, getting that big ol' check at the Sons of Charity dinner." He sat back, looking at her from cynical green eyes. "Voila!"

"What do you mean, 'voila?' You go from thinking I might know something about your condition to stalking in one easy step?" Holland couldn't help letting her annoyance show.

"Well, I wouldn't call it easy." He grimaced. "Hard to keep sane enough to stalk you properly, if you know what I mean. Or maybe you don't. How long have you had it?"

She frowned at him.

"Oh, yeah, I forgot. This isn't about you." He looked down to her knee touching his. "If this isn't about you, Doctor, why don't you break contact?"

He had her there. Damn. The professional veneer was all that stood between her and her own fear. Maybe it stood between her and what this man knew. Professionalism be damned. She didn't move her knee. But she did take a breath, for courage. "So you found out where I worked, and you followed me . . ."

"Only, when I saw you at the gym—no, when I *heard* you say something to the check-in guy—I realized it was your voice that had been the loudest of all those voices in my head. I thought maybe you yourself, not one of your patients, were . . . were what I was looking for. Then I thought maybe you were in on the conspiracy to drive me bats, or maybe that there was a colony of you and I could hear you all, and that maybe you weren't even human, or maybe I wasn't either. I've always had dreams . . ." He sounded insane now. Anyone listening to him would think so. Except he was echoing her own thoughts.

She searched his face, her fear cycling up inside her. His eyes were serious. They didn't flick nervously about. Maybe they wanted to, but he held them still. He was trying incredibly hard to pass for sane. But the green healing color of sanity bled out to the edges and all she could see (or did she mean feel?) was the brown streaked with orange that seemed like fear. It didn't matter that he was trying to sound sane, because what he was saying was too frightening, too horrible, and it was what she had suspected somewhere all along. Tears filled her eyes. Her breathing came fast and shallow. All she could do was nod.

He looked at her with some kind of longing she dared not recognize as familiar.

She swallowed and sat back. Only then did she realize she'd been leaning toward him, gripping her charts, her pen fallen to the cement among the wisteria petals. She filled her lungs. "What . . . what form to these dreams take?" she managed.

It was his turn to lean forward. The chains that held the leather cuffs to the chair clanked as he moved. "I bet you can tell me, Doc. I bet you know just what form they take."

Impasse. He wouldn't tell her if she wouldn't tell him. How badly did she want to know? Well, her sanity probably depended on it. She rolled her eyes up toward the tangle of ropy brown stems twining, dark and sinuous, through the pergola. They reminded her of Hieronymous Bosch's vision of Hell. Her throat was so full she couldn't speak.

His voice was soft as he took pity on her. "Those bruises on your neck?"

Her hand jumped to her throat. She'd forgotten that he would be able to see the bruises left by dreams too real to be dreams at all. She turned startled eyes to his face.

"I'm guessing it isn't a boyfriend thing. Didn't notice any boyfriend when I was stalking you. So . . . uh, *your* hand made the bruises?"

Tears spilled onto her cheeks. She nodded. That nod cost her all the vulnerability she would ever be able to spare.

He looked away, as though her pain was too terrible to witness. "Yeah. Well. For me it isn't a body part that seems inhuman, though I think maybe others feel that. I hear some of them talking about it, or thinking about it, or whatever." He sucked a breath into his lungs. "For me it's the whole enchilada. I dream I'm abducted by aliens." He took a breath. "I know it isn't real. Most of the time. But when

I come back to earth, I'm not human anymore. Not quite."

A breath shuddered into her. "What do you think it means?"

He chuckled under his breath. It wasn't as though he thought it was funny. But Holland felt, or maybe saw, the green again. "You tell me. Doc. You're the shrink."

"I don't know," she whispered. "I wish I did." She wasn't sure standard dream therapy applied in their case.

"Well, so much for psychiatry."

"What did you want to do when you finally caught up with me?" she asked. "It was you at my house that night, wasn't it?"

His eyes locked with hers. "I was desperate." He looked away. "I don't know."

"You left, though."

He licked his lips. "I could feel your panic. I . . . I didn't want to be the cause of that. And then there's the guy that is after me. Whoever it is. I didn't want to bring him down on you like I almost did outside the restaurant."

"Oh yeah, the person who's after you." The neutrality in her voice made him angry.

"You don't believe me?" he barked. "You still think I'm crazy paranoid, after all you know?" He must have seen the doubt in her eyes. "You *saw* him shoot at me, in front of that sushi restaurant. Don't you even believe your own eyes?"

"I didn't see anyone shoot at you. I thought you shot at me." Her voice faltered. Except he'd used both hands to run his fingers through his hair before he ducked into the alley.

"So, uh, nobody told you they patched me up here?"

"What?"

"I thought they might have made a little note in the chart." His voice was sarcastic.

She realized that she'd been so frantic to get to him, she'd only skimmed his chart. Ativan, Ziprasidone, intubation. Those kind of words tended to obscure the more mundane. She gritted her teeth. Could she have missed something?

"My shoulder." He shrugged it as if in proof.

Oh, God. She remembered the stiff, dark stain on his shirt at her father's house. Her hands moved up his body as she stood and undid the tie at the back of his neck. She could see the two strips of tape that held the bandage in place across his upper arm, just below the shoulder.

"Just grazed me."

She tied the tie with shaking hands. Somebody *was* shooting at him. "Why?"

He sighed. "Shit, I don't know. Maybe somebody doesn't like crazy people?"

Holland sat on the bench heavily, knee to knee. She couldn't meet his eyes. He was thinking someone was after him because he was evil, because he wasn't human. Because there was something strange about him. Something they shared.

She could hear everything he thought. Oh, this was just worse and worse.

She stared at the broken wisteria blossoms on the concrete. The edges had turned dark purple with rot where she'd stepped on them or where the wheels of McQueen's chair had crushed them. The silence might go on forever. Would that comfort her or drive her wild?

"What now?" he asked in that low rumble.

She drew her gaze up to his face. In that moment it looked so self-aware, so devastated, it could not help but indicate sanity. "You're the one with the plan."

He managed rueful. "My plan was to find you."

Practical. They needed to be practical. It was all very well to be talking about feeling evil and hearing voices. But how would they survive the next few days? "We need time to think." She looked around. "This place is as safe as any for a while. You are a patient and you can't be moved for seventy-two hours, except to another locked ward. That's just under two more days. No one can shoot at you inside a hospital." Her thoughts darted to the glint in the window. No, you couldn't let your imagination have free rein. She started again. "I can visit you at intervals to get us relief." Her hand crawled to his knee. It was the one that had left the bruises on her throat. "We can try to figure this thing out, what we should do." Oh, that sounded just so definite. Some plan.

"I don't think I can do another night . . . like last night." The words seemed torn from him.

"Okay." He meant another night with sound ramping up and voices whispering in his head. What he didn't say was that he couldn't stand another night without her. She didn't tell him she might not be able to do another night apart from him either. "I'll see you right before I leave for the evening. Eightish." Eight, to seven in the morning? Too long. "Or maybe I leave only to shower and change. Sleep hasn't been so good lately anyway. I come back at midnight, see you, then doze in my office if I need to." She nodded.

"Yeah."

The nurses would talk. Maybe she could come up with another patient as an excuse for her bizarre schedule. How long would that provide any cover?

"What happens after seventy-two hours?" he asked himself as much as her. "I can't go back out there. They'll kill me sooner or later."

Holland couldn't think. Then she could think too clearly. Something was about to happen.

"The cop is getting antsy." She knew he was right.

The cop stood and called, "You two about finished here?"

She glanced to McQueen. They'd known the cop would speak. "How?" she whispered.

"I . . . I heard him thinking about it." McQueen's eyes were wide.

She hadn't heard actual thoughts. Not like McQueen. But she'd known, just the same.

"Time to go back." Her voice cracked.

The devastation on his face would be comical if she didn't feel it too. It wasn't just brown, boiling fear. There was something else too, indigo blue.

She ran her hand up his thigh and jerked it to his arm, then slid up his bare biceps to his shoulder, the one without the bandage, covered still with the lap robe. "Let's get you a shave and a haircut. It will make you look a little saner, maybe feel a little saner."

He jerked his face up to hers. "You can't let them lock me up for good. And I won't be safe here forever. They'll find a way to get to me."

Well, there *was* a sniper after him. He had the graze to prove it. He might still be paranoid, but he had cause. That didn't make him less crazy. "Leave it to me," she muttered as she wheeled him up the path and made the dash toward the door the cop was holding open. "I'll work on it." The only problem was she had no idea what to do.

Chapter Eight

Holland reached her office with a feeling of surprising calm. The rush of water sounds in her ears was manageable and the certainty that there was another like her, however crazy they both were, gave some measure of comfort. Jeff McQueen's chart documented that his initial physical examination had revealed what was apparently a graze-type wound on his left shoulder caused by a bullet. At least he wasn't *only* paranoid. She was able to greet Chloe with a smile. Maybe the smile was a leftover glow from touching

Jeff McQueen. She could still feel the smooth, pale skin of his arm, the bunching of the muscles underneath, against her palm. She had revised her opinion of him. He wasn't just brave and perceptive. He might be the most courageous man she'd ever met. His plan to find others when his own sanity was under attack was really astounding.

Chloe lifted her brows and handed Holland a stack of messages on top of a cardboard box filled with file folders. "The lieutenant has been calling, Dr. Banks. And this box came by special messenger marked 'Urgent'."

Holland tossed the message slips back at Chloe. "I have his number." She took the box. She didn't have to look at the return address to know it was from her father. His work took precedence over anything she might have to do. He was expecting action and right away.

"Sniper got three more here in L.A., Dr. Banks," Chloe called after her. "Rhonda just heard on the radio. And they're falling like dominoes in San Francisco. One even in Iowa today."

"Calm down, Chloe. You have a better chance of getting run over by a truck than getting shot by a sniper." But all this talk of snipers resonated with someone trying to kill Jeff McQueen. Who would do that? How did they know about him? *What* did they know? Was it even connected to his condition, or was the shooter some enemy he had made chasing down frauds and smearing their indiscretions across a paper with a circulation of three million? The only thing she could say for certain was that someone *had* shot at him. His body bore the proof.

Holland plopped the box on the floor behind her desk. She had no time for research projects or lieutenants.

As a matter of fact, the lieutenant was a problem. He would be looking for a way to convict McQueen of assault. He'd want to know whether her patient was crazy. What could she say? *He is crazy by all clinical standards, but based on my personal experience he's sane because I have those same delusions and I'm sane*. Yeah. Great professional opinion. If she said he was sane, he'd be moved to jail. Jeff McQueen *must not* be incarcerated. As far as she remembered, visits to prisoners every four hours weren't regulation, and touching wasn't allowed.

And the lieutenant would know Jeff McQueen had stalked her, assaulted her father. Rich was still the doctor of record, but he'd document the transfer of care to her in the chart the next time he made rounds to absolve himself of responsibility for any violence on Jeff's part. If the lieutenant found that she was treating McQueen, he would know it was a conflict of interest and have her removed from the case. Maybe he'd have Jeff moved to County. If she refused to talk to the police, the D.A. would not be far behind the lieutenant. She hadn't watched all those reruns of *Law & Order* for nothing. The only answer was to get her father to drop the charges. That hadn't seemed very likely when last she talked to him.

She sat heavily into the hunter-green leather of her desk chair and let her head fall onto her hand. *The* hand. As she ran her fingers through her hair, she realized she could never trust that hand again. She straightened and looked at it. So ordinary! She straightened the emerald ring on her right hand with her little finger. She'd bought that ring for herself on a trip to Columbia. Her left hand was bare of jewelry.

A thought wormed its way into her mind. Maybe the ring was the source of the evil she felt. Who knew what ancient rite might curse that emerald? She took it off and put it in her desk drawer, then felt foolish. Lord! She was giving in to superstition as an explanation for her problems? Some bastion of rationality she was!

But what could explain her pain and her patient's except some kind of curse? The futility of that vain hope pried its way through to the pool of desperation inside her and set it free. Sobs convulsed her chest, and she covered her mouth with her hand so Chloe wouldn't hear her. *God*

103

help me! She was not religious but that came as near a prayer as she could make.

Maybe she and McQueen were both schizophrenic. Maybe what made them different was that they were defining a new kind of schizophrenia. One with group delusions. It was possible—and more likely than a cursed emerald. She pushed her mind away from that.

What if what was happening to them were real? McQueen was right. That meant there might be others out there, the ones they couldn't quite hear. Well, McQueen could hear them sometimes. And they had both experienced something more than just a feeling that the cop was going to break in on them. What did that mean?

And what about the feeling that they weren't human?

Holland's eyes darted about the purposefully cool and soothing office as tears streamed down her face. She was not a psychiatrist in that moment. She was a frightened child, pure and simple, one who might have some force or some mental disease growing inside her that could drive out the humanity, the Holland of her, totally.

Jeff McQueen ate lunch with a focus that he had seldom felt. It was regular hospital food, which wasn't to say real food. But the sound in his head didn't drown out the taste. It was that simple fact he was concentrating on, that and the memory of Dr. Holland Banks touching him. Every place on his body that had brushed her—the print of her hand on his knee, his biceps where she had gripped his arm to help him into the "wheelchair of the Inquisition"— all burned with the sense-memory of her. He felt like he had come back from the brink of . . . something. Something from which there might well have been no retreat.

He could hear the whispering more clearly now that she had made the wall of sound recede. The words were distant. Not like when the Doc talked. Then it was like he was singing along with the radio, like he was saying the words even as she spoke them. What was that about?

She had been so funny today, pretending she was in control when she wasn't. Far from it. Took some courage, though. He had to admit that. Especially when she was so afraid. Only he knew how afraid she was. He could see it, brown and red, glowing around her. He knew everything about her. It was his business to know. When he'd stalked her, he'd managed to use his research skills to find out about her, even through the noise. He knew she was smart, driven, and she had refused to trade on her father's name. She gave beaucoup bucks to charity, had a couple of high-profile dates who never turned into boyfriends, and now went to the required social events alone and unapologetic. Outside the social rounds she was private, even aloof. Her credit cards said she liked good wine, read all twenty of the stories of the sea by Patrick O'Brian and shopped on Rodeo Drive—not a huge spender but only the best when she spent. In short, not his type. But interesting.

What was more interesting was the effect touching her had on him. Yeah. The silence. Relief. But what about the rest of it? The kind of glowing feeling . . . Nah, not *that* kind of glow. Well, yeah *that* kind of glow, but more so—like his whole psyche as well as his body was healed by her.

He swung the metal arm that held the tray to the side. No time for that kind of drive. The important part was that he and the Doc shared the same problem. Whether it was based on a disease, a delusion, or experience . . . well, they must share that, too. They had to figure out what it was and what to do about it. He didn't rule out anything. Strange disease that presaged an epidemic of exploding brains? Maybe. Alien invasion of earth? Why not? Mass hypnosis? He'd go for that one too.

So, how did they find out what it was? How did they stop it? How did life get back to normal? He had to believe that life could get back to normal or he might just let the desperation churning in his stomach turn suicidal. He'd felt hopelessness circling the edges of his mind right before he'd decided to look for the voices, hoping to God there would be others like him. That feeling of utter despondency had scared him almost as much as the voices. He rubbed his hand over his recently shaved chin. The orderly had nicked the cleft, being not as practiced as Jeff himself was. It had probably given him another scar to match the one on his jaw. Still, the shower, observed as it had been by both an orderly and a cop, and the haircut and the shave had made him feel more human. The Doc was right. And the Doc hadn't let them cut off all his hair. It still fell over his forehead, even though it was shorter on the sides and back.

The door to the room rattled as someone struggled with a key. He could see the brown, curly hair of a nurse through the wire hatch of the window. She stuck her head through the opening door. An orderly behind her wheeled a chair. Was the Doc back already? A smile tugged at the corner of his mouth, unbidden.

"Visitors, Mr. McQueen," the nurse said in that bright tone reserved for the sick and children.

Jeff's eyes narrowed. He didn't want to see the guys from the paper under these circumstances. Didn't being on a locked ward spare you casual visitors? "Who?"

"Your parents." The nurse obviously felt she was giving good news.

"Here?" he asked, disbelieving. His stomach didn't disbelieve. It flipped and dropped.

"Well, in the visiting room." The orderly stepped on the chair brake to steady it.

"Uh, I don't think so."

The orderly moved around the chair. "You don't mean that, Mr. McQueen. They've come a long way to see you."

What were they doing here? "You have no idea how much I mean it," Jeff threatened.

The nurse put her hands on her hips, exasperated. The orderly hovered. "Sane people go visit their parents and behave nicely," the nurse cajoled.

"If I'm insane can I avoid visiting my parents?" Jeff growled.

The nurse looked nonplussed. "You should be grateful they're paying your way here," she finally sputtered as she unhooked the IV. "You don't want to be at County, that's for sure."

Ah, now she had hit on a way to blackmail him into seeing his parents. If they pulled the money, he'd never see the Doc again. At least not until he really *was* insane. He pushed himself up and swung his legs over the side of the bed. "Okay," he grunted. "Let's go." He got into the wheelchair. The orderly buckled his restraints and the cop followed them as they wheeled down the hall to the visitors' room. Jeff felt as if he had his own little entourage.

The door to the small interview room for the locked ward swung open on faces he hadn't seen in what, seven years? Ten? Closer to ten. His father's white hair, prematurely gray, fell over his forehead in a parody of boyishness. The jowls of his pudgy excess had begun to sag. The lips that called forth the spirits revealed a self-satisfaction forty years in the making, maybe more. His father's suit was rumpled from the flight. It was expensive fabric, but Jeff doubted he could button it across his waist.

All the old feelings washed over him, seeing his father like this; anger, shame, rebellion.

His father stood, frowning at the restraints buckled around Jeff's wrists and ankles, the hospital gown, the tidy bandage on his temple. "Well, boy, the wages of sin caught up with you."

"Donald, shush. Now is not the time." His mother stood. He had not noticed her until now. No one ever noticed her when his father was in the room. She had aged faster than his father. Her plain navy shirtwaist could not soften her angular figure. Her shoes were sensible—almost flat with thick heels. She wore no jewelry. His father had always wanted the kind of wife who brought in the crowds, like some other TV preachers had. The kind with stylish hair and too much makeup, divas in their own right. He had never appreciated the austere soul who kept the books and made sure the Ministry was making money, enough money to afford that estate in Tennessee, enough to afford keeping Jeff in Dr. Holland Bank's hospital. And of course, he wouldn't really have liked the competition from a glamorous wife. He was the one who gyrated in some pantomime grappling with the devil—he whose voice filled souls. But in some ways Jeff had always known his mother was more dedicated to the church than his father was, more single-minded. His father was the charismatic chrome detail, his mother the oily inner workings of the machine. It took both of them to make up the whole lie.

Jeff let the silence stretch. What could he say to these people? How could he have sprung from their loins? His father's brows were drawn together in holier-than-thou disapproval. His mother merely watched. You never knew what went on behind the opaque blue of her eyes.

"Come to gloat, then?" It was Jeff who looked away first. How could they be so sure of themselves when he was sure of nothing?

"I should think you'd thank us for getting you into a nice place like this," his mother scolded. "Your father wired money immediately when he got the call."

"You know I don't believe in all this psychiatric mumbo jumbo," his father muttered. "But it was jail or some hellhole run by the County of Los Angeles. The jail was full and they said the County place was worse than jail." He seemed to be saying that they'd have let him rot in jail as his just desserts, but that wasn't an option.

"Are they treating you okay?" His mother's voice was small, only a ripple in the stiff air between them. Her eyes darted between the bandage at his temple and the manacles.

Jeff shrugged. All the sullen rebellion of being sixteen washed over him, just as though he weren't twice that age and more. "They're past trying to beat the evil spirits out of inmates if that's what you mean." He stared at his dad.

It was his father's turn to look away.

"We'll get you out of here," his mother promised. "We'll get a lawyer."

"Nothing you can do, not for a while." Something under seventy-two hours, to be exact. Thank God for that. Except he didn't thank God anymore.

"We need time to arrange an exorcism anyway," his father intoned in his best preacher's voice, the one that made multiple syllables of the simplest word.

Right, it was the Devil made him do it. Couldn't his father get to some larger concept of the workings of the world? Jeff wasn't giving any ground. He let the silence stretch. *Exorcism?*

His father cleared his throat. Would he make an effort to connect, or did the silence just bother him? "So, uh, is it true, about the assault?"

The assault. As if it did not belong to Jeff. It was just some random assault about which there would be truth. Ah, truth. That was the crux of the difference between them. "You mean, did I assault someone?"

"Dr. Banks." His father tried to get himself together. He brought in his preaching voice. "Did you assault Dr. Banks?"

Jeff drew his brows together. Assault the Doc? No, it was her father. Oh, yeah. They were both Dr. Banks. He chuckled derisively. "I slugged him, if that's what you mean."

"Why, Jeff," his mother pleaded. "Why would you do that?"

His father put a hand on her arm as if to say, because he's crazy, that's why. But no, his father would never mean that. He did not believe in crazy. Evil. Possessed. But not crazy. "Never mind, Ida. Is there anything we can do for you, boy? Maybe bring you something?"

Jeff stared at his father. "No. Nothing."

Donald McQueen, the Reverend Don, could only say, "Well, then . . . I guess we'll work on getting you the help you really need." He turned up to the camera in the corner and raised his hand. Jeff hadn't noticed the camera. Of course the visiting room would be monitored.

Behind him the door opened. "Back to our room?" came the cheery voice.

"What help is that?" Jeff growled. "Spilling a little chicken blood and sticking some pins in a doll? Real spirituality?"

His father didn't answer. He just exchanged looks with Ida.

Jeff never let his eyes leave his father's until the wheelchair was turned from behind and the nurse pushed him out into the corridor. The slam of the door echoed in the hall.

By the time they got to his cell, Jeff was shaking. Damn his father! Damn them both to the hell and brimstone they believed in so much. All of his anger soaked him, remembering the rebellion against all the rules and the strap that accompanied any infraction. They had tried to beat religion into him. Well, his father had and his mother never once raised her voice in his defense. So, now they believed he deserved whatever he got. All this, "we'll get you the help you need" and "can we bring you anything"—that was all a ruse. If he was godless, that made him evil. Any help they brought, Jeff would consider hell. The word "exorcism" rang in Jeff's brain.

"Quiet now, Mr. McQueen," the nurse muttered soothingly, as she motioned for an orderly. She turned the wheelchair and put a hand on his arm. "It's okay. They're gone."

The hulking orderly, black this time, came in and unbuckled his ankles and then his wrists. "You be nice, now," he rumbled.

Jeff shoved himself up and onto the bed. "Yeah, that's right. Nice. That's how I'll be."

He was still shaking.

"I'll get a sedative." The nurse turned toward the door.

"No," Jeff called, panicked. "No sedative. I'll be fine."

She craned back and raised her brows. Jeff took a breath. "Call Dr. Banks, at least, before you give me anything." The nurse hesitated. "I'll be fine, I swear." He strove for a smile. "Parents. They get to you, you know?"

The nurse softened. "Boy, do I." She motioned for the orderly to follow her out. In a moment, Jeff was alone, listening to the bolt shoot home.

He crawled under the covers of the bed, feeling five years old. He concentrated on breathing. At least get me back to fourteen, he thought. By fifteen, he had been able to stand whatever the bastard had dished out. The rebellion, the anger, had saved his sanity.

Jeff ran a hand over his face. His forehead was damp with sweat. Yeah. Sanity.

A horrible thought occurred. His father had sworn Jeff was evil incarnate by the time he was fifteen—smoking, drinking, staying out, standing to the strap naked in the cool dimness of the church basement. Sometimes his father could get tears, but never a sound. Never after he was thirteen or fourteen. Jeff was his father's definition of evil. Maybe his father wasn't wrong. Maybe the man's definition of evil was just too small.

Chloe stuck her head inside the door, blonde locks flopping into her eyes. "Mr. and Mrs. McQueen to see you, Dr. Banks."

Holland looked up from the box her father had sent, box cutter in hand. She was getting on edge again, the whispers in her mind getting louder over the last hour or two. She wasn't sure she could handle Jeff McQueen's parents. What did they want? To deliver compliments on the care their son was getting? Probably not.

She sighed. Whatever it was, she had to manage it. They could screw the whole deal by moving Jeff. "Send them in."

Chloe's head disappeared.

Holland put down the box cutter and smoothed down the skirt of her white linen dress. It was wrinkled, and there was a smear of something pink like lipstick on the front. She just couldn't seem to keep it together these days.

The couple entering the room looked like some slightly skewed version of the American Gothic painting. What was wrong? His grin was too wide, almost like a politician with his hand extended to shake hers. The woman was wary, closed, the lines in her face severe.

Holland shook the outstretched hand, cool and firm. "Mr. McQueen, Mrs. McQueen. What can I do for you?" No, that was too abrupt. "We're giving your son the best care available." What a laugh. Rhenquist had just about killed him with drugs, and Holland herself was violating every ethics rule in the book in treating him. But she couldn't exactly say that.

"Reverend McQueen, ma'am. But you can call me Rev Don. We wanted to speak to the head honcho." The man's tone was ingratiating. "To get the straight story about Jeff."

She couldn't avoid this one. Couldn't refer them to Rhenquist, for instance. "What can I tell you?" She motioned them to the two guest chairs, elegantly upholstered in blue brocade with woven green geometric patterns. She sat at the desk, pushing the large cardboard box to one side.

"Well, you got to know that we don't hold with all this psychiatric mumbo jumbo." The man who called himself Rev Don sat heavily in the chair as his wife perched on the edge of hers like a nervous bird. His voice was rural south. Holland couldn't tell about the wife, since she hadn't spoken yet and didn't look as though she would anytime soon.

"Why did you have him committed?" Now that she thought about it . . . "And why here?"

"Wellll . . ." The elder McQueen stretched the syllable theatrically. "That had to do with the fact that it was commit him or send him to jail. That was the way the man explained it to us."

"And here?"

He blinked once. "Well, y'all are the best, ain't you?" He grinned again. "At what y'all are supposed to do. That's what folks told us. Now it's time we had a talk about what you're gonna say about young Jeff."

She went on her guard. Okay. She had to keep him here. What did people who didn't believe in psychiatry want to hear? "Your son is very disturbed, Reverend McQueen."

"In what way, exactly?"

"He hears voices. He thinks he's different from other people, maybe evil."

The woman showed signs of animation. "Devil has him. He's hearing the Devil's voice."

Holland pitched her voice at its most calming. "He is showing signs of schizophrenia, Mrs. McQueen, a disease that often manifests itself in otherwise healthy young people, especially young men. It is often present for some time before it becomes severe enough for friends and family to notice."

The woman closed down again, her face screwing into disapproval. Her husband maintained the same affable volubility. "And what do you propose to do for our Jeff?" he asked.

Holland hesitated. "There are medications that can help control the symptoms." What was she saying? What would happen when he left here if his parents believed he needed drugs?

"So, when he gets the drugs, can he come home?" Reverend Don was on a mission.

"The police have placed him on a seventy-two-hour hold. Based on our psychiatric opinion, they can hold him longer if they think he is a danger to himself or others."

"So you can tell them he's not a danger, and we'll take care of him from there on out."

113

She didn't want Jeff leaving in the custody of his parents. She didn't want him to go at all. But to keep Jeff here, she'd have to declare him insane. That had consequences for him. He wasn't insane, at least no more than she was. What could she say? "I think it would be ill-advised to remove him from care, Reverend McQueen."

The small eyes in the chubby cheeks went hard, as though the affability had been smeared away. Holland tried to find a trace of his son in that face, but she couldn't. "I think we know what to do for our boy, Miss Doctor. You're right that it started with him a long time ago. But Ida and I, we recognized it right off. He's got the Devil in him. He always did. Ain't no cure for that but throwin' that Devil out. We gonna take him home in the mornin' of the second day, and do just that."

Holland stood and placed her palms flat on her desk. "Not if I declare him insane and dangerous, Reverend McQueen. The court won't let you take him home."

It was the woman who stood in response. Her mouth had turned down for so long it had carved troughs in her cheeks. "But they maybe won't make him stay here." She almost spit the words at Holland. "We'll ask that judge to put him somewhere else with a good church-going doctor who sees the danger to Jeff's mortal soul."

"Some fundamental extremist retreat posing as a hospital?" Holland's anger welled.

"One that will take proper steps," the woman replied sullenly.

"Ohhhh, proper steps. Waving holy water over him, maybe a few choruses of 'Battle Hymn of the Republic'?" This was bright. Put them on the defensive about their religious beliefs. But her anger wouldn't be put down. Maybe it was the irritation of all that sound ramping up in her head. Her nerves were frayed beyond coddling and coaxing.

The Rev Don stood. His bulk filled the space. He let his voice boom out in the tone he used for his largest audience. "First the congregation will dunk him in the river in the presence of the words of the Lord Jesus, saver of the souls of men, to wash the Devil from his soul."

"That doesn't sound like something Mr. McQueen himself would embrace as a solution."

"If he refuses the Lord entrance to his heart, then we must beat the Devil out of him, until he accepts Jesus as the One True Way." The man's eyes had gone small.

Holland couldn't believe what she was hearing. They were going to take their son to some crackpot institution where they could torture him into accepting religion? These people were the evil ones! "Beating him would be against the law. It's called assault."

"It's our burden that we should've been firmer with him." The woman's voice sounded like dry twigs snapping.

"Well, you are going to have to fight me and the courts to get him. He needs care and concern, not half-drowning and letting a mob beat him!" Holland's voice rose with her anger.

"You are obviously not one who will be joining us in Heaven, Miss," the Reverend said. He turned to the door. "Come, Ida. We'll be back for Jeff on Thursday, or we'll see you in court." He flung open the door and pushed Chloe from her listening position as he strode out into the corridor, his sticklike wife walking stiffly behind him.

"Whoa!" Chloe exclaimed. "Are they for real?"

"Do you *always* listen at the door?" Holland said, annoyed at her poor handling of Jeff's parents more than at Chloe. She couldn't let them take him, but the only way to keep him out of their clutches was to actually declare him insane. And even that wouldn't keep him in her very expensive private hospital. It would only deprive him of his rights, smudge his character, lock him up unjustifiably, and . . . and keep her from touching him ever again. Then he *would* go insane and so would she. She sighed and turned back into the office. The sound in her head whined yet another decibel up the scale.

"I know," Chloe muttered. "Patient confidentiality. By the way, the lieutenant called."

Holland nodded absently, the noise almost overwhelming Chloe's message. She looked at the little crystal clock on her desk. It was nearly noon. Time for a trip to the locked ward. She'd better tell Jeff the bad news.

Chapter Nine

The nurse looked up as Holland strode by the station. Holland didn't even bother to sort through the charts. "He's, he's pretty upset, Dr. Banks," the nurse said. She knew just whom Holland was coming to see.

Her words jerked Holland around. She just stared at the nurse, not trusting herself to speak without shouting over the noise.

"He . . . Well, his parents came to visit . . ."

That was enough. Holland spun to unlock the door. Inside, Jeff sat on the bed, shoulders sagging, his eyes blinking rapidly. He was clean-shaven, his waving hair hanging over his forehead. She hadn't realized how classically handsome he was. There was a scar on his jaw to match the one through his eyebrow. They didn't mar his features, only defined them. The small bandage on his temple made him look even more vulnerable than the silly hospital slippers. Nodding to the young blond cop flipping through a magazine outside, she closed and locked the door behind her.

"Hi," she said.

Without even looking at her, Jeff reached out a blunt, strong hand. Holland sensed a gray, cloudy feeling of despair. She glanced to the camera in the corner. "The nurse said you were upset." She moved toward the bed, as though she felt nonchalant. "She thought it might be your parents' visit. Want to tell me about it?"

He turned up anguished eyes. The gray feeling she got was shot with red lightning, but it was still just a feeling. She wasn't seeing an actual aura.

"Want to tell me about *your* visit with them?" he countered.

How had he known that? She slid onto the bed beside him, ignoring his outstretched hand but pressing her hip against his thigh under the covers. The blessed silence fell. Holland heaved a breath, relief coursing over her. She wondered what it would be like to sleep in this man's arms, whether his touch could banish the dreams as well as the sound. His head lolled back against his pillows, his chest filling with the feeling of freedom from sound. He laid his arm along his thigh, but his hand touched her hip, as though for insurance. Only the fabric of her linen dress and the thin lab coat stood between hot flesh pressed to hot flesh. 98.6 seemed hot.

They sat in silence for a minute before she said, "Why do you think they visited me?"

"I heard you. Not them, but you. You were angry. Easy to hear. Your anger was orange."

Common delusion, okay for the camera. She should have warned him about the camera when they were in the garden. But they'd had other things on their mind. Then she registered his last comment. He saw the color of her moods, too? This was getting scarier by the minute. "Yes, well." She put on her best professional voice. "Would you like to tell me about your parents?"

He rolled his head in her direction. "You mean, will my pious old man take me out of here to put the fear of God into me? He'll take me out if he can." His smiled at her only with his eyes. They crinkled at the edges. The gray clouds she could see around his form flickered with soft colors like magenta and purple. Oh, God, the aura was back. "He has a poor track record, though, on the fear of God."

She wondered what his childhood had been like. She had to be careful here. "I'm not sure you will be certified at all. We will have to talk more before I can determine your prognosis."

"So, if I'm not psycho, I go to jail for assault. If I *am* psycho, you'll have to . . . what did you say to them? Use the courts to keep them from taking me to some fringe-group monastery posing as a hospital. Some choice."

Yeah, she thought. *Some choice.* "There's always bail if you're charged." But would they give a man with his record of instability bail? She wouldn't bet on it.

"Bail lasts for how long? I end the same."

She had nothing to say to that.

After a moment he continued, "So now you know my dirty secret." His shoulders seemed to sag again. Magenta faded to white swirling through the gray.

There were lots of possibilities for this one. "Your parents?"

"Rev Don and the little woman make the whole ministry run like a well-tuned money machine. Fleecing the flock, humbugging the ones who come for cures, using the pulpit to take political stands. It's all so easy for him to condemn anyone he doesn't consider righteous. And they follow him, even now that he's become a bad imitation of Elvis during the white leather and fringe years. The women especially. They bring their men, their children. Impressionable young minds eat it up—family values, right?" The crease between his brows spoke of years of pain.

"So, why didn't you eat it up, when it was all around you like that?" How could he have withstood the machine of the ministry when it had so dominated his life?

"Because he doesn't believe. Not really. Or her. They spout the words. But it's also a business to them, like a casino. It's a business that plays on the weakness of the human condition, people's desire to believe that there is an easy way to transformation. 'Hit the jackpot.' 'Diet without giving up macaroni and cheese.' 'Plastic surgery can make your life perfect.' 'Give to the ministry and your prayers will be answered.' " He turned to look at her. "We all love that stuff. It's what makes us easy marks." The gray dried to the color of mud cracked with ragged black.

Holland searched his face. "You think we're all easy marks?"

He didn't answer, as if the answer were too obvious to require confirmation.

"You weren't. You defined yourself apart from them. You, ah, rebelled, maybe?"

"Oh, yeah."

"Not easy to do."

"I was as bad as I could be, just to spite them." His mouth turned wry. Again magenta softened the dried gray mud color. "It's good to discover you have a skill."

"Must have been pretty hard on you."

He scrunched his lips and shrugged. "I finally left."

"How old?"

"Uh, sixteen, I guess."

She looked at him curiously, processing. "So, the investigative reporter thing . . . You search for truth for a living?"

He pursed his lips. "Nah, I look for frauds. That's different."

"Oh." But it wasn't.

"I find a lot of them. I broke the story on the Thai garment workers held as slaves in downtown L.A. Downtown L.A., for Chris'sakes!" His pride was carefully buried under anger, smudged with skepticism. "I cracked the round-trip selling game by power dealers to jack up the California energy prices in 2000."

"Those were good things you did," she remarked, giving him the approval he probably hadn't gotten much of in his life, and would swear he didn't need. She meant it, too. "You still a hellion?"

He breathed a chuckle. Warm magenta mist seeped into his mood. "Do I still jack cars?" He shook his head. "I can drink a little. Rough language. You've heard some of that. Mostly I just work all hours. I can get a little compulsive." Like he thought that was a revelation.

An uncomfortable thought intruded on Holland. She couldn't keep herself from asking. "No time for a relationship?"

He rolled his head to look at her. She hadn't hidden from him at all. She felt herself flushing. "You must mean 'relationships,' plural. A series of flings, no more."

She thought about the way he had touched her, gently. Here was a man who had it in him to love a woman. Underneath that hard exterior, that cynicism, there lurked a romantic.

"So," he asked. "How do you decide to be a shrink?"

She glanced away. "I like to help people."

"Bullshit. This isn't exactly the Korner Klinic. You don't get to be head of an expensive private hospital with lots of donors and a big research program without having a little more going on than deciding you want to 'help people.' " His tone was derisive.

She felt as if she'd been slapped. So this was what investigative-reporter mode felt like. "I'm sure you consider yourself an expert."

"So tell me." His eyes challenged her. She'd given a glib answer, while he had revealed as much as he could. His aspect had gone steel blue, yet there was a bit of the comforting magenta still lurking in the corners.

She took a breath. "Okay. My dad is a genetic scientist. He's very into truth. *Unlike* you, of course. He thinks truth is immutable. He is always so sure that the ultimate discovery that explains everything is right around the corner.

I . . . I thought truth might be more malleable than that. I thought there might be layers of truth, or versions, or maybe only a kind of endless compromise that, best case, yields something more true than the other choices you can see."

His hand moved on her hip. "So you became a shrink to find human versions of truth?"

"Maybe to help people compromise with the world. Maybe to help me compromise."

"And are you good at that—compromising?" He stroked her hip again—to soothe her, she realized with a start. His aspect was almost all magenta now, the throb of indigo pulsing behind it. She wasn't sure if that touch was meant to be sexual, but it sure stirred her in places she hadn't been stirred lately. He was coaxing her into revealing something she had never admitted to anyone, even her mother, especially her father.

"No." She took a breath and held it for a moment before letting it waft away. "I'm . . . I'm a little stiff, a little too fond of control." There, she'd admitted her failure. "Maybe a little more of my Dad than I'd like, a little less than I'd like of my mother." She huffed a silent chuckle. "My mother thinks I'm too compulsive—she's always trying to get me to take a vacation."

Jeff shook his head in sympathy. "Christ, do we have to be either of our parents at all?"

She nodded. "Yes. Yes, we do. At least a little bit. And we have to live with that and find our way in spite of it."

"You can reject it. I did." The stroking stopped. His aspect faded back to steel.

"They forced you into being opposite, but they still called the shots. You wouldn't be who you are without them.

"All right, I'm opposite." His teeth were gritted.

"And the same." She took a blind flyer. "They seem tenacious. Aren't you a little bit tenacious? Good trait for an investigative reporter."

"I don't want to think about that."

"It's no one's favorite subject." Maybe there was something she could do to help here. "Reconciliation with our parents takes us all our lives." She hesitated. That sounded so shrink-like. "But it's part of becoming whole."

"Reconciliation?" he practically jeered. "The only thing that saved me was hating them."

"At that point, yes. But the answers change over time."

"Well, they ain't changed yet, Dr. Freud." His voice was low and throbbing.

She shrugged. Only he could choose his path. She raised her head and rolled her neck to release the knots. The camera! She stilled, trying to keep down the panic. What had she just shown to anyone who cared to look at that tape? Was she acting like a psychiatrist? She had drifted from asking probing questions to answering probing questions—as though she and her patient were friends. What she had just displayed might *not* be professional, and it surely wasn't her usual therapeutic technique. It could draw attention to them.

"What's wrong, Doc?" The deep rumble broke the chains holding her gaze to the camera. He took her hand in reassurance. The camera would see that as well.

"Nothing," she managed. "I only realized I'm late for an appointment with another patient." It took all she had to pull back her hand and rise, breaking all touch. The rushing whispers shushed through her ears. She backed away from him, seeing the hurt look in his eyes. But she didn't dare stay. She had to think what to do. She would bet Jeff's parents were descending on the local judge for some kind of court order to remove him even now. If she said he was sane, it was a transfer to jail with no bail. And when the lieutenant saw the signature of the stalker's victim on the certification that he could stand trial? What then? Ruin of her career, at the least. There must be a way out of this dilemma. She just had to think about it. And she'd better do that before she revealed her relationship with Jeff McQueen to any more cameras.

Glancing up, she turned her back on Jeff's look of betrayal and practically ran from the room.

Yet, in the quiet of her office, she still couldn't think, because her distraction came with her inside her head. What to do? Okay, get another doctor on his case. Stafford. Paul would do it. He didn't like Rhenquist. He could interview Jeff, provide the opinion. That saved her career from ruin, but it didn't save Jeff.

No good solution. What did she want? More time with him. More time to figure out how to stop whatever it was that was driving them mad with voices not quite heard, or heard too clearly. What was happening? Jeff knew what she said to his parents when he could not have heard it.

She stopped stock still. She had been so intent on the problem presented by his parents she hadn't really absorbed just what that meant. He was hearing her in his mind even when she wasn't there. *Mind reading.*

There was no other term for it. A clearer version of what had happened to both of them with the cop in the garden.

Her intercom buzzed. Chloe's voice was metallic. "Dr. Banks?"

Holland slapped the intercom button. "What is it?" she snapped.

"You zoomed by so fast, I didn't get a chance to tell you that your father called."

"What did he want?" Holland felt like screaming.

"Uh, you know—the charts he sent by? I'm just the messenger, Dr. Banks." Her voice was full of stiff reproach.

"I know, Chloe, I know." She slapped the connection off.

The small box on her desk stared at her. She hated giving in to her father's pressure. But maybe it could distract her. Think about something else and let her subconscious solve the problem that had no solution. She picked up the box cutter. How to keep Jeff where she could touch him was only the tip of the iceberg. The real problem was how to figure out what was happening to them both, how to get back to a life without voices in your head that drove you crazy, before they both committed suicide.

Crazy . . . Suicidal . . . The words reverberated inside her head.

Oh, God! Wasn't that what her father said had happened to his research subjects?

She sliced through the brown mailing tape and jerked the box apart, fear and anticipation ripping through her. Why exactly was her father so goddamned anxious for her to review these charts? It couldn't be, wouldn't be. It was just coincidence. Then why did her heart flutter so? Because it would be just like her father, that's why, not to come out and tell her directly why he wanted her to review these records.

She pulled out the disks, hardly daring to breathe. They were organized by patient; the subject's name typed on each disk label carefully. She popped the first disk into the PDA chart reader always in her lab coat pocket, and flipped up the power to increase the readability.

Stazio, Anna Marie. Reports were listed by date. Holland couldn't make much of the first report she clicked open. "Attachments" angled over the top of the page in bold red script. The language was all scientific code words, some genetic analysis. She flipped to the next file. Her father had already told her these subjects had extra DNA, more than other humans. No, that wasn't exactly right. It wasn't extra. She clicked back to the first report and skimmed the pages again. The subjects attached the leftover DNA *everybody* had to their genome strands so they could use it. Ah, that was the meaning of the red stamp that said "Attachments." Still, they could attach the DNA, so they weren't like other humans.

She scattered the other disks from the box over her desk: Observations of the subjects entered by somebody, no several somebodies—the initials at the bottom of each page were different. Quotations from the subjects transcribed. She ran her finger down the screens.

"Like a waterfall—so loud I can't think."

Holland felt tears rise to her eyes. Her throat closed.

"Voices. At first they were just whispers."

"Not human, I'm not human anymore. Maybe I never have been."

She couldn't swallow. Everything was coming together with terrible synchronicity. She and Jeff McQueen had the same symptoms as the two subjects in her father's genetic mapping trial who'd committed suicide.

The tears spilled down her cheeks. Dread fought with relief. There were others like them. Had been others. Her father had studied these people. He knew what made them different. There might be a solution after all. And she and Jeff didn't have to commit suicide. These two poor souls had never found each other. They couldn't experience the relief of touching. Maybe they had died of ignorance.

Her father could help her.

More, he could help Jeff. Jeff didn't need to be declared insane. When her father found out that Jeff was another example of his precious genetic anomaly, he would drop the charges, just so he could study Jeff. There was still the matter of assaulting the police officer. But Holland would hire the best legal advice for him. A lawyer would explain the circumstances around his attack. Genetic defect—that would be his defense. Her father could offer proof. He could testify at a bail hearing.

Why hadn't her father dropped the charges already?

The room receded. The light of her desk lamp became too bright, the shadows in the office too dark. The contrast hurt her eyes. Her father knew about Jeff. Why else was he so insistent that she read the charts? Why hadn't he told her about the connection between Jeff and his subjects? She tried to think back to what Jeff had said that day at her father's press conference—what she had said, but it was a blur. Had Jeff said that she was like him, too? Did her father know about her? Only one thing was clear. She had to talk to her father. But first she wanted to look at all of these charts. She dove into the box again, separating the disks into piles by patient. Anna Marie and Barry Selway. She started reading through every file on the disks.

At the bottom of the box she found another file. Randy Nakamura. A third subject? Her father had only mentioned two. She scanned the file. Mr. Nakamura had not committed suicide. But the last file on the disk was a scanned newspaper article. It was about the sniper. Randy Nakamura had been shot by a sniper.

The intercom buzzed. Holland jumped.

Chloe's voice was neutral. "Dr. Banks, a Mr. Stemmons is here to see you."

Chapter Ten

Holland slapped the button with a shaking hand. Not now. "I'm engaged, Chloe."

A pause. "Uh, he's a lawyer representing the McQueens?"

Well, that was fast work. She exhaled. "Send him in, Chloe. Thank you."

She sat paralyzed behind her desk as the door opened. A slender man with graying hair and a suit with a reasonable, if off-the rack, fit, ducked his head apologetically.

"Sorry to disturb you, Doctor, but my clients' needs are pressing." His hair was a salt-and-pepper mop that made him look like an aging refugee from the sixties or late-night news programs. His face was lined with years of dealing with the seamy side of life, even if the dregs had money enough to hire him. His gray eyes looked as though they had seen the world and been scarred by it. Un-expectant— that was the only way Holland could think to describe him.

She went on guard. The lawyer's human expression of weariness was a trap. "What can I do for you, Mr. Stemmons?"

"I'm here as a courtesy only, Dr. Banks." He tossed a sheaf of papers on her desk. It wasn't a courteous gesture. "I'm filing a petition with the court to remove my clients' son, Jeff McQueen, to a more responsible institution that will provide treatment more in line with their beliefs."

Holland felt her anger rise. "If you think that care more in line with your clients' beliefs is medically responsible, I'd love to enlighten you, Mr. Stemmons."

"By all means, Doctor." The man smiled tightly. "I'm certainly looking for enlightenment. That's why I went to the Beverly Hills Police Department today. In fact, that's why I consulted Dr. Rhenquist in your doctors lounge."

Holland felt her stomach drop. All that in a few hours?

"Do you want to tell me why you have assumed the psychiatric care of a man accused of stalking you, a man who you tried to engage the police to arrest, a man whose alleged assault was against your father?"

The only thing missing was the bare swinging light bulb in the interrogation room. "It's just a transition until I can find someone else to take the case. . . ." Holland knew it sounded weak. Worse, she sounded ashamed.

The lawyer straightened, his face hardening. "This is the most blatant case of conflict of interest I've ever seen, Doctor. Not only will I get him out of here, but frankly, I wouldn't count on practicing psychiatry for very long." He nodded stiffly. "Good day, Doctor, for however long I may address you in that manner."

He was gone. The door swung shut on Chloe's big eyes and stunned expression.

Holland was stunned, herself. This guy would get his court order. Jeff would be taken away. No telling how soon. Holland began to shake. Her license . . . the foundation . . . her reputation . . . all she had worked for and whatever good she'd done were about to be flushed down the toilet. She had sacrificed it all to treat a man she should never have seen professionally. Treat? She hadn't been treating him. She'd been treating herself. It was the worst kind of professional lapse. The damned lawyer was right.

Of course, Mr. Stemmons had no idea what was really wrong with Jeff McQueen, and she did. God help her, she understood only too well.

She took a breath. Her eyes came to rest on the computer disks that held the records of the other people who understood: her father's subjects. Come to think of it, her father understood, too.

That was the only way now. Her father had to drop the charges against Jeff. He hadn't dropped them already because he was trying to blackmail her into entering his little research project and his world. Okay. That was the price? She'd pay it.

Her father knew governors and senators. If he put himself out, maybe he could get the police to drop the charges, too. Still, something nagged at her. Why hadn't her father told her about the third subject with the anomaly?

She glanced at her watch. Nearly four. She must have spent more time on the charts than she'd thought. She turned to the desk and dialed a number by heart.

"Dorothy? Holland. Find him for me?"

"He asked me to interrupt him if you called. He's in West L.A. at a board meeting. Hold please."

He knew, at least about Jeff. She hoped to God he didn't know about her. She thought again about the press conference. Jeff had said, "You know." She remembered that. He'd asked about her patients. He'd mentioned hearing voices, too. Her father had heard all of that. But would he have concluded that she had the problem too? And how was that possible?

"Holland?" Her father's voice was crisp with anticipation. Yeah, he knew about Jeff all right. At least Jeff. She could hear it in his voice. "Did you read the files?"

"Yeah, Dad. I did."

"And, what's your opinion?"

She hit it head-on. "I think you ought to drop the charges against Jeff McQueen and get that cop to dismiss his charges too."

"It's true, isn't it? He has the same symptoms!" Her father's voice was excited. "I knew it. I'm in the car right now. I'm on my way over."

The phone clicked dead in her ear before she could ask him about Randy Nakamura. At least he hadn't accused her of having the symptoms, too.

She stared at the cell phone in her hand. Something . . . something wasn't right. It was impossible just to sit here and wait for him to arrive. And she'd better prepare Jeff for an assault by her father. In some ways it was the price of freedom for both of them.

"Chloe," she called, as she trotted through the outer office. "Call Admissions before you go home. Tell them to have someone escort my father to the locked ward and call for me." She was already clicking into the corridor. "He'll be here in about fifteen minutes."

"Yeah, sure, Dr. Banks," came the bewildered girl's voice behind her.

Jeff was reading a newspaper when she got downstairs and through the two locked doors. She warned the nurses to expect her father, and to escort him to the visitors lounge.

"Good sign," she said as she moved to take her now-accustomed place at Jeff's bedside. "You're taking an interest in the world."

The room shushed to silence around them as she pressed against his thigh.

"This rag?" he asked, smiling. His eyes crinkled.

Magenta shushed over her. What was this color thing? The colors didn't obscure her vision of him. A series of impressions just glowed around him—like an indicator of his moods and meanings that amplified what he was saying. She breathed out with a shushing sound. Mind reading, colors. God, she hoped her father *could* explain this to them.

"Nothing in here worth reporting, now that I'm out of action—unless you want to know what percent of men get testicular infections after surviving the flu, or unless you're fixated on the sniper stuff. Then this rag is just your cup of tea."

"I've got some better news. Could be good, at least." She wasn't going to tell him about Stemmons. Why upset him when the solution to all their problems was on his way?

He raised his brows. His look was soft. Indigo throbbed through the magenta.

"My father. He's coming here."

Jeff pulled back physically. "Isn't he the guy I decked?"

"One. I think he's going to drop the charges."

Jeff's thick, expressive brows drew together. "And . . ." He had heard her reservations.

She cleared her throat. "He might know what's wrong with us."

Jeff sat up and grabbed her hand, careless of the camera. "He knows about us? How?"

The touch of their bodies, even through cloth, could banish sound. But when he touched her flesh to flesh, the shock was almost stunning. She looked at him and saw his face as though she had never seen it. The puckered lips, the green eyes that had seen everything and believed nothing, the cleft chin that spoke of artificial good looks, but somehow seemed so natural, the hair—still too long for fashion—waving over his forehead. This face spoke of faith. Not his father's faith, but faith that his strength of character could make a difference. Had she not known that face forever? Could it possibly relate to the fearful visage she had seen outside Matsuhisa?

She could see him examining her face in return, with wonder and with . . . fascination. Some alchemy drew them to each other, whether they would or no. She gathered herself.

"He's been working with the human genome. He found some subjects who could bind in extra DNA, but . . ." She swallowed. "They always went crazy and committed suicide." She didn't mention the article about the sniper. That was probably just a mistake.

Jeff raised his brows and swallowed. "He thinks we're like that? Why?"

"I don't think he knows about me. But he heard what you said to me at the press conference—the stuff about not being human, hearing voices. Those are almost direct quotes from his test subjects about their symptoms."

"Why didn't he say so?" Jeff scowled. "Could have saved some time and anxiety."

Holland blushed. "I guess I haven't always believed in him, and . . . uh, I'm a little rebellious. He probably thought I wouldn't help him if he just told me. But he gave me the charts of the subjects." She leaned forward, pressing his hand. "I read them this afternoon. They were just like us, Jeff."

He nodded, and she nodded with him.

"But they committed suicide." His voice was low, thoughtful, his eyes serious.

"That's the bad-news part. But I'll bet they didn't . . . connect to each other like we can. If they never knew each other, if they were alone with the noise and the voices, and dreams . . ."

"I'd be crazy by now if we hadn't found each other." He said it steadily. "I might have done myself in. I don't know."

"So, he's coming." She cut the speculation short. No use dwelling on how much worse it could have been. It was bad enough anyway.

"And . . . you want to tell me what about that?"

Damn him for being an investigative reporter. She couldn't speak for a moment and found herself wondering if he saw colors that revealed her mood, her fears. "He's . . . difficult."

His eyes were wary. "So, this is where you give me the 'meet the parents' speech?"

She managed a deprecating shrug. "No. But . . . I have my problems with him, just like you have problems with yours."

He began stroking her hand with his thumb. "The 'I'm a little rebellious' part?"

She realized she was frowning. "I guess. I'm asking you to talk to him . . . about you."

Jeff raised his chin, then nodded. "I get it. Okay. About me."

She nodded. "I'm not sure I'm ready to tell him about me. Let me do it in my own time. I . . . I'm not good at admitting things to him."

The intercom beside the bed buzzed. "Dr. Banks, Dr. Banks is here. Uh, you know what I mean. Edna will take him down to the lounge."

"Thanks, Sally. You want to have Sam get a chair?"

"You got it, Dr. Banks."

They sat there in blessed silence, storing up resiliency, while they waited for the orderly.

"My father is very observant," Holland said as she heard the key in the lock.

"Got it. You saying no PDA?" His thumb hesitated on her hand.

She nodded—then suddenly shook her head. She didn't think she could do a visit with her father under these particular circumstances with sound making her crazy. "No. Not that. But discretion is the watchword here."

Sam wheeled in the chair. Holland rose, breaking the connection. The shushing waterfall returned. She could hear the whispers in it more clearly today, faint as the waterfall was. Yeah, right. Discretion. The camera had certainly recorded their speculations and conclusions. She'd have to find a way to lose that tape. Her vigilance was slipping. With luck, they wouldn't have to dissemble much longer. Jeff was almost home free. She only had to get her father to the police station before a court order to move Jeff came through.

Jeff slid into the chair and Sam buckled the restraints.

Her father could figure out how to get them back to normal. Maybe you could just cut off the offending DNA. Wouldn't there be some drug therapy that put them back the way they were? She hardly dared hope. But if anyone could do it, her father could, bastard that he was. She took the handles of the chair. A little surge of pride made her smile as she pushed Jeff's chair out the door and down toward the visitors lounge.

Chapter Eleven

Jeff let the sound bathe him as his touch with the Doc broke. The whispers were so much clearer now, even if they softened after he had touched her. They spoke of terrible things—fear, and destruction, most of them. But he could hear other voices, too, sometimes. They seemed . . . whole, not fragments of wild resistance or cringing resignation and withdrawal. They breasted the roll of sound like the masters of sailing ships or surfers on the big Australian waves.

He wanted to hear those voices more clearly.

But now, he must get up out of the bed like a sane person and climb into the torture-chamber–looking wheelchair. He heaved himself up and swiveled into the chair a bit too heavily.

"That's right, Mr. McQueen," the orderly boomed. Jeff lifted his forearms to the sheepskin-lined restraints and watched the big black hands buckle them around him, then bend to fasten his ankles. It was beginning to feel almost natural. He looked up at the Doc. She was nervous. It was more than the sounds in her head. She had a sort of fog around her, shot through with yellow lightning bolts of nervousness.

He understood the feeling. Parents. He wouldn't reveal her secret. That was up to her. What had she said about her father? That he was sure of truth. Well, they could use a little sureness right now. What hand of fate or God or accident had connected them to the one man who knew what made them what they were?

The orderly pushed Jeff's chair. The Doc clicked along behind him. She couldn't really touch him until they stopped rolling. He admitted to himself that he longed to touch her for more than just the silence. Maybe it was the curve of her lips that belied the icy professional exterior. He liked that curve. She tried to hide her vulnerability. It didn't work. What must it be like to be smarter than all the men you knew? He glanced around to reassure her, to make the little yellow lightning bolts disappear. She was smart, and kind and driven, strong and vulnerable. He'd gotten on her case for telling him she wanted to help people. But she probably did. It just wasn't the only reason she did what she did. The Doc was one complex lady.

His feet in the chair kicked the swinging door to the lounge open as Sam wheeled him through. The man pacing the small room impatiently was . . . straight. From the cut of his suit to his posture to the hair rising up and back from his forehead, he was straight. His lips were pressed together. Even his tie was straight. He was sure and controlled. Jeff knew immediately what the Doc found disconcerting about him.

"Sam, you can leave us." The Doc's voice was only trying to be cool and collected. As the orderly left, she took his place behind the chair and leaned in, so that her abdomen, probably, touched his shoulder. The silence sounded like wet snow in a graveyard in the dead of a January night. He craned around to see her. Gray fog was trying to keep the yellow bolts in check. And there was a new red glow. The Doc was angry with her father, low level, maybe all the time.

"Dad," she said behind him. "This is Jeff McQueen."

He saw the man's arm twitch as though to extend before the elder Dr. Banks realized that men whose hands were strapped to their wheelchair could not perform the social niceties. "Dr. Banks," Jeff said, trying to make his voice relaxed, cordial—sane. "Sorry about the left hook."

The man rubbed his chin ruefully. The shadow of a bruise was just visible along his jaw. But his eyes never left Jeff, except to shoot a penetrating glance at his daughter.

"Guess I wasn't myself." It was the only excuse Jeff had to offer. He hoped it was enough to get the guy to let him off.

Dr. Banks nodded. "Not being yourself—that's what I wanted to talk to you about."

"The Doc here says you think I've got some kind of genetic anomaly."

"That's one way to put it." Mr. Scientist's voice went into 'gentle explanation' mode. Jeff bet that annoyed the Doc a lot. Hell, it annoyed him. "Now that the human genome has been mapped, we expected to find only the changes in the genetic structure that denoted individuality. You know—hair color, facial structure, body type, and of course, the rogue revisions that indicated disease or deviation. When this particular gene has this particular deviation, you get multiple sclerosis or Parkinson's. That's what we were looking for—deviations that could be corrected, so that drugs or the insertion of new genetic material could improve the human condition." He smiled a very straight, controlled smile. "Drug companies are branching out into genetic manipulation. It's a marvelous opportunity to invent a whole new industry. I was working on a mechanism to insert the revised DNA when I discovered the subjects with the extra strings of DNA. Quite a successful mechanism by the way."

The guy wanted to be asked about his success. Well, Jeff could do that. A little greasing of the old ego wouldn't hurt in this case. "How were you going to deliver it?"

"A re-usable viral vector," Banks said triumphantly. "You hook the DNA to a virus, infect the subject, and the virus carries the new DNA to every cell. A real advance over the single-use vector, and very profitable."

Jeff glanced to the Doc who had moved to the side of his chair. She still gripped the back, though, and that scraped her knuckles across his back. He saw the look of derision and disappointment in her eyes.

"I didn't know you were working for drug companies, Dad." Anyone who didn't know her as Jeff did since he touched her would think she was master of the situation. But he could see the glow of red, and maybe sort of a baby-blue regret around her edges.

"They're the ones who have the money for R&D, Holly. R&D is the business we're in."

Holly? Jeff thought, intrigued. *He calls the doc Holly? That's a far cry from Dr. Holland Banks.*

"You forget the government. They don't expect a monopoly in return for their money."

"No." His voice was flat. "I don't forget the government. But they do want a monopoly."

Both Jeff and the Doc stared at her father. Jeff could *feel* her staring. She felt what he felt. Something wasn't right.

There was a painful silence. What was it? What was going on here?

Dr. Banks broke the silence. He turned to a black bag on the table behind him. "So, a simple blood test is in order. Do I have your permission, Mr. McQueen, to take a sample?"

Jeff looked at the Doc. She was still nervous, but she nodded.

"Yeah. I guess that's okay."

Dr. Banks the father fiddled with a syringe and some plastic tubes. The Doc came around and bent over Jeff. The sound shushed on again, and then was silenced as she unbuckled the restraint on his right arm, touching him as she did so.

"Clench your fist, Mr. McQueen." She balled his fingers into a fist and held it.

Her father passed over a rubber tube and she fastened it around his upper arm. Every caress of her flesh sent shock waves down his spine. He schooled his features to stony disapproval, his mouth tight, and was very glad that Dr. Banks Senior couldn't see aura colors right now. He jerked his gaze to the Doc's face. Could she? Oh, he didn't like that. What if he didn't want her to know what touching her did to parts of him that had a mind of their own? What color would that look like?

Maybe it would look like magenta, with pulsing indigo behind it. That was what the Doc looked like now. She was studiously holding his clenched fist, not looking at him.

Behind her, her father brought the needle up. The Doc slipped the knot on the tube. "Relax your fist, Mr. McQueen," she said, her voice low and a little throatier than usual. He unclenched his hand, but that was all of him that was relaxed. He told himself he was nervous about what her father was doing. But that wasn't true. Dr. Banks wasn't going to inject any unknown substance. He was collecting with an empty sample tube. Jeff could spare some blood. As a matter of fact, it seemed right now that he had too much of it, the way it was pounding through his body. No, it was Banks's daughter who made Jeff tight.

Jeff hardly saw the needle slide into his bulging vein. The Doc moved around behind him. The sound shushed on and off again. The tube filled with thick claret. A new tube was snapped onto the syringe and it filled too.

Dr. Banks was saying something. "I'll have this analyzed. We'll know within an hour if you have the attachment factor."

"What then, Dad?" the Doc asked. Her voice sounded frail and distant, as though she could hardly concentrate on what she was saying.

"I'll want you to come to the laboratory at the Foundation tomorrow morning. We'll start testing immediately." He sounded excited, even though he focused on the filling tubes. "You seemed to have the full-blown symptoms the other night. Yet today . . ." He glanced up at Jeff, speculating. "Today you seem remarkably calm. Are you able to control the symptoms?"

"I guess you could say they come and go."

"What about the charges, Dad?" the Doc asked impatiently. "Unless you drop them he's not going to show up in Malibu." Jeff could hear her panic rising.

"Yes, Holly, yes," Dr. Banks murmured. "I'll get down to the police station first thing in the morning." He withdrew the needle and pressed a wad of cotton into the crook of Jeff's arm.

"And there's the matter of the other officer Mr. McQueen hit. He'd have to drop his charges, too. That could be tougher."

Dr. Banks shook his head. The man was totally self-confident. "I'll take care of it." Jeff believed he would.

"As a matter of fact," the Doc said slowly, "this really can't wait until tomorrow morning." Jeff raised his fist and Dr. Banks taped the cotton in place with a strip of tape from a roll dispenser as he glanced up to her. She was worried all of a sudden. Her aura had gone chartreuse.

"What do you mean?" her father asked sharply.

"All this paperwork could get crossed up. It will take time for the D.A. to get the charges dropped. And Mr. McQueen's parents have already been working on getting custody of him. They want to transfer him to another facility. If their lawyer shows up with an order before the D.A. says I can let him go, I'll have to release him to their supervision."

"They're not quite up on modern psychiatric theory," Jeff shrugged in explanation. "They have something a little more spiritual in mind. I just won't go with them."

"They could be here any time with an ambulance and a couple of big orderlies, Mr. McQueen," the Doc said. "It's not like we're going to have a choice." Real fear lurked in her voice.

Dr. Banks straightened. His lips hardened into a line. "We can't have that, now can we? We'll get the charges dropped tonight." He gestured with the vials of blood. "First I have to get this to my lab. We need to know whether the anomaly is present." He held up a hand as the Doc started to protest. "The bureaucracy can move quickly with the right stimulus. We can have him out of here in a few hours, Holly. No one is going to show up in the middle of the night."

He pressed the three claret-colored vials into a cooler bag about the size of a woman's evening purse. Jeff saw him go still for just a moment. It wasn't much, just a hiccup in his movement. But Jeff sensed the worry that emanated from him.

When the man looked up, he smiled. "But we need to keep you safe, young man, and healthy until you can get to the lab tomorrow. Why don't you let me put you up at the Foundation? We have several overnight rooms."

"Uh, I don't think so, Dr. Banks. Not that I don't appreciate the gesture." He felt the Doc's warning hackles go up, just as his had. Dear Daddy wasn't quite on the up-

139

and-up here. He didn't know how he knew. It was more than just investigative reporter's sixth sense. No, he was *sure* about it. Right up there with the colors—that sure. Something was going on here. He could smell half-truth in the air. And the Doc could, too.

"No, really, Mr. McQueen. I wouldn't want you to suffer any relapse, any depression. Please let me extend this courtesy. We have a doctor on staff at the Foundation twenty-four/seven. It would be the safest place for you."

Was he really just concerned? There was concern there. And his other patients had committed suicide. Cause for concern. He didn't know someone had tried to kill Jeff, and that wasn't on the revelation agenda right now. No, Dr. Banks's concern was something more than fear Jeff would do himself in before morning. "I'm not suicidal, Dr. Banks. And we reporters are independent cusses. After being locked up in your daughter's lovely accommodations, I'd like to get back to my own place."

"My house? My wife is an excellent hostess . . . unlike my daughter, I suspect."

That hurt the Doc, Jeff could feel it, even though it was meant as a joke.

"If it makes you feel better, Holly could come with you. Just to reassure you that I have no nefarious designs on your person, in retribution for your left hook." He glanced to the Doc. She was looking mutinous. Dr. Banks was wary. He wanted her to come, but he was used to the fact that she didn't do what he wanted.

"Nope," Jeff said with finality. "I'm afraid it's home sweet home or bust." Would the guy still spring him if he couldn't lock him up in some new way? That was what was going on here, Jeff was fairly sure.

Dr. Banks turned away, his back ramrod straight, to seal the little cooler. "Very well, Mr. McQueen, though I must tell you I feel rejected. A car will be waiting at the front door at eight tomorrow morning to bring you to the Foundation laboratory. We'll get at what's wrong with you, and what we can do about it."

Again, Jeff felt the tingle of something going on below the statement. "Okay," he drawled. "That's great." It wasn't, somehow. "You think you can do anything about what's happened to me in the last couple of months?" Jeff had to know that, whatever was below the surface, this guy could really help him. Them.

"Well, it hasn't actually 'happened to you in the last couple of months,' Mr. McQueen." Dr. Banks snapped the black bag shut and zippered it. "It may have manifested itself recently, much like schizophrenia waits to strike in young adulthood." He nodded in his daughter's direction. Her hand was on Jeff's back where her father couldn't see it. "But the capacity to attach junk DNA has been with you since birth. We just can't identify that capacity until the attachments actually start to occur."

Jeff had a nasty thought. "If the blood test shows I don't have attachments? What then?"

"Then you are on your own, Mr. McQueen, with the law and the psychiatric system."

He strode past Jeff and his daughter and out the door without a single glance back. Jeff and the Doc craned around to see him go.

The Doc let out a breath as the door banged shut behind him. "I warned you he was difficult. But if anyone can help us, he can."

He was more than difficult. But Jeff couldn't put his uneasiness into words that didn't sound as paranoid as his chart said he was. So he just kept silent.

"Let's go to the garden for a while, and wait," the Doc muttered. "I need some thinking room." She sounded uncertain. Maybe because of what she had felt from her father. Jeff was pretty sure she had felt it too. He wondered if she realized that she had begun rubbing his shoulder the minute her father had left.

"Just keep out of the sight line of that apartment building straight back from the door," he said under his breath.

Chapter Twelve

The garden of the hospital was turning to shades of gray in the last light of the day, the blues and purples of the princess flowers and the agapanthus fading into monochrome. The young blond cop sat by the door, pulling out a cigarette. Over the edge of the garden wall the apartments and the office buildings that faced Wilshire loomed. Lights blinked on in some windows. The wheelchair bumped quickly across the pebbled concrete of the patio toward the pergola. Its heavy fall of wisteria looked like a woman brushing out her hair before bedtime. The wisteria's flowery scent overpowered even the faint drift of disinfectant from the hospital and the fainter smell of gasoline and exhaust never really absent in the city. Holland willed herself to relax. It was all falling into place. Jeff's blood would prove he had the genetic anomaly. Her father could pull strings better than just about anybody. Jeff would be free by midnight.

So, why didn't she feel good about it? Maybe it had to do with how funny her father had been acting. But when she passed her mind over exactly what had happened in the visitors lounge, she couldn't put her finger on anything specific. It was just a feeling she had that something wasn't right. Or maybe all her perceptions were skewed by the nearness of Jeff. That whole thing had been coming on slowly, but she couldn't ignore how his touch had affected her in the visitors lounge. It had been all she could do to keep up a facade of calm in front of her father.

She sat on the wooden bench underneath the wisteria and leaned over to unbuckle the leather cuffs. "Let's not pretend anymore, what do you say?"

"Fine by me," he growled and rubbed his wrists. The restraints hadn't been tight enough to restrict circulation, but the gesture seemed a natural reaction to freedom. She bent and unbuckled his ankles. When she'd finished, he reached out and took her hand. His strength coursed through her. She'd never realized how strong he was or how comforting that could be. He'd been frightening; he'd been weak and sick. But he wasn't either of those anymore. Or maybe he *was* frightening, but just in a different way.

"So, I guess you'll be out of here by midnight," she said, as much to herself as to him.

"In some ways that simplifies things," he said. In the growing gloom she made out the wry smile and a twinkle she had only glimpsed before. "Your place or mine?"

She chuckled, a little wearily, then stiffened. What would happen without the decorum of hospital protocol and the fear of discovery to restrain their need to touch? Holding hands was all very well, but what if he wanted more? She hadn't been so nervous about the prospect of being near a man since she had first dated in high school. Always she had been in control of the situation, having liaisons when and where she would, then sending the men away before they could get close. But she didn't trust herself to have a shred of restraint when it came to being near a man whose very touch brought sanity. And she wasn't exactly sure that more of that touch would bring more sanity. It might bring less. Much less.

"What?" he asked. "Is it your father?" He moved his hand to the back of her neck. "I felt that something was wrong. I think you felt it, too."

She jerked her gaze up to his. Her throat filled, so that she could only nod. That was the part of her uneasiness that she could admit to him. Then there was the part about how his parents, a lawyer and some orderlies could show up before midnight.

Jeff's eyes darted around the scene. She couldn't really see an aura in the twilight, but she felt yellow. He definitely *felt* yellow. He was all investigative reporter now. "How much do you know about his work?" He practically leapt from the wheelchair to pace.

A *pfff*ing sound whizzed past her ear. What was that?

Jeff whirled, scanning the garden, then ducked and grabbed for her. "Come on!" he yelled, as another *pfff*ing sound sent chips of concrete flying from the block wall behind her.

She was on her feet, scrambling after him. They ran for the door.

"What *was* that?" she panted as they collapsed against the enamel of the corridor wall.

"Shots," he said, peering out through the glass pane in the door. "They came from that office building, the one that can see the back wall." He turned back to her. "Time to exit."

"The sniper?" she said.

"Or my personal paranoid fantasy."

"Dr. Banks!" the big black orderly said, running up. Two nurses were several steps behind him. "You okay? What's going on here?" His eyes roved over Jeff, who strode back to stand behind Holland where he could touch her and give them both the silence they needed to think rationally and banish the panic she still felt choking her.

"Somebody was shooting at us, Sam," Holland said as calmly as she could. She saw concern and disapproval in his eyes as he stared at Jeff. "Hey, if I'd still had him strapped to the wheelchair he'd probably be dead by now."

"The sniper is here?" Terror filled the nurse's voice.

"I'll call the police." The second nurse turned on her rubber-soled white shoes and ran.

"And I'll take Mr. McQueen back to his room," Sam said in his best imitation of James Earl Jones's command voice.

Can't let him do that. Jeff's voice sounded in Holland's mind. *We've got to get out of here.*

He was right. She felt it. She cleared her throat. "I . . ." but she couldn't think of a plausible excuse. Bad, this was bad. "Sam, get the officer who's guarding Mr. McQueen. Have him call in the sniper attack. That will get us action. I'll supervise Mr. McQueen."

"Too dangerous," the orderly protested.

"Do it, Sam," she repeated, her voice low. That got the job done. Sam disappeared. "Alert Ernie and the nurses stations to the sniper. Tell everybody to stay inside until the police get here," she said to the other nurse.

Mrs. Hernandez nodded. "Yeah, you're right, Dr. Banks. All hands on deck in an emergency." She dashed down the hall.

The corridor emptied. Jeff pulled her toward Ward C. "Got to get my clothes."

"We can't just walk out. We don't have the order for your release," Holland protested.

"So, we're a little ahead of the paperwork. A sniper is after me, here." Jeff's thin cotton gown gaped ahead of her where it was tied across his back. The cotton slippers provided by the hospital shushed against the linoleum. Holland scurried behind him in her clicking heels. She pulled back, hard, forcing him to turn toward her.

"You're safe as long as you stay inside." Except from Mr. Stemmons.

"What?" he said. "What aren't you telling me?"

His green eyes were penetrating. His brows drew together. "My parents . . . a lawyer . . . They're coming for me any minute, aren't they?"

Damn! She'd never told him that. "I don't . . ."

"We're getting out of here," he growled. He grabbed her hand and dragged her forward.

She dug in her heels.

145

"You don't understand. I let you walk out of here before the paperwork arrives, and there'll be an inquiry. They'll check records; find the tapes of our conversations. My career will be over. You can't just let patients on a seventy-two-hour hold walk out the door."

"Even if you walk out with them? I'll be under your personal supervision." He was trying to joke her out of her growing panic. It just made her angry.

"I've built a reputation—," she started.

"And you think you can just keep your life all controlled and perfect when you have some kind of genetic defect that makes you hear people in your head?" His own anger was rising. "Some shmuck is trying to kill me. Think there's a connection? Think maybe if they knew you had it too, you might be on some list? And then there's your father."

"My father will protect us." She didn't mean to sound so defensive.

"Yeah. So he can study us—me, rather, since you didn't 'fess up that you have it too."

"Let's just wait for the police." She wanted to feel that was the right thing to do. But she didn't. Or maybe Jeff was mixing her up. She could definitely feel what he felt so clearly.

"Maybe paranoia is striking deep here, but I think you're not telling me everything. My parents are about to show up. That sniper could have an accomplice inside. Everyone knows where I am. I'm not feeling too secure."

"We have the best security around . . ."

"I say we go."

"Go if you want to." The words were said before she knew she would say them.

He stared at her. The red pulse flared up around him. He swallowed once and let go of her hand. Sound shushed over her. He'd made his point.

God, it was like being in one of those movies where you were handcuffed to some stranger with everyone after you. There would be questions she couldn't answer if they left

146

now. She looked down at her hand. He had been holding the one that always felt evil. She raised her eyes to his face. The red pulse of anger was gone now. Replaced by . . . hurt and urgency. Colors were swirling around him, pulsing orange and jagged yellow with a glow of magenta. He believed with all of himself that they had to get out of here, and he wanted her with him.

"Okay." He held out his hand, but she refused it.

"It can't look like we're together."

He nodded slowly, then turned down the hall. "Clothes."

She followed briskly in his wake. The cop outside his cell was gone.

"Dr. Banks?" The nurse's voice was shocked that Jeff was unrestrained.

"Have you heard about the sniper?" she called. "In the garden." She fumbled with the lock while Jeff stood at her side, scanning the hall as though the bad guys were about to crash through the door.

"The sniper? Here?"

"Do *not* leave the building," she said. "The police are on their way."

The door swung open. She and Jeff left the babbling nurses behind. Holland stood under the camera. Jeff pulled open the doors of a cupboard where his belongings were kept. The carefully laundered plaid flannel shirt and jeans hung on a hanger. The boots were lined up straight under them, socks balled and stuffed inside. There was a little basket with his wallet and car keys. Jeff scooped them up and headed into his room.

"Be quick," she whispered, over the sounds in her head.

"Don't worry."

He dressed without self-consciousness. She was a silent witness, along with the camera, to a flash of chest and bare buttocks as he leaned over to pull on his jeans. Biceps stretched and bunched. Pectorals clenched. Muscles and sinew moved under the skin of shoulders and back. Nice. Too nice. What was she doing running off with this guy?

He was more a danger to her than . . . than what? She had no idea why she felt the same panic he did. But she surely shared it. "Hurry," she whispered.

"I'm hurrying." He sat to lace his boots.

"We're going to be sitting ducks when we go out the door to the parking lot."

"Hospitals have roll-around laundry baskets, don't they? And really big laundry bags."

"Oh," Holland sighed. "Oh, no. That can't work."

"Sure it can. I used it once to do a story on kickbacks in the hotel business." He straightened. He didn't look like a patient. He had only the dreaded plaid shirt to remind her of her stalker—that and the strength, the maleness that had made him frightening then, and now.

She had to admit it might work. The hospital sent its laundry out each morning. The room where it was collected in the basement would be empty. There was a stairwell just outside the door to Ward C. Everyone would be in turmoil. But . . . there was another problem.

"Where will we go? The police will hit your house and mine as soon as they find you're gone, if I'm seen to leave with you. Hotel?"

"Not using our credit cards." He unzipped his pants to tuck in his shirt, revealing an alarming V of hair. No underwear. His aura was the gold of logic, his investigative training working overtime. "Okay. You don't leave with me. You stay and talk to the police. We have some third party load the laundry into your trunk. You join me when you've answered all their questions. When your father comes through to drop the charges, we're home free. You got enough cash to take me out to dinner? Let's hide in plain sight."

She nodded numbly. She should be telling him to wait here, in the hospital, for the charges to be dropped. She shouldn't be throwing her life away for nothing. But in some ways it had already slipped through her fingers—no longer hers to control. She watched him zip his jeans and buckle the worn leather belt, trying to find some defense against feeling defenseless. He slipped his wallet in his back pocket and fastened a little medallion on a chain around his neck. She sighed. "Let's get you down to the laundry room."

"Whaddya want? He's locked up where I can't get at him." Guy was busting his chops over something he couldn't help. He cradled the tiny cell phone as he strolled down Wilshire.

"You had a clear shot and you missed. I thought I hired an expert marksman."

"First, the light was bad. I'd moved to a new building, been waiting for two days—nothing. Then they finally come out when it's dark and I don't have my scope. And plus, the guy is a fucking jack-in-the-box. I thought he was locked to the chair, and he starts leaping around."

"So, I guess I have to get somebody to do the job you can't. You lose a hundred grand."

"You ain't paid up for the first four."

"Aw. I thought you were doing this for its value to humanity."

Sarcastic bastard. *"I don't save humanity for free, dude. I got to live after I'm done."*

"Yeah, well. Checked your account lately? It's in there."

He grunted. *"It better be. My target's got to leave this looney bin sometime."*

"Maybe I better find someone more effective to save humanity."

"Go for it." He clicked the phone shut. Get somebody else? Yeah. They could do that. With what was in the papers, they already had several somebodies doing their work. And they paid good for hits on people who didn't even have any security. Information had been perfect up to now. It was easy street. Except for this one. This shoot was turning into a nightmare. He could just walk away. But with how these money guys seemed to be connected, that might not be a

healthy thing to do. The healthy thing to do was make the hit.

He sauntered among the crowds heading for the trendy bars with little intense lights and martini menus a mile long. Look cool, dude. *That was the way to blend in.*

"I found one, Doug, and I know where there might be another one, just waiting to hatch. This might be the break we're looking for." Leland paced the white linoleum of the huge central room of the lab out in Malibu, his headset on. The lab was empty this late. Nothing moved. It made the glare of the lights on all the white even more pronounced.

"They're easy to find these days, Leland. They seem to be everywhere."

Leland ignored the barb. Time enough for that later. Doug never saw the significance of a thing until you pointed it out to him. "No, this is different." Leland glanced toward the huge microscope looming over the little lighted slide. "He seems pretty sane today, and he was remarkably insane two days ago. He looks like he's thriving to me."

"You think he can help you stop this thing? We need to do that, Leland."

"We'll find out."

"There can't be anything to this jogging thing. It sounds insane."

"Could be the release of endorphins. I don't know. But this guy today hasn't been doing any jogging. He's been locked up in solitary at a psych hospital for three days. There must be another reason he's able to cope."

"Then find it. Lendreaux's solution will only take us so far—*if* he's not lying to us. We need to counteract this thing if we can't keep it from spreading."

"I'll come up with a solution. If the guy doesn't get killed by a sniper first."

"So, call the sniper off."

"Tried. But I don't seem to be having any effect. Talk to Lendreaux. He listens to you."

"That guy is nothing but trouble. But he is *your* trouble. I am not getting involved."

"The announcement didn't raise a ripple," Leland noted. Let Doug realize that he knew what he was doing. "Hardly made it off the science pages, except for the *L.A. Times,* and nobody else has picked it up yet."

"That might just be because the front page is taken up with sniper activity." Doug let the accusation hang in the air just for a moment. Then he hung up.

Leland jerked off his headset. How dare Doug hang up on him? Doug was in this thing at least as far as Leland himself.

Leland got a grip on his anger with difficulty. He couldn't lose perspective. All right, Doug knew the thing was accelerating. But he could tell Doug that most of them would self-destruct. That would even be true. And Lendreaux would take care of some of them. What he wanted was the ones who knew how to thrive. Lendreaux could help him find them. He recounted the reassurances while he breathed slowly in and out.

He needed time. So much had to happen. They had to eliminate the defectives, then study the survivors under controlled conditions. If he could establish a genetically diverse colony of what he liked to call 'thrivers', he might just figure out how to stabilize the effect of the anomaly, know its full effect and extend it to himself. Yes. He sighed, the longing welling up as it always did. If he could start a colony, he might be named, if not the father of genetics, its brightest star. And then his secret hope might be realized: He might father a new, improved, human race—both figuratively and literally.

Holland parked on a side street in Beverly Hills, three blocks from Wilshire. The sound rushing in her ears had begun to talk to her in distinct voices. Someone shrieked about hearing voices. Someone else was contemplating suicide. This was getting worse. It obliterated her concentration. Still, she was careful to avoid the streetlights. She popped the trunk and got out of the car, glancing nervously around, waiting for some sign she'd been followed. The street was quiet. Lights glowed in expensive dining rooms as people sat down to dinner. That routine comfort seemed far away, here in the dark, with the voices in her head. Three blocks away the traffic on Wilshire was a dim whine.

By the time she got around to the back, Jeff had scrambled out of the trunk. He must have wiggled out of the laundry bag during the drive. He slammed the trunk lid and ran both hands through his hair. "Voila," he announced. "It worked." He reached for her arm. Silencing the voices gave her a small version of heaven.

She puffed air out between her lips. Her voice was only a little shaky as she said, "Ernie would be appalled to think he helped load you into my trunk."

They turned toward the lights of Wilshire Boulevard. Jeff's hand stole protectively around her shoulders. "I've been meaning to tell you, you've got to learn to lie on your feet better."

"Hey, I got us out didn't I?" *She* should be better at lying? With noise in her head, and interviews with the police about the sniper, wondering all along when the alarm would be raised that Jeff was gone or Stemmons would show up with an order and an ambulance?

" 'I'm taking home some extra towels. I have guests coming for the weekend?' " He raised his unruly brows. "I could do better than that."

He was so damned sure of himself. "And what would you have said, Mr. Big-time Investigative Reporter? Why does the president of a hospital and a research foundation put a very lumpy and abnormally heavy laundry bag in her trunk?"

"I don't know . . . Uh, lab coats being donated to charity?"

"Lame."

They walked down the darkened street between the houses of normal people with normal lives, something that might never be theirs again. "Not up to my usual standards," he rumbled beside her. "Guess I need the rush of the moment to really strut my stuff."

She'd chosen the new Panache Bistro because it was crowded and everyone there seemed in a rush—not normally her criteria for a good time. But maybe no one would remember them. The room was gray and copper, the surfaces metallic and shiny, just like the people. How many little black dresses could you count? How many of the newest twisted knit neckties, or leather jackets? Jeff's plaid flannel shirt didn't fit in. Maybe this place would end up a mistake. He steered her through the crowd to the maitre-d's stand, rifled through his wallet and slid a fifty-dollar bill under the seating chart.

"I'm sure you'll find a table somewhere secluded," he murmured.

Holland frowned. Now everyone would remember them.

Jeff glanced to the upholstered benches where others waited and scooped up a newspaper. A girl in the tiniest leather skirt Holland had ever seen and thick-soled boots that made her ankles look like sticks led them to the back. Her eyes were lined in black, her lips vaguely purple, outlined in black as well. She'd look dead except for the roses in her cheeks.

"You're wrong," he whispered. "We don't care if they remember later, only that we can sit here for a few hours." She stared up at him. How clearly could he read her thoughts?

"It fades in and out," he answered. He motioned her to sit at the granite-colored booth, and slid in beside her instead of across the table, one arm draped across the back of the bench and touching her shoulder. They took the menu from the girl too young and vibrant to be dead.

"Is this a new development?" she whispered when the girl had gone. Well, she meant to whisper, but the place was too noisy for whispers. At least she didn't shout.

"Pretty recent, yeah. New stuff all the time . . . especially when we're together."

She thought back. He was right. She could hear him more clearly. His thoughts were more complete. And she had started to sense things about others. Just not as clearly as he did. Like about her father. She squirmed against the hard booth. What was happening? She didn't dare let Jeff know she felt uncertain about her father. She had told him her father would protect them.

"I'm uncertain about him, too," he said. "He wasn't telling us everything."

She shot him a look. This was going to be massively inconvenient. But she sensed his discomfort with her father's proposition for supervising him until the car showed up the next morning. He didn't want to put himself in her father's power as a research subject, either.

"What choice do we have?" she asked. "He's the only one who might be able to help us."

"I know."

When the waiter came and introduced himself, he wanted to recite a long list of specials. Jeff put up a hand. "What we need here is a Jack Daniels straight up, and . . . for the lady?" But he answered himself. "For the lady a Sapphire martini, straight up with olives. And she does want vermouth in it. Just don't get carried away."

Holland looked at him, shocked. How could he know what she was about to order?

"Doubles all around," Jeff muttered. The waiter, named Ethan or Nathan or whatever, drifted away through the animated crowd.

"Look at them," Holland mused. "They're talking about what Suzie wore to the theater, or baseball stats, or what the latest hot stock is. Don't they know everything has changed?"

"It hasn't changed. Not for them. Just for us." His voice rumbling in her ear, the closeness of his body: both comforted her and made her acutely uncomfortable.

"What are we going to do?" she breathed, knowing he could hear her, though her voice was swallowed by the noise of the crowd.

"We're going to have dinner and wait for your father to spring me." His green eyes were serious. His gaze moved over her face, searching it for something. He looked as if he didn't know what it was, and she couldn't tell him.

"I'm not hungry," she said, "and you know that's not what I mean."

"Then tomorrow I'm going in to let your father figure out what's happened to us."

She was acutely aware that she had not played her part in that little drama. Her courage had failed her. "I'll go with you." She didn't say she'd tell her father that she shared Jeff's malady, and she knew he realized that fact. It was the best she could do right now.

He nodded. "Yeah."

The drinks came: Jeff's in a squat cut glass and hers in a long tube sheathed in an ice cylinder. The waiter made a show of pouring half of it into the frosty martini glass he'd brought. "Let me know when you're ready to order," he said, and disappeared.

"To answers," Jeff said and clinked his glass to hers.

She only hoped there *were* answers.

Jeff shook out the newspaper he'd claimed at the door and spread it across the table. The front page focused on the sniper attacks. But Jeff was drawn to a smaller article in the lower corner. He flipped to an internal page and sipped his drink.

"What's up?" she asked. How could he read the newspaper at a time like this?

"Just checking to see if we're famous yet." He pointed to an article.

The article, as it continued, read: ". . . the new discovery has some scientists frankly amazed. John Landry, head of the private wing of the Genome project, said, 'I'm astounded that new strings have been expressed in some subjects. I will, of course, have to examine the evidence itself, but Leland Banks is no crackpot society claiming they've cloned a baby. He has invited several of us to examine his research.' But what does this mean," the article continued, "for the future of humanity? We asked the head of the Health and Human Services Senate Subcommittee, Senator Emile Lendreaux. 'I would have to look at the evidence, gentlemen, before I could comment.' But Liam Talbot, President of the Society for the Preservation of Humanity, thinks that this discovery is of the greatest significance. 'Who knows what capabilities this genome will give humans? More, what can the ability to attach junk DNA to existing genomes portend? We are on the verge of a new and frightening human society.' "

Holland raised her eyes to Jeff's. "So, I guess we made the papers."

"Yeah. I can't say that's a good thing."

She was playing with her spoon at the edge of the berry cobbler they'd shared when her cell phone rang about two hours later. She fumbled in her purse for it and flipped it to her ear.

"Holly? Where the hell are you?"

She knew Jeff could hear. "Did you get the charges dropped, Dad?"

"Of course I did, including the ones by the officer. I even brought a lieutenant to the hospital to get Mr. McQueen released. Mr. McQueen's parents were there with their lawyer and transfer papers. The only person missing was the guest of honor."

156

"Does the lieutenant know I was involved?" Holland asked. He would know sooner or later. But the answer mattered for tonight.

"No, Holly," her father said. "He thinks McQueen escaped while you were talking to the police about the sniper."

Jeff smiled in reassurance. "Good. And it won't matter now that the charges are dropped." The smile lit his green eyes and softened his lips. Holland wanted to see more of that smile someday, when things weren't quite so dire. If that day ever came.

"Why couldn't you wait, Holly? Do you know what this could mean to your career if they found out?"

"There was the little matter of the sniper," Holland snapped. "You must have heard about that."

"The police were searching the surrounding buildings." She could almost hear her father thinking. But not quite. "Did the sniper hurt anyone?" That wasn't what he wanted to ask.

"No."

"Who . . . who was the intended victim?" And why wouldn't he think the attack random? Wasn't that what the papers all said—that there was no connection between the victims?

"Mr. McQueen was the target, I think." She waited to hear what he would say.

A hiss of breath sounded from the other end of the line. "Where are you now? You need protection."

Jeff shook his head and put a finger to his lips. She glared at him. She wasn't that dumb.

"We're fine, Dad. Maybe it's best if we don't say where we are on an open line like this."

"My offer of security for the night still stands."

"I think he's safest someplace anonymous like a hotel. He'll meet your limo at his place in the morning." She had just lied to her father. It didn't feel good. Jeff stroked her shoulder.

"Are you in a restaurant? You always liked the Polo Lounge at the Beverly Hills Hotel."

"Give it up, Dad. See you in the morning."

She flipped the phone shut and turned it off. "Just in case anyone's listening, they'll start searching hotels. That could take a while."

"I know that was hard."

The feel of his hand on her shoulder was intimate, promising, threatening. "I'm trying to take advice from a professional, learning to lie a little better." She made her tone light.

"The upshot is that hotels are out." She was just inches from his face when she turned to look into those sad eyes that only seemed like they belonged to a hardened journalist. "So . . . your place or mine?"

Chapter Thirteen

"Get this stopped immediately." Leland barely controlled the fury in his voice. "I don't care if you have to put a yellow alert on freeway signs. Call off your dog or I'll have your hide, and I am not speaking euphemistically, you understand?" He clicked off the connection on the tiny button that hung from his headset cord.

Damn! Wouldn't it just be the act of a perverse universe to strip him of his first and maybe last opportunity to study another thriver? He couldn't even find the guy, or his daughter. His daughter might finally be ready. She was hiding something. And only he knew what she might be hiding. She had always been a late bloomer. But she might just be about to bloom. He was sure the sniper was after the guy, but might shoot his Holly by mistake. These shooters weren't infallible. He didn't want to lose either one of them. It was going to be a long wait until morning.

He spoke into the headset. "Dorothy, I want you to check every hotel in town for . . . I know it's one in the morning. What I want is to check registrations for credit card use by Holland Banks or Jeff McQueen . . . I want it real time—you understand?"

It was after midnight when they parked her Mercedes at the neighbor's house across the street. The neighbors were in Italy for the summer. The driveway meandered downhill toward a garage below street level, overhung with an ancient California live oak. The car was almost invisible from the street above. Jeff took Holland's hand and led her across the street at a stealthy jog.

They'd decided upon her house, in case the limo arrived early for spying purposes at Jeff's apartment. He'd admitted gruffly that he hadn't been much of a housekeeper during the days before the press conference. She hadn't been much better, but the choices were limited.

Still, she hesitated before pushing open the door. Who had been inside her house, except her mother? She didn't think Maria, who came to clean every other week, counted. Did she even have friends? Lisa was more of a colleague, though they had lunch once a month. And she'd never brought one of her dates here. She suggested their place or the Beverly Hills Hotel—maybe the Four Seasons, so she could leave when she was ready. Of course, Jeff wasn't a date. Definitely not a date. They were hiding out, for God's sake.

What was he? More frightening than a date, less predictable.

"What?" Jeff murmured, sensing her mood, but obviously not her thoughts. "You think someone's inside?"

159

She shook her head and stepped through the doorway to punch the security code into the keypad in the foyer. "No. Just remembering the mess I left." He might just know that wasn't the truth. He didn't say anything, but followed her in. She was acutely aware of the dry warmth of his hand clasping hers.

She flipped on lights, seeing the wood floors, the carpets, the mementos from her travels all meld into something that said things about her she might not want to reveal. Jeff blinked against the brightness, though the sconces left soft shadows. Chinese take-out boxes lay scattered across the coffee table in the great room. Shards of the smashed pot from the Acoma reservation littered the floor near the entrance of the dining room. The rough pickled-wood shutters were still closed against the night.

"Nice," Jeff was saying as he moved into the room. His aura was magenta, but shot with tiny yellow streaks of tension. "Not what I would have imagined your house would look like."

"What *did* you imagine?" she snapped.

He looked down at her. Speculation lurked in his eyes. "Something . . . huge and white and angular hanging off a hill. Sealed concrete floors, brushed steel fixtures, that sort of thing."

"You been moonlighting in the Art and Architecture section?" But that was exactly the kind of house she thought she should have.

"No. Just seems to go more with linen and pearls than this one." He looked around again. "Not that I don't like this one." He dragged her over to the bookshelf. He must know books said more about you even than your house. She couldn't let him see her books . . .

"Wait," she said, wondering what words would come out. "I . . . I want to see what shattered my pot that night you were outside." She pulled him away from the bookshelves. "Unless you did?"

He shook his head, hovering over the shattered pot, then fingered the shutters behind it, finally flipping one open. "Look here."

She peered around his shoulder as he fingered a smooth round hole in the glass.

She jerked upright. "That's a bullet hole!"

Abruptly, she lunged for the light switch, pulling him with her. "God, what was I thinking?" she said as the room plunged into darkness. "We can't leave lights on."

"You're right." He took her hand in both of his. The darkness seemed blacker than before. She could practically feel her pupils dilate in a search for light. Slowly the shapes of the furniture emerged. "Steady now. The police are on a full-court press, looking for this guy. He's taking care of himself tonight, not after us."

"You don't know that." She could feel herself tremble—whether in sympathy for the danger she had been in several nights ago or for the possibility that danger still stalked them, she didn't know.

"If he'd wanted to pop us, I think the walk down Wilshire in the open was a better chance than trying to follow us up here and guess where we are in the house with all the shutters closed and the lights off." His tone was so matter-of-fact, the humor lurking just behind it so sensible, that Holland exhaled. "Why don't we go to the back of the house?"

She took a new deep breath. "Good idea." She started through the kitchen, Jeff in tow. "Be careful, there's broken glass in here."

He pulled himself closer to her as they picked their way across the tile. "I'll follow you."

That was just what she was afraid of. Follow her where? She was leading him toward her bedroom; there was no doubt about that. They needed sleep. The revelation that her father knew what was wrong with them, his visit, the sniper, escaping the hospital, the long dinner hiding in plain sight while they waited for freedom. And now, skulk-

ing into her house, afraid to turn on the light because of
. . . of fear. Fear of what they were, of who might know. It
had been a long day. She should make him sleep on the
couch. But how could she bear to be parted from his
touch? She stood, almost trembling, in the hall outside her
room.

He reeled her in with a hand on her shoulder until she
was clasped against his body—so strangely bulky, hard in
places she was not. His hands slid around her belly. His
scent suffused her senses: hospital soap, the fabric treatment the laundry used, and there, beneath everything else,
his smell, the scent of a particular male, aroused. The hard
swell of his arms bound her close to him. The length of
his body was solid against her back, her buttocks. "Shush."
He soothed into her ear. "We have enough to worry about
without worrying about that. You don't have to do anything. Just hold my hand." She could feel his smile in her
hair, trying to reassure her. How did he know what she
was afraid of?

But if nothing was going to happen, why were they
pressed together, with shock waves shooting down between her legs? There was no way she could pretend it
was a "fluttery stomach" the way heroines always did in
books. No, this was raw sexual attraction making her
throb, multiplied by the need that had grown to touch Jeff
over the last days, fueled by the healing she felt when she
did. And something else. She liked him more than any
priggish stockbroker or self-important shrink she'd dated.
She liked his wry smile, his practicality, the vulnerability
that lurked beneath his cynicism. She liked the quality of
his masculinity, so opposite to white lab coats and red
power ties. For her part, there was no room for pearls and
linen in what she felt right now. She had no choice, no
power at all. The fact that they would sleep in her rumpled
bed, touching, meant that she could just give up any
thought of "nothing happening," because if she was touching his hand, she would want more—more than she had

ever wanted from a man. She turned in his arms, but she didn't draw back. Even in the semidarkness she could see the pulsing, roiling indigo around him. She let her breasts brush his chest, felt her nipples harden, knowing he would feel them too. His hands fell naturally to her buttocks and caressed their curve. His eyes glowed in reflected moonlight through the one open shutter. She knew that glow. It didn't matter that he promised restraint. He wanted her as much as she wanted him. She raised her arms around his neck and felt the throb of his wanting rise inside his jeans.

"Doc . . ." His voice was throaty.

"You're not my patient anymore." Her colleagues would not think a few hours from discharge justified that claim. Okay. She was about to have sexual relations with a patient. No one outside could know how much more than her patient he was. . . . "Call me Holland."

"Not Holly?" His lips moved over her throat. She thought she might faint.

"Only my father calls me that." Once, thinking about her father might have upset the mood. But nothing could upset *this* mood. It was like a freight train with a hundred engine cars on a slick track that led only one place. She leaned in against the bulge in his pants. A small smile curved her lips to hear his breath quicken. His chest rose against hers. Underneath the plaid flannel, his flesh was hot.

His hands roving over her buttocks clenched her against him; his breath became a groan. He bent his lips to hers. She opened her mouth to him. His restraint was almost painful as he kissed her gently, his kiss all the more passionate for the cost of that restraint. He licked her lips, outside and inside. It made her shiver.

"Holland," he whispered. It echoed inside her head, more intimate than any other man's speech had ever been, could ever be.

This was so much a mistake. But she wanted it, for reasons too primal to name. Because he was different than her other boyfriends, or because he was different than her father? *Stop the shrink-talk!* she told herself.

She had better get him to the bed before she just hiked up her dress and pulled down his pants and made him take her standing. That's not what she wanted. She wanted the sweet pain of his restraint for herself. So she pulled away, running her hand over the bulky shoulders she couldn't wait to see under that flannel shirt, and took both his hands.

"God, Holland, are you sure?"

"You know the answer to that." The bedding was strewn over the floor from her last nightmare. She didn't care. She kicked off her heels and reached behind her neck for her zipper.

"Let me do that," he muttered, reaching around her. His lips brushed her hair.

She did her part. With trembling fingers, she slipped free the buttons of his shirt, one by one. The ripping sound of the zipper was followed by the tickle of air on her back. The light that bathed the room was dim, the moon probably waning. But she could see the coarse curling hairs on his chest. A little medallion glinted just under the vulnerable place in his throat where she could see his blood beating. She pulled the shirt from his belt and pushed it over his shoulders. He released her only long enough to wiggle out of it. She hardly noticed the shushing in her ears as they parted. Her pounding blood obscured the sound. She shrugged out of her dress, watching the play of muscle and sinew under his smooth, pale skin as he reached for his belt and the button on his jeans. He was beautiful. The thick hair that waved gently over his ears, the green eyes, glowing now with lust, and the body, heavy with muscle, reeking of male. She wanted him so much it hurt between her legs. How long had it been since she'd let dating progress to sex? A while. Now she knew why. She'd never felt this animal attraction before. That was what it was. Only animal attraction. The perfect combination of body type, and pheromones, and . . .

He reached for her hair, feeling for pins. The massive muscles in his arms, the hair peeking from his underarm—almost overwhelming. She slid her thumbs under his waistband and pulled apart the jeans. She knew he wore no underwear. She slid the jeans over his hips, the silky skin beneath her thumbs bringing a little moan to her lips from a place at the base of her spine.

Hair fell down her back. Jeff ran his fingers through it and slipped the catch on her bra.

"Boots," she whispered, urgency throbbing in her throat. He sat in the disarray of the bed and she pulled his boots off, then stood before him, studying his nakedness as she slipped off her own remaining clothes. She wasn't disappointed in him. How could she be? His thighs were full and muscular. Of course, his erection promised fulfillment, ached with restraint. His body excited her as she had never been excited. But the tug she felt inside her was more than that. The fulfillment Jeff promised was new in a way she couldn't imagine. She could feel it lurking behind his big eyes and shallow breathing. He felt it too. She felt his excitement, his wonder, his fear as strongly as she felt her own.

They stood there, not touching, sound cascading over them like a waterfall in the background. But it was no longer important. What they were about to do was.

He swallowed, his solemn gaze never leaving her face. His brows asked a question, tentative. She pressed her lips together and nodded.

He held out a hand, as he had already done so many times before. She placed her own in his, so slender compared to his square strength. He didn't use strength, though. He pulled her gently toward him in the renewed silence. She sat beside him, turned in toward him so their knees touched. He smiled as he fingered the string of pearls she still wore. She couldn't help the answering smile that rose to her lips. The height of refinement, at least if she weren't naked, eager for this equally naked man to take her with all the force he cared to muster. His hands descended to her breasts. She strained against them.

He was everything she wasn't. She knew he could be crude, violent. He was unabashedly sexual. But he wasn't violent now. She could feel the restraint threatening to make the indigo of his passion boil over. There were no little yellow lines of tension now. It was only blue swirls shot with bursts of black and carmine. His lips brushed hers even as his hands explored her body.

Not that her own hands weren't busy. She ran them over the small muscles in his back that slid over the larger ones. She could feel them move beneath the smooth sheath of his skin. He rubbed her ribs, her back. His breath in her hair bathed her in his scent. She felt the ridge of his spine and then she went lower to the swell of his buttocks, so silken, and the soft depression between them.

"Holland," he breathed over her, the word echoing inside her mind. *"What's happening?"*

She knew what he meant. She felt his passion, his need for her seep inside her with a sureness that was totally different from any other experience she'd ever had. He must be feeling the same. It was more than sex. Something pulled them together and she couldn't explain what it was.

Since she couldn't answer his question, she pressed her lips to his, searching his mouth with her tongue, letting her nipples tickle across his chest. She wanted him, all of him, body and mind and soul. She had felt the tug of him from the first moment she'd seen him, but mistaken it for other things. With a small sigh she acknowledged that want. She wanted him. With a whoosh, his soul seemed to engulf her. She had never truly known what maleness was, but she felt it inside her, felt what it was to be male and strong, even as she felt female, strong in her giving. She pulled him down onto the bed.

Then restraint was gone. With a groan he suckled at her breasts as she arched to meet him. His hands kneaded her buttocks. His erection pressed against her thigh. She felt his need, his focus on wanting her. With one hand, she reached to caress the flesh of his maleness, lightly. She could feel the drops of liquid oozing at its tip. She smoothed the juice over its sensitive head as he groaned into her. His own hands slipped over her belly and down to test her readiness. She could feel the wet of her own slickness on her thighs.

He touched her moist folds and she opened her knees, her longing for being filled with him almost pain. He ran his fingers over her swollen flesh, feeling for her nub of pleasure even as his mouth found hers. Her feelings drew to a fever pitch almost immediately, the ramp-up so steep she thought she would explode.

"Take me," she hissed into his mouth. "I want you in me." In that moment, she gave herself to him. It was a decision, a commitment.

She rolled into him and he rolled her back, his hips now squarely between her knees, his cock pressing at her entrance. "I want you. All of you," he whispered.

He gave himself to her. She could feel it. He opened to her, even as he penetrated her.

He was in.

He filled her in all the ways she could be filled. He thrust inside her physically. At that instant, his whole personality penetrated her mind as well. She felt the fire of his passion, his need for thrusting. Behind that she felt his rage, the hurt of rejection, the drive for success, the fear of himself, his need to control his rages, the despair when he could not, his pride in what he did beneath a veneer of cynicism about the value of it, the hatred for his father, for his father's religion . . .

It overwhelmed her. She wanted to push it away. Her eyes widened. His eyes stared back, half in horror, half in fascination. But he could not pull back from the brink. Another stroke and the cataclysm was upon them—so fast it seemed to engulf them without warning. The colors around Jeff went from indigo shot with white-hot flares to only white—a nimbus of light that flared out and eclipsed the room.

The scream was bass and treble together, reverberating in their heads. It echoed in the room beyond. Holland's consciousness wavered before blackness shadowed everything.

Chapter Fourteen

Holland woke slowly. Her brain felt like she had blown a fuse. She opened her eyes on darkness. The sounds in her head were clearly voices.

"Great oysters, man. Make you hard as a rock. Nothin' like the Acme." The voice was southern, maybe black.

"How can I go to school tomorrow and pretend to teach?"

A shriek. "Evil!"

The voices multiplied. Holland shook her head, hoping to make the voices go away. The clarity of the words just made the cacophony harder to ignore. She put a hand to her head, groaning and tried to sit up. Where was Jeff?

Jeff! It all came back to her: the passion, the attraction bordering on insanity, the moment she had decided to open herself to him, the sex that made her feel like she might explode. And the unmistakable feeling that he had given himself to her in return.

What about the feeling of invasion—the violation of having all of him inside her mind? Had he felt that from her, too? She shuddered and looked around.

He was standing, naked, in the dark in front of the slider over the deck. He'd opened all the shutters. The summer moon was almost set. It gleamed in a bulging crescent as it hung over the city lights. It must be near dawn. She'd been out for hours.

She clutched the sheet to her breasts as though that could protect her from the voices now so clear in her mind, or from what had happened at the moment of orgasm.

Holland.

He didn't turn, didn't speak. But she heard him just the same. Holland took a breath. Fear showered her, half her own, half his. Whose fear was it?

Wrong—this must be wrong.

She felt the same way. He would know that. He had felt overwhelmed by her, just as she had felt overwhelmed by his mind, his experience, his soul.

"What happened?" She purposely asked it out loud.

I think we fused some circuitry.

The dim feeling of distance, despair, and acceptance of that despair was the most natural of emotions, and it washed over her. Was it from him, or was it hers? She couldn't tell. The feelings mixed together in a way that frightened her. She couldn't see an aura around him either. Maybe it was black, like the dark room.

"You think it will fade?"

Maybe. He didn't believe it any more than she did. At least when he spoke inside her mind the others faded a little. *You can hear them now, can't you? Clearer than before.*

"Yeah. I hear them. This was what it was like for you?"

His agreement washed over her. He still hadn't moved. His back was silhouetted against the moonlit trees. How had he stood that terrible multiplicity of thoughts at all? In the silence, she heard them all talking at once, some more loudly than others. Maybe she could just refuse to listen to individual words. Maybe she could make it go back to sounding like a waterfall. She tried to let them melt together, the voices. But words still emerged from soup.

"Wife—crazy—my house—president . . ." And then there were the shrieks of despair.

Holland found herself standing beside the bed. She wanted to touch Jeff. He turned to her. He wanted to touch her too. So much. The need emanating from him was physical, emotional, spiritual, matching her need. The tug between them was increasing. She reached out her hand. His silhouette heaved with his breath. "Holland," he whispered.

The need for him was almost pain. She took a step, and then knew she couldn't, shouldn't, wouldn't close the distance between them. The fear she couldn't know was his or hers circled the room.

He could feel it too. *Can't. Won't. Dare not. Not right now. Not until we understand.*

She agreed. Somehow she stopped walking toward him. The need for his touch must be denied. The touch wouldn't stop there. Not with him naked in her bedroom with the moon limning every undulating muscle with light and shadow, and each fiber of her body wanting him. Who knew what would happen if they had sex again? They might lose their slim tether to sanity altogether. They might merge entirely, or blow out their neurons in some ultimate ecstasy that left them brain-dead shells of themselves.

"How long can we go, without . . ."

Touching? I don't know.

"I don't want some collective consciousness," she whispered. "How would you get privacy? How would you maintain who you are?" She felt the panic ramping up.

Do you think that's what's happening here?

"I don't know. I only know I can hear you. I can hear others. I can't stop it." Her voice was hoarse in her throat.

He spoke aloud. "Me, too. You're here inside me. I think I invited you in."

He was right. She had felt him take down his guard, open himself to her. It had happened when she wanted him so badly that she opened to him, mentally as well as physically and emotionally. She had invited him inside her, too. She shuddered. Not a violation. But she different than she had been before she had joined with him. More? Less? God, what path were they on?

"Are you sorry?" The words were torn from her. Why did that matter?

"I don't know."

"At least I didn't have the dreams again."

"Me, neither."

But maybe the dreams are better than what actually happened, she thought. She didn't mean to think that, but she couldn't help it. And she heard the glum echo of his agreement.

He flipped out his cell phone. Better admit up front he hadn't found the guy. Maybe the moneyman knew something he didn't. He sat down on a park bench in the morning sunshine.

"Yes?" The voice on the other end of the line was curt.

"How'd you do getting somebody else? Need some help?"

"Actually, no. Guy's going to be where I can get to him whenever I want him in about an hour and a half."

"That mean my ride is over?" He didn't want the ride to be over. A hundred grand a pop, he figured he was good for at least ten. He was already a serial killer. What did more matter?

"The name of your next target and all that info will be waiting when you claim your lost library card at the Beverly Hills Public Library. They open at ten. Same deal as before."

"Great." That meant he was out of the hit from hell. Maybe the next target would be some mousy girl who worked at a video arcade or something.

"Let's hope this one is a little easier, huh, Eddy?"

"Cut it out." The moneyman knew he shouldn't use names on the phone. *"Consider it done."*

He flipped the cell phone shut and looked around. The library was on Santa Monica, wasn't it? Yeah, Santa Monica.

The promise of sunlight erased the setting moon. Jeff had dressed in his jeans and the red plaid flannel shirt, Holland in slacks and a cashmere sweater. She rolled her hair into a chignon and carefully pinned it, then stuck a comb under the roll. He removed the bandage at his temple. The wound had scabbed over, leaving a dark, cracked spot.

They hadn't spoken again. It was all Holland could do to keep herself from going to him, handling him, running her fingers through that thick wavy hair. What *was* this attraction? It was physical as she had never experienced physical attraction, but it was more. She could hear his desire for her. Disturbing. He liked her breasts. That wasn't what he called them. She should hate that. She could feel the images of his hands on her buttocks in his mind. He loved the curve of her breasts, her buttocks, even her calves. She caught glimpses of the chaotic images that darted through his mind. He refused to look at her, but that didn't stop an erection. He couldn't hide that from her either. He was afraid of going to her father's lab. He was afraid of snipers. He was afraid of the fact that he could hear her in his mind. And he was confused.

He was confused about the sympathy she felt for him. He didn't want her sympathy. The tender thoughts she had about him made him nervous. He was afraid of having opened himself to her and that she would use that against him.

Lord, was this what a male mind was like? The thoughts about sex were ubiquitous. His mind came again and again to the feel of her body, and what that did to his own. And she knew he could hear her dismay about that. Not that he probably wasn't getting signals of her own arousal loud and clear. But he reveled in his, and she was afraid of hers, afraid that arousal was all it would be, that she couldn't handle it being anything more. He could sense her doubt that she could feel the way she did about some guy she'd known three days, her fear that she had opened herself to him and he would use that against her.

There was *no* way this situation was tenable. They couldn't go on, knowing everything the other thought, felt. Sometimes she couldn't tell his feelings from hers. The more she tried to hold herself in, to prevent him from hearing her, the more she felt his concern that she was afraid of him knowing. It was all too much!

The aura had returned around him with the light. The colors were clearer than ever. The nervous crackling green was shot through with brown bubbles of fear. She wondered what he saw when he looked at her. She looked up at him and knew he saw the same. She'd never have to wonder what he saw again. At this rate she could practically see it with him, through his eyes. Was she her looking at him, or him looking at her? She wanted to shriek her refusal of this whole mind thing. He was as close to screaming as she was. But there was nothing to be done, not right now, and they both knew it.

So they walked out the front door. They didn't have to tell each other it was time to go meet her father's limo at his apartment. She didn't have to ask where his apartment was. They just turned toward the front door.

Outside her house, the black limo waited like one of Darth Vader's Imperial Destroyers. She felt her shock echoed by Jeff's own. They stopped, frozen on the doorstep as the driver got out of the car.

Guess he finished going through the list of likely hotels.

She heard him clearly. She nodded. Her father had been looking for them all night long.

He must want to be sure we catch his ride pretty badly.

She didn't answer. She didn't have to. Her father might be the only one who could help them. She looked at Jeff.

It was up to him whether they got in that sleek black car or not.

He set his mouth and stalked down the brick path. The driver held open the limo door.

"Mr. McQueen, Dr. Banks," the driver murmured. He crackled with green nervousness too. The aura was pale but discernable. Holland glanced at Jeff, who stared at the driver in shock. It was the first time they had seen an aura on anyone but the other.

"That's us," Jeff growled as he got in the car. "I guess you know where we're going."

Holland slid in beside him, careful not to touch him as the voices in her head cackled on about Mildred's mother's cancer and the fear of what was happening to them, and the despair that they might be insane, and the chick some guy banged last night. The last was as bad as Jeff, she thought. Were all guys like that? She pressed down the voices as best she could and leaned her head against the cool glass of the smoked window. It would be more than an hour to the lab in the hills of Malibu. She wondered how she would stand the drive with Jeff less than two feet away from her. Two feet? Two neurons.

She could feel his fear as the words *Here's looking at you* echoed in her mind. He was acting tough. The car pulled off. The driver was safely locked behind the smoked glass. He couldn't hear. She had to try to allay Jeff's fear. It wasn't like they were going into some torture chamber. It was just her father's lab.

"He's just going to ask you questions about your experience," she murmured, around the voices in her head. He had those voices for distraction too, but it wouldn't matter how loudly they spoke. Her voice would be louder.

"Yeah, and how much should I tell him?" Jeff asked, between clenched teeth.

"I don't know. How bad do we want the truth?" That pretty much said it.

"Okay. And after that?"

"Baseline testing."

"Great."

"Some MRI, some body scanning, some neural activity testing, probably."

"What's that?"

"Like an EEG. You've heard of that. It's fancier now. That's all."

"No surgery, no lasers?"

She managed a chuckle. "You've been watching too many documentaries."

"No, I saw *Marathon Man*."

"The worst that happens is that you get tired of getting stuck with needles. They'll probably inject some dye for contrast in the imaging."

"Dye? What kind of dye? Where does it go?"

"Wherever they want it. They have the kind that seeks out neural pathways, or capillary concentrations—that one is for tumors."

"Shit, yeah. That makes me feel good."

"It's no big deal." She tried to sound matter of fact.

"Then why don't you admit you've got it too, and we'll do it together?"

She looked at him and knew that he could look back and see inside her. Maybe he could see the truth when she could not. What could she say—because she didn't want her father to know this about her? Because she was afraid it would disappoint him yet again that she was somehow defective? Or was it something else? Maybe she wanted to maintain some small ability to be objective about what was happening to them. As part of the research team, partner with her father, she would be privy to his research techniques and his conclusions. He would treat her as an equal. That would feel good. But it would also give her and Jeff an advantage. If she were a subject, she'd know nothing.

She didn't have to explain. She could see in his eyes that he saw it all. And he agreed with her. His role was subject. Hers was stealthy research partner.

"We're going to need some periodic quiet to keep our wits about us, though. Think we can touch without jumping onto the nearest gurney?"

"You're asking if I can touch you without trying to fuck you?" His voice cracked with his realization of her disapproval. "Yeah, I think I can manage it. You're not that good looking."

"Well you're not exactly God's gift," she hissed. But she knew she was lying, and therefore he knew it. And come to think of it, he had just lied about how he felt about her, too. What they both were was confused and afraid. Oh, this was insane!

He reached out a hand and covered hers on the leather of the limo seat, where she had braced herself stiff against her emotions. The silence shushed through her. Relief cascaded over both of them. She let a ragged breath tear into her lungs and blinked slowly as she relaxed into the seat.

"Let's see how long we can do this before things get out of hand." His voice was a sensuous rumble, as he too sank back, head lolling on the seat. His hand was warm and moist against hers. He had broken out in a sweat trying not to touch her.

She nodded. Sweet torture: to need his touch and have that touch be the very thing that threatened her sanity. Or maybe his touch was the only sane part of life, crazy as it had become. The car swung off the I-10 onto Pacific Coast Highway. She only knew that it was still forty-five minutes to Malibu, and she would have the relief of silence, the shock of hearing his thoughts and fears and the threat of losing who she was in the melange of experience they had exchanged, for three-quarters of an hour.

"Welcome, welcome!" Dr. Leland Banks shook Jeff's hand too vigorously. Her father's aura was pale but it was there. He was electric yellow with excitement and there was a peachy glow of pridefulness around him.

He had met them at the mounded beds of impatiens planted in tiered shades of white and peach and persimmon in front of the Foundation's lobby. The driver had called ahead to announce their arrival. The security station waved them through. Security guards stood on each side of the entrance. Behind them, the huge pentangle buildings of white stone that were the laboratory marched up the hill, brown now in summer.

Jeez, she could hear Jeff thinking, *donors pay for all this?* Seen through his eyes, it was an impressive operation. Jeff must have heard her thinking. *Too impressive,* he responded. *The kind of donors who can afford this setup aren't the kind you want to know about.*

Holland was outraged that he could accuse her father of shady dealings. The last thing her father was, was shady. He might be taking R&D money from drug companies, but he was funded by think tanks and foundations, too, as well as individuals. It wasn't like the Mafia gave her father money or anything. As if to reassure herself, Holland turned to her father.

He was impeccably dressed, as always, and attended by three pasty specimens in white lab coats. Their auras might be described as avaricious, eager. They were streaked orange and hard-edged. But there was nothing evil about them.

"I'd like you to meet Dr. Yoshimora." Leland Banks introduced the Asian gentleman with stripes of white in his hair, but didn't bother with the two assistants. "He'll be working with you while you are here. Of course," he added, "I'll supervise your debriefing myself."

"I'd like more information about what exactly you have in mind, Dr. Banks," Jeff said carefully. He was trying to think around the noise. They dared not hold hands. Their connection, and the fact that they had been wrapped around each other in naked abandon last night, was a secret they had to hide from her father.

177

"We're going to interview you, Mr. McQueen, before we decide what tests are most appropriate." Her father raised his hands in mock defense. "Don't get me wrong, we have some idea what we're looking for, but we're going to start at the beginning."

"Holland said you interviewed others."

Dr. Banks placed a hand on each of their shoulders and herded them in through glass doors that slipped aside for them. Several more security guys hung around the lobby. Holland didn't remember her father being quite so security conscious in the past.

"Interviewed might be an exaggeration. If Holly hasn't told you, my former examples of the genetic anomaly you share are dead, by their own hand or another's. That's why I'm so anxious to work with you. And why I didn't want to leave you on your own last night. You aren't in danger of committing suicide, are you?"

"No." Jeff shook his head as he swallowed a chuckle. "Not right now." His thoughts slipped back to their love-making of last night. Fair enough. Holland herself had just been thinking about it.

"Well, keep it that way."

"Someone else seems to want my hide, though."

"The sniper? Oh, I wouldn't worry about that, Mr. Mc-Queen. My security is excellent. This is the one place you have nothing to worry about." Her father smiled. His aura was so self-satisfied, his grin might well have belonged to the Cheshire Cat.

That's my father, his strength and his weakness. She felt proud and ashamed all at once.

At least you can be proud of yours sometimes.

They trailed the researchers through rooms that looked pretty much like what Jeff expected. Holland, of course, had been here many times. Was that why Jeff expected it to look like it did? There were gleaming linoleum floors and machines both huge and small, scurrying assistants in lab coats and lots and lots of stainless steel. The light was neon, hard. The smell was pure disinfectant. There was, perhaps, a faint whiff of cigar somewhere.

He led them out through a corridor and down to a door that looked like the wooden front door to a house. Inside, that's what the room looked like—someone's living room, in contrast to the sterile laboratory outside. It was filled with oriental rugs and soft lamps, deep leather couches and mahogany bookshelves. A mirror on one wall was framed in ornate rococo gilt. There was no desk. It was just a room that looked as if it were made for conversation.

"Sit down." Her father gestured magnanimously. "Holly?"

They sat. The couches were almost too deep, too self-consciously comfortable. "I'd like to record our sessions." He wasn't asking permission. He leaned over and flipped a switch embedded in the coffee table. "Holly, feel free to ask anything that comes to mind."

Holland had almost forgotten her role as co-researcher. She nodded, trying to press down the voices that had been ramping up in her mind, and trying to suppress the swirl of emotion between her and Jeff.

Her father took out a small notebook and his Waterford pen. He obviously wanted to compliment the tape with his own observations. The assistants had disappeared. With a start, Holland glanced to the mirror. She bet she knew where they were. Jeff didn't seem surprised at her conclusion.

"Now, Mr. McQueen, why don't you tell us about your first symptoms?"

Jeff took him through it, leaning forward as if to reject the comfort of the couch. He told about the tinnitus, the voices that emerged, the rising sense that he was going insane, the reaction of his friends and coworkers. He spoke of his suspicion that the voices he heard were others like himself, of deciding to try to find them, of stalking Holland. He just left out realizing that Holland was like him.

179

"And what happened to change the distress you were experiencing? You seem remarkably calm compared to that time you graced my home with your presence."

Holland felt like she'd been slapped. Why hadn't they realized that was where the questions would inevitably lead? What could Jeff say? She watched his eyes dart around the room. It made her nervous.

"I . . . I don't know," he said. "I . . . just got past it." He managed to look her father straight in the eyes. "New symptoms started appearing, and others just . . . seemed to bother me less. I guess your other subjects never reached that stage."

Oh, he was good. All that lying you had to do as an investigative reporter came in handy.

"What other symptoms appeared?"

"Well, the auras."

Yes, Jeff. The auras would be good for a real detour.

"Auras around what?"

"That would be around whom. They're halos around people—they seem to be a special language of color. They match the person's emotion, as far as I can figure. It takes a while to get the hang of it, because the combinations are endless. Kind of like kanji script."

"Do you read kanji?" Her father was surprised. His aura said that his self-satisfaction was a little shaken. He must not have thought Jeff smart enough to read kanji.

"My work means I need to speak languages, and read them when I can. I do Spanish, of course. Can't get along in L.A. without it. French. I hail from Louisiana purchase lands—Creole, you know. A little Mandarin, Japanese. L.A. is the Pacific Rim. That's why the kanji. Portuguese, Italian—so close to Spanish and French they were easy."

Okay, so he laid it on a little thick. Her father deserved it. Jeff shot her a sheepish glance.

But her father had moved on. "So . . . these auras. Do I have one?"

"Sure."

Her father looked a little nervous. "You want to tell me about it?"

"You just got nervous. That's sort of a grass green. It crackles a little."

Her father sat back in his chair. But his scientific fascination overcame his feeling of violation. He leaned forward again. "Excellent," he said slowly.

"There, see? You just got excited, that's little yellow streaks, and those orangey-red patches . . . I don't know. Ambition?" Jeff looked up at him seriously. "Maybe you think this research is going to make your name."

Her father chuckled, uncertainly. "My, that makes it a little hard to hide your intentions, doesn't it? Don't tell me! I just went crackly grass green again."

Jeff just smiled and nodded. "Come to think of it, I bet it gets a little harder to lie."

Holland felt the rebellious twinkle in Jeff's eyes more than saw it. "Well, it would certainly make it easier to treat patients with psychosis," she spoke up, suppressing her own smile.

Her father glanced over to her, obviously having forgotten she was there. He gestured with his pen. "What about Holly's aura?"

Jeff shook his head, his smile now bubbling at the corners of his mouth. "I feel a lady ought to be allowed some secrets, Dr. Banks."

Don't you dare imply I'm having lecherous thoughts about you, she thought sternly.

You don't *have lecherous thoughts about me?* His eyes went dark green like the sea when clouds passed over it. She noted the magenta bubbling with indigo. She knew what that meant.

Careful, even my father can see that look. There. Take that.

"We'll come back to the auras." Her father cleared his throat. "Do you still hear voices?"

"More clearly than ever. Lots of them. Maybe the fact that they're clearer makes it easier to handle." He was trying to give her father some reason for his sanity—besides the fact that he touched the man's daughter.

"What do they say to you?" her father asked Jeff. He glanced to Holly, disapproving. He thought she should have asked that question.

"I did ask it, Dad, a long time ago." She answered his accusation. "Mr. McQueen?"

"They don't talk to me at all. I just hear whatever they're thinking at the time."

Her father's brows drew together. "And that would be?"

Jeff glanced up and to the right, concentrating. "Mildred doesn't feel able to cope with her mother dying of cancer when these voices are screaming at her. Some woman just shrieks. I don't think she's going to make it. There are a lot of those. Some guy is thinking about this lady secret service officer. I won't get specific there. Another guy thinks the sazeracs Floria makes at the Two Sisters are just about enough to drown out the sound." Jeff looked back at her father. "That sort of thing. Those are just the ones I can pick out right now. There are lots of others."

Her father looked at Holland again and lifted his brows in question.

"It's possible he's making it up, of course, even though it is very detailed." She put on her best psychiatrist voice. "Minds can invent and sustain whole personalities. He could be inventing the auras, too, based on a complex system he's worked out and some sensitivity to other's moods. He could make up all the detail about what he hears. But weigh that against the fact that he has this extra DNA string, and he's saying pretty much the same things as the other people who have that string, and . . . Well, that's a lot to just write off to psychosis." They'd never find out anything if her father just wrote Jeff off as crazy.

"It's much too soon for conclusions anyway, Holly. A serious seeker after truth should not leap to them." He flipped shut his notebook. Holland was stung by his rebuke. Suddenly she was fighting for control among the voices in her mind. She found herself swallowing hard.

Shusshh, she heard, in her mind. *It's okay. You were great.*

She clenched her lips together. *So were you. Kanji. That set him back a pace.*

He met his match, girl. Rebellion can heal. You know rebellion. Try a little.

Easy for him to say. What an ego! But it wasn't easy for him. No, she had felt all his history, all that his rebellion against his father had cost him. But it had been the only way for him. And somehow he had grown into a competent, intelligent man who did what he could in the world. Not bad. She looked at him, and saw his smile. Her father should not see that smile.

He didn't. He was rising. "There will be many hours to explore this, Mr. McQueen. I want to examine the coping techniques you are using to continue rational interaction with the world. Holly can help us define those. Learning to control the response to your situation could be crucial to helping others with the anomaly survive and enjoy relatively normal lives."

"I'm not sure there is going to be a normal life for people like me, Dr. Banks." Jeff's aura darkened. "Have you thought what it means, not only to individuals, but to the world, to have people be able to hear each other think? Doesn't that scare you, Dr. Banks? It sure scares me."

Holland saw peach bubbles in her father's aura turn hard orange. "Yes, I have thought about it. But the discipline of science requires that we know what we're dealing with before we decide to be frightened." He turned to the door. That wasn't what he meant. He was excited, ambitious, unbelievably determined. She felt his personality hardening as they spoke. Worse, she felt something familiar about his attitude, his voice maybe. It raised an echo she couldn't place.

He thinks this is going to make his name, big time. Jeff was a little frightened of him.

Holland was frightened too. Why was she getting flashbacks of a similar fear? Why was it connected to her father? It came to her suddenly. When she was sick, in ICU—that was when he'd felt like he felt now, a little frightening, overbearing, pushing her, controlling. They shouldn't be here! The feeling was overwhelming. Her father had a hidden agenda they wouldn't like. That was what her father had been hiding.

Her suspicions echoed through Jeff's mind as well. But they both knew it was too late.

"Why don't we start getting those baseline readings we need?" her father continued. "By the way, have you ever had an MRI or any kind of neural scan?"

"Motorcycle accident outside Columbia, Missouri, once. Ended up in the hospital with some broken bones and a pretty good concussion. I think they did some tests." This was still their best chance for answers. Those answers might just come at a price.

"Excellent. I'll request your records right away. They'll make a good comparison point."

Holland managed to touch Jeff's elbow as she guided him out the door in front of her. The people at the mirror wouldn't suspect anything from that. And the relief it gave both of them was just a bit of fortification against the trial to come.

Chapter Fifteen

Holland sipped an iced tea as one of the technicians, a pretty Asian girl, supervised Jeff getting onto the narrow gurney. She kept a watchful eye on the surrounding equipment and bustling techs, but she couldn't detect anything out of the ordinary. Jeff was clutching his paper gown where it gaped at the front as though his life depended on it. She smiled at his discomfort and felt him bristle.

You try wandering around all these people with your ass hanging out, darlin', and see how you like it. He lay back on the gurney, straining his neck to see how much of himself was revealed—at the moment, only his bare feet, hairy calves, and quite a bit of corded thigh. She was pretty sure he was in for a surprise, though.

What surprise?

"Mr. McQueen, we'll need to remove that gown," the little Asian girl said. She looked as if she were twelve. She held up what Jeff thought was a microscopic cloth. Holland could feel his disbelief. "You can lay this over your hips." She handed it to him and turned discreetly away.

"This? I get to cover myself with this?"

"Well, only until you're inside the machine. I'll take it before the scan starts."

"You'd think these powerful machines could see through a little cloth," he grumbled, holding the tiny towel to his groin and slipping out of his paper gown. Holland noted with a smile that it was torn in several places where his shoulders were too broad. He laid back down on the

185

gurney, glaring up at Holland. She moved to his side.

"They're a new kind," she said. "And it isn't the worst thing in the world, Mr. McQueen." She patted his arm and let her touch linger. His barrel chest, revealed now, was as massive as she remembered it, his nipples as vulnerable and soft, his shoulders . . .

His eyes went soft. Images of her own body beneath his flickered across his mind. She practically broke contact— the vision of her as he saw her, the feel of her own flesh stirring his. *Stop this,* she ordered, *or that cloth won't be big enough to conceal what you're thinking about.*

With a start, she realized that the pokerfaced twelve-year-old beside her wasn't as impassive as she made out to be. It wasn't just her aura, which had gone magenta, shot with darker red, lust-red, not the indigo that meant . . . meant something else.

Nice. Really nice. I wouldn't mind some of that action.

Holland heard it clearly. So did Jeff. He turned toward the tech, who was staring at him frankly, before her aura suffused with pink embarrassment.

They were hearing the technician's thoughts.

Was she one of them? Holland turned toward her, breaking her contact with Jeff.

I understand her interest of course. "You been hearing voices, young lady?" Jeff asked as the lab assistant went to the foot of the gurney and pushed him into the round tunnel of the giant scanner.

"Me?" the young woman snorted. "Not likely. That's your department, Mr. McQueen."

Holland touched Jeff's hand as he slid by, surreptitiously.

This guy's bats. No matter what they say, the tech was thinking. "Now, you might feel a little claustrophobic. The tube is meant to be tight."

Jeff disappeared slowly inside the gullet of the machine. He was a little afraid. Holland could feel it. But he pushed it down. *She's not like us.*

You're right. But we hear her.

Yeah. He handed out the towel at the lab tech's insistence. The machine made a little humming sound. Holland could practically see the rotating scanner just inches above Jeff's face, feel the massiveness of the metal around him.

But only when we touch. They had just entered a new era. Holland shuddered.

Leland Banks stared down at the records they'd downloaded from the hospital in Columbia. He held up the scan, translucent like an x-ray but shaded with multiple colors. It showed brain activity. Entirely normal brain activity. He held up the scan they'd just taken of the same brain, Jeff McQueen's brain, today. The colors shouted with intensity.

Yoshimora, looking over his shoulder, took in a sharp breath. "I expected a change after the onset of the anomaly. But none of the others showed *this* level. This is amazing."

"Yes." Leland glanced at the series of scans again. This was unexpected. "He's going to make quite a subject." He tossed the film on a table and glanced through the one-way glass down into the room where a technician was just pulling McQueen out of the full-body scanner. They'd been keeping McQueen, and coincidentally, his daughter, quite occupied, so they would think the tests going on on the lab floor were the only ones occurring. Now he could do something he'd been wanting to do for . . . well, years. Holly had come to the lab at last.

"Now, what about the difference in intensity level between the scans we took today?" Yoshimora wondered aloud. He picked up yet another film from the table whose colors shouted. "What could be causing those tremendous spikes in activity?"

Leland grabbed the garishly colored sheet. "Do you see any pattern in the surges?"

Yoshimora moved to a tape that was being spit out of a shiny box attached to what looked like a long-range camera lens. The tape curled in piles on the floor. "I thought we might be getting surges when his anxiety ramped up— you know, a new test starts, or he gets a little claustrophobic in the MRI tube. He definitely shows periodic signs of anxiety. But . . ."

"What is it?" Leland snapped. "No time for reticence here."

"Well, have you noticed how frequently your daughter touches him?"

Leland nodded his head, his lips pursed. Only he knew why she might find herself so attracted to McQueen. He cleared his throat. "Just so you don't have to say it, I think she's been screwing her patient. That about it?"

Yoshimora shrugged. "I don't know and, frankly, I don't care. But she makes any excuse to touch him, however briefly. That's when his brain activity spikes."

Leland turned from watching his daughter, who was brushing McQueen's hair off his brow. "Now, like now?"

Yoshimora held out the tape. The spikes crisscrossed the tape in a frantic scribble of ink.

Leland slid the tape through his hands, staring. "Some kind of response to sexual urges?"

"I have no idea what it is, but his frequency goes wild every time she touches him."

"Great, my daughter just brings out the best in him." But this would provide the perfect excuse to ask Yoshimora and company to perform the tests on Holly. She wouldn't even know what had been done. "All right. Let's take her scans as well," he said. "Maybe there is an equal or even opposite reaction." She should have been exhibiting effects before the age thirty-four. Was it just late in her? Well, they were about to find out what he had longed to know for years.

Sariya, a lab assistant who still spoke with a marked Indian accent, stuck her head in the door. "Senator Lendreaux on the line for you."

Damn and damn! The last thing he wanted was Lendreaux right now. The senator would not be avoided. His funding committee in Congress provided all the money to create and sustain this place. In spite of what he let Holly and others think, the drug companies had no part in this little action. And Lendreaux's other talents were so crucial to the project. Too bad the senator could or would not provide all the answers they needed. That would have simplified matters. Well, he'd handle the gentleman from Louisiana. The man was transparent in his simple avarice for power.

Leland pushed off the table and past Sariya toward the privacy of his office. The senator's "personal" involvement in the project needed privacy. Privacy. Leland chuckled. If he had his way, privacy might just be a thing of the past.

Holland was almost as exhausted as Jeff was. It was nearly seven, and they'd been at it one way or another all day. The brief respites of touching weren't enough to keep the voices at bay. And if they touched, not only did they feel that dangerous attraction, they might just hear the thoughts of those around them. It felt wrong, like eavesdropping. And then there was the fact that when they were both afraid, or anxious, Holland sometimes couldn't tell her emotions from Jeff's.

"Hey, don't you believe in time off for good behavior?" Jeff growled as one of only two remaining lab assistants attached the cuff to take his blood pressure for what seemed like the hundredth time.

"I think we're done for the day," Holland said firmly when the tech had recorded her reading. "We have time for a nice dinner down in Santa Monica and an early bedtime. We're still an hour from Mr. McQueen's apartment."

Holland glanced up to see her father swinging through the double doors at the end of the lab. "You don't need to go into the city, Holly." He was looking at her so strangely, fear and pride mingled in his eyes. "I've ar-

189

ranged to have a lovely dinner catered in the private dining room here tonight. And you know there are excellent subjects' quarters here. Mr. McQueen can be very comfortable here tonight. We want to get an early start tomorrow. You're welcome too, of course, Holly. I'd like to have you stay as well." His voice was almost humble as he addressed her. It was as close as she had ever heard him to asking, rather than commanding. It made her seriously consider doing what he wanted, for the first time in a long time.

I don't think so. Jeff's aura had little frissons of brown fear around the edges. What he said was, "You're too generous, Dr. Banks. But I prefer my own bed."

"Sariya, you and Joseph can go. Oh, Sariya—can you bring in Mr. McQueen's clothes before you go?" The assistant nodded and turned out of the room without speaking. Joseph gave a mock salute and left. Her father waited until they were gone. Holland could see the orange of his ambition pulsing behind the yellow-green of uncertainty.

Her father sat down on the nearest chair, carefully adjusting the creases of his pants at the knees. "Look, Jeff. I don't need an aura to tell me you don't trust me. But you've got to realize that you are the most important thing to happen to genomic research in . . . I don't know when. You may be the most important thing to happen to human kind." He glanced again to Holland, and she saw a smile play around his eyes. He was proud of her. What was that all about? "I admit I want you where I can see you. I don't want to lose you to snipers, to some sudden impulse to kill yourself, whatever could go wrong. We made good progress today. But we're not done by any means. Don't endanger that."

Holland and Jeff knew he was telling the truth as he understood it, even though they weren't touching. His aura suddenly reeked of blue-green sincerity.

Her father shrugged. "A little caviar, a little champagne, a little duck a l'orange, a good bed. Is that so bad?"

Jeff glanced to Holland.

He's not exactly a mad scientist. Just a little intense.

A little!

Like you're not when you're after a story? Bet you're just the same.

Sariya ducked her head in and set a carefully pressed and folded stack of Jeff's jeans and his plaid shirt on the counter.

"See?" her father said. "Even cleaned your clothes."

"Okay. One night can't hurt," Jeff growled. He was thinking about snipers, and about the need to protect her.

Her father didn't seem to notice Jeff's grudging acceptance. "Holly?"

She nodded. If Jeff was staying, she had no choice.

"Excellent!" He radiated satisfaction. "Now, Holly and I will go see to the arrangements while you dress." Holland helped Jeff off the gurney, though he didn't need the help. The moments of silence fortified her for what promised to be a long dinner. She hoped to God there was some way to see Jeff tonight without her father knowing. She was going to need his touch. But his touch would bring its own threat. When it came down to it, could she muster any control?

Her father ushered Holland into a dining room that looked as if it could be in any expensive West Side home. The interview room they had used this morning seemed to be part of a wing that looked pretty much like a series of luxurious apartments. Several caterers were setting out a sideboard with warming pans. An ice bucket filled with a bottle of champagne sat beside an antique breakfront with a pullout shelf now lined with smoked salmon, caviar, broiled and stuffed mushrooms, and other tidbits.

Her father held the bottle of champagne aloft. "Cristal, Holly. That still your favorite?"

"I haven't changed that much." Oh, but that was a lie. She had changed right down to the cellular level. She felt her face heat. Why could she never lie to her father?

"You're right, much better quality than Dom."

"But you always serve Dom . . ."

"Name, dear Holly. Dom has the name. You want people to recognize your generosity."

That pretty much said it. Appearances were very important to her father. He wanted to be accepted, worshipped, valued above all others. If that meant serving champagne he knew wasn't the best he could do, then he would, without question.

"You look tired."

"No more tired than you," she bristled.

"It wasn't an accusation, Holly. Relax." He examined her quizzically, a little smile playing around his lips. She was getting that fearful feeling again, the one that echoed the time she was so sick. "You're really coming into your own, now, realizing your full potential."

Praise? From her father? She watched the ambition and the pride marble together in his aura. What was with this? "So, what did you find out today?" Holland changed the subject abruptly as she took the glass he held out to her.

"We charted the pattern of increased brain function. I expected a change in the section that is devoted to hearing. But the activity is located primarily in the left brain. There's also some increased activity right down by the hypothalamus. The hypothalamus itself is operating at a higher level than normal all the time, which is what we've seen in others, but there are some astounding peaks. Tomorrow we can try some interactive testing, where we track the activity as he performs certain functions. He appears to go through periods where he becomes more agitated, followed by periods of those spikes in brain activity. We'll start monitoring saliva production, sweat. I'd like to know why he gets agitated and why he calms down, and what that cycle has to do with the increased brain activity. We'd also like to test his eyesight, examine some of those rods and cones that can suddenly see auras."

192

Holland nodded, digesting. The anxious periods were the ramp-up of the noise level. She always made some excuse to touch Jeff when their mutual distress got too bad. So the periods of spiked intensity were when they touched. When they could hear other people thinking.

"What are your conclusions on the psychiatric front?"

Holland snapped her gaze to her father's face. He had never asked for her psychiatric opinion. He lifted his brows. She sighed. "I think he's sane. Stressed, but sane."

"You said he could be making all of it up—living in some kind of constructed fantasy."

"Yes. Absolutely." She raised her chin. "But in my opinion, he's not."

"Is that based on more than just opinion?" Her father couldn't believe psychiatry had rules too. It made her angry. Her father almost always made her angry. Or maybe her anger was fueled by the fact that she couldn't tell him the one reason she knew for sure that Jeff was sane.

"Look," she said, allowing condescension into her voice. "If he were truly schizophrenic, the voices would be more sinister. They'd be berating him, telling him to do things to protect himself, or prove himself. The voices he's reporting sound . . . mundane for lack of a better word."

"What about the people who just scream?"

"I think he's hearing other people with the anomaly."

"So do I," her father said. His aura sparked with nervousness. What did that mean?

A white-jacketed caterer opened the door for Jeff. "Here you are. I got lost." He smiled.

Holland couldn't help but smile in return. She wondered if he knew how that smile softened his features. What would his laugh sound like? She wondered if she would ever hear him laugh. She suddenly thought that green eyes, glowing with intelligence, vulnerable under their cynical veneer, were about the most attractive feature a man could have. Or maybe puckering lips that looked unruly, like they said something about a man he wouldn't

193

want just anyone to know. She felt the tug between them grow into a throb. His eyes jerked over to her. Those eyes registered surprise, and then his aura deepened into that magenta, shot with indigo. She blushed. He'd caught her thinking some very carnal thoughts.

"Well, you're here now," her father said. "Have some champagne." Her father played the magnanimous host and poured a glass. "We've got some '85 Opus to go with the duck."

Jeff eyed the hor d'ouvres hungrily. "All this testing has made me famished."

Do men always think about food?

Jeff glanced up at her. *Complaints, complaints. I thought you'd like compulsive food thoughts better than constant sex. Guess I was wrong.*

Holland smiled and looked at her shoes. When she raised her head she caught her father looking at her strangely. His aura pulsed with tiny bursts of orange-yellow. What did that mean?

"So, Dr. Banks—can you put me back the way I was? I may be getting used to this voice thing and the colors are all pretty, but I've got to say I'd rather go back to the way I was."

"I'm afraid not, Mr. McQueen."

"Jeff, call me Jeff. You already started."

"Jeff." Her father sipped champagne thoughtfully. "It's not like you have some tumor we could cut out. Change has occurred on a cellular level. You have new strings of DNA attached to every cell in your body."

Holland could feel the edge of Jeff's disappointment, and the swell of fear. "No radiation . . . no laser thing . : . ?"

Her father shook his head. "This change, whatever it is, is permanent."

"Then how did it happen? Was I born with it?"

"Probably. At least with the capacity for attaching the new DNA." Her father's aura was showing those little black circles she just couldn't place.

"Why didn't it show up until I'm thirty-six?" Jeff was in reporter mode, focused, probing.

"Like schizophrenia shows up only in young adulthood," Holland interjected. "The tendency can be there in certain individuals, but it lies dormant until . . ."

"Until what?"

"Ahh, that we don't know, Jeff." Her father shook his head. He looked thoughtful. "Holly, does schizophrenia show up *only* in young adults?"

"Yes, almost exclusively. It's as if the condition doesn't 'take' in subjects outside a certain age range. I think it's related to the pruning of dendrites in the brain during adolescence." Her father's aura had the same dark red that Jeff's had shown a moment ago. "Does that disappoint you?" she asked.

The green of nervousness pricked through the colors around her father's form. "Why should it?" he asked, too jovial. "There might be a similar phenomenon at work in this case. All the subjects with the extra genomic string are in their late twenties or early thirties."

A young man came in from the kitchen dressed in a black jacket. "Shall I serve, Dr. Banks?"

They sat to eat at the table laid with white cloth, sporting silver and crystal.

Jeff's mood turned dark. Holland could hear him chewing on the problem mentally. She felt his fear of needing to touch her constantly, of the connection he found overwhelming when they did. He was trapped by this condition, just as she was. Finally he said, "What's the point, Dr. Banks? If I can't go back to what I was, what's the use of all the poking and prodding?"

"Truth," her father said. "We want to *know* what has happened. That in itself is worth our trouble." Of course her father would say that. Maybe it hit home with Jeff. Jeff thought truth was important, too.

"I guess." Despair danced at the edges of Jeff's voice, just like the black around his aura.

"Then there's the fact that you are an anomaly on top of anomaly. Sure we want to know what you can do with your new protein strings. But we also want to know how you are living with this change when others can't seem to. You can help people who share your condition."

"Dr. Banks, don't give me that 'science as humanitarian aid' crap. Most people aren't worth helping." Jeff savagely cut into his duck.

"I'm sure you're right. And that's why you're an investigative reporter, right? You just take on slave labor rings for the joy of it." Her father's derisive tone was calculated.

"I like exposing frauds." Jeff stuffed a forkful of bird and dressing into his mouth.

"I'd think you'd want to figure out ways you can control the sensory input even more effectively than you do now, Mr. McQueen," Holland said. If they could learn to control it in some other way besides through each other, they would be free. Freer, anyway.

"If your father's going to call me Jeff, I guess you can, Doc."

"Okay, Jeff." Inside, she could feel the voices ramping up. *She* wanted to find ways to control it, that was sure, and if her only respite came from touching Jeff she would be in constant danger of doing what they'd done last night. Her eyes raked over his body, remembering what it looked like beneath the red plaid.

His thoughts flickered over last night, too: the burning desire, the need to join more powerful than either of them had ever felt it. No, that kind of need was more than just the need for sex. He thought that, too. She could feel it. For all his seeming preoccupation with sex, last night was as different for him as it was for her. It had been too powerful, too wonderful, too much of a fusion. Both of them were afraid of any more fusion.

"All right," Jeff muttered. "I want to control it better."

"Maybe the others can teach you," her father said. "How many voices do you hear?"

"Lots. Too many."

Holland had a thought. "You said your subjects were both suicides, but there was a third guy. He was shot by a sniper. Bad luck. Were there . . . ?" Her question petered out.

Her father's aura had gone murky aubergine ringed with black. That felt bad. Very bad. A flicker of . . . something, passed over his features before he schooled them. Jeff reached across the table for her hand. She meant to protest, to pull away. She could feel her father's startled disapproval. *I want to hear him.* The warmth of Jeff's palm slid over her knuckles.

They heard.

"So the sniper shooting your subject wasn't an accident?" Holland asked in a small voice. "How many more were shot?"

"Some." Her father peered at her, then at their joined hands. There were those black dots bubbling up through his aura like mud pots around a hot spring.

Sixty-eight, he was thinking.

Sixty-eight others who had the anomaly she and Jeff had were killed by snipers? Holland felt the bottom drop out of all her rational thinking. What did that mean? Wasn't that almost the whole total of people killed?

Jeff looked at her. *The snipers are killing us—our kind.*

Her father took a breath and controlled himself. But not entirely. *He'll be here, any time now. He'll know what to say to them.*

Jeff looked at Holland. What the hell did that mean? Who would be here? *Ask,* she thought. But they couldn't. Not if they didn't want her father knowing they could read his thoughts.

Her father practically threw his napkin on his plate. "Don't worry, either of you. Snipers won't get you. Not here."

"How can you be sure?"

"We're prepared here. I thought you were safe when I got you admitted to Holly's loony bin. I was wrong. But that's because I couldn't let the hospital know you were in danger."

"*You* got him admitted there?" She snatched her hand from under Jeff's in surprise.

"You thought a judge remanded him at three in the morning by accident? Who do you think called his parents? I pulled every string I had when I realized what he was. Pressing charges got him off the streets. But jail didn't seem exactly a secure location."

"You knew what he was all along."

"Well, he was spouting pretty much the same language as our other subjects that night at the press conference. And of course, he looked crazy as hell. It was an easy bet to make."

Jeff was breathing hard. So was Holland. "So, how secure is this lab, Dad?"

"I've got twice the security we usually have, and we're not slouches in the security department. No one is going to get Jeff here. Why do you think I wanted him to stay? Who knows what could have happened last night with you two gallivanting around town and then going back to Holland's place? Too predictable." He downed his glass of wine in one gulp.

Which meant he almost choked on it when the two men pushed open the door and strode into the cozy dining room.

Holland recognized Brad Weller from her father's press conference. Top aide to . . . Senator Lendreaux, who followed him through the door. He was lean and sinewy under his perfectly tailored suit. His hair just grayed at the temples, but it was premature. Everyone knew he was the youngest man to reach the Senate since Dan Quayle.

But that wasn't what startled Holland and Jeff.

The senator swept his eyes over them. His aura was steel blue. *Well, well, well. Him I expected. But not you, my dear.*

The senator was one of them. They could hear his soft southern accent clearly, in spite of the fact that they weren't touching. He obviously knew about them. Both of them. And he was ever so sane.

"How?" Jeff murmured. *How do you turn it off? Do you touch someone?*

Holland heard Jeff thinking, and knew the senator could hear it, too. She wanted to tell him to cut it out. But how could you stop thinking?

Jogging does it for me. How do you do it? You said touching?

I don't know.

Liar.

"Senator Lendreaux." Her father rose. "Here so soon?"

"My pet research project calls, and you just know I'm gonna come runnin', Dr. Banks."

But Holland and Jeff heard the chuckle in his mind and knew that there was something else going on.

"How flattering, Senator."

"Well, when I hear that we finally have a subject worthy of research, I just had to come on down and see for myself. Now, I find you got two. We don't want to take any chances with Mr. McQueen and your daughter. Can I provide y'all with a little security? Gov'ment is mighty good at that. Got a military base right up the street at Vandenburg. Or maybe we could borrow the Navy at Point Heuneme. Just state your pleasure, Doctor."

"Well, I don't think that's necessary, Senator. We have excellent security here."

"So I heard you saying."

Don't tell my father! He couldn't find out about it like this. Her gaze was pulled to her father's face. She didn't have to read his thoughts to know that he knew about her. "You knew?"

"Have for a while, honey," he said, almost sadly. "Just waiting for it to take hold." He smiled a crooked smile. "You're a late bloomer, like I always said."

199

"But how do you know it's active now?" Fear coursed through her. Had this senator that could hear thoughts been keeping track of her? Had he told her father?

"We scanned you today, as well as Jeff, here." He saw her look of disbelief. "You don't think we need to put you in a metal tube to do a brain scan these days, do you? I can afford the latest equipment."

"So, all this talk of helping you with your research was just a bunch of bull. Wasn't it, Dad? You didn't want my help. You wanted me where you could scan me." Anger rolled up from her belly into her throat. "How long have you known?" she accused. She didn't wait for an answer. "You could have told me, so I wouldn't think I was psychotic when I started to hear voices. And you must have known the real reason Jeff was stalking me. Why didn't you come out and tell me, so I could get some help? I thought I was schizophrenic! Do you know what that felt like? It felt like shit!" Holland couldn't stop. She shouldn't be revealing this to some sinister government official she didn't know and his lackey, but she couldn't help herself. "And the sniper! If the sniper were after people who have the anomaly, he could have been after me!" She finally sputtered to a stop and waited. Her father couldn't say anything that would excuse him.

"I wasn't sure it was inevitable. I was looking for a cure. Should I have frightened you and told you you were a mutant?" He shook his head sadly. "I didn't think so." He was lying again! The little black bubbles in his aura said so.

"If I could interrupt this tender family scene," the senator drawled, "I'd just like to say that I would like to provide protection for both of you—Miss Banks, Mr. McQueen."

"That's Dr. Banks, Senator," Jeff corrected. It would never occur to her father to do so.

The senator smiled. "Of course. Dr. Banks. A psychiatrist, yes?"

NAME: _____

ADDRESS: _____

_____

_____

TELEPHONE: _____

E-MAIL: _____

_____ I want to pay by credit card.

__ Visa   __ MasterCard   __ Discover

Account Number: _____

Expiration date: _____

SIGNATURE: _____

Send this form, along with $2.00 shipping and handling for your FREE books, to:

Love Spell Romance Book Club
20 Academy Street
Norwalk, CT 06850-4032

Or fax (must include credit card information!) to: 610.995.9274.
You can also sign up on the Web at <u>www.dorchesterpub.com</u>.

Offer open to residents of the U.S. and Canada only. Canadian residents, please call 1.800.481.9191 for pricing information.

Holland nodded, drained. The future that now opened ahead had frightening possibilities. The senator obviously had very good reasons for supporting the study and good reason for keeping his own mutation secret. Not exactly a vote-getter these days, mutation. But she and Jeff weren't secret anymore. And if the senator wanted them studied, they would probably be studied. At least they'd be safe from snipers. Maybe the devil you knew . . .

But we don't, Jeff had a milky haze in his aura. Wariness?

"But you will," the senator said. Again with the smile. It was a campaign smile, not one that lit his eyes, like Jeff's.

"What?" her father asked.

The senator ignored him. "Well," he said, rubbing his hands. "Brad, I think Mr. McQueen and our fair Dr. Banks are more comfortable here. Where we have such fine laboratory equipment. Let's just beef up the security with some secret service and maybe some MPs? The combination of military brute force and Secret Service paranoia makes for excellent security."

Brad ducked his blond head and withdrew, clicking open a tiny cell phone.

"The more everyone insists I stay here tonight, Senator, the more I want to go home," Jeff said with deceptive calm. The senator knew he wasn't calm, though, just as Holland did.

"Ahh, boy, we'll have to think about your safety for you, won't we?" The senator smiled.

"And what about your safety, Senator?"

"I am an expert in security. These days an elected official has to be."

"So that's why the sniper won't get you?" Jeff turned to Holland's father. "I wonder why you aren't using the senator as a guinea pig?"

Don't, Holland thought. *We need to think about this.*

But Jeff was in his reveal-the-fraud professional mode. "You know that your patron is a mutant, too."

"Of course." Her father merely shrugged.

201

The mask fell away for a moment from the senator's carefully constructed persona. He glared first at Jeff and Holland and then at her father. "Kinda nice to have a friend in high places, wouldn't you think? Guarantees my interest in Dr. Banks's research here. Guarantees my interest in your safety, too." He saw Holland's father about to speak and interrupted him. "The Doctor here knows I can't be a research subject. I have more important things to do. Besides, what would happen if my status leaked out? My ability to help you—any of you—would evaporate."

Holland heard the threat, but felt the truth of it even more viscerally from his thoughts and the deep purple intensity of his aura. He would do anything to keep his secret. And that aubergine color in his aura was one he had in common with her father. What was it? Commitment? Ruthlessness?

The senator looked around, changing the subject, though his thoughts still raged. "Aren't y'all going to offer me some of that lovely duck? We might as well start getting to know each other."

Jeff was shooting warning barbs at her, but there was nothing to be done. Holland sat down. She and Jeff said little throughout the senator's lusty enjoyment of the meal. Her father looked at her with pride, and something almost like avarice. The senator regaled them with stories of political wars and favors asked and answered. It was just the campaign smile that bothered her. Behind that smile was the aubergine color she found frightening. Knowing that the senator could hear what she was thinking didn't help. She felt violated in a way she hadn't really felt before; even though Jeff could hear her, too. It made her squirm as she second guessed her thoughts, tried to suppress them, failed. Why was it the one thing you didn't want to think about was the very thing you always thought about? She didn't want to think about Jeff, for instance, and what they had together.

The senator glanced her way, his brows lifted.

Holland panicked and lowered her gaze to her plate. Duck. Why was it always orange sauce? She didn't even like marmalade, so why did she like this duck sauce? Oh, this was just insane! She couldn't listen if she was preoccupied with focusing her thoughts on stupid things. The senator only came through in snatches. He was speculating about how he could turn the situation to advantage. He was thinking about being president. She glanced up to him, and saw him watching her. He was thinking that someday, he would be the only one who had the "gift" as he called it in his mind.

Shit! Okay, back to food. Cornbread stuffing. It was so southern—the senator would like that. She never had. Give her regular stuffing with herbs any day of the week. She was breathing hard with effort.

Jeff's feelings about the senator throbbed through her attempt to entertain only banal thoughts. He hated the senator at first sight, and that hadn't abated. Jeff was calculating, wondering just how the senator could look so calm with all the voices in his head. As Jeff thought that, she saw the senator smile—a secret, knowing, almost vengeful smile.

"That's what we're going to find out, Mr. McQueen. Banks here is going to figure out how we survive it, and then we can replicate that. Right, Banks?"

Her father nodded, eyes narrowed. His aura shared Jeff's red flashes. They both disliked the senator.

The pressure of suppressing her own thoughts while trying to pick out Jeff's and the senator's in the mishmash of sound in her head made her want to scream. She found herself standing. She looked around the table at the three men staring at her. "I'm . . . I'm sorry, Senator, Dad. I'm exhausted. If we're going to stay here tonight, I'd like to retire."

The senator stood, followed by her father. Only Jeff remained seated. Rebellion oozed from every pore. *I'm not letting these guys have any kind of control over me.*

203

"Of course, Holly," her father said. "Yours is the second on the right, just outside that door." He pointed to the way the senator had come in. Two caterers came in to take their plates. "Senator, will you stay the night? We have one more suite."

"Not a chance, Banks. I'm at the Four Seasons in Santa Monica."

Holland made her way out of the room, trying not to feel relieved. She hoped to God Jeff would take her lead in spite of his feelings. She needed some respite here.

He must have felt her plea. "I'm with her," Jeff said tersely, and nodded briefly to the others before he followed her.

"I hope you had the catering staff checked, Banks," the senator was saying as they left.

As the door swung shut behind them, Jeff strode up and took Holland's arm above the elbow. "Jesus, Holland. What have we gotten into?"

"I need some space to think." She turned toward the door to the suite, but an ugly thought intruded. "There won't be any privacy. Not when Dad's got two-way glass and security cameras everywhere, and that damned senator can hear what we're thinking. How can we decide what to do with everyone watching us?"

Jeff shook his head. "Doesn't that reptile have to go vote on something? Maybe with distance we can avoid him."

They both heard the chuckle inside their heads. *Not a chance. Nightie-night.*

Holland suppressed a moan and dashed down the hall. She leaned her head against the second door and just tried to breathe. She had never felt so claustrophobic.

Jeff turned her toward him, both hands on her upper arms. She could feel the tug toward him almost physically, though it wasn't a tug of bodies and hormones only, but something larger. The silence fell. The senator faded. There was only Jeff.

I won't be locked away from you tonight, Holland. Cameras and windows be damned.

He was right. There was no way she could do a whole night on her own. Of course, if he were in the room with her she would be tempted to repeat something perhaps even more dangerous to her well-being. This was going to be a test of willpower like nothing she had known. She said nothing, tried to think nothing. She just pulled him inside the door to Subject Suite number 2. She felt embattled on every side. Worse, she'd just let up the portcullis and allowed one of the siege engines inside her battlements.

Chapter Sixteen

Inside the suite, neither Holland nor Jeff moved to turn on the light. She could hear his fear growing. *If they get the army out here, and the Secret Service . . .*

They're only concerned for our safety, she reassured him. He must know she wasn't sure herself. Damn, but this ability to read minds was going to be inconvenient!

I don't like having no choice. You really think Senator Snake is on the up and up? Come on, Holland, he's got your father in thrall with money or power, and he's got his own agenda.

She wasn't sure. She didn't say anything. But Jeff gathered her into his arms as though to comfort her. She had meant to stay away from him until the voices screaming in her head made her touch him, and then she had intended only to hold his hand. But there she was, enveloped in his strength, her cheek pressed against plaid flannel, smelling the clean fabric and the earthier scent of man beneath it—a man she liked, a man she understood. Her fear slowly subsided into the silence. The voices faded once more into the comfort of his presence. His fear whooshed slowly away as well. For a moment, with the fear and confusion gone, Holland felt strong—maybe stronger than she had ever been, and it felt good.

Physically, she wanted Jeff. The thrum between her legs wouldn't be denied. Some bit of her also wanted that moment of fusion again, in spite of all the more rational parts that feared loss of self and the possibility she would incur all the psychological damage she had ever read about in any book. She had been overwhelmed by contact with all of who he was. It had been frightening. Some parts of her said it was dangerous, but some part said it was also right somehow. She had to admit she had never felt such perfect comprehension of anyone before that moment, let alone a man. Strange for a psychiatrist to say that . . . *Not* that she necessarily liked what she understood. My God, the ego, the tendency to violence, the constant concern with sex . . . But then there was the vulnerability, the tenderness, the anxiety. Who knew what to think?

She was concentrating so on her own feelings that she hardly realized her concern and her temptation were echoed in Jeff until she felt his hand move through her hair. He was calmer now. She didn't need to hear the echo of his desire. She could feel it swelling against her belly.

He pressed her head to his chest. "Okay. All right. We've got to get some control here." He murmured it into her hair. "We can't just sit here waiting for the axe. We can't give in to what we want, either." It was a mantra. "We need to hear what they're saying."

"He can hear us, too."

"So what?" She felt rebellion rise in him and knew it was his protection from fear. He held her out from his chest. "Turnabout is fair play." He took two breaths. "We've got two choices. Touching, I think we can probably hear your father if we try. He's not that far away. Or if we let the voices in, I bet we can hear Mr. Big Ass Senator. He's the one with the accent whose been lusting for that secret-service chick. I'd lay money on it."

She nodded. "I vote for the senator." She felt creepy listening to her father, and more than a little anxious about what she might hear.

Jeff nodded and took his arms from around her waist. She took a single step back, prepared for the flood of voices. Jeff's glance ricocheted around the darkened room as he listened. "Got it," he whispered.

She shook her head. She couldn't pick out one voice among the others.

"It's louder, just a little," Jeff encouraged. "I'll concentrate on it."

That helped. A single voice jumped to the foreground of her mind.

"If you play this game, there's a big grant and a lot of prestige at the end." Scorn, derision. *"If you don't, the train stops here, buddy."* The senator listened, genuinely anxious. *"I've got to figure out what's going on. He's powerful, up a factor of ten from others. At least I think it's him. Hell, I don't know . . ."* Listening again to something her father was saying. Grudging acknowledgment, impatience. *"Okay, so you're on the trail. Show me the data."*

Holland and Jeff both felt Lendreaux shift his focus to their thoughts. A flash of fear consumed him as he realized they were listening to him. He had never really had that experience before, Holland thought in surprise. He just heard the general soup of noise and voices. Or maybe he was so used to being the predator, it felt odd to have the prey turn when it was cornered. There was a hungry feel about the senator. She and Jeff recognized it at the same time. Holland shuddered.

"Brad, where the fuck are the reinforcements?" they heard him say. Must be on his cell phone. His dismay that

it would be at least an hour came through loud and clear.

Holland felt Jeff's blaze of resolution. *We're not waiting,* he thought.

Holland felt the senator recoil at Jeff's vehemence. Jeff lunged for the door.

We'll never get out of here, Holland thought. What was Jeff doing? There were security guards everywhere, no doubt with orders to keep them inside the lab.

Don't bet on it, baby. Jeff's determination and his subtle confidence suffused her.

Hurried steps sounded in the corridor. Someone was coming to lock them in. Jeff grabbed the doorknob. It still turned. The steps were louder. Fear collided in Holland's mind, hers and the senator's. But Jeff wasn't afraid anymore. The door swung out as he put his weight behind it. It caught whoever was in the corridor full on. Jeff grabbed Holland's hand and pulled her into the hallway as the silence fell.

It was her father who sprawled in the hall. The senator hurried up. Jeff used his elbow like a battering ram and the senator collapsed against the wall. His head hit with a thunk. Jeff thought, *Maybe we should just get rid of him. Solve a lot of problems.*

No way! Holland was revolted. How could he? She pulled Jeff over her father. She wanted to stop and see if he was okay, but there was no telling what Jeff might do.

"Okay, okay," Jeff yelled at her. "We're out of here." She felt his flicker of shame. Her anger flashed, but there was no time to indulge it. "Which way?" he called.

Holland panicked, disoriented, before the sense of where they were settled around her. She nodded to the right. "Through the lab." Jeff pulled her into a trot. "The lobby is just beyond."

Jeff slowed, shaking his head. "No lobby. Loading dock."

She nodded. Maybe there would be fewer of her father's rent-a-cops back there. "Uh, let's see." She looked around.

"Still through the lab. Use the back door." Jeff powered into a run, Holland in tow. "Up through the lab modules to the back. There's a big storage area." She panted. "I think the loading dock is back there." Then there was no more breath for words.

Words weren't necessary. She thought her directions, and Jeff got them just fine. They pushed through swinging doors and up a short flight of stairs to the next lab module that marched up the Malibu hills. Finally they stumbled into a darkened room lined with rows of floor-to-ceiling metal shelving stuffed with boxes. Careening around a corner, they almost tripped over several crates, then skittered onward into the blackness. A door to the outside was here somewhere. Jeff felt along the wall, until the edge of a door met his fingers. The latch gave a click as he leaned into the exit bar. Garish light from the flood lamps on the loading dock sliced in through opening door. They were out!

"Hey!"

The bulky middle-aged man in uniform tossed his cigarette onto the concrete platform and reached for his nightstick. He never got a chance to take it from his belt. Jeff let go of Holland's hand. She felt his anticipation of violence in a soaring rush of adrenaline. He had no question about the outcome in his mind. In one smooth move he turned and stepped into the guard. He planted his boots and balled his fist. The blow was low, from the hip, into the guy's paunch. It was over right then, for all intents and purposes. The guard doubled over and met Jeff's left fist with his chin. Jeff motioned her forward even as the guard sat heavily and lolled against the wall.

They looked around. The light that bathed the dock seemed to scream their presence. Jeff pointed. A beige Honda Accord at least ten years old was parked at the far end of the building. Jeff grabbed for her hand. They started down the concrete ramp at a run.

Behind them, a shout of protest echoed. Jeff just ran harder. *Not locked, not locked*, she heard him think. Holland looked back, even as she stumbled on behind. Another guard hurried after them, his two-way radio held to his mouth. Oh, that was bad.

Jeff reached for the door handle even as Holland crashed into him from behind. The *snick* of the opening door sent relief flooding through Jeff. "Get in!" he yelled to her and let go of her hand, motioning her around to the passenger's side. She scurried over the asphalt, her eyes only for the guard, who was almost upon them. Still, Jeff wasn't afraid. Confidence flowed through him, born of experience. He'd fought before. He turned to face the guard. Three punches and it was over, even though this one was younger and in better shape. The guy even managed to land a punch himself. Jeff wasn't bothered, though his head jerked back. It just fueled his rush.

Holland slid into the car. They wouldn't have much time now. The empty key slot on the driving column sent dread snaking through her. No keys!

Don't you worry, darlin', Jeff reassured her as he knelt and swiveled to lie on his back on the seat. His thoughts had acquired a southern accent almost as pronounced as the senator's. He fumbled under the steering column.

"Jeff," she warned. A patrol vehicle rounded the far corner of the building, moving slowly, its searchlight swiveling. Jeff didn't answer. His focus was absolute.

It didn't take long for the car to spot them and begin accelerating. With a roar, the engine of the Honda leapt to life. "Woo-hoo!" Jeff shouted, and bounced upright behind the steering wheel. His right hand was throwing the car into reverse even as he punched the gas pedal. The car fish-tailed, door swinging wide. "Seatbelts, everybody."

Holland's eyes grew wide as she realized they were now facing the navy blue security cruiser head on. The Honda lurched into second gear as Jeff accelerated toward the other vehicle. Holland gasped and fumbled with her shoulder harness. *Crazy!*

"You bet, baby." The other car seemed to lunge at them, they converged so fast.

"Jeff!" Holland shrieked, bracing herself against the dashboard. She could see the eyes of the two guards inside the opposite vehicle go wide. Just as she thought there was no way out of a head-on collision, the other car swerved. Its bumper clipped the Honda's open door, which shut with a bang. They were past.

Jeff giggled as he hunched over the wheel. "Yeah, baby," he gasped. "Guess they never played much chicken." The Honda squealed around the corner of the building and practically went airborne as the driveway curved sharply downhill. Holland felt her stomach lift.

"Jeff McQueen," she shouted. "You are going to kill us!" She felt shaken and angry.

Jeff was still giggling. "Kill us or set us free." She could hardly hear him over the roar of the engine as it accelerated down the long incline to Pacific Coast Highway.

At the bottom of the hill, the guard station glittered white in the floodlights. A security guard stepped out of the box. He, too, was on the phone. A new wisp of fear curled in Holland's stomach, among all the other fears. Then she realized that Jeff had no intention of stopping at the guard gate. The dread of being stopped morphed into fear of imminent bodily harm. She leaned back into the seat, bracing for the shock, hoping the broken gate wouldn't smash the windshield.

The crack of breaking wood was closely followed by the whoosh of the red-and-white striped plank as it sailed over the car. They were away! The Honda's tires shrieked as they careened onto PCH. Burning rubber was the sweetest scent Holland had ever smelled.

"Yes!" she screeched. "Yes!"

Jeff was laughing, his head rolling back on his shoulders even as they streaked through the night. And then Holland was laughing too, until tears rose to her eyes. She was right. She loved his laugh. It was more of a cascade of giggles, not at all what she'd imagined from the rumble of his voice. There was not a shred of cynicism in that giggle.

When finally she could breathe, she choked, "So, that's what it feels like to jack cars."

"Absolutely," he rumbled, glancing over at her, his eyes still bubbling with adrenaline. "Ought to do it more often. I damned near lost my touch."

"You looked pretty good to me."

"Yeah, but what do you know about jacking cars?" he grinned. "There was a time I would have had that baby sputtering in less than ten seconds."

She shook her head, her own laughter subsiding only slowly. "That was less than ten seconds. It only *seemed* like a year and a half."

"Yeah . . ." He breathed out the last of his laughter, and looked around. PCH was pretty much it, this far up. Few roads branched off. The lights of Malibu proper glittered ahead. The black sea swelled and crashed somewhere to their right. The waves were hidden below the cliffs just here. Jeff swerved around another car. His face turned serious. He glanced up at a green highway sign above their heads. "Santa Monica, fourteen miles," it said. "I don't think we want to be here," he muttered. "Too exposed." They swerved between two slower cars and squealed onto a tiny road going inland.

"Where is this?" Holland asked. The road was not in great condition. They jolted among the potholes. This seemed like a bad idea.

"You may be right," Jeff answered the unspoken doubt. "I think this connects to Big Rock Canyon Road up here, or maybe Kanan Dune."

"Oh, *that* sounds like a sure thing," she muttered.

They lurched along in silence through the hills. Lights only occasionally winked from mammoth mansions, or modest farmhouses that predated the Malibu land rush. They couldn't go fast here. Holland wondered how long it would be before someone came after them.

"They can't just call the police. Maybe they can get the army. It doesn't ask questions."

"They *can* get the police. All they do is make up some story about you assaulting someone. You have a history."

"They don't even have to make it up. I did assault someone."

The fact that they were on the run and had no destination sank in for Holland. "The senator and Dad just want to know about us. Don't we want that, too?" Suddenly, she was sure it had been a mistake to panic. Where were they escaping? To a world where snipers shot people like them? A world where they were alone? "We need them."

"Maybe. But I didn't much like the senator. Neither did you. He didn't feel right."

"Then let Dad protect us from him."

Jeff just looked at her. He didn't need to say that her father hadn't seemed heroic back there, or that her father hadn't felt right either. "There's no way back, Holland. Your father said it." Jeff's voice was a rumble in a darkness broken only by the dashboard lights. Scenery careened by them, lit by their headlights then plunged into black and gray behind them.

"Dad could get us access to the scientific community. Believe me, there are guys out there who are more than a match for the senator."

"Holland," Jeff snapped, exasperated. "What do you think is going to happen when Joe from the first truck stop east of Elko, Nevada, figures out that some people have a mutation that lets them read minds? You and your father think we'll have some place of special treatment and recognition, admiration. Well, I can tell you that the American public's first impulse is to kill anything they don't understand. And that's going to include some pretty powerful members of your 'scientific community.' You think you've seen hate crimes? That ain't nothin'. Those people were just black or Muslim or Jewish or gay."

And we're something worse, more dangerous. She finished his thought. Despair crept into her mind.

The headlights hit a green street sign at the top of a hill. Kanan Dune Road. "Okay," Jeff breathed. He swung left onto the smooth asphalt and eased off the gas pedal. "Let's blend in."

They were through the sheltering slopes of the Santa Monica Mountains and onto the 101 Freeway south when they heard the senator's thoughts kick back in. He must have been knocked out. Holland couldn't hear him all the time, just sputters of him, but as she recognized the accent and the anger, she turned to Jeff.

Jeff's mouth set grimly. He heard him fine.

The senator was ordering the army to find the car.

How will we ever escape if he can hear us?

Jeff gave a little shrug, not looking at her. "We'll be faster than he is." She knew he was not sure of their escape at all.

He swerved into the right lane and got off the freeway at White Oak. Scooting into an alley just behind all the shops and restaurants lining Ventura Boulevard, he cruised to a stop and parked the car behind a tiny Thai restaurant. There were still some cars in the lots along here, late diners or the restaurant help.

"Stay here," he ordered curtly. She could tell, though he didn't want her to know, that he was trying to keep her out of it, should he get caught. She didn't argue. Jacking cars was his specialty, not hers. Best to let him focus on it.

He found a battered old Jeep Wagoneer unlocked about half a block down. He opened the door, disappeared, then popped back up immediately as the engine ground to life. He motioned to her with a grin and she hurried over the slick asphalt and slid in beside him. The Jeep smelled of cigarettes and stale beer. "Lovely," she said.

"Hey, people never bother to lock the old ones," he said in defense. "This is an eighty-eight—a classic." Right. Wagoneers weren't classics. They pulled out of the alleyway and joined the crush, even at eleven P.M. lurching along the Boulevard. She laid her palm across his thigh. It had been over an hour since she'd had relief from the noise.

Now that she could think better, their situation seemed even more tangled. They were on the run to nowhere. With the army after them, or the secret service, and the senator able to hear their thoughts, there couldn't be much doubt to the outcome of all of this effort. Holland sighed.

Jeff nodded in agreement, but he was not despondent. He was calculating. "Your father said something I've been thinking about."

She raised her brows. *One thing?*

He brushed her off. *Yeah, okay. More than one thing.* "But there was one good suggestion in there. He asked why we didn't go to others like us to tell us how to control this thing better."

She nodded. That was interesting. "Maybe he was hoping we could tell him where others were."

"Maybe. But he was right. That was my original plan when I went looking for you. I think it still stands. The question is, who and where."

"Well, it's probably somebody sane. That lets out the shriekers."

"I haven't heard that woman who was shrieking loudest lately anyway," he said.

That gave them pause. She must have done herself in, or been done in by somebody. A sniper? If she'd just been incarcerated, they could probably still have heard her somewhere, even muffled by drugs. Holland shuddered. Was that the way they'd end? Just drop off the mind-map? She gathered herself. Best she follow Jeff's example. She couldn't afford despair.

Jeff managed a wry smile. "Who then? You're the specialist in sanity."

She smiled grimly. "Actually not. They never teach us much about sanity, happiness, or any of that sort of thing.

We specialize in abnormality. Humanity's got plenty." Still, she took her hand away and let the voices wash over her. "All right." She let some of Jeff's resolve sluice through her. "They're going to be the ones who think about mundane things. No suicidal thoughts, no utter despair. If they've learned to control it, they're going to sound more . . . comfortable." She began sorting through the voices.

Jeff's eyes were glued to the road. "They might be the ones that are clearer."

"You're probably a better judge of that."

"If you hear them at all, they must be strong." Excitement danced behind his words.

She sorted memories, to find the ones she heard over and over again that sounded unique. There were so many! Finally she went with her gut. "There seem to be a lot of strong southern accents, using . . . I don't know, maybe black dialect kind of words? I'm not really sure. Street language anyway." She touched his thigh again.

"Yeah. I thought you might pick those. One or more, I don't know. And they come from . . . from someplace I know."

He had thought about New Orleans. He pronounced it N'*awlins*. "How do you know that?" She hadn't picked that up at all.

"I heard them talking about Acme Oyster House, and sazeracs from Floria."

"I did too! Does that mean they're in—"

"No, don't think about where. Let's call it, uh, Chicago in our minds, okay?"

She nodded, wondering if that was possible or if the senator had already heard. She felt Jeff stretching out to search for the senator's thoughts.

I want every resource of the army at my disposal. We're going to find them, General, and we're going to find them tonight.

Holland felt her eyes go big.

216

*They're fading in and out. Sometimes I hear them some-
times they just shut down . . . No, I'm getting nothing now.*

That might be good. Now if only they could find a way
to control that.

"That means he doesn't know where we are." Jeff whispered, as though that would keep the senator from hearing
them. He took a breath and let it out, and consciously
relaxed his white-knuckled grip on the steering wheel. "But
to continue, I do know where they are, darlin'. I grew up
there. Well, not really. The years I spent there were as they
say, 'formative.' Anybody who knows anything in . . . Chicago . . . knows Floria makes the best sazeracs in town
down at the Two Sisters." He didn't have to look to see her
confusion. "Oh, sazeracs—the first cocktail. Pharmacist
made them up as a 'restorative.' Rye whiskey, bitters from
up country called Peycheaux, and anise flavor. Used to be
made with absinthe, so I guess if they didn't cure you, at
least you didn't care you weren't cured." He chuckled.
"We're going to Chicago, darlin'."

She nodded. It was as good a destination as any other,
though she didn't have much hope they could elude cap-
ture, or snipers for that matter. The world had become a
dangerous place.

"Now, as to the how. We're gonna keep jacking cars. If
we're careful we can stay ahead of the senator and friends.
Good thing I have a skill, isn't it?"

Holland was breathless. She was about to break more
rules than she had ever broken in her life. As a matter of
fact, she had already broken more rules than she'd ever
broken in her life.

"Can't we just fly?"

"Not unless you've got some good quality fake IDs
handy. They're going to have the airport security guys
watching for us. They might even let us get on the plane.
But there'd be a welcoming party we wouldn't like when
we got off."

"I am *not* going to turn into Bonnie and Clyde."

"Daddy's little girl find stealing a little tough?"

Damn, but it was inconvenient that she couldn't hide from him! "I am not Daddy's little girl, any more than you're Daddy's little boy." Let him chew on *that* a while.

Yeah, she's got a point, he thought. "Now, we have to talk about money. That's where you come in, Ms. Leader of a Big Foundation who probably has check-writing authority and withdrawal privileges. We may get down to buying fake ID's, even leaving the country. We are going to need some serious cash money."

"Right. No credit cards, no debits, that goes without saying."

"Cash."

"Uh, we could go to my house. We need clothes anyway."

"Nix." Jeff shook his head. "They're posting watchers at our houses even as we speak. I would be." He peered out the windshield, and swerved into the parking lot of a bank. "Come to think of it, they've probably staked out the hospital, and they're now putting a hold on those foundation accounts as well as our personal accounts." He pulled up to the drive-through automatic teller and fumbled through his hip pocket for his billfold. "Okay, we both get our daily max. A couple thousand is better than nothing. But it won't get us to . . . Chicago."

"How do we get more, without leaving a trail?"

He grinned as he slipped his card into the machine. "Robbing banks is too high-profile?"

She felt her heart skip a beat. Robbing banks?

"Darlin', quit being quite so serious," he chided as he fanned his money and then held out a hand for her card. "Humor is a great relaxer, isn't that some kind of psychiatric truth?"

"You are *so* ill." But her mind was working. Where could they get money in the middle of the night? If they used credit cards or tried to cash a check, they'd leave a trail a mile wide.

The answer came in a flash and she let it go. "Get on the 405," she said.

Jeff just looked at her, and patted the hand on his thigh. His grin faded. He nodded.

Chapter Seventeen

The stock of his rifle was slick with sweat. Wasn't San Diego supposed to have perfect weather? Well, it was hot here. Too damned hot. He crouched, sweltering, on the carpet in the back of the van, its window open only a crack to admit the gun barrel. A bead of sweat rolled out of his hair and down his temple. Yet, it wasn't the heat he was upset about, and it wasn't the quality of the shot. He couldn't miss today. This was a big target. Overweight Mamacita with two kids in tow—one maybe two, one maybe four. They were crying already, and Mamacita looked disheveled, crazy even. She was wearing a shapeless purple sweater even in this heat. It hung off her shoulders, revealing her massive arms like hams busting out of her sleeveless dress. Her hair was all snaky and greasy. Jesus, Mary, and Joseph! A wetback mother. He would have enjoyed putting another baby machine out of action, if it weren't for the kids. You couldn't down a mother in front of her kids, good for humanity or not. Could you?

Damn, fuck, piss. He couldn't screw this one up after his failure with that guy at the loony bin. There was the hundred K, too. He blew air out through his lips. Maybe he should wait until her kids weren't with her. But women like that, all they had was their kids. She probably took them every-where.

Ah, what the hell was he thinking? Kids that young wouldn't even know what had happened. Mama would fall down and look like she was sleeping, except for the black hole in her forehead. She'd fall back with the impact, so they'd never see the mess at the back of her head. Yeah. Mamacita was just going to go to sleep and never wake up.

The little parade of Mama and kids came out from behind an SUV in the parking lot of the Walmart below him. Slowly, he squeezed the trigger. For the good of humanity and for the cash.

The old Jeep chugged up the silent street in Pacific Palisades.

Here, Holland thought, trying not to think about anything else. Jeff was not surprised by their destination. When 10 turned into Pacific Coast Highway going north, it had been apparent where they were headed. She could feel he wasn't sure about this.

Neither was she.

She got out of the car, breaking their silence, and motioned him out too. The double thunk of the doors slamming was loud in the quiet of the sleeping neighborhood. There were still lights on in the house, though it was after midnight. Holland knocked. Jeff craned to see down the side yard. He was expecting camouflaged special forces or something.

Holland's mother came to the door, peered through the etched glass panels, and opened them.

"Holly!" She glanced to Jeff, then jerked back to her daughter. "What are you doing here?"

"It's okay, Mom. He's okay."

"Uh, hi, Mrs. Banks." Jeff ducked his head, trying to look innocuous.

"Can we come in?" Holland was already feeling the stress of the noise.

Her mother hesitated only a moment, then stepped back and let the door swing wide. "Of course." She closed the door after them. "Can I get you anything?"

"Ever the perfect hostess, Mom. Jeff?"

Jack Daniels. A stiff belt.

"I think we could both use some water." Holland frowned at Jeff.

Her mother led them into a cozy little sitting room where she'd been watching *Nightline*.

"A flu epidemic is sweeping the nation," the set was saying, "gaining momentum over the last month. The Center for Disease Control has announced that the current flu shots are not effective against it. It is a particularly potent virus often resulting in testicular infection in male patients. Let's go to Atlanta, where our own Mariel Whitcomb is with Dr. Eldon Grimsby."

She waved at the set, which turned itself off, and went to fetch the water.

"I'm not sure this was a great idea," Jeff whispered.

Holland chewed her lip. "It's our best shot."

Her mother returned with several bottles of Perrier, and some ice in glasses that she set on a low table, and poured for them. There was also a triangle of brie and some imported water biscuits. She was dressed in a black stretch lounging outfit, with long sleeves. It set off both her blonde hair and the huge diamond ring that matched her stud earrings. *The picture of elegance, even when there's no one around to see*, Holland thought. She shook her head to clear it.

Jeff glanced at her as he took his glass, willing her to calm down.

"Now, what can I do for you?" her mother said as she sat down and crossed her legs. "I assume this isn't a social call at this hour."

Holland took a breath. How to begin? "How much do you know about Dad's project?"

"Just that he's found some extra genetic material. He's very excited."

That was good. "He's excited all right. He found two subjects who have that extra material and he wants to study them."

Her mother lit up. "Oh, good. He was worried. He couldn't seem to find subjects . . ."

She looked from one to the other of them. She was not a stupid woman. "Oh." She wasn't sure she wanted her daughter to be a research subject. More, she was probably not quite sure what that extra DNA was all about, and whether she should want her daughter to have it.

Holland leaned in to brush Jeff's shoulder and heard her mother thinking, wondering why her husband hadn't told her that her daughter had a mutation. That's what she called it in her mind: Mutation. And she was wondering whether she was responsible. Fear and guilt washed over the woman.

Holland jerked away from Jeff's arm. She didn't want to hear her mother's fears and doubts. She didn't want to hear why her mother stayed with her father, whether she really loved him—none of that. She wasn't strong enough to take it right now.

Instead, she nodded. "Yeah, Mom. It's us. And it's not a good thing."

"Why not?" Her mother lifted her chin. "You and your father, working together . . ."

Jeff took over when Holland couldn't bear to dash her mother's illusions. "Your husband is mixed up with that senator from Louisiana. I think the senator is calling the shots, Mrs. Banks, and neither Holland nor I feel like putting ourselves in his hands right now—not until we can figure out what this means to us."

"What *what* means to you? What is this mutation?" Her mother skipped over the part about what they needed to do to the part they least wanted to explain.

"I don't want to tell you, Mother. You'll think I'm crazy. We just need to get out of here without anyone being able to trace us, and we need your help for that."

Jeff looked at Holland. *You maybe skipped a few steps in there somewhere, like the part where you convince her.*

Her mother sat back in her chair stiffly. "Holly, if something has happened to you, you need to let your father help you. Senator Lendreaux helps Leland get funding, that's all."

Tell her. We're committed now.

Holland pressed her lips together for a moment. Finally she shrugged. "I guess I'll just say it. We can hear thoughts. We can hear each other, and we can hear others like us, and if we touch, we can even hear people who aren't like us."

Her mother's brows came together. "You mean you can read minds?" Her voice held all the skepticism Holland knew it would.

Holland nodded. "Yes, I'm afraid so."

She glanced to Jeff. *It sounds like a parlor trick even to me.*

"Holland's thinking that it sounds like a parlor trick even to her, Mrs. Banks." Jeff reached out for Holland's hand, and turned back to her mother. "And you . . . you're wondering if Holland is imagining being able to read minds, and remembering how stressed she'd been lately, and how you've been lately, and how you've been trying to get her to take a trip to Scandinavia. And now you're thinking that of course I would guess that you were thinking about how stressed she is. So think of something else, Mrs. Banks. Something I don't know about."

The woman's eyes went wide. Jeff gazed at her, steadily, with those green eyes that could look so calm and sure and sane. He nodded. "You're thinking of an image from your past—an exciting time for you, full of possibility. A little blonde girl is wearing a red bathing suit, laughing and playing in the sprinklers in a yard. The yard is grass, and there's one of those blue plastic pools in the background with . . . the Flintstones, I think, on those tube parts that you blow up. And you're thinking about your neighbor. I think his name was Fred." Jeff paused. Holland could feel his shock, but she wasn't sure why. She hadn't been concentrating on her mother, only on Jeff.

What?

Jeff continued with only a catch in his voice. "And now you're frightened because you know it's real, what's happened to us." He jerked his hand away from Holland's.

"We're frightened, too," Holland said. Her mother opened her arms, eyes welling. Holland slid out of her chair to kneel and hug her mom. They just rocked like that.

"We think people will be afraid of us, Mrs. Banks—want to lock us up, control us, kill us, even. Hard times ahead. We don't have much time. The senator has the world looking for us."

Holland broke the hug. "Lendreaux is one of us, Mom. That's what's so scary. He can hear us, if he listens. Dad can't protect us."

Or won't.

Holland didn't acknowledge Jeff's revision.

"What can I do?" her mother asked, sniffing.

"It's pretty mundane. We're going to find some people like us. Maybe they know how we can deal with what's happened. We need money, and we can't use our credit cards."

Her mother nodded once and rose with a jerk. She walked to where her purse lay on a side table. "Your father will be looking for you. He'll want to help."

They watched her pull out a stack of bills and three credit cards. "And you can't tell him we were here, Mother. Not even if he asks you directly."

Her mother looked a little scared. Natural. And a little doubtful. Not as good.

Jeff stood. "Call the card companies and say you'll be using the cards a lot on a trip you're taking, so they won't call for verification and get your husband. And Mrs. Banks, can I see your driver's license?"

She looked puzzled, but she slipped it out of her wallet and handed it over. Jeff let out a relieved sigh when he saw it. "Couldn't be better," he muttered. "Looks enough like you, Holland, and *H* is her middle initial."

That would be because her middle name is Holland.

Jeff turned to her mother. "Can we take this? Holland can use it for ID."

Holland would not have thought of that.

Her mother nodded, more frightened now that Jeff was talking about the sordid details of their flight so calmly. She didn't know about jacking the cars, but she'd realized that using another person's identity and credit cards was technically fraud. More than technically.

"And if you meet the senator, Mother—we don't know whether he can hear anybody else besides the ones like us, but just in case, try not to think about the fact that we were here."

"How do I do that?" There was an edge of hysteria in the woman's voice.

"Think about something else." Jeff made his voice matter-of-fact. "Something that will distract him, like how you're surprised that in person he really doesn't seem like presidential material, or maybe wonder if he had to have someone else coach him in how to dress, anything that will upset him."

Holland smiled at Jeff as she put the credit cards and the driver's license in her purse. "You really are devious. Is it the investigative reporter thing, or the male thing, or . . . what?"

"Probably from my preacher father, lying to the faithful." His eyes crinkled at the edges, even though his mouth was serious. There was definitely some indigo in his aura.

"That's *not* what you're thinking." Holland was not about to say aloud what he had been thinking. She turned to see her mother glance from one to another with recognition in her eyes.

225

Her mother nodded with a little more certainty. "You'd better get going, you two. I can't imagine not knowing how you are, but I know you can't call me." She reached out two hands and grasped one each of theirs. Holland could feel Jeff's surprise. He wasn't used to motherly affection. "I can't imagine what this must mean for you, for all of us . . ."

Holland gathered her mother into one last hug.

Her mother still clasped Jeff's hand. "I'm not sure any of us knows, Mrs. Banks."

Jeff reached for Holland. Silence fell. With one last backward look, they slipped into the night. As they walked out to the car, Jeff said, "She'll tell him if she gets cornered, won't she?"

"Probably."

"Then we'd better max out the cash advances on these cards fast."

Jeff trotted around to the driver's side of the Jeep and flung open the door with a creak.

"Where are we going to find a place to give us that much cash at this time of night?"

Jeff's head ducked inside the car. "Las Vegas, of course."

Holland drew a breath and let it out. *Okay Just in case the senator can hear us, let's call it . . . what? Seattle?* She slid into the front seat. Could you lie to people who could hear your thoughts?

Leland Banks watched Senator Lendreaux pace back and forth in Banks's office at the laboratory, barking into his cell phone at some head of the Navy Seal unit stationed at Port Heuneme. His assistant, Brad, stood leaning against the wall next to the potted ficus, unobtrusively. Brad's initial efforts to engage all known forms of authority had not gone well.

Leland had slipped into the lab proper to call Doug. Doug made things happen. Because the senator, blowhard that he was, was right. They couldn't let Holly and her reporter just leave.

The whole might of the armed forces, as well as local police, were now looking for Holly and that crazy reporter. Leland felt old. Worse, he felt passed over. Holly and Jeff McQueen were standing on the edge of a new world no one understood, while he was only an observer, a recorder. It was what he had always been.

At least Holly's genome strings were finally active. He'd been waiting for that, ever since he discovered the phenomenon. Holly. She was such a source of pain, of anger, even after all this time. He blamed Carol. She had destroyed their relationship, though he and his wife had kept that from the world, even from Holly.

Holly would be the perfect subject, incredibly bright. She was a natural, just like this Jeff, like the senator. They'd had the strings forever, was born with them. That's what all these early manifestations were—naturals; the ones who would have started the slow process of transforming the human race across twenty generations or a hundred, passing the anomaly from generation to generation in ever-increasing spirals of frequency. Or they might have all flamed out in suicide and the mutation would have ended with them.

But it wouldn't end like that now. His virus would see to that. He'd hung that genome string on the best carrier viral vector his research had turned up. And he'd made sure the virus was infective. He'd collected the strings carefully, combined them with the virus until the lab had hundreds of little red petri dishes filled with the future of the human race.

The first escape had been accidental. The senator had thought he could control that one. All the lab assistants between twenty-five and forty were dead. They had discovered right away that it only thrived in hosts between about twenty-five and forty-five. Others could carry it—the damn thing was pretty hardy and could live outside its artificial dish environment for as much as ten hours. It was airborne, which meant it could spread quickly. Still, by using the techniques identified by the Center for Disease Control for stopping epidemics, and with the help of the senator to identify the naturals, they could have wiped it out.

But Leland didn't want it wiped out. Let nature take its new course, helped along by the father of the future, Leland Banks. He'd started the second wave of infections himself. Soon now his very own epidemic would end in testicular infection in males—much like mumps, only milder. But instead of leaving the men sterile like mumps, this virus would infect the germic chromosomes and all those little X's would pass his changes to the next generation. A triumph. He closed his eyes to savor it. Leland Banks would have changed the world forever. He could keep the senator thinking that he was in control. He could keep Doug thinking that he was trying to find the "cure."

But he wasn't. He was spreading this as fast as it could go. He would barricade a colony of thrivers somewhere safe who would point the way to surviving the mutation. The world would be dependent upon his research. And he would find out how he could give it to himself. Then . . . *then* the new world would belong to him wholly. He would not just be a spectator. He'd be part of the truth, not a witness to it.

Leland had no illusions about the senator's motives for helping him. The man was sure that if he were the only one left with the gift the genome sequence gave, he would be invincible. Not exactly a reliable ally. But he was more than willing to identify his fellows.

The senator didn't matter. He couldn't stop the spread. Not anymore. When he began to realize that fact, he would become dangerous. And Doug? Doug wasn't enough of a visionary to affect the outcome. He'd be overwhelmed by what would be happening in the outside world and turn to Leland as the last defense against the chaos ahead.

Leland sucked on his cigar and watched it draw. The world was changing. It would be changes of his making. His thoughts returned again to Holly. Why had she run?

It was the reporter's fault. But Holly had gone along with it. He had believed she was stubborn enough to go her own way, not just trail along after this guy when he made a break for it. There was only one explanation for her lapse. He'd seen the looks between them. His little girl was confused by sex with this guy. She *was* his little girl, in spite of everything. A surge of pain coursed through him, familiar after so much time. He pressed it down. That low-life bastard was using sex to drag Holly into something way over her head.

The senator snapped his cell phone shut and handed it to Brad. "Let's hope they don't do any more than corner them." His gaze locked on Leland's face. "You know your little girl better than anyone. Where are they likely to be going?"

"Can't you tell?"

The senator looked put out. "They're flashing in and out. I can hear them sometimes, in snatches, and then it just goes dead. They don't fade into the other voices. They just blink out."

Leland eyed him narrowly. "Have I got a defective on my hands, Senator?"

Lendreaux's eyes went small and nasty. "Careful, Banks."

Such a child. "All right. We don't know everything there is to know about the phenomenon. Maybe something is causing interference. So, where would they go? I'd say the reporter was calling the shots. You've covered his apartment?"

"And her house. I've got MPRI getting over to the hospital."

"MPRI?" Leland had never heard of that unit.

"Government contractors. Vendors, shall we say?" When he saw Leland still looking puzzled, he added, "You might

229

call them mercenaries. They do all kinds of jobs for the military. Especially jobs our own forces might not like."

"Jesus, Lendreaux, the army has mercs after my daughter?"

"I trust them more than I trust the police. They're not excitable. I just hope a sniper doesn't get her."

"What? You were supposed to call the sniper off when McQueen was admitted. You bungled that. If you're playing a game, Lendreaux . . ." Leland let his voice go quiet.

"These guys are hard to just call off."

"You have to identify her to put her in danger, Lendreaux. If you fingered her . . ."

"You may be the one who has endangered her, Banks," the senator snapped. "It was you who told them to go to some of their kind to find out more about themselves." He narrowed his eyes. Leland noticed that there were little pouches around them, from dissolution rather than age. "They go find some folks who've been targeted and they might just get themselves in the way."

Leland felt himself go cold; his blood pooled in his stomach. For once he was speechless.

"Anyway," the senator continued briskly, "your little girl is safest under study right here in the lab. We agree on that."

They did agree on that. He had to get Holly back here, where he could figure out how to survive the mutation, and how to catch it if you were too old.

"Then let's find her." Leland didn't want the senator to know it was Doug who had made his efforts to mobilize the army bear fruit. Let him think he was in control. He turned his mind to the problem of where Holly might be going. "She may not have a coherent plan about how to find those like her. But she's going to need money. I'd try to catch any credit card use."

The senator looked disgusted. "Got it covered, and we froze her on-line accounts, and his, if he's got anything in it. Reporters rarely do. We'll cancel all credit cards and put a notice to call the police on them. We'll cover his parents, see if he's got other family. We'll get down to his paper and find out if there are any other Oliver Stone types he can count on if he tells them there's a conspiracy against him. We'll know what size BVDs he wears by tomorrow morning at ten. She got any siblings, girlfriends?"

Leland shook his head. "Doesn't make friends. Only child. But you'd better pay a visit to the board members on her Foundation. They've got money and they trust her."

The senator nodded to Brad, who, Leland noticed, had taken out a notebook. Leland examined the senator. Lines of tension were drawn around his mouth, his eyes. "Brad, where are my running clothes? I need to get out for a run."

Brad nodded and disappeared.

"At this time of night?" Leland asked. "You're going for a run now?"

"Yeah. I'm going for a run now," Lendreaux sneered. "I need a little quiet. Now why don't you leave me alone, so I can concentrate on finding our runaways."

The senator was essentially ordering him to vacate his own office. The prick. He really thought he was in charge. Leland felt his throat tighten. He put down the anger that threatened to boil up from his gut. There was time enough to show the senator who was boss, so he got up stiffly and walked out without a word.

He hoped to God that the mercenaries found Holland before the senator's snipers did.

Chapter Eighteen

The highway east of Barstow stretched out into the night as though it might snap. The desert on each side flattened into a great dry plain, featureless, timeless. Holland couldn't really tell they were making progress, in spite of the flickering needle on the speedometer. Jeff was keeping it at sixty-five exactly, so they wouldn't attract attention. The only distraction from the sameness was the occasional car that whizzed past at eighty or ninety. Maybe going sixty-five was what would make them stand out. Her head had gotten more crowded with voices; they droned away and made her blink.

She resolved she'd talk out loud, rather than just think things Jeff could hear. That had gotten a little too weird. The confusion of their emotions when they felt the same thing was weirdest of all. She looked over at his profile in the dark. He was tired. So was she. Why not? They'd just had a day when everything about their lives changed forever. Maybe she should talk to keep him awake. Maybe she just needed to talk.

"So, where'd you learn to fight?" she asked, because she knew what he was more entirely than she had ever known anything or anyone, including herself, but not necessarily all the facts that led to what he was. "That standard-issue training for investigative reporters?"

He sucked at his lips for a minute. She'd seen him do that before. He glanced at her, saw her distress, and draped his arm across the seat to touch her shoulder. The silence made her suck in a breath and hold it. "Put myself through Stanford boxing smokers."

She exhaled. "So, uh, you had an advantage because their lungs were shot?"

"It's a kind of club. People come to watch two guys go at it. Not too many rules."

"Novel work-study program. Sounds like those awful cage fights they do at the casinos." She caught flashes of a darkened gym with fancy padded seats and an audience up to the rafters disappearing into the dimness, screaming for blood, waiters moving among them with trays loaded with drinks, a lighted ring, a black guy with muscles bulging out all over him, his red leather gloves grotesque in size. She shuddered.

"Draws a crowd, though. Fighters split ten percent of the door. Trick was not to use it up on doctor bills. Easy if you're the winner, not so easy if you weren't."

She kept silent. Remembered adrenaline, remembered pain, washed over her along with something else she hardly recognized in its intensity. Rage. She flinched. The scar on his eyebrow, the one at the edge of his chin made more sense now. She wondered there weren't more.

"I did pretty well. Most guys weren't too bright. Sometimes that gave me a break." She needed some distraction from the tug his touch engendered.

When this time he seemed disinclined to break the silence, she prodded him to go on. "That still doesn't tell me where you learned to fight. You must have known how before you started fighting for money or you would've gotten killed."

"I worked out at a gym some. I'd beefed up working summers on my uncle's ranch in Colorado. Bucking hay is better than a Bow-Flex for building muscle. Guy at the gym thought I might be able to fight. He was a broken-down fighter himself. Gave me a lesson or two."

"Why did he think you'd be able to fight?"

"We doing twenty questions here, or is this Madame the Shrink coming out?"

His flash of irritation might be justified. "Just wanted to know how you got to what I felt last night. Is that so bad?"

He didn't answer. He was thinking about how completely he understood her. That frightened him. "He thought I could fight because he saw the anger in me. There's a certain combination of fury and . . . I don't know . . . cold resolve, maybe, that makes a good fighter. I guess it's another version of the outrage and calculating nature that makes a good reporter. Anyway, I had it in spades back then."

He still had it. "So, you didn't hate having to fight for money?" Unimaginable. Holland thought how afraid she'd be, how degraded.

"Nah. Kept me from beating the rich snots at the Stanford fraternities to a bloody pulp. Kept me out of actual jail."

She couldn't help but know the other benefit—the one he was thinking about but not mentioning aloud. Not everyone who came to watch two men strip and fight were male. Images of pretty, predatory women flashed in his mind and were gone.

"Kept you in sex, you mean. That pay well, too?"

"Steak dinners, sometimes new clothes. I never let them give me money."

"Oh, well that's okay then." Damn. She wished she hadn't said it just that way.

"Like *you* never sold yourself? Let's have a little self-awareness here. Hmmm? What about those scholarships I'm sure you had? What about how your little foundation gets money? Aren't you selling yourself every day?"

He wasn't going to let her off the hook. "Okay. I do. Is that what you want to hear?"

He looked over at her, still expecting a fight.

Not going to get one. Not when you're right. Boy, that was hard to admit.

"Well, that's disappointing." He grinned again.

God, she loved that grin. It said he had the self-awareness he was demanding from her. That was a little rare in her experience. Maybe that's because she hung out with sickies and guys who thought they were really important. Jeff didn't. The bravado was a cover-up. He could be smug about being attractive to the opposite sex. He was good at his job and he knew it. He just didn't think that was enough in this world. Nothing he would be would ever be enough. Ahhh . . . she knew that feeling. That came from his parents.

"Sorry to disappoint you," she said. "I'm no match for a guy who boxed smokers."

"Just remember that." He glanced over at her again. She was sorry it was too dark to see his aura. "Those summers with my uncle got me through adolescence. He was a great guy. Simple. Wife had died. Ran some cattle west of Denver. He was a bit of an antidote to my parents. When they figured that out, they stopped the summers. That was their revenge."

"Did you go to him when you ran away from home?"

He nodded. "He stood up to my dad for me. Uncle Jed was my dad's older brother, and he never let my dad get all righteous on him. Just said it was better I was at the ranch than on the streets shooting drugs and whoring myself to get the money for it."

"Whoo. That blunt?"

"Uncle Jed was blunt." She could feel the sadness, see the flashing images of the funeral, and a glimpse of the little medallion around his neck.

"He give that to you?" she asked, reaching for it. It was a St. Christopher's medal.

He shook his head. "I took it. The only thing I took when he died."

"What happened after that?"

"I went to uh . . . Chicago and lived wild. Hey, why not? In a world where people like my father lived and my Uncle

Jed died at fifty-eight of stomach cancer, there didn't seem much point doing anything else. Nasty way to go."

Chaotic sensations of sickness, the smell of rot, the feel of carrying a big man who weighed hardly anything in his arms, echoed through Holland. Jeff had cared for his uncle to the last, though he must have been only seventeen at the time. Now that was a whoo. Holland felt humbled, so she changed the subject.

"How did you get from living wild to Stanford?"

Jeff lightened his tone deliberately, pushing down the images of Jed. "Now *that* had to do with a little girl named Ella Sue. Oh, yeah. Ella Sue."

Holland tightened at the memories that came floating through that satisfied voice. "This I've got to hear."

"Ella Sue liked Faulkner. She was going to LSU, and she lived in the Quarter, right across from where Faulkner once lived. He and his friends would get drunk and throw things from their balcony at the Ladies' Literary Society members as the meetings disbanded."

Holland smiled and raised her brows. "That must have been inspirational."

"She used to read Faulkner to me while we were naked in bed, and those lovely interminable sentences just trapped me, really. One day she moved on to this jock who played football or basketball or something. But she left me with Faulkner. I had to get out of N'aw . . . Chicago. But I took Faulkner with me—and all her other books, too. Just took them and went as far as I could go. West Coast was farther than East Coast, so I landed at Stanford." Like anybody could just show up at Stanford. But she already knew he was smart.

He looked over at her and by the dashboard lights she saw the look was soft. "Guess Faulkner was some kind of bridge between my father's religion and what morality could really be. Austere, unblinking, even unforgiving— but transforming in a way. You choose who you are, even if you choose the worst in you like Joe Christmas in *A Light in August.* But whatever you choose, you have to live with. Faulkner's full of that. He showed me some kind of road out. All Ella Sue's books did. Kinda balanced things."

That was just about the most eloquent tribute to the power of art Holland had ever heard. She had nothing to contribute about her life to compare with that.

This isn't a game of "I'm more twisted than you are," she heard him think. In the darkness she couldn't see his aura, but she knew it would be magenta. She'd come to think of that as the color of softness, maybe of caring.

She was embarrassed for feeling competitive. "It's the revelation part that makes me jealous," she said. "You transformed yourself."

"No, darlin', I just took forks in the road." Again the flash of the medallion.

She got it. St. Christopher was the patron saint of travelers. Through that medallion, Jeff hung on to some vision of goodness given to him by his uncle and chose his roads accordingly. It had pulled him out of his cycle of self-destruction. "You chose."

"We all do that, every second of every day." But he had chosen the harder way, the better way. He had gone to school, developed a stubborn addiction to truth, done something with it.

"So, what do you want out of life? I mean, what did you want before you got some new DNA strings? Wife and family? Settle down? Pulitzer prize?"

"I don't need some certificate." He grinned. "Though money is always nice." He sobered. "I don't have time for steady relationships."

"No urge to procreate? Even men have ticking clocks."

"Absolutely not. I never wanted kids."

He was afraid of having children. With his parental history that fit the pattern. She let the silence stretch, wondering whether he could hear her diagnosis.

He must have, because he changed the subject. "You did your job. I'm awake now. Why don't you try to get some sleep before we hit 'Seattle'?"

"I'm not wild about sleeping lately. Bad dreams." She knew he had felt those dreams too.

"Didn't dream last night, did you?"

Last night. Was it only last night they had made love in such overwhelming ferocity of oneness that she had actually passed out?

"Me, neither." He moved his hand to her thigh and let the silence fall around them. "I'll see you get some peace and quiet here. Give it a try."

She closed her eyes tightly and laid her head back on the cracked naugahyde of the seat. His hand stroked her thigh. That was not the way to peace. But she was tired. And soon she was thinking about whether her mother would hold out against her father, and whether her father would think to ask if they'd been to the house. And then she was wondering if her father had ever really liked licorice. He kept a jar on his desk but it was always full. And then she drifted off.

"God, what a night, Carol." Leland Banks slid his tired bones into the overstuffed chair beside their bed. It was covered in wildly flowered chintz, with ruffles to match the feminine, romantic decor of the room. It didn't look like a man was half of the pair that lived here. But the house was his wife's job. He paid for her expensive decorators, and everyone said it was gorgeous, which was the important part. So he had a bedroom in which he felt like an interloper. "I'm surprised you're still up. It must be five in the morning."

"I couldn't sleep," she said. But the book lying on the bed wasn't even within reach. She hadn't been reading either.

He didn't hesitate to tell her what was on his mind. Of course, he never discussed the details of his work. Her mind was not scientific in any sense. But she had always supported his decisions, never questioning, only murmuring encouragement, ever since the incident. She had become a comforting source of affirmation, like a mirror that revealed a reflection you knew would be handsome. Besides, she would very likely hear about the whole mess anyway if the press picked up on the frantic search going on. He considered briefly saying that Jeff had kidnapped Holly. But that would upset Carol too much, worrying that the crazy guy would kill her. He had that much affection left for his wife. Or maybe he was thinking of his own comfort. Hysterical women were not his style, so he told her the truth. "I'm afraid I have some bad news, Carol. Your daughter has run off with that reporter she was treating."

Of course, that wasn't the worst of it, but he'd ease into things slowly. Carol didn't look surprised. She looked worried. She always got that little crease between her eyebrows when she worried. But of course she'd worry. A little worm of resentment ran through him. Damn Holly for getting cold feet about the research! Now he was back to having no subjects to study. "It will ruin her career." His voice was a little more vehement than he intended.

"I'm sure it will."

"Are you taking a 'girls will be girls' attitude? Well, I can tell you I'm not. I've got everybody out looking for her."

"Why, Leland? Did he kidnap her?" But she didn't seem worried enough to believe that.

"No, no, of course not. She actually helped him steal a car as far as we can figure." *That* would shake Carol up. His wife was taking this much too calmly. He almost wanted her to be hysterical about her daughter's behavior. Then, when he slipped in the part about mutation, it would just be one of many catastrophes. Or maybe he just wanted her to share his outrage.

But Carol only nodded. "Love makes you do strange things."

"What?" Leland's voice ramped up. "We're not talking about anything as lofty as love."

"She must think she's in love, in order to run off with him." Carol looked at him over her glasses. Her rose-

239

colored gown picked up the pink in her cheeks.

Carol should be as angry with Holly as Leland was. "I should think you'd be horrified that your only child has thrown away all her opportunity, her reputation, *and* that of her foundation for a little thrill-seeking. How could she be in love with the guy when she's only known him four days? And remember, he's her patient. She's not supposed to be in love with her patient at all. It's unethical."

"He's not in the hospital now, is he? He's been discharged from her care?"

Leland didn't like this pushy attitude. It wasn't like Carol. "Since last night. One day doesn't exactly make her suddenly a shining example of objectivity."

"Okay, so she pushed the boundaries a little. I believe she loves him." Carol reached for a book and opened it. If he didn't know better, he'd think the gesture was defiant.

"Stealing cars, Carol? Even you must draw the line at that. I think she's snapped."

"Maybe," Carol said, a little too thoughtfully. Then she looked up at him. "Anything else about this situation you want to tell me?"

Leland cleared his throat. "She's ruined my study. The reporter has the extra genome string. Without him, we're not going to be making any progress on defining it, cataloging consequences—nothing. All my work, wasted."

"You'll find others."

How could she be so calm? Her reassurance was maddening. She should be hysterical. Her only daughter was missing, in the company of a man she had last seen attacking him. Holly was committing crimes, her career and reputation in shreds. Leland got up and began pacing the floor. Should he tell Carol about the mutation in Holly? That would get her thoughts appropriately hysterical. She wasn't mirroring his anxiety at all, and that felt strange. Unless . . .

He rounded on her. "You've seen them, haven't you?" His words dropped into the quiet of the bedroom, an accusation so unthinkable, he could hardly imagine it.

She stared at her book, but her eyes weren't moving and her knuckles were white.

Leland marched around to her side of the bed and sat heavily. "Don't think you are not going to tell me the truth, Carol, because you know you will."

"When you're not telling me the whole truth, Lee? Turnabout is fair play."

"All right! All right. Holly has the anomaly, too."

"And that's why they've gone, isn't it? They're afraid of some senator."

"They *have* been here!" He looked wildly around. Why had they come here of all places? And to Carol? What could she do for them? "What did they want? Money! They needed money." He stilled. "Where are they, Carol? I can't help them if I don't know where they are."

She smiled. He did not like that smile. "I don't know. They wanted it that way."

"How much did you give them?" That might tell him how far they could go.

"What I had." She was enjoying telling only what he asked. She was enjoying the fact that she wasn't just murmuring encouragement.

"Damn you, Carol, this is not the time to hold out on me!" But wait, Carol never kept that much on her. There was nowhere to get money late at night. His eyes widened. He turned and strode downstairs to where Carol's purse always lay on the table in the foyer. He ripped the snap apart and fumbled with her billfold. Opening it, he took a long breath.

He heard her come up behind him. "So, credit cards, driver's license, as well as all your cash," he said softly. He rounded on her slowly. "A second little betrayal? You always manage to do the wrong thing. They may be right about the senator, Carol. I'm all they have to protect them. And you've just put them beyond my reach with your little

241

rebellion. They'll pay the price for your lack of trust in me."
He had the satisfaction of seeing her face fall. "Let's hope
we can track them when they first use the cards, and get
your daughter back where she's safe."

Chapter Nineteen

The colored lights of . . . Seattle glittered on the edge of
the desert like a child's vision of heaven. *The promised
land,* Jeff thought. The sky was not quite black behind it
and off to the right. It would be dawn soon. A quick couple
of stops at casinos and they could be off again.

He glanced over to where Holland slept, his hand on
her thigh. What had happened to them was so big he
couldn't comprehend it. How many movies had he seen
where people, or aliens or animals or somebody, could
read minds? It seemed so cool, so easy. Yeah, right. It was
nothing short of awful. All this noise in your head, and no
way to shut it off except to touch a woman and then hear
her thoughts so clearly and know she could hear yours.
. . . God, but it was a miracle the sexes *ever* got together!
He had felt her contempt for some of the things she heard
him thinking. What did she expect? She was a beautiful
woman. He was a guy. Even now, his hand on her thigh,
even tired as he was, he could feel the attraction to her.
That was more than just sex. It was the "more" part that
scared him. He put it down forcibly. If he weren't this tired,
he wouldn't be able to put it down. She didn't accept a
lot of things about a man, like how fighting could make
you feel powerful, and his rage scared her. Uncomfortable

at best. Plus, how could you be macho if she could hear your doubts about yourself?

Even sex was ruined if you got that explosion that turned into an invasion of your soul. In the moment they had fully joined he'd felt all of her, her insecurity about her value to the world, the certainty that someone would discover she was not as smart, as competent as she made out to be—stupid insecurities. She was fastidious, too; finicky even. Thank God they hadn't gone to his place that night. And stubborn. Probably had lived alone too long. Too used to getting her way. She'd probably treat him like he was her secretary, or her patient, ordering him around. Hell, she'd already treated him like a patient. Thought she was always in control. Well, she wasn't.

Finicky or not, she did like sex. In fact, she was very sensual. He had thought her cold—a calculating psychiatrist. He'd been wrong. His thoughts strayed to the way her body had looked that night and dwelt on that for a while; the curve of the underside of her breast, the full roundness of her bottom. She had very attractive knees and ankles— not clunky. That was important to him. Soon he realized his thumb was stroking her thigh, even as other parts of him awakened. Maybe he wasn't tired enough. He stilled himself. In some ways he knew more about her than any woman he'd ever known, including Ella Sue.

She lifted her head, groggy.

"Sorry," he said. "Didn't mean to wake you."

"No, that's all right," she said, sitting up. She touched her hair to see that it was in place. It wasn't. Four or five strands escaped her chignon and trailed around her face. With a little moue of her mouth, she unclipped the comb. Tossing it onto the dashboard, she ran her fingers through her hair. It hung loose on her shoulders in untidy strands that showed a dozen shades of gold. That was better. Her hair looked good down.

"You sleep okay? Dreams?" He stopped his thumb from stroking her thigh.

She shook her head.

"We're almost there," he said, then felt stupid. She could see that. The horizon was filled with tiny blinking lights, glowing pyramids, towering columns of lighted hotel rooms. "Seattle" was the circus midway of the world. Already, around them, houses had sprung up, mostly singles, standing alone against the desert, but occasionally in groups. He wondered what it was like to live at the edge of a town that lured people to dissolution, encouraging their worst impulses.

"Why the worst? For some it's just fun," Holland said.

Case in point. Why he hated this whole thing. Now he'd have to explain himself.

"So, don't explain," she said, miffed.

Christ Almighty. You couldn't even have a discouraging thought without her catching it.

"Yeah. It's really hard to pout or feel self-righteous, too. It's put a big hole in my behavior patterns."

He glanced over and caught the smile. Nice smile. You'd never know she was a shrink when she smiled. "You're right." Only half-grudging. Then he chuckled. She *was* right. Better change the subject in a hurry. "You think maybe we've stopped having bad dreams entirely?"

"How should I know?"

"I thought shrinks specialized in dreams."

"Some place more importance on dreams than others." She pushed herself down in the seat. "Okay. Here's a theory, if you're into theories. Maybe all those dreams about not being human were because on some level we knew about the gene mutation. Not specifics, mind you, but we felt we were different. Now that we know that consciously, we don't need the dreams shaking our mental cage to let the truth out anymore."

"And what about the evil part?" In some ways that was scarier than the alien part.

He could feel her apprehension. "Not so easy. Maybe the constant conflict with the shadow in all of us superimposed itself onto the other impression that we weren't human."

"The shadow. Oh, you mean the part of us that does scary things we can't accept."

"You should be a shrink."

He grinned. "Enough of shadows. It's dawn, and we've got a job to do."

She sat up in her seat and squared her shoulders. What must it be like for a woman who had trod the straight and narrow all her life to be on the run and breaking laws? "Pick a casino," he said softly. "You fancy pyramids, the Roman Empire, old England, New York, the Circus?"

She put a finger to her mouth. "The Mirage. I like the white tigers."

Perfecticy cats. You would like those.

Holland actually shrank away from her. He got a flash of young men in white coats, laughing. They had called her "ice princess." It had hurt her then, it hurt now.

She sat back up, and got angry. *Right, I'm such an ice princess that you're afraid to touch me because we'll end up in bed.*

Shit. Why did I think that? "Uh, sorry. Not fair. You're right, when I think about it." He glanced over at her. "You can't have right thoughts all the time, you know. You can just sort the thoughts you have and choose what to believe."

A man who acknowledged he was wrong? He felt her anger drain away. *Must not have a high opinion of men.*

"It's the preoccupation with truth," he said wryly. "Guess it has an up side."

"Boy, this is hard."

He thought about the prospect of hearing the mistaken thoughts rather than the sorted ones, on both sides. She was thinking about it, too.

"Whole new world," he said, thoughtful. How could they get used to it? How could you keep friends or lovers when you could hear their thoughts, even the angry, spiteful ones? He glanced over at her. All she wanted to do was change the subject, fearing she would hear her name attached to either friend or lover. Or that she wouldn't hear it attached to either. What to think about that?

"So what's *your* choice of casino?" she asked, a trifle louder than was required. "We need a couple of targets."

"Ancient Rome."

"You like the debauchery or the gladiators?" She was on the attack now, accusing him of being violent and debauched.

Maybe he was. "I thought you'd like the gladiators." It might offend her, but it would also show he didn't think she was an ice princess.

She grinned. "Maybe. We'll see if they're up to my standards."

The glitter of the Strip was overwhelmed by the pinkening sky as they drove east.

They'd gotten twenty thousand off one of the cards in a cash advance from the high-rollers cage at the Mirage. Holland had been so nervous handing over her mother's ID and the cards, she'd thought she might wet her pants, even though Jeff had made her practice the signature and promised no one would look really closely at the picture. The picture itself helped. It was twelve years old. California was saving money by not retaking driver's license pictures every time you renewed. Carol Banks and her daughter looked enough alike to pass. As they were walking away from the window, the cashier wished them luck. Holland was just happy she didn't faint. Now they were on their way to Caesars Palace.

You know we could win big at blackjack. Poker maybe, too.

Holland suppressed a chuckle. *Oh, now we're going to do the what-could-you-do-with-this-gift routine?* They were pushing through the casino, the crowds seven-A.M. thin, past beautiful young people with skin painted to look like statutes, who were striking classic poses.

Sure. If we touch, we can hear everybody thinking about their cards. Sure thing.

You better be glad those security guards over there can't hear you planning to cheat.

He took her arm and glanced down at her in the letup of the voices multiplying in their heads in the last days. *Not even tempted?*

All I think about is getting caught.

Who'd believe we could read minds?

So, it would be okay because we couldn't be caught? She held his gaze. They stopped in the middle of the roulette tables. Some winner's shout faded away behind them.

He rolled his eyes. *Women!*

But she heard that he didn't really mean it. He'd been dreaming, planning, imagining how good it would feel to be a winner. He didn't really want to carry through on it. But he didn't know how to back down. A male thing. *That's us females. Party poopers all around.*

"Come on." He dragged her through the crowds. "Let's find the high-rollers cage. It's probably off that private poker room over there."

They passed one woman in skintight leopard-skin spandex displaying an impressive décolleage. Holland heard Jeff's mental intake of breath.

Jesus, Mary, and Joseph! Look at that. I bet she'd really . . . He jerked his gaze to Holland as a string of very graphic images slowly faded to black.

Not slowly enough. "I can't *believe* you!" Holland protested as the woman pushed past—but not before throwing an appraising glance at Jeff. Holland didn't have to be touching Jeff to read the woman's thoughts. She was as eager as he was, for about the same kind of thing. "She's forty-five if she's a day," Holland whispered furiously. "Her boobs aren't her own, and she wears leopard spandex." She could feel through all her righteousness that he really didn't care about what the woman wore or whether her anatomy was natural. He shrugged, his aura turning pinky-lavender in places.

"Don't look all embarrassed, for God's sake," she said, now annoyed at him on so many levels she couldn't seem to distinguish between them. "It seems to be a ubiquitous subject for you—and probably for your whole sex."

"Hey, I thought you were supposed to be a psychiatrist. You know the tangled nature of the male psyche." Jeff took her arm and led her off toward the bowels of the casino.

"There's knowing, and having it shoved down your . . . your brain," Holland muttered.

"Besides. Doesn't mean I would have done anything about it. Just looking, so to speak."

"Well, you were looking pretty graphically."

"Sorry. But you were ready to condemn the woman because of what she was wearing and the state of her breasts. Not exactly enlightened, milk-of-human-kindness stuff. Are all women so judgmental?"

"So, you're saying she's a whore with a heart of gold?" Holland snorted.

"Maybe."

Holland was suddenly uncomfortable in so many ways she just stayed silent. The possibility of being judgmental—over clothes, no less—like her father; the remote chance that there was some jealousy involved; the real possibility that she would be exposed to all these male impressions—not only the sex, but violent impulses and that kind of crowing ego she felt sometimes, just made her freeze.

Even worse, she could feel Jeff's own dismay at the topic of conversation and their future prospects pretty clearly. There was no melding now. They felt like they were from different species. He stared at her, then shook off his thoughts and pulled her through the last forest of slot machines to a discrete door. They stepped up to the gentleman in the dinner jacket who stood in front of a red velvet rope.

"You have any chairs opening up on the five-hundred-dollar table, my man?" There were only two tables with players at this time in the morning.

"One, or two chairs?" the man asked deferentially, in spite of the fact that they weren't dressed for the occasion. At least Jeff wasn't. Plaid shirts were not the order of the day here. Holland was glad she was wearing her pearls and that at least her sweater was cashmere.

"One," she answered. "I just want to watch, if that's okay."

"You'll have to stand behind the line, Miss," he said as he took Jeff's subtly offered bill and motioned them in.

See, they wouldn't let us touch, she thought. *Too bad. No cheating this morning.*

"We'll just see the cashier first," Jeff murmured as they passed.

The young woman acting as cashier didn't even sit in a cage. Cages were too unsophisticated for the rarefied atmosphere of the high-stakes poker room. She simply stood behind a counter that looked like an old-fashioned wooden bar, polished and shiny. She wore a very short toga no Roman woman would have worn. Jeff nodded to Holland.

"Twenty thousand, dear?" she asked as she stepped up, card and driver's license ready.

"That should be fine. I feel my luck changing."

Holland passed the second of her mother's cards across the bar. The girl nodded. "Thank you, Miss." She ran the card through a reader and handed it back. "May I see some identification?"

The girl gave her mother's license a cursory look and waited for the machine to beep.

It didn't beep. The silence stretched.

"Trouble with your verification line tonight?" Jeff asked to cover the gap. Holland could see by his aura that he was getting nervous.

"Not that I know of. Perhaps another card?"

Holland felt all the shame of being unworthy of the room. She was about to produce the third card, when the machine beeped. The girl glanced over to it, smiling and taking the tape that spewed from its slot. Then her smile froze. Unconsciously she peered more closely at the tape.

Uh-oh. Holland and Jeff felt the impending doom at the same time.

"Darlin', did I ever show you the private room at the Luxor?" Jeff asked. "I have the strangest feeling I'll be lucky there tonight." He was already steering her away from the bar as the woman motioned to someone, a security guard, no doubt. "You can cancel that transaction, miss," he called over his shoulder.

Shit! They're on to us.

I guess Mom caved.

Hurry, darlin'. They picked up the pace, nodding to the doorkeeper and then plunging into the forest of slot machines outside the door.

Jeff jerked her into a small dark bar as three security guards trotted by on their way to the poker room. "Better get out of here pronto," he whispered. "Not enough of a crowd to hide us."

Holland wanted to run but Jeff tugged her hand. *Just walk to the exit, nice and calm.*

The place was huge. It seemed like a couple of miles to an exit. They were making their way toward the doors where they'd entered when they saw the Las Vegas police coming down the main isle in a phalanx. Jeff pulled her toward the shopping area, open twenty-four hours. He looked around frantically. Holland dragged him into one of those candy shops with clear bins from floor to ceiling filled with odd treats like watermelon sours. "Excuse me," she asked the bored girl behind the counter. "Where's the closest exit?"

The girl pointed. "At the Steak and Potatoes. Take a right. It leads to the parking lot."

"Thanks." *See? Asking directions is a virtue.*

She felt Jeff's snort of derision, but he was off toward the exit at a run. No time for calm now. They hurried down the hallway, past the restrooms, out the double doors, and into a sea of cars sparkling in the morning sun. It was already hot. It would be a scorcher.

"I don't think this is where we parked," Holland said uncertainly.

"You think we want that car back? If they know about the credit cards, they might know about the car." Jeff tugged her into the rows of parked cars. "Split up. Holler if you can find one unlocked."

The fifth handle she pulled opened. *Jeff!* She called silently, and saw his head pop around to look for her. Then he was jogging toward her. She knew what would happen next.

Now she was really an accomplice. She'd found the next car they were going to jack.

As usual it was a matter of moments and they were driving with maddening slowness toward the exit booth. A sleepy attendant with acne swept open the window on his booth. A blast of cool air whooshed over them.

"Ticket?"

"Uh, we lost the ticket." Jeff's aura crackled with tension.

"Lost ticket pays full rate," the attendant warned. "Eighteen bucks."

"Here's a twenty, keep the change and let us out of here."

"You in some kind of hurry, Mister?"

Jeff smiled. "Can't miss the buffet breakfast at Bally's. They only serve 'til nine."

God, but he was a cool customer! She felt him preen a little under her admiration. "Okay, Mr. Ice Under Pressure. Let's get out of town while we can," she said under her breath.

It wasn't five blocks before they heard a siren screaming up behind them while they were stopped at a light.

Shit. Jeff's eyes darted to the rearview mirror. The tension in his body echoed her own. Her aura must also reflect his—bright green with yellow crackles through it. They were busted, big time. Jeff was about to hit the accelerator and make a run for it. Holland darted a hand to his arm. "It'll just bring down more of them on us. Maybe you can talk your way out of it."

She craned around to see their nemesis approaching.

The cop car showed no signs of slowing. For a frantic moment Holland thought, it was going to ram them. Then it swung out around them drunkenly and careened off through the traffic at the intersection.

Holland and Jeff locked eyes. Relief washed through him. His aura faded to a blue-gray.

"Not for us," he rumbled.

The light turned green. He took a breath and urged the car slowly ahead. "Low profile," he murmured. Then he looked across at her. "Thanks for your vote of confidence, but I couldn't have talked my way out of that."

"I don't know," she said, laying her hand on his arm as they wended their way through morning traffic on the Strip. "You're pretty smooth under pressure. Must be all that undercover work."

"Yeah. Okay. See if you can find a map, will you? We're headed for . . . Chicago."

Holland grinned. Out of "Seattle" for real, headed for Chicago, proxy destination. Why did she feel so free? They were on the run, had barely missed being caught at the casino. The last cop had either missed them or was on some other errand but it wouldn't be long before the highway patrol, or the army, or the police in some one-traffic-light town took his place. All her life as she had known it was gone.

Her gaze was captured by a convoy of camouflaged vehicles rumbling past them, going back toward the casinos: Hummers and trucks with their side flaps up to reveal men in battle garb sitting with guns propped between their legs. It looked like an enemy invasion.

"This is bad," Jeff said, then glued his eyes to the road ahead.

"They can't be after us, can they? It's just a coincidence, like the cop."

"Yeah. Must be."

She listened to the wash of voices in her head. That was funny, she hadn't been that aware of them until she focused. But now that she listened, she could hear a woman swearing in Spanish, several voices joined in a guttural song, and there, at the edge, was someone thinking about how long it was before he would reach LAX and when he could get a flight to Washington.

She turned frightened eyes on Jeff. "The senator. Do you hear him?"

Jeff's eyes flickered. "Yeah."

"Do you think he's called off the hunt?"

Jeff set his lips. "No."

She put a hand on Jeff's shoulder. "Does he know where we're going?" The words she didn't want to think flashed through her brain. *New Orleans*. Impossible. It was impossible to lie to yourself, and so you couldn't keep the truth from him.

"I don't know, darlin'." Jeff said. He didn't hold out much hope.

It was morning. No shower, no breakfast, no any ritual of her life. She went stiff. No little yellow pills that she had to take every morning of her life in order to live, ever since she was in intensive care for exaggerated immune reaction. Fear showered through her. There were more immediate consequences than the fact that the senator knew where they were. She might not make it to the senator finding them.

"What?" Jeff asked. "What pills?"

"Allergy pills," she said, pushing down her fear.

"Oh. Can you get along without them?"

"Guess I have to."

Chapter Twenty

The saguaro forests around Tucson and the plains filled with feathery Palo Verde trees and squid-like Ocotillos, bright red flowers like suckers at the tips of their spiny stalks, had given way to desert hosting far less life and almost no greenery. Next stop was El Paso and a different car.

"This place is just butt-ugly," Jeff muttered as he settled into the passenger's seat of their current vehicle, a Chevrolet of some kind, probably from the mid-nineties. Holland had slept for a few more hours out of Las Vegas, but Jeff was looking red around the eyes. When he'd almost sideswiped a car he was passing, Holland commandeered the driving duty.

"Austere beauty?" Holland asked. She fastened her seat belt, adjusted the mirrors, and tossed the empty coke cans and the greasy wrappers from burgers and fries over the back seat.

"Not likely." Jeff rubbed his temples. His scab was beginning to crack.

Holland pulled out into the lanes of Highway 10, headed east. It was mid-afternoon.

"So, why don't you miss the landscape show and get some shut-eye?" Holland asked.

" 'Cause I'm so wired with Coke I'm not sure I can sleep."

Holland pressed the Chevy up to seventy. Five miles over the speed limit wouldn't attract attention. "Okay. Radio?"

"Last I looked we had the choice of one of the ten stations playing top country hits, the ten Spanish language band, or the national First Channel pabulum. What ever happened to regional radio? Can't we hear some old-fashioned blues or something?"

"Not responsible for the content of the airwaves, guy." Holland glanced in the rearview mirror for anyone behind her and pulled out and around a Winnebago.

"Yeah, I know."

She glanced back to Jeff and saw an aura almost itchy with orange and green. He was fraying at the edges. "Want to talk?" She put a hand on his thigh and steered with her left hand.

The silence fell around them, but his breathing was still shallow. He shook his head, as though he couldn't decide. "God, Holland. I was thinking while you were asleep, about where all this could lead. I mean, have you thought about the consequences of what's happening to us?"

She cleared her throat, feeling a pull toward Jeff McQueen in mind and body. "Sure. Snipers, and people who want to study us, and people who will be afraid of us because we're different."

He scooted back in his seat and sat straight up, rubbing the nape of his neck. "No, no—it's really more than that. It seems to me that there are new voices appearing in my head all the time." He glanced to her and raised his brows.

She nodded. She'd been feeling it, too.

"It would mean there is a community of people like us. We wouldn't be alone."

"*If* enough of us survive snipers and suicide."

"Yeah. But if we do survive—the voices have been getting clearer for me."

"Me, too. Though I think I'm behind you a bit."

He nodded, thoughtful. "And one of us is a senator. We're going to find others in our government—why not other governments? Genetics isn't circumscribed by national boundaries Or in the CIA maybe, or . . . secret research."

"Yes. So?"

"We can't lie to each other, Holland. No more lies, no secrets."

She didn't say anything. The implications of what he was saying washed over her. Government, industry, military . . . religion? Scams? Criminals? "My God . . ."

"Yeah." He slumped in his seat and scanned the sparse landscape of sand and creosote bushes and the occasional Cholla cactus. She could feel his anxiety ramping up, even through the silence they created together. "And what if we can all touch each other and hear the thoughts of people not like us, if they're close by? That seems to be how it works for you and me."

Holland hardly saw the asphalt, the limitless horizon, the sky hung with cutout clouds, the blue Dodge she was passing. "A new world," she breathed. "It would change everything."

"And before things settled into some kind of new order, there would be absolute chaos," he said, his voice hoarse. "No business deals where everyone doesn't understand the consequences, no cheating on your spouse, no little white social lies. No hiding the budget deficits, no bamboozling people about your intentions, in government or in private life. My God, can you imagine it?"

"The world will come apart. Or maybe we'll make it a better place." She wasn't sure of that. It seemed like such a sixties love-everybody thing, something her mother would say.

Jeff didn't believe it, either. "If there were enough of us. If we end up with only a few . . . I don't think we'd have much of a chance." She glanced over to see him chewing that wonderful, full lower lip. His aura had turned dark, almost black. "What I know is there will be people, institutions, companies maybe, who will do anything to prevent that, once they figure it out."

"Yes." She took a breath and let it out slowly. "So you're thinking that maybe some of them already have figured it out."

"Yeah, and we're not just talking Senator Lendreaux."

The bleakness of the surrounding landscape suddenly echoed her mood. What chance did they have, damaged and unsure of themselves as they were, against a whole world that would hate what they were with the vehemence borne of self-preservation?

Jeff strutted down Decatur Street past the House of Blues. Summer rain made the black wet of the streets glow in circus colors of reflected neon. House of Bullshit Blues is more like it, he was thinking. The real stuff blasted out from tiny stages in courtyards off Bourbon, or in clubs on Basin where fashionable people never went. Blues was gritty, not homogenized for shows at seven and ten, standing room only, two-drink minimum. Jeff felt strong, powerful. He strutted past the crowd waiting outside the ticket office. The faceless people in line seemed to realize just how dangerous he was. They glanced away, humble in his presence. Yeah. That felt good. Little did they know, he ruled this town, maybe this world.

In spite of the encroaching banality, New Orleans was his town. Not the House of Blues New Orleans—that had been polluted beyond hope by the tourists. But the New Orleans of the Napoleon House belonged to Jeff McQueen. The Napoleon House hadn't been painted, inside or out, in a hundred years, and the patina of age on the walls, the classical music, the chipped black-and-white floor tiles, and the slow courtesy of the waiters made you stop to let the flow of time pass over you while you relished who you were. One afternoon he had sat inside, drinking Pimm's Cups until twilight, the shutters open on the rain falling just outside the awning. You didn't have to do anything there. You could just be.

And right now what he felt like being was powerful. The powerfulness inside him welled up until he thought he would burst. He pushed one of the black kids always tap-dancing for money with bottle caps pressed into their shoes. "Outta my way, kid."

He realized he had a knife in a sheath on his belt. It was one of those curved blades that meant serious business. He took it out and it gleamed in the neon. Passers-by drew back from him, gasping in horror at the knife. As a matter of fact, Jeff was very skilled with that knife. He could practically feel it gutting one after another of the stupid tourist cows and letting their blood flow warm over his hands.

Somehow he found himself at the back door of the Court of the Two Sisters on Royal. The streets were strangely empty. Everyone had disappeared. Probably because of his knife. You never ate at the Two Sisters. Total tourist trap. He hated it and what it stood for. As a matter of fact, he hated anyone eating there. They had to be tourists. But the bar at the back made the best Sazeracs and the best mint juleps in town, thanks to Floria. She should have retired years ago, an old black woman, imperial ruler of the bar rather than the bartender. The way she spun those glasses in the air to coat them with Herb Sainte before she poured the rye whiskey and the Peycheaux bitters . . . Sure it was for show. But it also left just the right anise flavor in the glass. Don't try this at home, boys and girls. Floria was powerful in her own way. But not as powerful as he was. He felt the rage against the tourists rise in his throat until it was likely to choke him, and the only way he could breathe was to go through that bar, and into the courtyard where the tourists were all sitting, laughing loud and ordering hurricanes, pecan pie, and let his knife tell them what he thought of them, and what they had done to his town . . .

He pushed inside from the Royal Street entrance. In the comfortable gloom of the Two Sisters, sitting at the bar, was Holland. And she was wearing the loosest of gowns, diaphanous, so that it fell over the barstool, like she was a fairy. She smiled at him, like she had been waiting for him for a long time. His knife was gone. Had he laid it down some-

where? It didn't matter. New Orleans was hot outside, and rainy on summer nights, but inside here it was cool, and he thought about maybe getting a hotel room at the Royal Sonesta over on Bourbon and Bienville and walking Holland over there under a big umbrella in the rain. . . .

The senator's eyes snapped open. "Got it," he said, to the ubiquitous Brad who lounged in a chair in the executive terminal at LAX where the private jets arrived and departed. "They're on their way to New Orleans." Triumph coursed through him. He couldn't understand why he hadn't been able to get it before. When he could hear them, they were loud and clear. But he couldn't hear them very often. Disturbing. He didn't like the possibilities.

"How do you know it's New Orleans?" Brad asked, folding his newspaper with a snap.

"Dreams, my boy." Senator Lendreaux murmured. "They say things we would never speak out loud. So I know who they must be going to see. Hmmm. That could be bad."

"We know they're driving. No signs at the airports or train stations. They're probably heading out Interstate 10—it's the main route through the Southwest." Brad rubbed his chin. "Shall we try to intercept them?"

"Call Amstead at the Secret Service. He'll coordinate resources along the 10. I want our guys in the Quarter. Our runaways will stay there. Check the Royal Sonesta."

"I'll see who's in the area."

"I want backup, too, Brad. If the military picks them up en route, fine. But if they make it to New Orleans, I'd rather have them out of the picture entirely. Am I making myself clear?"

Brad nodded his blond head and stood, flipping open a tiny cell phone. "Check."

The senator leaned back in the airport lounge chair as a woman in a maroon suit and striped tie leaned out of the service window.

"Your plane has been authorized for departure, Senator." She smiled.

Lendreaux rose. "Get on it, Brad. The people's business calls me."

Jeff jerked his head forward into wakefulness. The voices in his head clamored, intruding on the silent landscape. The desert outside El Paso was black and gray in the night, like the landscape on the moon. Holland, both hands on the wheel, was passing a livestock truck.

"Hey," she said softly. "You awake?" Her hand slipped back to his thigh. The voices slipped away, leaving only the silent desert night and the thrum of the engine.

"Yeah, I guess."

He could feel the tenderness in her thoughts. There was this whole maternal thing going on about touching him while he slept that made him nervous. She was thinking about her parents, for Christ's sake, and how her mother felt about her father. She was wondering if once, before they compromised, they had ever felt like she did about him. He hated when women got like that. Pretty soon they were talking baby talk and wanting commitments. He'd managed to avoid that for thirty-six years. But he couldn't avoid her emotions. They washed over him constantly. Did he want to avoid them? He certainly didn't want to be swallowed by them, or by her personality. He felt like they'd been getting closer and closer, ever since they'd had that supernatural sort of sex. Damned uncomfortable. But, like dancing with the devil, there was something attractive about it too. It wasn't just the physical. He sucked in a breath—but oh, the physical!

Looking at her there in the half-light, she looked ethereal. The word fairy came to mind. With that tumbled blonde hair and perfect profile, she looked like salvation, but a salvation that made his cock hard. He swallowed and closed his eyes. Any man's dream, right? Close up, it was scarier than that. He might be dancing with the devil.

She glanced over at him. He knew she knew he was getting hard right next to her in the car. *Yeah. Let that chase away those damned maternal thoughts.* Why couldn't you have just the pieces you wanted instead of the whole uncomfortable package?

He swept his hair back off his forehead and looked around. They were driving a Toyota he'd jacked in a hospital parking lot in El Paso. Since that was the car-jacking capital of the world, he didn't think anyone would notice. Holland had volunteered to drive again and he'd let her. That first stretch of being awake for thirty hours had taken its toll, what with the emotional strain of all that testing in her father's lab, and the chase to Las Vegas. Now the desert night around them seemed blacker, more filled with stars than he had ever seen.

"Don't see nights like this in L.A.," he remarked, to keep her tenderness at bay.

She peered up through the front windshield. "No. Seems fitting, somehow, that we get a whole new kind of night along with a whole new kind of brain."

A whole new kind of brain . . . Yet he felt like he was taking all his old brain with him, hardwired as it was. Trapped between what he was becoming and what he couldn't help being, he took a breath and retreated to his best defense. "So, Harvard or Yale?"

"What?" She glanced over to him in surprise.

"Did you go to Harvard or Yale to become a shrink?"

"Yale," she answered slowly. "How did you know?"

"Hey, someone as concerned with appearances as you are had to go to one or the other."

"They're good schools," she snapped. "That's what's important."

He couldn't see her aura in the dark. But he could guess. This was more comfortable. The prickly exchange of information reluctantly given was what he was used to. "And I'll bet your father was keen on your going to one or the other."

261

He felt her shrink away from that. "Yes," she almost whispered. The guilt she felt, the fear at that truth, made him feel small.

"Yeah. Good schools," he said. An impulse to give her some room to wiggle came over him—something he never gave his interview subjects. "So, you and your father don't get along?"

He felt her relax at that certainty. "No. Never have." He thought she wasn't going to give him any more, given what a cad he'd just been, but slowly she continued. "He wanted me to study the hard sciences. Follow in his footsteps—that sort of thing. He was . . . very disappointed when I entered a soft field—that's what he called it—like psychiatry. A pseudoscience."

"You rebelled."

She gave a half-breathed chuckle. "I guess you'd call it that. He was into absolute truth. I followed more in my mother's footsteps. She was a social worker, you know. Dad never respected her for that—mushy thinkers. But I thought she did a lot of good before she retired into being his personal hostess and social chief-of-staff."

"And you were into . . . ?"

"Well, psychiatry is a blend. It has a hard science side—chemical imbalances, hormonal influences, the effects of drugs, that sort of thing. But I think the role of the psychiatrist is really to allow the patient to find on his own that compromise between his need to live in the real world and the demons that drive him. It's a relative thing. No hard and fast rules. Some solutions better than others, but no perfect outcome. It's a series of compromises, which in the most positive outcome, allow the patient to live in some degree of normalcy."

"Not something your father could appreciate," he murmured. "I understand that." There was a silence while they looked at the stars, and the blackness and the sand glowing gray-white in the night. He had his body under better control now. He could also feel her sureness that she had told him what she knew of the truth about her life. But something niggled at him.

"So, do you apply those principles to your own life?" he asked, almost against his will. He knew what would happen. He felt her sureness dissolve.

"What do you mean?" Her anxiety washed over him. He had felt that anxiety a lot—as much for her relationship with her father as for the predicament they were in.

"Well," he stuttered. But he had no choice but to go on. "I mean, at the hospital you said you have trouble compromising. Do you compromise with your demons to get along?"

"Everybody does." She knew that was a pat answer.

He cleared his throat. He was committed now. "I was just thinking how hard you try to be what your father wants."

She sat straight up in the old Toyota seat. "I do *not*. I am constantly wrangling with him. I am not at all what he wants me to be and I don't care in the least." The anger he felt from her, the total denial, was absolute, and therefore vulnerable. When you could hear everything, there was no alternative but truth. She cared, all right.

"Really? Why the linen sheaths and pearls, the careful hair? You look like a parody of what your father thinks you should be. And the workaholic thing? You are trying so hard to be the perfect psychiatrist. Do you think that might be just a little bit to please your father?"

"More like to spite him!" she retorted. But she knew that wasn't true.

"Let's say . . . to prove to him that you're as good as he is."

"At least I don't break into rages and beat to a pulp other people in lieu of my father." In spite of her tone of voice she was appalled at what she had just said.

"The difference between us is that I know that's what I do," he said softly.

He heard her sharp intake of breath, her outrage and then collapse. "Doctor heal thyself?" she asked, managing to mock him. And then he heard the echo in her mind that said she knew he knew her vulnerability.

He said nothing.

"I've told patients a thousand times that you rework your relationship with your parents throughout your life, even after they're dead. I help people do that." Her spirits sank. "I just can't help myself. Because of his disapproval, I've always felt any achievement was a lie." She gathered herself. "He has affairs, you know." She tried to make it sound casual. "Doesn't think it has anything to do with the fact that he loves his family. Sort of a separate thing entirely."

"Feels to you like he doesn't think his family is enough, though," Jeff said matter-of-factly, saying what she felt. "And that's just like telling you you're not good enough."

"He has a double standard. Mother strayed when I was young. Our neighbor."

"Yeah. Fred. I heard her thinking about him as she was watching you in the pool in that memory. She didn't mean to let Fred slip in, but he did. Your dad was a little angry?"

"Woo, yeah." Holland tried to make her voice light. "They almost split."

"But they didn't."

Holland thought about that. *Why not?* Jeff heard her ask herself. *It wasn't that their love came through stronger than ever.* "Habit? Maybe," she said softly. "Maybe he didn't think he could find a perfect hostess who would support him unquestioningly."

"What about her?"

"Fred got cold feet when Dad found out. He moved. I heard from an aunt that he never really wanted to divorce his wife. So, I guess Mom would have been adrift on her own if she'd left Dad. Don't think that was the kind of life she imagined."

He was saddened by the story. "Maybe there's such a thing as too much compromise."

She didn't want him to feel sorry for her. "Hey, they buttered their bread, now they have to lie in it. But I refuse to go the same way." She might be so much like him that she couldn't make that refusal stick.

"So, I guess I shouldn't call you Daddy's little girl?" He, too, tried to lighten his tone.

She managed a smile. "Why not? It's what I've been trying to be all my life."

"Because you're more than that. It's an easy phrase that doesn't tell the whole truth."

She looked away from the ribbon of asphalt stretching away from their headlights into the darkness and examined his face. "And you're all for the whole truth."

"Aren't you?"

"I guess, but that's probably the one way in which I truly *am* different than my father. He thinks there is a perfect answer if only we can find it."

That made him think about where he stood. "You don't. I can go with that. As long as we can agree that there are shades of gray so deep that they require action."

"Like the slave labor rings in the L.A. garment industry?"

"I actually believe in the death penalty." Now *there* was an admission for a politically liberal reporter. That ought to make her feel better.

"You're kidding." She was surprised and a little appalled.

"Not like we apply it today. We should save the death penalty for the worst of the worst, not any black guy that pulled a robbery and shot somebody." He paused before the explanation of this most difficult opinion. "But there *are* people so depraved, some crimes so heinous, that the penalty should be death."

"So, who judges the worst?" She wasn't judging him, yet. But she didn't agree with him.

"I think people know. The guy who kidnaps an eleven-year-old girl, tortures and rapes her, and then kills her really slow? That guy should die. I think people know."

He could feel her protest and then her realization that it was a protest against her own agreement. She couldn't agree. She couldn't even nod. But he knew, just the same.

"There is one thing you're going to have to change," he said. Maybe it was the pushy reporter in him coming out, but he couldn't let her out of confronting her dilemma.

She glanced over at him. Even in the dark, he could see her skeptical eyebrow raised in inquiry. "And that is?"

"You've got to stop trying to be perfect. Make that rebellion against your father real. You know? You're okay just like you are. Good, even."

"Always easier said than done." He felt her tentative smile more than he saw it. "But, hey, I'm jacking cars and committing credit card fraud. Don't think Daddy would approve of that. . . ."

"Maybe there's hope for you yet." A puff of true tenderness toward her overcame him. He pushed it down in alarm. No room for that!

He felt her confusion. Her feelings for him were all bollixed up with the terrible things that were happening to them, the uncertainty of any future at all, the fear that they'd be caught. She broke contact, grabbed for a map in self-defense and tossed it to him.

"There's a little town up ahead." She was careful not to name it, tried not even to think it, if that was possible. "Maybe we can get something to eat."

When the contact broke, the voices intruded. Among the debris of commentary Jeff heard a voice he knew.

New Orleans. Are you ready along the Interstate? They've got to be going that way.

His gaze jerked to Holland. She had heard it too. "He knows," she whispered.

"Don't panic. Probably had to be. Doesn't mean we can't still get there."

"Yes it does, Jeff!" Panic rose in her. "He can pick us up any time he likes."

"Maybe ... maybe not." He was catching at straws, drawn by her fear to reassure her. "He said he can't hear us all the time. We blink in and out. He was frustrated at that." The realization was simply there in his mind. He didn't have to say it. She would feel it too.

"He can't hear us when we touch." She stated it simply.

"It's the only reason I can think that we would blink in and out for him."

They knew it was true. They reached for each other. Their hands were both clammy.

"Okay. We've got a chance."

"Even though he knows where we're going?"

"Yeah. Now that we know the key." *Courage, darlin' ol' Jeff ain't beat yet. It's only round five.*

She nodded. Her attempt to focus all her courage on what they had to do touched some place inside him that he didn't let be touched very often. A yellow sign flashed past with the silhouettes of a woman and two children running. "Watch out for people crossing the highway," a follow-up sign said.

"We must be on the border." He opened the map. It was folded wrong. They always were. He saw her questioning look. "Those signs. They mean that there's a border patrol station ahead." They both felt the danger at once.

"Let's get off the road."

"Can't, darlin'. There isn't any other road around here. That's why they put the checkpoint here." Sure enough, the signs saying "Prepare to Stop Ahead," seemed to rise up out of the road.

"Jeff." Holland was really afraid now.

"No choices here," he said. "But I bet the car hasn't been reported stolen yet."

"If it's as bad as we think, they'll be looking for people of our description. You can't just drive through—they'll be all over us. And in a chase, they'll win." Holland was almost babbling, and she slowed way down, as though to delay the inevitable. The road signs seemed to rush at them. Ahead, several other cars were also slowing, in spite of the late hour. The Interstate was the only thoroughfare around.

He held up the map and oriented himself. "Change places."

"What?"

"Crawl over me. I'm driving." She didn't question again. They scrambled over each other as they approached the glaring lights. "Okay, you're asleep. Let your hair hang over your face." He reached for the pack of cigarettes on the Toyota's dashboard, shook one out, and planted it in his mouth. Then he felt in the back seat for the baseball cap he'd seen there and jammed it on his head. The three-day growth of beard would help conceal his mouth, which was always pretty distinctive. He was willing to bet that the pictures distributed by the authorities had Holland with her hair up, looking impeccable, and his newspaper ID which showed him absolutely clean-cut and Ivy League. Thank God, the Toyota was an old clunker. Holland hunkered down in the passenger seat and shook her hair over her face.

An officer in a khaki uniform waved the cars ahead of them through. These guys usually looked bored as hell, but this guy was scrutinizing faces. Not good. Jeff rolled down his window. "Hey, dude. Got a recommendation for a place we can get some breakfast in Van Horn, or we gonna haveta go on in to Pecos?" He mumbled around the cigarette, thinned his lips and crinkled his eyes up as best he could.

"Nice little diner on the far side of town," the guy said, looking in the window.

Jeff followed his gaze over to the lump that was Holland, apparently asleep, her hair in disarray. "Looks like I might haveta wake her up. But hell, a man's gotta have some sustenance if he's gonna drive all night."

"Where you folks going?" The trooper's eyes still roved the car. The glare of the lights from the booth and the arch overhead cast his face in ugly shadow.

"Got a little place outside Haskell. Been gamblin' in Vegas."

"You win?"

Jeff grinned, making his eyes crinkle up even further. "Temporarily, you might say. Don't nobody ever win permanent, less you stop going."

The border patrol officer chuckled sympathetically and tapped on the roof of the car. "Y'all take care. You got a ways to go if you're heading to Haskell."

Jeff touched his hat brim with two fingers and drove slowly forward. As he passed the booth he saw the paper with both their photos tacked to the wall. It took all he had not to gun the Toyota. "Stay down," he whispered to Holland.

Holland waited for a mile or so before she sat up.

"Jeff? Your brain is going a mile a minute. You want to sort for me, here?" He was scaring her. He could feel that.

"Okay. Give me your hand." He reached for her. "Here's the deal. We've got to get off the Interstate. Just in case that guy back there jumps to the fact that it was us, I let him believe we were going up 20 toward Dallas. Find us a route that parallels the Interstate 10 as soon as you can. Just in case I'm wrong about the touching thing, don't tell me what it is."

She shook out the map with one hand. He could feel her fear. "Got one," she said. "It's a ways."

"Now, you just guide me. Just say, 'turn here,' when we get to a turnoff, okay?"

She nodded. "Is this about the picture of us you saw?"

He'd almost forgotten he couldn't hide from her, even to protect her. "Somebody mobilized the Border Patrol specifically. That means they know pretty much where we are."

"Unless we're just international criminals and they notified everybody." He didn't find that comforting and neither did she.

"Which brings me to the second point. The senator from Louisiana couldn't mobilize military and civilian authorities against us, across all those agencies. Big deal, he's head of the NIH funding committee. He doesn't just put in a call and then the Border Patrol and the LAPD and the Army for Chrissakes sit up and say, how high, sir?"

"So, what does that mean?"

"That there's somebody behind him. Somebody who *can* put in a call."

"Who would that be?" She was truly frightened. He wished he weren't.

"I don't know. I'm not sure I want to find out." For the first time, he really didn't care about the truth. He just wanted out of the trap.

Leland was home with Carol when the senator called.

"You don't call my house," he said bluntly as he picked up the extension in his office and slammed the door behind him.

"I call you wherever I damned please, Banks," Lendreaux growled. Whoever said a southern accent was soft? "This thing is getting way outta control."

"What do you mean?" It rankled Leland that he needed the senator in order to keep close to the pace of the phenomenon.

"I mean that there are thousands of them out there. More everyday." The senator's voice grew tighter. "It's a goddamned roar in my head."

Leland was silent for a moment. His flu epidemic was successful. In the young and the old it was just flu, a virulent batch—some deaths, lingering illness. In young adulthood, it gave those it infected a new strand of DNA. It infected germic chromosomes. He rolled his lips between his front teeth, biting down until he tasted blood. The change had not begun with him, but he had ensured that it would take hold—not only in this generation, but in those to come.

"Banks! You understand what I'm saying?" the voice in his ear shouted.

"I understand your solution isn't going to work, senator." Leland managed to keep his voice flat. "It's gone beyond that now. You can't take out an entire generation."

He could hear Lendreaux's rasping breath. "I won't have to. Suicide will get most of them. I just have to take out the ones who figure a way through it. Believe me, there won't be many. It's getting worse all the time."

Leland had a vision of mass suicides across the nation, a generation decimated. And what would happen when the teenagers of today turned twenty-eight and thirty? Would the fact that they had had the flu this month mean that they were able to attach junk DNA when they matured? He shut his eyes. Was this the end of the human race as he knew it—or the beginning, for everyone but those of his generation? He had to call Doug.

"What do we do?" The note of hysteria in Lendreaux's voice was unmistakable.

"Do? There's nothing anybody can do. If I were you, I'd try to stay calm. Wouldn't want you committing suicide, now would we?"

Chapter Twenty-one

Holland had never been to . . . Chicago. Jeff drove in through a hard rain shower, off the 10 and down across Canal Street into the Quarter. She wrapped her hand under his arm, her fingers playing across his bicep under the flannel shirt. Crazy. Like those times in adolescence when she could stay wet for hours thinking about her favorite heartthrob. Not a time she especially wanted back. Still, sitting next to Jeff, she felt more alive than she had in years. They'd spent the last day and a half on the back roads in a Ford pick-up, but Jeff had gotten lucky and jacked them a nice Lexus, an '01 Holland thought, as they hooked up with the Interstate again in Baton Rouge for the drive into the city. The back roads seemed slow but safe compared to the major cities. You might see a sheriff's deputy coming out of a diner, or a patrol car here and there, but there was no mass movement of troops that had scared her so in Las Vegas.

And she'd had no adverse reaction from not taking her immune suppressant medication. It was strange. She felt tired, frightened, but physically fine. Maybe this new gene string had some side effects. Maybe she was cured.

Now, as they crossed Canal street, two- and three-story buildings crowded in on the narrow streets, lace iron balconies hanging over tourists thronging on the sidewalks even this long past midnight. The tourists, mostly young and mostly drunk, wandered aimlessly from bar to bar, drinks held openly in their hands. The street itself breathed an elegant shabbiness that spoke of aristocratic decay. She caught a street sign. Royal Street. Still not an atmosphere Holland could respect. It was as though this part of the city wore hand-me-downs, once fine but now faded. She was more comfortable with the clean-lined hotels of the business district across Canal Street. Jeff loved it here though, and more strangely, wanted her to love it.

"Damn! I missed it," Jeff muttered, and honked at some woozy pedestrians who had apparently decided to re-group in the middle of the intersection. "Bourbon Street is barricaded until morning. I'll have to come up Iberville."

"There are so many people on the streets," Holland remarked.

"This isn't even prime tourist time," Jeff said, peering at street signs. "That's in February for Fat Tuesday and April for the Jazz Festival. Summer is muggy and sort of sluggish, the way only the bayou south can be."

"Thanks for driving," Holland said.

"No problem. I'm not wild about sleep right now anyway."

"It's the dreams, isn't it?" She didn't want to let her concern show, but there was no helping it, of course. She felt his resentment that she should doubt his invincibility, his disgust as he thought she had good reason to doubt, and his sudden realization that she might know exactly what he was dreaming.

"You're the expert," he muttered as he swung the car right onto a one-way street. "They're not exactly the same as they were before. But as you are probably well aware, knives figure prominently. Really macho knives. Definitely not Disney material. And I'd thank you not to whip out the analysis right now."

"Wouldn't dream of it." But it was no use. Her mind cranked out possible explanations. He was still feeling that there was a dark side to what they were, or could be, if they weren't careful. Anyone could become a monster. They could use the gift like the senator. She changed her tack. "But since I can't seem to help it, why don't you talk about something else?"

He looked around wildly for a moment before he said, almost at random, "N'awlins is the northern-most Caribbean island." His voice was a rumble in the dark. "It's surrounded by water: the Mississip, Lake Ponchatrain, the Gulf. It practically floats, the water table is so high."

She swallowed. "Guess it doesn't matter that we say things like that."

Jeff turned stricken eyes on her. "Shit!" He breathed. "But it doesn't matter. He already knows."

She felt his dogged determination to not be afraid. His aura had gone brown again, with red flashes. They were so tired. The few hours they managed of uneasy sleep in the passenger seat wasn't enough to keep their fragile psyches together.

"I hope you're right about the touching. Might keep him from knowing where we're staying." She said it to be reassuring. It wasn't.

During the last two days, the voices in their heads had begun to multiply in those brief stretches where they dared not touch each other. There was a base chorus of shrieking. Those were the ones who wouldn't make it. But the voices they could identify had been getting louder, stronger. Including the senator's. If they broke contact with each other, they could hear him yelling at his aides on Capitol Hill, talking with her father about the search for them. And there was something else, too. The senator was hiding something from her father. He talked to Brad about their "guys" and felt satisfied, but that was all they could decipher.

It's not as if they had any choice but to be here, and to try to find those voices that talked about music. Those voices held hope. Of course, Holland and Jeff had to break contact to hear them. They sounded the most mundane, and therefore the most sane. And they were here, somewhere in this city.

"Let's just find them quickly." Jeff took another right. Holland looked up toward the sign at the corner ahead—Bourbon Street. It was filled with five times the revelers of Royal. From what she could see Bourbon Street was truly tacky. No other word for it. Sex shops, frozen daiquiri bars, and different kinds of music blaring from every doorway. The car glided to the side of the street before they reached the corner. A black doorman in a green uniform with gold braid opened her door. Holland stepped out over a gutter clogged with soggy litter.

"Welcome to the Royal Sonesta," the doorman said.

He stepped off the plane and immediately, even in the jetway, he could feel the sticky air. Way worse than L.A. Shit, if he hadn't been promised quintuplets at the minimum, he would have told them they could stick this job where the sun don't shine. And no more mothers with kids. He'd told the dickhead that for sure. He pushed his way through people hugging and kissing right where people needed to get off the plane. Damn fools. Like stopping at the top of the escalator. Somebody ought to teach them a lesson. He grinned as he stuck an elbow into a girl's ribs. They were lucky he didn't have the tools of his trade with him.

That made him nervous, actually. Why the hell the hurry? He'd had to fly? Give him a few days, he could've driven down here with his whole bag of goodies. He slung his canvas gym bag over his shoulder and headed for the taxi stand. Get to the hotel and get the instructions on where to pick up the car and his equipment. He wasn't going to do a job like this with borrowed goods. He needed his own sweet baby to make music in a strange place. Good ol' FedEx.

In line for the taxi, he saw a guy three people ahead of him with a black leather jacket and a kind of a hooded look about the eyes. If it wasn't Jimmy Greaseball. They called him that on account of his hair. Surprised it didn't fall in his eyes when he was tryin' to sight.

Now, what was Jimmy Greaseball doing here? Two shooters coming in at the same time? Not luck. Looks like Mr. Dickhead Moneyman might be hedging his bets.

Jimmy bounced up and down on the balls of his feet as he waited for the cab, then cut in front of two ladies to slide into it. Jimmy never did have no class.

The Royal Sonesta was a cool marble oasis of quiet once the front doors had closed on Bourbon Street. Jeff took Holland's hand and led her toward the registration desk. The silence in her head was echoed in the sudden quiet around them. Custom carpets laid into the floor, huge flower arrangements, a darkened bar off to one side of the lobby, a subtly lighted central courtyard filled with rain forest—all gave it a feel of money. New money, maybe, but money nonetheless. Holland relaxed. She'd been afraid Jeff would want to stay in some rat hole he would claim exuded charm.

"We'd never get a room here except in July or at Christmas," Jeff muttered. "But it seems your style."

Holland wasn't sure. It was the style that matched her linen suits, but not the jeans she now wore. How long had it been since she'd worn jeans? Maybe forever. Still, she had to admit she'd been drawn more to the business district than the Quarter. Maybe he was right. That depressed her somehow. "Ask for two doubles," she whispered. She wasn't taking any more chances than she had to tonight.

Jeff made a sizeable cash deposit in crisp hundreds. Holland was touching him, so she heard the desk clerk speculate that they were having an affair and didn't want to leave a trace on a credit card. Fine. Let him think that.

Soon they were stumbling into a lovely room. It was all a bit of a blur. Holland wondered if she had ever been this tired in her life. At least she was sure that nothing would happen between her and Jeff tonight. The bellboy brought up the roller bags with the clothes they'd bought in Austin. What a job she'd had talking Jeff into stopping! But Holland was not going for more than forty-eight hours wearing one set of clothes, and she wasn't wild about sitting next to Jeff if he was going to do it, either. He had been afraid she was going to shop. What a stereotype! She'd been very directed. It was Jeff who tagged along and gently led her away from the slack sets and over into the jeans and shirts. He didn't have to explain that she stood out like a sore thumb the way she was dressed. And she'd forced him to buy three or four of everything for himself, so they'd have enough for a week.

They didn't unpack. Jeff turned on the light only in the bathroom. Breaking contact, Holland threw herself across one bed, face down. Water splashed in the bathroom.

"Shouldn't we try to find the guys we came to see?" she called. How would they do that? The voices buzzed in her head, but they were a blur. She wasn't even sure she could lift her head from the quilted spread.

Jeff's voice echoed from the bathroom. "I'm not picking out individual voices. Are you?"

"I can't even hear myself think," Holland murmured. Her eyes were closing of their own volition. But that only left her alone with the cascade of voices. She was too tired for anxiety, but the blurry voices shouted at her. She felt Jeff approach. One eye opened. He was standing over her, stripped to boxers in some dark color, maybe green. They were snug.

Oh, dear. He rubbed a towel over his face and around his neck, over his wet hair. His heavy shoulders, the biceps that worked the towel, his barrel chest, the taut belly, and then lower down, the thighs—all conspired to spark her body to awareness. A quiver of apprehension shot through her.

He stopped tousling his hair. The towel dropped to the carpet. His aura pulsed with indigo against the light from the bathroom behind him. She could feel his need rising. No images this time. His thoughts were focused steadily on her. Tenderness lurked behind the fact that he, too, had desire coursing through him.

"You must be tired," he said. His voice was a little hoarse. He cleared his throat.

She nodded. "Yes."

"Let's hit the streets tomorrow, then." His ambivalence cascaded over her. He wasn't suggesting they delay because he wanted sex. He was as afraid as she was about what would happen if they started down that path toward physical joining again. Ramping up of powers? Total loss of self? Not enticing.

"That's a good idea." She wasn't sure. She only knew she was exhausted, and she was trapped in a hotel room with a man she didn't dare let close, no matter how much she wanted it, and that she did want it. A lot. And if they didn't touch, the bad guy could hear them. Or maybe he heard them anyway. Not relaxing, actually. She didn't know anything right now.

Jeff's hair spiked out in all directions. She liked it that way. It suited his prickly character. "You think maybe we could hold each other, just to cut out the voices?" His aura was tentative.

"I'm afraid to try that right now."

He looked around, then dragged the spread off the opposite bed and bunched it on the floor. "How about I sleep right below you? You can drag your hand over my shoulder when things get too bad." He didn't mention what he was thinking about the senator being able to hear them if she didn't touch him.

"Good idea." Like hell it was. He laid himself on the bedding and pulled one edge over his body against the chill of the air conditioner. Holland closed her eyes and tried to sleep, but she could feel him there. It was torture having him so close, and yet having to endure the shout of voices in her head was worse. How would they get strength enough to find the ones they sought if they couldn't sleep and couldn't touch, and couldn't escape the racket?

Finally, she let one hand hang over the side of the bed until her fingertips just touched his shoulder. Hardly even a real touch. But it brought quiet. She felt him stiffen in response, heard the iron self-control he put behind his thoughts.

That's better. He wasn't sure he meant it.

Now let's see if we can avoid letting anything get out of hand here.

That provoked an image in his mind she didn't like much, but she had to smile. The very act of smiling made her shoulders sag into relaxation. Before she knew it, she was knowing nothing.

* * *

On the front seat of the car, he found the instructions, along with the precious FedEx package. Shit! He was supposed to do the same guy he'd missed in L.A. Only now she was included in the package. There were pictures in the envelope and the address of a hotel in the Quarter maybe six blocks from the cross street of the house they'd rented for him.

His car was a Caddy—man, one of the new ones. Not pale lemon yellow. That woulda been too good to be true. But, hey, you can't always get whatchu want, but sometimes, (do, do-do, do) you get whatchu need. He hummed the old Rolling Stones tune. The Caddy was black. Lower profile than pale yellow. And no one could say he wasn't stylin'. Black goes with everything. The narrow streets and the pedestrians didn't really allow him to test its power. But he practically got a hard-on just knowing all that engine was there. He followed the little computer map on the geo-tracker until he saw the address of the house. The garage door to the side of the wall opened automatically as he got close. That was cool.

The house was one of those strange Quarter situations, fancy iron gate in a wall that hid you from the street, courtyard with some plants in pots, then the house itself, walls straight up against the neighbors. It was nice inside, rugs and paintings and stuff, and private as shit, in spite of how close it was to the next-door houses. No windows shared either way. Good setup, all in all. He tossed the FedEx package on one of the sofas and went in search of the booze cabinet. There had to be one in a house like this, and it was probably stocked with the good stuff.

He didn't like the fact that the first two vics were the ones he had been trying to do in L.A. They had history, you know? But he'd been promised at least five, so if he had to get through these first, then he would. At least they were here in the Quarter. It was a little place, compared to L.A., all cramped-up like. Had to make it easier.

Goddamn! Grey Goose, Bombay Sapphire, Courvoisier— the lattice doors on the cabinet went from floor to ceiling, and held a pot of gold. He grabbed the bottle of Courvoisier. He didn't bother with the glasses on the center shelf. Stuff like this was best straight. And straight might just as well be direct from the bottle.

He thought some about Jimmy Greaseball, as he threw himself on one of the couches and upended the bottle. Maybe the Payer-Man had promised Jimmy the same five. Or maybe Jimmy was backup in case he shot blanks. Well, Jimmy wasn't going to get his five, or the hundred K that came with each one. He looked around and took another slug of brandy. He kind of liked living like this. You could prob'ly live just like this on what he was makin' on these jobs. That was sounding pretty damn good.

Chapter Twenty-two

"Housekeeping."

Holland cracked open her eyes. Light filled the room. Jeff moaned lightly in his sleep. She glanced down and saw him shaking his head convulsively. Unmistakable tears were leaking from the sides of his eyes. She got an impression of evil on the rampage, of Jeff doing horrible things he would be sorry for later and not caring. A knife glinted somewhere. Holland jerked her fingers up, away from his shoulder. The sound of voices shushed over her.

"Housekeeping." This time the call was followed by the noise of a key in the lock.

Jeff started awake, gasping, and struggled up on one elbow, groggy.

"Not yet," Holland called, shaken, just as the door hit the little U of metal that supplemented the lock.

"Sorry," the maid called. The door slapped back.

"Forgot to put out the 'do not disturb' sign," Jeff muttered. He sat up and ran a hand through his thick hair. He must have felt the tears leaking down his cheeks because shame washed over him and he rubbed his hands over his face.

"Dreams getting worse?" It wasn't really a question. They both knew it.

"Yeah." He glanced over to her. "You're not having dreams?"

"Mine are pretty much gone, as long as we touch. At least the evil part." She wondered about that for a minute. Why were her dreams of being evil and not human gone?

He nodded. "If yours are gone, how come mine are getting worse?"

"Dreams are normal." She tried not to sound like a shrink.

"Sure." He didn't believe her.

"Hey, we're under a little stress, don't you think?"

"Then, why aren't you still trying to choke yourself?" He attacked because he was frightened. She knew that.

She shrugged. "Maybe it was a relief to find that there really *was* something different about me. I wasn't imagining it. I wasn't alien, and I wasn't evil. Just had a little extra DNA."

He collapsed back onto the floor. "Yeah. Well, maybe the evil is still to come. Maybe we'll turn into that senator, corrupted by the possibilities."

She managed a chuckle. "Worst I saw you do was figure out that we could cheat at cards. And you didn't even follow through. Not exactly prime time as far as evil goes."

His eyes came to rest on hers. "You haven't been having my dreams." There was no making light of the look in his eyes. She thought about saying that maybe the guys they were going to see could tell them how to control what they had, that probably what he was experiencing was the fear and the anger at being out of control, but she didn't. Those seemed like easy answers that didn't match the magnitude of the situation.

He got up without a word and went to the bathroom. The shower hissed on.

Holland rolled over and clasped her hands behind her head. They hadn't pulled the draperies shut last night. The walls were palest gold. The spread she lay on had a jungle pattern of deep green leaves and some golden-colored flower like hibiscus. The furniture was dark and delicate. French reproductions, she thought, and the mirror had an ornate gold frame that must have cost a fortune if it were wood, not a plaster knockoff. The painting in the corner was ornate, with a Mardi Gras theme that managed to tie the tropics and the French flavor together in shades of green and gold with purple accents. Mardi Gras colors.

When Jeff emerged from the shower, he had rinsed more than the sweat from his body. He had himself back in hand. "Holy shit, it's ten o'clock," he said, glancing at the alarm.

Holland stretched. "We must have needed the sleep."

"Time to find our quarry."

Now that she thought about it, she was hearing voices more clearly again. She could pick out individual ones. She tried to sort through until she heard the ones she wanted. She could feel Jeff do the same. One by one, she pushed aside the ones that weren't right. There!

Keep it comin', bro. Yeah, roll yo' guitar in there.

Flyin'. I'm flyin'.

Good as that sweet lil' sugar drop I had las' night. Coulda licked her 'til she melted.

Holland was staring at Jeff. His green eyes stared back at her. He heard them, too.

Acme for lunch? I'm gonna puke if I smell any more sweet.

282

Damn straight, man. I got needs, and oysters make you strong.

That woman gonna be the death a you.

I'm jes' sicka tourists is all. When we off?

It was like they were talking to each other.

"They *are* talking to each other," Jeff said slowly, "but in their minds."

"So, they've got control of it."

"Yeah."

Holland leapt from the bed. "My turn in the shower. How are we going to find them?"

"We know they'll be at the Acme Oyster House. They're playing music somewhere. Somewhere that serves something sweet to tourists."

"Where could that be?" Holland called over the shower as she stripped off her clothes.

"About a hundred places—restaurants serving bread pudding for brunch or pecan pie, or some candy store making pralines and they're playing right outside . . ."

Holland stepped into the shower and pulled the bubbled glass doors shut. The water made her tingle. She turned up the heat even more. Heaven. Who knew showers could be orgasmic? She saw Jeff's shadow push her roller bag in, set it on the toilet and unzip it. She was very aware of his mostly nude body just beyond the glass. As a matter of fact, some glass and some steam were the only things separating his mostly nude body from her entirely nude body. And she was feeling better than she had last night.

"Don't think those thoughts, darlin'," he murmured. "We've got miles to go and promises to keep this morning."

"I'm not thinking any thoughts," she said, useless as the lie was. She soaped herself vigorously—in penance or in rebellion, she was not sure which.

"Of course not." She could hear the grin in his voice. She opened her eyes in spite of the soap and saw his aura go magenta. "Neither am I."

But he was and he didn't care if she knew it. Cracks of indigo opened in the magenta. She poured shampoo into her hand from the little plastic bottle and rubbed it through her hair with her nails grating on her scalp, just to take her mind off other things. "I'm just hungry, is all."

His retreating laugh was followed by a rush of cooler air as he left the bathroom door open on his way out. "I could take care of that."

"No, you won't," she called after him. Curse him for being quick.

"What—I can't show you what we eat for breakfast down here?"

"Yes, you can—assuming that it's food."

"Done and done. Your wish, etc." His giggle trailed off. It was a good laugh: genuine, un-self-conscious. At least it was, better than leaking tears. She rather liked it. No one had laughed at her at the hospital. Of course, had she joked? The only laughs she could seem to remember at all were her father's, either condescending or derogatory, and those of her fellow students, always meant to cut like shards of glass. She had never really considered it before.

She got out of the shower. The return to the ritual of daily ablutions made her remember her allergy suppressants. She hadn't taken one in more than three days. It was too late for anxiety. She'd always thought that if she didn't take those pills, the level of suppressant in her blood would drop, her immune system would start fighting anything and everything she ate and drank, and she'd be back in some intensive-care ward pronto.

But the suppressant level must have dropped. And nothing had happened.

She stared at herself in the steamy mirror, her reflection dimmed by fog. She'd eaten from truck stops and sipped Cokes from fast food places. She'd ridden in cars with who knows what kind of germs crawling all over them. By now she must have pretty much no suppressants in her system at all.

Had she gotten over the allergies that had once almost taken her life? How long had she not needed the pills she took every day, or the monthly visits to Dr. Grayson to draw blood? This was good news. She was freed from the tyranny of drugs whose side effects included heart disease and liver damage. But there was something disturbing about that freedom, too.

"Dr. Banks, I've got you booked on a flight, but you'll have to hurry." Leland's secretary handed him his itinerary. He glanced up at her, then went on packing his briefcase. She was the picture of efficiency as well as style, right down to the glasses perched precariously on her nose, and her fashionable spike-heeled boots.

"Uh, shall I expect you back for the donor board meeting Wednesday? Or would you like to reschedule?" She must be able to see he wasn't in the mood for questioning.

"I have no idea. We can cancel later," he said tartly. The cell phone at his belt buzzed. He nodded his dismissal, and tapped his tiny earphone to receive the call.

"Banks?"

"Yes, Doug. It's me, since that's who you called."

"Banks, this thing is getting *way* out of hand. Have you looked at the suicide rate?"

"No," he said, interested. "Is it up?"

"Is it up?" Doug barked. "It's off the charts. It's everywhere. How in God's name did this become so widespread? We're never going to stop it! I thought we might have to deal with a few hundred people. Do you realize what we're talking here?"

Leland sighed. It wouldn't do to let Doug see his relief. All he had to do was keep the satisfaction out of his voice. "It does look like the infection is spreading more rapidly than I had supposed."

Doug was silent for a moment. "You're not an idiot, Banks. That leaves another possibility."

Leland thought it time to change the subject. "The whole phenomenon is in the process of extinguishing itself. We just have to ride out the course of the disease, that's all."

"The ride is rougher than you promised, Banks. There better not be any more surprises." Doug clicked off.

Okay, Doug was unhappy. That was fine. Leland wanted to stave off the ultimate realization as long as possible—until Doug was in too deep to disavow it, until Doug had to be part of the solution and not part of the problem.

They sat in the steaming heat under the great, green-and-white striped tents of Café du Monde as the waitress poured, of all things, hot coffee. Their hands touched across the table. A sign on the front of the restaurant just off Jackson Square said it never closed.

"You're kidding," Holland said bluntly.

"Nope. Not kidding. Taste before you reject it. Didn't your mother ever tell you that?"

Holland's mother had told her that a thousand times. As a consequence, Jeff knew that. Holland knew Jeff's mother had never encouraged him to try new things. That was why he had tried everything when he was young. All this burden of knowledge from their mutual thoughts hung on Holland's sip of coffee. How could she bear it? How could she stand how well she was likely to know Jeff, and worse, how well he was likely to know her? There could be no cool, professional mask with him. He knew all her steaming chaos. And she knew his. She wasn't even sure which was which sometimes and that was scariest of all. She raised the plain, thick gray-white mug. It smelled of cinnamon. She sipped. Smooth. Actually, really good.

"It's the chicory. Best coffee in the world." Jeff slouched back in his rickety green metal chair, the ornately curved kind they had in ice-cream parlors or back yards. His fingers barely touched hers. He had finally shed his plaid flannel in the muggy heat for a tank top she'd bought him in San Antonio. It was cooler of course, but it left his arms bare, the shoulders, the swell of biceps. That could be bad.

"They usually have music here in the morning. Really good jazz or blues sometimes."

"They're on lunch break," the waitress said as she set down a pile of plump golden dough smothered in powdered sugar. "For them that means about eleven to two." She shook her head, disgusted. "Musicians . . ." She apparently felt the accusation was self-explanatory.

Jeff smiled as the waitress left, still shaking her head. "Beignets," he said, sweeping his hand over the little treats as though he were presenting a crown roast on a silver platter.

"How are you supposed to eat them?" Holland asked. She looked at them from several angles.

Jeff pulled about two dozen paper napkins from the dispenser. "With your fingers. And spread all available clothing surfaces with these."

He took no precautions, but picked up the top one, heaps of sugar and all, and went at it.

Holland smoothed a paper napkin over her lap. Looking down at the vibrant blue and green print of the full skirt on the sundress she'd bought, she couldn't think what had come over her. Must be all the country music in the air in Texas. Sleeveless, with straps that crossed over her back, feminine full skirt that hit her just at the knee, narrow waist with a turquoise belt—this dress made her feel exposed in ways she couldn't quite name. But free, too.

She gingerly plucked a beignet from its fellows and shook it gently. Powdered sugar floated into the air. One bite and she was hooked. Doughnuts, but lighter; filled with air. And the cinnamon-chicory coffee was perfect to wash them down. She felt Jeff's grin, and looked up. His face, newly shaved this morning, was dusted with a clown smile of powdered sugar. She couldn't help but laugh, then realized what he must be grinning about. She snatched up a napkin and rubbed at her face, not caring if she smeared her makeup. The table, her dress, and all of Jeff were unevenly dusted with powdered sugar, in spite of the napkins.

"Never, never try to have an illicit assignation at Café du Monde. Everyone will know just where you've been." He chuckled. He looked around for their waitress, but his gaze was caught by an abandoned newspaper on the table next to them. He snatched it up, his eyes riveted.

"What is it?"

He tossed the paper into the center of the table, raising a flurry of powdered sugar.

Suicide Epidemic! the headline screamed. She picked the paper up, scanning the text. There had been hundreds of suicides in almost every city across the nation in the last two days. Los Angeles was up to almost a thousand. Morgues were full. Television stations were broadcasting pleas to get psychiatric help. Psychiatrists were in short supply. Hospitals were full up with flu cases and the infections. People were complaining of noise, that they couldn't think. Some just screamed. Drug companies were making free tranquilizers available. The AMA was protesting that only doctors could prescribe medication, but the Center for Disease Control had recommended dispensing the drugs at local pharmacies, beginning today. The article ended with an interview with a guy from the Center who said that readers should proceed to their nearest pharmacy if they were experiencing feelings of despair.

Holland raised her gaze to Jeff. *This is awful!*

Jeff's eyes were stricken, his aura a painful yellow-orange. He jerked his gaze away. Outside the café in the heat, they could hear someone shouting. Suddenly it seemed ominous. They couldn't hear what he was saying, but two policemen loped by, nightsticks drawn. *Oh, God!* Jeff was thinking. *It's happening to everybody.*

Chapter Twenty-three

They strode through the plaza in front of St. Louis Cathedral, aware of the chaos beginning around them. *What are we going to do?* Holland thought.

Jeff put his arm around her as a sobbing woman dragged a little girl out of the kite shop past the tarot card readers and the caricaturist. "It's okay, Mommy. I didn't want the kite," the little girl was saying in a parody of a mother comforting a child. A man ran past, yelling.

I don't know. I don't know how to help them. She could feel his panic. Jeff drew a breath. "So, we do what we came to do. We find the guys who seem healthy and we see how they do it. What else can we do?"

She shook her head. She didn't know any more than he did.

Resigned, she listened. Jeff glanced around, and she could feel him focus, too. They were listening for echoes of the thoughts they'd heard earlier. At first they searched for thoughts of music. But there were no musical themes in the voices now. She sorted as best she could. She could feel Jeff doing the same. There they were! The clearest of them was talking shop. Literally. He was checking orders of some kind. There were only about a million tiny shops in the Quarter, of course.

They passed the balcony of the house where Faulkner and Ella Sue had revealed the world to Jeff. They poked into every store they could, from the one that sold Cajun and Creole cooking supplies, to a store that sold hand-made masks made out of everything from leather to rhinestones to feathers. Up St. Louis Street and down Dumaine—it seemed a hopeless search.

As they passed a worn little corner grocery, Holland felt Jeff stiffen. A poster, stapled on top of three or four layers of tattered older posters, made him stop in his tracks.

"Come on," he growled, taking her hand and dragging her forward.

"What? What is it?" She craned her neck behind her. REVIVAL TONIGHT! the orange-and-red poster screamed. "Reverend Donald McQueen preaches the Word in Metarie."

His father was in a suburb not twenty-five miles from the Quarter! Holland didn't say a word. Jeff dragged her toward the nearest shop, not caring what it was, his anger erasing any other thought.

Holland looked around. The shop sold voodoo paraphernalia. Their guys couldn't be in here. But as they crossed the threshold, she and Jeff both felt something click into place inside their heads. A back door slammed somewhere behind the counter.

Neither Holland nor Jeff had any eyes for the feathered dolls, the books, the gris-gris pouches hanging in strings from wrought-iron displays, the small offerings of food and cigarettes in front of manikins dressed in flowing robes. All their senses snapped to the back of the store.

Oh, ho, pretties. So you here at last.

Shit, Jeff thought.

My God, it's one of them, Holland echoed.

A very tall, thin black man pushed through the beaded curtain, wearing an African dashiki over matching pants. They were a kind of royal blue shot with black in a pattern than looked like wax transfer. The man's cheekbones poked out under black eyes you could lose yourself in. He had creamy coffee skin and a wide mouth. His eyes slanted until he looked almost Asian. His face was distinctive to the point of being disconcerting, even evil-looking, or maybe he was handsome; Holland couldn't decide. His aura was very defined and glowed out around his whole body. Right now it was blue and mellow. It was hard to tell how old he was, but he couldn't have been more than young middle age, because that was when the anomaly asserted itself.

"You right," he said. "I'm thirty-two. That's in this life, of course." He didn't believe the mumbo-jumbo reincarnation part. They could tell that.

He laughed. It was the most infectious laugh Holland had ever heard except for Jeff's—natural, ingenuous, joyous. His aura shot with multicolored cloud shapes that Holland had never seen. "You right about that, too. Oh, y'all got it, right and tight. You two got it in spades."

Jeff reached for Holland's hands instinctively. As silence fell, the man's eyes widened.

"Shit, yeah. You got it. Ain't never felt that before." His face went serious. His aura darkened. "Why you come here?"

"Looking, uh, looking for answers." Jeff was not exactly in investigative reporter mode. He sounded tentative, both in voice and thought.

"Yeah, well, there ain't no answers, 'cept ones y'all don't want to hear." He looked them over. "But maybe you got something I want to hear. You that shrink, ain't you, honey?"

Holland nodded.

"I been hearin' you. Yo daddy a science dude?"

Because she thought she could do no more than nod, Holland made a supreme effort, cleared her throat and croaked, "Yes."

The spectral black man nodded. His eyes were opaque. Holland let go of Jeff's hand. He was thinking he could use them.

Behind them, the shop door tinkled. The black guy glanced up. Neither Holland nor Jeff took their eyes off of him. "Shaleen," he called. "Customers." Then he swept around the counter. "Come on. Let's go someplace quiet."

He walked past the pasty man in shorts and sandals worn with white socks, and past the man's lumbering wife whose flowered dress seemed to take up the whole shop, and was out the door almost before Holland and Jeff could gather their wits enough to follow.

The man's legs were long, and he was striding north on Dumaine so fast—even in the midday heat—that Jeff and Holland had to trot periodically to keep up with him. The sky looked as if it were about to arrange an afternoon downpour. The air was too thick with moisture even to breathe. They met several people who seemed distracted and distraught, hearing voices.

Sweat soon rolled between Holland's shoulder blades, soaking through her sundress. West on Dauphine, north on St. Louis—where the hell was this guy taking them?

She and Jeff were both trying to keep their thoughts at bay, impossible as that was, but fear gnawed at their minds, exacerbated by each wild-eyed sufferer they passed. At Rampart Street their guide suddenly turned on them. "They two quiet places up here. You got Cemetery Number One, and you got the Church."

Holland looked at the sky. "I'll take the church. At least we won't get rained on."

But it did rain on them. They dashed down Rampart and up Conti as the drops turned from splatters to downpour. As they pushed into the quiet vestibule of a plain little church with a white steeple, Holland was gasping and so was Jeff. Their guide seemed barely winded. Holland was soaked. Her sundress clung to her calves. She could feel Jeff's discomfort behind her. Churches held bad memories for him. It took a moment for her eyes to adjust to the dim interior. The usual arched stained-glass windows lined the nave. Ubiquitous pictures and marble figures of the Madonna proclaimed its denomination Catholic. White statues of saints stood solemnly in their niches above. The pews were polished but unadorned wood. Beyond, down the red-carpeted aisle near the altar, hundreds of flames danced from candles lit in prayer. Lots of parishioners needed either hope or guidance right now.

"This here is a plain-people's church," the black man said. His aura had gone a darker, more serious blue. "Not yo big white people's cathedral down by the river. People find help where they find it." He pointed up to the statue above him as Holland came to stand beside him. The statue was labeled "St. Expedite," with quotation marks around it.

"I've never heard of *that* saint," she said tentatively, not wanting to offend him.

" 'Course you ain't. When all the boxes came, with all the statues in them, last century or so ago, didn't none of them have labels. People could mostly tell who they were, though."

Jeff peered up at the saint, solemn as all the others. "What's he holding?"

"Don't nobody know. He was extra. But his shipping box had 'expedite' painted all over it, so they called him St. Expedite. People pray to him if they need help real quick."

"The power of superstition," Jeff said. The bitter thoughts behind his words were probably clear to both Holland and their guide.

"Yeah," the black man said. "People transform their institutions as much as their institutions transform them. Catholic in Louisiana is as much voodoo from the old country as anything Rome would recognize."

Holland looked up in surprise. Their guide had changed his diction very suddenly. No matter what he wanted others to think, there was no way he'd been educated in the projects. And he probably felt he was as much an impostor as she did. It was his effort to blend in. He was right, of course, about people transforming institutions as they needed. Look at Jeff transforming his uncle's medallion into a guiding talisman.

"You mean, they're going to cut off a chicken head at the next communion?" Jeff's voice was still tense with derision, and he didn't agree about the medal.

Their guide turned and walked down a side aisle. "I mean belief is a strong thing." He ducked into a tiny side chapel and sat, lounging, on one of two pews, bathed in the rich, multicolored light of a single gothic arch of stained glass.

"You don't believe that voodoo stuff you push." It was the ultimate accusation for Jeff. "And you aren't the street tough you pretend."

Holland turned apologetically to the black man, wondering how she could erase Jeff's derision. She felt most clearly that he did believe—if not in voodoo, in something. She felt Jeff's surprise echo her own.

"What?" the black man asked. They could tell his shock was only for effect. "You don't believe the spirit of the world can live through symbols?"

"You better believe somethin'," the black guy said. His accent was back. " 'Cause we are comin' to a time when belief the only thing gonna keep us from being the mos' evil we can be, 'steada the mos' good."

Holland shuddered, remembering her dreams, and Jeff's. Their guide motioned them to the other pew.

Holland and Jeff sat, hips touching, and watched the guy's eyes go wide again. "There are things we want to know," Jeff began, trying to retrieve his investigative reporter mode in spite of the fear he felt.

"And you think I know the answers. Fair enough. They things I wanna know, too." The man nodded graciously. "You first."

Jeff cleared his throat. "We hear several voices here in the city. These voices are about the sanest of any right now. One of them is yours. We want to know how you . . . how you get that peace of mind."

"Don't know how to answer, since y'all don't take to the 'belief changes all of us' thing."

Holland saw his aura get little rose-colored barbs around the edges. He was baiting them. "Okay, fair enough." She used his words back at him. "Let's start at the beginning. How long have you heard the voices?"

"Months."

A straight answer. "So you know that they get clearer, and that there are lots more now."

He nodded. Holland looked at Jeff.

"So, we thought you found a way to regulate the voices—cut them out, maybe stopped the progress of the anomaly." Jeff was thinking aloud. "The whole thing doesn't seem to bother you much."

"Don't seem to bother you two much either," he countered.

"Not all the time. We get peace when we touch," Holland almost whispered.

A smile suffused the man's face, banishing any impression of evil. "Oh, that's good, that is." He looked at Jeff sharply. "You grabbed her hand when you first saw me, yeah?"

"Yeah."

He nodded thoughtfully. "Yo power ramped up big time. An' you touchin' her now. Maybe you joinin'."

He had felt something similar to what they felt. "What?" Holland encouraged. "Joining?"

"Evabody who got this thing got to find a way to deal, you know?" He was being straight now, as straight as he knew how to be. His aura was pure, dark blue. "But they find different ways. I heard people say they get quiet when they run—like joggin', you know? Or yoga, or playin' video games. That one gets me." He chuckled. "Me and my friends, we get the quiet with music. Best with the blues. I can sometimes get it prayin', but the others—they cain't. It's just with the music for them."

Holland was thoughtful. The senator had said he ran to get the quiet. "So . . . it's a kind of focus?" she said slowly.

"Something that transforms you or takes you out of yourself," Jeff agreed.

"Maybe it has something to do with endorphins. Chemicals released in your brain." Leave it to Holland to think of the pseudo-scientific explanation.

"I ain't never heard that anyone got the quiet by touching. Think I might like that," the black guy said.

"Don't get any ideas," Holland admonished. And yet . . . that was one experiment it wouldn't hurt to try. She leaned forward.

Don't do it, Holland. Jeff's protest accompanied a flash of alarm.

I ain't gonna take yo woman, white man. He reached forward, eager for the experiment.

Holland broke contact with Jeff and let the crash of all the voices hit her like a blow. Then her finger touched the long bony digit of the black man. She locked her eyes to his, expectant. Nothing. The voices continued to clamor around her. The man raised his brows. Holland shook her head. "Sorry."

"Me, too," he said, sitting up. "Looks like you two got what they call 'chemistry'." Again his chuckle transformed him. "And I'm back to playin' the blues."

"Is that when you get what you call 'joinin'?" Holland asked.

"Yeah. When the music is jest right between us, then the energy flows. You get, uh, close to the other folks."

That was an understatement. Holland leaned back into Jeff where he had turned in the pew and laid his arm along its back. Soothing quiet reigned again. She felt him relax. He wanted touching to be theirs alone, and yet she could feel his flicker of fear at what that meant. He was thinking about Felipe's assumption that she was his woman. He didn't know how to feel about that. Neither did she.

"So," Jeff said aloud. "When you play your instrument, and you get this 'joining,' can you hear regular people?"

"Yeah," their guide breathed. "I wondered if you'd get to that. Not everybody can. Only certain ones—the ones that got more juice, I call it. My partners, they cain't."

Jeff leaned forward in the pew. "But if you only get the quiet when you're playing . . . I mean, if we don't touch for a few hours we get pretty edgy. You seem . . ."

"Calm," Holland supplied.

"Yeah, how is that?" Jeff asked. She could feel his flicker of distrust.

"Oh, they somethin' you don't know yet, boy?" The black man enjoyed the moment. Holland could feel Jeff's anger.

"We don't know lots of things," Holland said to cover for him. "Tell us."

The black man sat forward, suddenly intense, his aura swirls of blue and red until he matched the rich corona around Christ's head in the glowing window behind him. "I *am* gonna tell you. I'm gonna show y'all how to do it. And you know why? Do you?"

Jeff went wary behind her. Holland was frightened of this strange man's intensity, but she shook her head. *Go on,* she thought. *Tell us why.*

"Because we are the different ones, fools!" he practically hissed. "All we got now is each other. All these voices in yo heads, they either gonna get it or they gonna die. They dyin' right and left. You know that. But they more all the time, too. The world is changing and don't nobody know how it's gonna end."

The black guy smiled and sat up. "Now, it's my turn. What's with us? What's this about? You know. I got a glimpse of it at the store." He looked from one to the other. "Yo Daddy figured it out?" he asked Holland when neither spoke.

"Yes." She breathed. She could do this. "We have a genetic propensity to attach specific junk DNA to the human genomic string. It manifests in early adulthood." She had regressed to the language of her comfort, jargon and all. Still, the black man nodded thoughtfully.

"Had to be something like that." He sat back and slapped his knees. The accent thickened again. "So, we X-Men."

"Not exactly," Jeff corrected. "The X-Men had lots of different mutations, with different results—one could raise storms, one was magnetic. As far as I can figure, we all pretty much got the same mutation. Maybe with little variations, maybe just at different points along the same line. What we've got is the ability to read thoughts, see auras—basically a connection to others."

"Well, shee-it. That's a doozy of a mutation, ain't it?"

Both Holland and Jeff nodded.

The guy sighed, then glanced at the very expensive watch on his wrist. "Woo! I am one late mo-fo."

"Lunch at the Acme Oyster House," Jeff said.

The guy looked surprised.

"Heard you making arrangements this morning."

"Yeah. No more secrets, man. Ain't that just the bitch of it all?" He stood and put out his hand. "Felipe Laveau."

Jeff shook his hand. "Jeff McQueen."

Felipe turned toward Holland. "Doctor?"

"Holland Banks." She extended her hand. Instead of shaking it, he bent and raised her fingers to his lips. Because of his name she guessed, "You have voodoo running in your blood?"

"Ahh, great-gramma and her mama before her—both Marie Laveau. The first Marie, she buried in Cemetery Number One out behind here. Misunderstood, both of 'em, but easy in their souls about using they power."

Jeff spoke up, his tone tight; "What power was that? Sticking pins in people?"

"They used the combination of their knowledge of the white community's political intrigue and their spiritual leadership in the black community to influence the course of their times." Felipe's accent disappeared entirely. "I always admired that."

There was a pause. "I'd like to see their graves," Holland said, half to prevent Jeff from insulting Felipe's ancestors. She knew why Jeff did it—because he thought his father

298

was just as much of a crack-pot as he believed Marie Laveau was, and his shame was spilling all over Felipe.

"No time today." Felipe lifted his head as if listening. "Rain's over. Better get down to the Acme."

Chapter Twenty-four

"You missed the four o'clock call, Doug." Leland drove his new Infiniti down the payline lane on the 405. He'd be back in West L.A. in half an hour. He glanced over at the poor schmucks sitting in the regular lanes lurching ahead at five miles an hour. Thank God you could pay for speed in this town.

"You're not having to listen to the FBI accusing Defense of knowing more about these sniper shootings than we're saying. Things were rough today, and you're out there in La La Land . . ."

Leland stopped the voice in his ear short. "I don't care about the FBI, unless they can find my daughter. You understand a father's love, Doug. You have two kids of your own. We both know she's in New Orleans. She can't be that difficult to find. And I want Jeff McQueen, too—both of them alive and well."

"We're mobilizing our forces now. We'll use the safe-haven laboratory we prepared for the colony. When we do find them, let's get them someplace secure."

"Excellent. Arrange it, Doug. I'll meet you in Virginia."

Now this was getting somewhere. Leland punched the connection closed.

*   *   *

The Acme was two blocks over to Iberville and roughly four blocks down to just past Bourbon. The narrow street in front of the restaurant was torn up, almost entirely blocked by a truck carrying equipment and orange traffic cones. Holland had to scramble around heaps of wet dirt and blocks of asphalt to join the line waiting for a table at the Acme. Jeff held her hand in an almost courtly fashion as he helped her through the mess. It was an unpretentious place: red-checked tablecloths, plastic baskets for the fried oysters and clams, neon beer signs for decor. The combination of frying oil, the wafting odor of onions and sizzling butter, and the rich scent of simmering red beans and clam chowder smelled great. To the right of the line was an old-fashioned bar set with cracked black-and-white tile. People sat at high stools in front of a huge mirror. Next to the mirror was a board that showed the records for dozens of oysters eaten at a sitting, and the dates and survivors of each ordeal. Holland thought she saw the number thirty-six. Several young black men wearing red aprons and gloves shucked raw oysters right onto the bar as fast as the diners could down them with Tabasco, horseradish, or tomato sauce. The half-shells skittered across the tile, spilling oyster juice as they went. It was a very untidy affair.

Felipe shoved through the tourists in the line for tables and waved at two black guys at the end of the bar who raised their arms in salute.

They white? one was thinking, apparently appalled. He'd just realized that Jeff and Holland were the ones he had been hearing in his mind.

You heard 'em talkin'. They sound black to you?

The two had saved a seat for Felipe, and, as though fate intervened, the two truck-driver–looking guys next to that seat got up and left their tip on the bar. *Whoa, they powerful mo-fos!*

Yep. They sho are. They joinin'. "Sit down," Felipe gestured politely. "Meet Lemon and Rusty. This here's Jeff and Dr. Banks."

Holland slid onto a stool gingerly after one of the shuck-ers ran a rag over it. "Holland. Call me Holland," she mur-mured. She didn't touch her knee to Jeff's. She wanted to be able to hear them. So did he.

"A dozen and a Dixie for the lady," Jeff said to the guy behind the bar. "Same for me."

"Me, too, Jack," Felipe called.

"Oooh, he been here before," the one called Rusty said in mock respect. Dreadlocks about four or five inches long sprouted over his head. He oozed distrust; his aura was a suspicious red-orange.

"Lived here in the late eighties for a while," Jeff ex-plained.

"Only way to eat your oysters," Lemon declared. He was a small man, and looked almost comical next to the tall and gangly Felipe. *Calm down, Rusty. Jess' cause they white . . .*

"You forgetting 'em po'boys at Johnny's?" Jeff asked as he cracked the top from a long-necked beer the bar guy slid to him. He passed it to Holland, who looked around only briefly for a glass.

"Oooh. He really *been* here before." Rusty examined Jeff closely. The red-orange faded, but only a little.

"Yeah, but they *fried* oysters at Johnny's. A man needs raw oysters, if y'all know what I mean." So, it was Lemon who'd been concerned with his ability to perform.

"I ain't," he protested. "I perform just fine." Then he grinned. "I jes' got a lotta performin' to do." Flashes of his favorite past performances hung in his mind.

Holland smiled in spite of herself. These people seemed normal, except they could hear her think.

Once she got over the initial horror of having raw oysters shucked at her while she drank beer from a bottle, she got into the whole thing. The guys ordered her a white clam chowder that she shared with Jeff. It was too rich for her to finish alone. And the black guys pooh-poohed her when she inquired about whether they served salads at the bar.

"Y'all can *not* order a salad at the Acme—even if y'all *are* a girl." Rusty declared. "It ain't natural." He upended a shell and let the oyster slide down his throat. "Say, you guys hear that guy talkin' Chinese or somethin'?"

Jeff took a swig of his Dixie. Holland could feel him listening. She listened too.

Jeff nodded. "I got it," he said.

She closed her eyes and tried to shut out the noise of the restaurant around her, to just let in the noise of the voices. Sorting. She had to sort. She threaded her way through the screamers. She was actually getting used to that, if you could believe it. She pushed away anything that sounded familiar. And there it was. *Ching ni gai wa y bei p 'jio.*

Holland nodded, a smile growing that almost brought tears to her eyes. "I heard," she whispered. "I heard somebody speaking Chinese." It was such a signal of the universality of their plight. They were so clearly not alone.

"He just asked for a beer," Jeff said.

"Hey, man, you speak fuckin' *Chinese?*" Rusty blurted.

Jeff shrugged. "Mandarin. Easier than Cantonese. I know about enough to order beer."

"What more y'all need?" Lemon laughed. "Well . . ."

They all heard what he was thinking. Holland blushed.

"Nope!" Jeff interrupted the images. "Don't know how to order that."

"Sorry, uh, miss." Lemon shrugged in apology.

"I'm a shrink, guys. I've heard it all." She just wished she hadn't blushed.

She ate two dozen oysters and drank three beers, but inside she was waiting, waiting for what these strange examples of her new kind could show her. She realized if she could control her reaction to the voices in her head, she might be able to break the bond that held her so inexorably to Jeff. Did she want that?

There was no pressing the men. When Jeff tried to raise the subject of sharing knowledge about their condition, everybody just clammed up. Rusty's thoughts raised warning signals every time she thought Felipe might be about to speak.

"Whoa, we gotta get back to the café," Rusty said abruptly. "We on this afternoon."

They all got up, tossing bills on the tiled bar.

"Wait," Holland asked. "We need your help. And maybe . . . we can help you in return."

Jeff put a hand on her arm. He didn't think her entreaties would do any good. All three black men glanced up, then shared glances and raised eyebrows. They had felt Jeff and Holland's power ramp up as they touched.

They do it when they touch? That was Rusty. He wanted to know how.

Woo, boy! Jes' think about them possibilities. Lemon had his usual subject in mind.

You gonna tell them, Felipe? he thought.

Don't you go tellin' them. This from Rusty.

She axes too many questions.

Goddamn. They white.

The rust of thoughts almost drowned Holland. She'd pushed too hard.

Felipe's eyes narrowed. He must know their need, their anxiety. *We need them as much as they need us with what's comin' down.*

The protests filled Holland's head. She could feel Felipe's anxiety. He turned to her and Jeff. "Old Absinthe House tonight at nine. We talk then."

"Tony Moran's?" Jeff called as they walked to the door.

"Hell, no. The original. They ripped out the daiquiri bar. They rebuilt the real one 'bout three years ago. It's back in all its glory. Corner of Bourbon and Conti."

"I hate Tony Moran's. Damn tourist trap," Rusty said.

And then they were gone.

Jeff took a breath. "Well, maybe we passed the test," he muttered.

"Why didn't they just tell us now?" Holland asked.

"Think they needed a batch of blues to settle them. Or maybe Felipe needs time to convince his partners. Don't think they expected us."

A young black woman in the corner of the noisy room stood up suddenly, upending a table, and pressed her palms to her temples.

Jeff exchanged a look with Holland, then shoved his way between the tables toward the woman before she could stumble away. Her companion was looking startled and a little frightened. Jeff turned the black girl toward him and took both of her arms firmly.

"Can you hear me?" he asked. The young woman's aura turned brown and orange with fear. Her eyes were wild as she searched Jeff's face. Holland came up to stand beside him.

"Can you *hear* me?" Jeff repeated, shaking her a little. The room had quieted around them. People were wondering whether they should intervene.

"Hey," her companion shouted. "You let her go, you hear? I'm gonna call the police."

"He's going to help her, Miss. We both will if we can. I'm a psychiatrist." Holland glanced around and saw people writing off the woman as a psycho, returning to their meals.

The companion stared, big-eyed, for a moment. "She *has* been feelin' poorly."

"So have a lot of people," Holland said, in her most soothing voice.

Jeff nodded encouragement to the woman whose arms he held. She swallowed and nodded. "I hear you. Inside, outside. I hear you."

Jeff smiled. "Good," he said simply. "That's good." He glanced at Holland, and so did the black woman. "I'm like you. So is she. You'll be okay. What's your name?"

"Mary." The woman choked, tears rolling down her cheeks, her dark eyes filled with pain. "The buzzing . . . I think sometimes it's voices. I can't quite hear what they're tellin' me."

Jeff grinned again. He wanted to make it easier for her. "They *are* voices, and it's okay that they are. You'll hear them more clearly in a while, and it gets easier." He wasn't sure he believed that, so the woman's eyes grew frightened again. She could sense Jeff's thoughts, all right.

Holland put out a hand and touched the woman's forearm. "What do you like to do, Mary? What makes you feel good?"

The woman looked at her blankly.

"You have a husband, a boyfriend?" Holland pressed. Mary shook her head. "Do you like to run?" But her chubby frame said she wasn't a runner. "You don't play music, do you?"

"I . . . I like to knit."

Holland glanced under the table to where a canvas bag bulged with colorful yarns. *Why not?* "You forget yourself when you knit?" She took the nod as encouragement. "You maybe get a little hypnotized by the flash of needles and the colors and the texture of the yarn?"

The woman nodded again. "I guess so. I lose track of time . . ."

"Well, I want you to sit down and knit whenever the voices get too much for you, understand? Let it take you away."

Jeff was grinning. "Knitting! Yeah, lady. Knitting is gonna give you peace and quiet."

"Am I crazy?" the woman asked, bewildered.

"No." Holland answered unequivocally. "No more than any of us are."

"You're part of the new generation," Jeff whispered, and he kissed her on one tear-stained cheek. "Now, you sit right down. Have some more of that Dixie beer and just knit up a storm."

The woman nodded and sat down.

Holland sighed as they turned to leave. *Think she'll make it?*

She has a better chance than she did five minutes ago. Knitting! Whatever, I guess.

A siren screamed somewhere close. *We just can't help them all.* It was overwhelming. Despair ate at Holland.

"I'll be happy if we can just help us," Jeff murmured. He opened the door for her.

"Hope Felipe and his friends know what we want them to know," Holland whispered. "And that they decide to tell us. What do we do until nine?" She could think of several things that she wanted to do, and she was afraid she couldn't refuse the call. The pull of Jeff . . .

"I've been hearing the senator every time we break contact, haven't you?

Holland didn't have to nod, but she did, out of habit more than anything.

"My guess is that he's about a half-step behind us," Jeff said. He frowned. His aura went darker. "We pack."

Chapter Twenty-five

He delivered flowers to the Royal Sonesta about noon, but they hadn't registered under their own names. He left with the flowers, shaking his head, and asked the bellman about a description of McQueen and the good doctor. The clerk went blank at the question, refusing to be drawn into speculation. But the flicker in his eyes said he had seen the burly guy and the ice blonde. Gotcha.

They were probably out touring. He'd get some shut-eye and catch them on their way out for dinner maybe. He looked up at the balconies that hung over the street. Excellent.

The doorman at the Royal Sonesta loaded their roller bags into the trunk of the Lexus. "Y'all come back when you can stay longer," he said as Jeff pressed money into his hand.

Jeff raised his palm in salute. Holland knew they might never come here again. The future was looking a little grim. She just hoped they made it until nine tonight.

Jeff got into the driver seat and pulled into the narrow street. He laid one hand on her thigh to keep out listeners. Down a few blocks he turned right, and right again on Royal, and coasted into the indented curb in front of the Monteleone Hotel. Huge flags hung outside the hotel in brass holders, still now in the afternoon heat. Holland recognized the American flag and the French one. Some guests looked more idiosyncratic, like they might be local. The Monteleone presented a grander facade to the street than the Sonesta, but inside it was just as serene, just as cool, just as studied in elegance. She and Jeff were not serene. As they had to break contact to get out of the car, the voices cascaded over them. Those voices were growing in number, and the new ones were definitely in distress. All that anxiety was oppressive.

They rented a room, as before. At this rate, they'd stay in every hotel in the Quarter within thirty days. She felt Jeff's doubts they'd make it that long. He took her hand and led her to the elevator.

In the room, they stood, looking at each other. The afternoon stretched ahead. Outside, the sultry heat of New Orleans beckoned them to strip for comfort. But the heat was sensual, too. Combined with the atmosphere of charged sexuality in the Quarter, it was almost too much to resist. Was it the sex shops on Bourbon, or the Blues and the Zydeco blaring out from every open doorway?

Whatever it was, it was a heady combination. One could say, dangerous.

Jeff broke contact. She could feel desire rising in him, his fear of what might happen if they couldn't resist the call of their bodies. The voices chorused around them. Which meant the senator could hear them.

Jeff threw himself onto the king-size bed. The spread was crisscrossed with gold stripes lined with red on cream. Indigo had crept into his aura, coupled with little yellow darts of tension. *All I have to do is make it through the afternoon,* she heard him think.

That was all. Gingerly, Holland lay down on the opposite bed, trying not to think.

But she couldn't do that. Better to cover with talk. "So . . . when we get what they've got to give us, what do we do then?" she asked. He wasn't looking at her.

"Been thinking about that."

"I know. What's the verdict?"

He made his decision, tried not to think about it. She caught a glimpse of a private plane, though. "We have to figure out how to get some more money."

"He knows where we are, doesn't he?"

"I think so. Let's listen."

Holland went inside her head and listened to the voices. It was harder now that there were more, to pick out only one. But she could feel Jeff sorting too. He latched onto the senator's voice, and that brought it to the forefront of the noise in her own head.

The bastard's thoughts held a note of triumph. *Okay. Yeah, they've changed. I saw flags. Monteleone. Brad, make the call. Watch the exits, but don't storm the place. They have to come out sometime.* There was a pause. *Leland? Yeah, call Leland. If our guys fail, he can send in the troops to pick up the pieces.*

Holland practically jumped out of her skin. She sat back abruptly. "Jeff, we've got to get out of this place!"

He sat up slowly. His green eyes were serious, maybe even sad. "Won't make a particle of difference, darlin'. He knows we're moving from hotel to hotel. Say we go to a restaurant. Think he won't recognize it from our thoughts? Every time you hit the restroom or we get out of a car, he hears us. At least they're going to wait until we come out."

"Then let's go now!" She couldn't think straight. Fear was shorting out her logic. There wasn't a whole lot of hope in his thoughts, either, or in his aura, which had darkened to a charcoal gray. His mood infected Holland. "They're going to get us, aren't they?"

He didn't bother lying. "Can't see how they won't, sooner or later." His voice was husky. "Can't get out of the country. Security is just too tight at airports, docks. Maybe wouldn't do any good if we did. Government has got a long reach, especially when it can read your thoughts."

His eyes lifted to hers. How could he feel desire now? But he did. She could see it in his aura. It was magenta, shot with indigo. She was pretty sure hers would be a match, if what was happening between her legs was any indication. And they hadn't even touched yet.

But they would. Nothing mattered anymore. They had so little time.

He reached out his hand to her, as he had so many times before. Life slowed. Voices cascaded in her head. She was aware of every detail of his hand: the square-cut short nails, the light brown hair curling so faintly on the back. She could even see the small misshapen callus on Jeff's middle finger that said he still liked to write with a pen sometimes. He didn't wear a ring. As a matter of fact, his only adornment was the little St. Christopher medal. Holland liked that: Jeff was naked except for the symbol he carried and the power he invested in it. She had never been so aware of another as flesh and bone, as well as complicated mind and spirit.

She breathed. It was almost a gasp. And then she shrugged.

She took his hand. The hallowed silence fell in that sweet relief she had come to expect. Only Jeff's thoughts still echoed in her head, and those thoughts were mirror images of her own; a wanting that accelerated up some incline with no end in sight, coupled with hopeless resignation.

She ran her hand up his forearm, feeling the thicket of hair tickle her palm. The light sweat of the New Orleans afternoon was banished by the air-conditioning, but somehow the sultry atmosphere of the bayou lingered. Maybe it was the faint musk of male and female left over from the heat. Maybe it was just the Quarter, calling to them from a time when it had been home to town houses for the planters, and for the octaroons behind balconies of floral iron, fanning themselves as they waited for their lovers.

Holland's hand caressed the fullness of Jeff's biceps, and ran over the soft skin that lay in the hollow where the muscles joined and the shoulder bulged anew. His eyes were green fire, his thoughts burning. He knew the danger here, that they might join so intensely that all the rules might change again. They might become some new thing entirely, one they didn't recognize. They had been afraid of that for days—had *wanted* it for days.

The scales tipped. She smiled. All was lost. Gladly.

He smiled in return. *Is there anything to do on the way to the gallows but laugh?*

Yes, Holland thought. *There is.*

Before she knew what he was about, Jeff lunged up on one elbow and took her in his arms. She was before him, pressing her mouth down against his, opening his lips with her tongue. Her loins were throbbing until they ached. How long had she ached for him? Months, years, days, minutes? All her life, more like.

There was no time for delicacy. He crushed her against his chest. The violence of his need would once have frightened her. She could feel the hardness under the zipper of his jeans as he pulled her to lie beside him and wrapped his arm around her bottom. She arched against him, pulling away from his lips to bare her throat in some primal instinct to show him that she longed to give herself to him. To hell with what would happen to their psyches. What would anything mean when they were dead?

Jeff startled her by ripping the front of her blouse with his strong, square hand. Buttons popped and soared. Nor did he bother to unhook her lacy white bra, though it fastened in front. He just pulled at the center until it gave and her breasts hung free. She did not hesitate, but shrugged out of her clothes, naked to the waist of her jeans.

She grinned at him and grabbed the neck of his tank top and pulled with all her strength. She got a little rip. His eyes went crinkly, then he took up where she left off and tore the remaining fabric asunder. They were both naked to the waist. She nestled close, conscious of her nipples rubbing against the light hairs of his chest, sending sensation cascading through her body to pool between her legs.

I want this, she thought. *More than I have ever wanted anything.*

Not just the sex. I want the joining, *too.*

That startled her. She could feel his fear. He hadn't disregarded the consequences as she had. He embraced them. Could she do less? She was hurtling down some corridor that had only one entrance, and only one exit. "So, let's join."

Frantic pulling off of boots and shoes, belts undone and jeans unzipped—they couldn't do it fast enough. Nakedness was their only object, the only object of the expanding universe. And then he pressed the heat between his legs to her thighs. He burned her. Were all men so hot? She felt like the ice princess she hated, her skin so cool against his throbbing heat. Yet before she could allow that wound to open, Jeff hushed her, holding her close, kissing her hair, radiating the thought that she was not what everyone thought, that she was whole and real and sensual.

She turned her face up, and he descended to her lips again, hungry for her—all of her. He wanted not only her body but her soul.

And she wanted his. She gave freely in order to receive in kind.

Thus she opened her legs to him, and felt him groan into her mouth. He entered her and the sweet pain of opening against his first thrusts filled her with satisfaction, filled her with him. This, *this* was right.

"Banks! What the hell took you so long?"

Leland wondered if the senator knew that he was shouting into the phone. "I do have other things going on, Lendreaux," he said coldly. "I took your call." He was not about to tell the senator that he had taken a call from the Pentagon after he knew Lendreaux was on the line.

"You're damned right you took my call! You're nothing without me, Banks. You're a guy who has no way to rectify his failure to control this, if I don't help you. Remember that."

"What's the problem?" Leland did not acknowledge the threat.

"I'm getting an incredible increase in power, Banks. Incredible."

"What do you mean? You're not making sense."

"I mean your precious daughter and her reporter friend. They were offline for a while. Then I get a burst of power from them that went off some scale I've never felt before."

"What?" Leland snapped into focus. "What are you saying?"

"I'm saying that all of a sudden their thoughts are louder than any others—by a lot. They're broadcasting on wideband in my head. What does it mean?"

"I don't know." Leland fought frustration and annoyance. "We saw spikes in their brain activity when they were touching. Maybe it's an amplification of that. I won't know for sure until I bring them in."

"How close are we? Banks, we have to nip this in the bud."

Ah, now he understood. What the senator was saying was that Holly and McQueen were more powerful than he was. And that meant that he might not want them around to upstage him. "We're close. The army will be in position in about an hour. We'll let the NOPD go in first. If we don't have to figure prominently on CNN headline news with photos of tanks and machine guns in the French Quarter, I'd rather not."

"I do not think we have the luxury of waiting, Banks."

"Calm down! We'll retrieve them. The fact that they are generating unusual output should make us both more eager to have them as part of our experiment. Don't you agree?"

"When can you get them?"

"Tonight, sometime. Don't get yourself into a knot."

"Not good enough, Banks. They're thinking about private airplanes."

"Don't do anything we'll both regret, Lendreaux," he warned. "If I don't get these subjects one way, I'll get them another."

There was a silence on the line. "Are you threatening me, Banks? Because if you are, I don't think you know who you're fucking with."

"Of course I do, Senator. I know you very well." Leland made his voice hard. "Don't think you're invincible, and don't think you're in control. Don't even bother to think that you're the one who called in the military. My friends at the Pentagon did that." He let a silence stretch. "Toe the line, Lendreaux. You have your uses. But if you dare put your hands—or anyone else's hands—on my daughter, you are expendable. Am I clear?"

The line clicked dead.

Holland gasped and rolled over onto her back, letting the cool air from the vent above dry the sheen of sweat on her body. At least she hadn't passed out this time. She rolled her head to look at Jeff. His fine male body was stretched out beside her, ribs defined, belly flat, and the thatch of hair between his thighs clustered around a member that was slowly subsiding. As she watched, Jeff flung his near arm up and pushed his hand behind his neck.

Well, she had certainly never had sex like that. She wasn't sure *anyone* had ever had sex like that. Unable to help herself, she rolled into him nestled her shoulder into his armpit, then let her hand creep across his rib cage.

Jeff gathered her into his side and looked down at her with an aura glowing around him that was entirely magenta. "You okay?" he asked. His lips brushed her hair.

"Yeah. It was more manageable this time."

"Mmmm. But no less. . . ." He searched for a word that could possibly comprise what they had experienced. After a pause he gave up, and just spewed out comparisons. "Wonderful? Frightening? Completing? Hell, I don't know what that was, Holland."

She sighed against his side. "Neither do I."

She'd felt it all again, all the incredible complexity of him: the compassion he tried to hide, the bravery he'd drawn on to run away and make it stick, the cynicism that came from being ashamed of his father and horrified that people could be so gullible, the secret determination to make a difference. She'd felt the anger at his father, too, the fury that was born of standing physical as well as mental abuse for years. He had tried to deal with that anger; thought he'd it conquered, but it kept coming back on him. And then there was the puzzle of the emptiness he'd felt in the center of his life, the tentative diagnosis he now made, wondering almost timidly if he had been missing the softer influence of love. That was probably more frightening to her than all the rest. How had she ever thought she'd understood how complicated people could be? If all shrinks could experience what she just had, they'd be a humbler group.

He stroked her flank, his thoughts compelling her to look up. He was thinking about what he'd felt in her in equal awe. "We were two halves of one whole. Is that possible?"

"I don't know," she mumbled into his chest. "I'm not sure anyone has ever felt this before." Silence fell as they thought about that. New territory. They were a new version of the old species? How big was *that*?

Holland bit her lip as a thought crossed unbidden to her mind. She was joined, just like Felipe said. She was joined to Jeff McQueen in ways no woman had been joined to a man, ever. More than attraction, more than "I promise to love, honor, and obey." Her destiny was Jeff McQueen, intertwined, inextricable. But that didn't feel bad.

She wanted to stop thinking, right there. Because she was a psychiatrist, she knew that wanting to stop thinking was not a good sign, besides being very hard to do. Destiny meant no choices. There would be no privacy, ever, between them. They *were* on some road to becoming one being, two halves of one whole. But what if you wanted to be your own woman? What if you didn't want to be half of a whole, but whole all by yourself? What if the torn psyche you brought to the joining was a burden to the other half? She wanted to lighten his burdens, not add to them.

She raised herself up on one elbow, looking at him. His doubts echoed hers, washed over her. She and he just stared at each other, listening to the dialogue of doubt in their minds. He doubted himself and felt unworthy of what had happened to them. Lord, weren't shrinks supposed to help you accept yourself, make you feel whole? She'd never felt so inadequate.

Jeff cleared his throat. "We better get out of here," he said, and his voice was filled with shame about his fear, and about his retreat from what they had achieved.

"Are we on the run?" Their bodies cooled in the circulating air.

"I guess. We'd better be elusive until nine."

Holland glanced at the clock. It was four. Five hours. Maybe there was one thing she could do for Jeff, even if she couldn't do it for herself. "I know where we can go."

"What?" Jeff's voice was sharp. He must have caught a glimpse. "Absolutely not."

But he needed this. Acceptance? Maybe not. But maybe he would get a little peace.

"We've got to go somewhere. Argue later. First we find a way out."

Chapter Twenty-six

Getting out of the hotel through the kitchens and the laundry occupied their minds, but as soon as they got in the cab, Jeff's resistance blossomed. She grabbed his hand to keep their destination secret from anyone listening in. "Metarie," she said, and the cab took off.

"I am *not* going to a goddamned revival," Jeff said through gritted teeth. She could feel his anger flare, and knew that only its surface focus was on her. His hands balled into fists. He was reliving moments with his father, and each scene made him angrier.

"I've never seen one," she said mildly.

"And I've seen a hundred. Maybe a thousand. Don't get on the Interstate, driver," he called. "We're going back to the Quarter."

The driver slowed, looking in his rear view mirror.

Holland said, "Well I *am* going, Jeff McQueen—unless you want to hit me over the head and drag me back to the

316

hotel." She held his gaze a moment, letting his rage wash over her. "Driver, you can let him out at the corner, but I'm still going to Metarie."

"Make up your mind, folks," the driver drawled. "I'll just drive around in circles here."

Jeff looked away, his eyes flicking to the cars around them. He somehow pushed his anger down. He was ashamed of the rage. Vicious circle, that—shame and rage.

"Good place to stay out of the way for a couple of hours," she ventured. "Or you could spend the time telling him what you think of him. We don't have to be back until nine. That should give you some scope."

"I've got nothing to say to him." He took a breath. "But you're right. No one will think of looking for us there. Not if they've ever read my thoughts."

Holland lifted her brows. Jeff nodded. "Metarie," she said to the driver. Then they were on the Interstate, driving east. Jeff's hand was warm, its human contact comforting. Holland leaned into his flannel shirt, layered over his tank top. She'd put a light cotton sweater on with her jeans and clogs. She could hear the driver thinking that his kid needed braces, wondering how he was going to pay for them.

The cab got off at a huge mushroom of a water tower and drove north toward the lake. A striped tent rose in the center of sports field; filled with cars parked on the packed dirt.

Holland kept hold of Jeff's hand as they scooted out of the cab and paid the driver. Jeff was wound tight. His aura crackled with green and red. His eyes searched the stragglers who hurried toward the entrance flap, as though he might know them. Holland heard the nearest, clearly excited about seeing Reverend Don. Jeff and Holland followed. It was bright July, but in the muggy air of the Delta breath was hard to come by. They could hear the crowd chanting in call and response inside the tent. Shouts of

"Amen," and "Yes, Lord," carried above the din. She and Jeff stood in the flap entrance, torn between the punishing light outside and the murky dark of the interior. Holland felt like she was going blind. But she could smell sweating humans—too many in too small a place—and feel Jeff's bitterness. And then the thoughts of all the people nearest to them washed over her.

Lord, save me.

Make my husband love me, Jesus.

Get me work, Lord, I can't take being shiftless anymore.

What was this? Holland felt Jeff tremble. Was this some ramp-up of their power since their joining this afternoon? The spotlight shining on the stage brought Jeff's father into focus. The man stood with feet shoulder-wide, his powder-blue suit fairly glowing in the light. He raised his arms slowly to shoulder height, his face upturned into the dim recesses of the tent. As Holland's eyes grew accustomed to the gloom, the crowd emerged: families and older people, the youngsters mostly women.

"And the Lord Jesus said unto the multitude, 'I am the reason. I am the life.' " Jeff's father slowly opened his eyes and lowered his gaze to the filled bleachers that surrounded him on three sides. "And he will *be* the reason and the life for some in this humble tent tonight. Who has come here with affliction?"

A chorus of muddled assent rose from the bleachers. The thoughts around Holland and Jeff were filled with such yearning, it was almost unbearable. Jeff almost staggered beside her. He broke contact, letting in thoughts of their own kind. Was there no refuge from their gift?

"Who needs the forgiveness of our Lord Jesus this evening?"

The chorus swelled. Reverend Don circled the arena with a piercing gaze, his arm outstretched, finger pointing to the crowd. "Whose heart is pure in worship of our Savior? For only such may be healed of their afflictions, spiritual, or physical. Who will it be tonight?"

318

His finger seemed to flutter in uncertainty before it jabbed out at the crowd. "You there! You, boy, come forward. The purity of your belief will be your salvation tonight."

Behind the Rev Don, the emaciated man who played the organ pounded its keys in a background crescendo. Holland saw Jeff's mother standing in her plain dark dress in the wings. She blended into the blackness, her pallid face floating above the ground in a sort of limbo.

A boy in about the fifth row of the house pushed himself erect. He walked with two canes. He made his laborious way to the aisle. "Please, sir, did you mean me?"

Jeff turned his back on the scene and shoved his hands in his pockets. "Don't be taken in," he growled. "He's a plant."

"How do you know?" Holland was riveted. The crippled boy made his way to the stage.

"Because I played that part in every new town for most of eight years," he muttered, gazing out the door behind her. "I was healed maybe a thousand times. You'd think it would stick." Silent, he stalked out the door.

"Okay, we won't watch," Holland said, turning to follow. Jeff's back was stiff. She could hear his distress; the shame, the anger just beneath the surface. He'd been used, and he hadn't liked it. When he protested against his role, he'd been beaten. Whoa. Coming here had not been such a good idea after all. Even though . . .

"What? Not a good idea?" He was trying to breathe slowly, his face turned up. "I thought playing shrink again was your favorite thing." He swallowed a chuckle and lowered his head. He knew what she had planned. At least part. She could see him try to relax. She wanted badly to knead the muscles in his back and shoulders until he turned and took her in his arms.

"Sometimes revisiting the painful parts of childhood when we're adult and more powerful releases the anger." Boy, did she sound like a shrink.

319

"Yeah? Seems like it just makes me angry all over again." They sat on a hay bale, one of many drawn up to mark the perimeter of the parking area and create a path into the revival tent. Jeff and Holland let their hips touch, knowing it was the only way to hide. That let in the normal people's thoughts—though fainter with their distance from the tent. Rev Don's exhortations floated out behind them.

Neither spoke. Holland could hear Jeff's thoughts more clearly than ever since their joining. A flood of memories cascaded over him, and Holland shared them all. She tried to seem supportive, accepting, even when, inside his calm exterior, he envisioned himself pounding his father to a pulp. For a moment she thought this, too, was a memory, before she realized he was creating this vision, one he had probably imagined before, to ward off his feelings of helplessness. His head jerked to the sun, setting behind the bridge that arched over the huge lake to the north. She felt him shake himself mentally, admonish himself to get hold of his emotions.

People started flooding out of the tent, chattering about the experience they'd had, praising Rev Don, feeling transformed. Their thoughts grew louder as they approached. Jeff turned to Holland. "We don't have to stay here with all these people. Want to grab some dinner?"

"A crowded restaurant?" She wondered how to say something to him.

"Just say it."

She looked into the green intensity of his eyes. "I think you should see your parents before we go."

"I managed just fine not seeing them for years. Twice in a week is pushing it."

"May not have another chance, you know. Who knows what will happen?"

"Start using shrink words like 'closure' and I might lose those oysters we had for lunch." Jeff stood and shoved his hands into his jeans pockets.

Holland shook her head. "Gonna feel just as bad if you walk away now." She let the words hang in the air. But she was thinking that she'd stand by him no matter what. She got up, too. She felt him make up his mind.

"Oh, what the hell. The old bugger can't say anything to me he hasn't already said."

Holland tried to be positive, too. She and Jeff made their way like salmon fighting upstream against the tide of people gushing from the tent. Once inside, it was easier. They made their way between the bleachers toward the stage. Several stagehands were testing the microphones.

"Two hours 'til the next showtime," one yelled. "Get the second jenny hooked up."

The lights dimmed, then flickered back. Jeff and Holland trotted up the three steps to the stage holding hands, wended their way between the speakers and around the piano, then pushed through the curtains at the back. Jeff's father was changing his blue suit for a sunny yellow one.

"No jacket yet, Ida. I'll sweat all over it in this heat."

Ida McQueen draped the jacket carefully across a chair. "Looked like a full house," she remarked. The glow of self-approval surrounded both of them.

"We'll have standing-room only tonight. It's them snipers. Puts the fear of God into folks."

Then Ida noticed Jeff and Holland standing inside the curtains. She touched her husband's arm to get his attention. He turned and followed her gaze. For a moment the four of them just looked at each other. Holland could feel Jeff's turmoil. He didn't know what to say. They both felt his parents' shock and disapproval.

"I'm surprised a fugitive from the law would show his face somewhere he's known." Jeff's father's voice was stiff.

Holland felt Jeff recoil. They had both been concentrating so much on his relationship with his parents, she'd forgotten there were more practical considerations.

"Guess you didn't have time to hang around L.A. to see if I was alive or dead." Jeff went on the attack. "If you couldn't get me to one of your brainwashing centers, I wasn't much use, right?"

His father finished loosening his tie, his aura bitter chartreuse. He was disappointed in his only son. He thought Jeff had blighted his life. Jeff cringed under Holland's hand on his arm. "We had obligations," the reverend said, "*which* we dropped at a moment's notice to bail you out of a fix you'd gotten into with your godless ways."

"Like your ways have anything to do with God." Jeff turned around. "Come on, Holland. We should never have come." He pulled out of her grasp and made for the door. He shouldn't do that. The senator would hear everything.

"I'm glad you're all right," his mother called. Jeff stopped and glanced back. His mother's gaze darted to Holland, then back to Jeff. "They came around asking after you. We didn't know where you were."

His father stared at Holland, eyes narrowed. "Doc, is it usual to go gallivanting around the country with a patient you're supposed to be curing?"

"I don't think he needs much curing, Reverend," Holland answered calmly. Telling the truth seemed the only option now. "He just hears voices. So do I. So do a lot of people these days. It has to do with a genetic mutation. We have an extra bit of DNA." Holland went up and deliberately out her hand on Jeff's arm. It was important that he hear his parents' thoughts.

"You telling me you're both mutants?" The Rev Don's voice rose.

Holland smiled. "Yes. Don't you read the newspapers?"

That took him aback. He *had* read the papers. The story was spreading.

"That's us," Jeff agreed. "Among others. Lots of others."

Holland watched Jeff's father rearrange his thoughts. He didn't like the fact that there might be an explanation other than Satan's power for his son's behavior. He wanted Jeff to be evil, *needed* him to be evil. He'd based so much on that fact. Those thoughts shouldn't have shocked Jeff, but they did.

Rev Don made his decision. "The most evil among us are given into Satan's power. Those who have offended God, sinners, are sacrificed to preserve the ones who hold Him in their heart."

"Or maybe we're part of God's plan for humankind. Have you thought of that?" Holland had to challenge this man, because she could feel Jeff giving in to old feelings of powerlessness in the face of his father's accusations. "But no. You wouldn't want that, would you? Because your son, who dared to question your faith, would be the one to take the step into God's future. By the way, do you *really* have faith?"

"He was always godless, no matter what I did to teach him," Rev Don said, his voice tight. He ignored the question of his own belief. They could hear his anger that he had failed. He pushed the anger onto Jeff and Holland.

"Hey, you did your best to beat belief into him. What more could God want?" Holland stared at him, all his venom harmless for her if not for Jeff. She smiled, a strong smile. "You know, I don't even think God wants those kind of converts." She paused. "A son is a precious gift, Reverend. One not to be wasted."

Jeff was rigid with memory and resentment. The Reverend's thoughts flickered. He was remembering his own father's abuse, the terrible fear, the tears and promises to be a better boy. He was thinking that what he'd done to Jeff was just what fathers did to set their boys on the right path. But now doubt flickered beneath his righteousness. He wondered if there was anything else he could have done to save his boy.

Holland looked at Jeff, whose eyes were wide. He'd never really considered what demons drove his father. Now he was hearing them all. He heard his father's need for God to be powerful. In fact, the Rev Don was so desperate in some corner of his soul for God to be the Great

Protector, he'd made up the protection he wasn't sure was there. The healing routine, the faked intervention of the divine . . . he believed he was giving people hope that he needed himself. He never allowed himself to express the doubts that cowered in the dark of his mind, which was why, when his son had rejected the very thing he himself wanted so badly—the protection of faith in something larger than himself—the Rev Don had feared for his son's soul enough to try to beat belief into him. It was the only way he knew.

Jeff glanced to his mother, wondering, and only then did her thoughts come through. "Why didn't you help me, Mother? Why didn't you once take my part?" She seemed to shrink a little, and guilt washed over her. Her usual implacable demeanor was a cover for an overwhelming feeling of inadequacy. She was only too aware she had no beauty. She didn't think herself smart, and she was so shy as to be paralyzed in front of people. She did not know why her charismatic husband had chosen her; did not love him, did not expect love in return. She'd been grateful to be chosen, by the grace of God. So she had cultivated the one trait she could manage; support for her husband's calling. In that she was steadfast, because it was obviously God's will that she be chosen by this man.

Jeff was staring at his parents, seeing them for the first time. Who expected parents to have their own demons? You only knew they were responsible for yours. Holland felt pity creep into Jeff's mind. She looked over and saw that a soft, green aura had replaced the jagged red.

They're small, she thought. *They needed to be bigger to overcome what drove them.*

He turned to look at her. *Like, I'm so big?*

His parents hadn't said a word. Now the Rev Don shook himself. "The Lord requires hard things of us, boy." It wasn't his preaching voice.

Jeff took a breath. Holland felt him decide.

"Yeah, Dad. He does." He broke contact with Holland and held out his hand. What courage that took. He gave his father room to be humanly frail, if not absolution, with those four words of agreement.

His father reached out and clasped Jeff's forearm. Holland could feel the pain between the two, but also a glimmer of healing. "We'd better be going. Fugitives and all." Jeff turned to his mother, still standing gracelessly in her husband's shadow. He simply gathered her into his arms.

"I know you never liked this much, Mom. But sometimes it works better than words." They stood that way for a while.

He broke away and turned, holding Holland's elbow. They walked through the curtains, out of the stifling tent, past the lines beginning to form for the next show, without looking back.

There are all kinds of healing, Holland thought. She was so proud of him.

Did I just forgive them? He was wondering. His aura had a glimmer of magenta.

You understood them, she reassured him. *Things like forgiveness happen a little at a time.*

Maybe now the dreams of being evil, likely driven by rage and his father's disapproval, would subside. That was what she'd hoped to give him.

It seemed wrong somehow to jack a car from among the faithful, though how that was different from what they'd been doing all along Holland couldn't say.

Jeff pulled her toward a yellow school bus parked at the edge of the dusty lot. Emblazoned on the side was Quarter Foursquare Church. Jeff called up to the driver of the bus. "You going back to the Quarter?"

The huge black woman whose bottom enveloped the seat nodded. "Climb aboard, Pilgrims. Yo car break down?"

"We took a taxi out and now we can't get back," Jeff said, truthfully. He was thinking that the senator and his cronies could have traced the cab. Calling a cab now and waiting for it . . .

"Jest trust in the Lord to provide." The black woman laughed, a big throaty laugh. "And he done provide. Climb on in."

They settled in one of the few remaining empty bench seats among the throng of chattering women and children, some men, most black. Jeff slid in beside Holland, thighs touching. Immediately she could hear all the thoughts of those around them cascade through her mind. She jerked against Jeff, the onslaught was so strong.

"Jesus!" he gasped. *How much of this can we stand?*

"We are gonna have to avoid crowds," Jeff muttered. "Well, hang on." The bus closed its doors. "It's about an hour into town."

They rolled out onto the Interstate. About half an hour later, she felt Jeff's shock. He was looking behind her. She turned. A convoy of camouflaged vehicles pushed through the late traffic, the lead vehicle honking, going in the opposite direction.

"A convoy for some military base around here?" she asked without much hope.

"They're not usually in such a hurry," he said grimly. They no longer dared risk even a moment where they didn't touch. The sky was deepening into dusk as they pulled up in front of the unassuming stucco building north of Rampart in the projects labeled Quarter Foursquare Church. It was less than an hour until they were to meet Felipe and company at the Absinthe House.

Chapter Twenty-seven

He'd taken up his position in a storeroom over a sex shop on Bourbon, just across from the Royal Sonesta. He'd been watching since five, but he hadn't seen the targets leave. The streets were crowded, but he couldn't have missed them. From this corner, he could cover both the front and the side entrance. Once he saw them, he couldn't miss. The money guy should've called him this afternoon. He wanted to ask about Jimmy Greaseball. Too late now. He never carried a phone when he was staked out. He needed to focus. This damned place was hot. Way worse than L.A. His t-shirt was sticking to him. The window was open, of course, so he could get his gun up at a moment's notice. But that didn't help.

Just at dusk, he saw Jimmy Greaseball walking up Conti. What the fuck? He was even more surprised to see Jimmy, dressed real nice in a leather jacket and slacks and carrying a briefcase, duck into the side door of the Sonesta. He glanced to the street, surveying the crowd for his targets before transferring his attention to the hotel's main entrance. Was Jimmy going to take out the targets before they could get out the door and into range? But that would mean close work, and Jimmy didn't like close work any more than he did. No matter how he figured it, this was bad. His glance flicked up to the upper stories of the Sonesta, thinking maybe Jimmy was just going to walk up to their room and take them out. He'd get caught, wouldn't he? Silencer? Maybe not. Maybe he could make it out the door. But the brief-

case—that was sure a broke-down rifle in there.

In the corner room of the third story, draperies cracked open. The corner room faced both Bourbon and Conti, so its green, wrought-iron balcony wrapped around. He could practically feel Jimmy Greaseball behind those curtains, casing the street just like he was. What the hell was this about? Jimmy couldn't get them from inside the Sonesta, 'less he knew something Eddy didn't. Lights went on around the Quarter. Jimmy Greaseball appeared on that third-floor balcony. Ignoring the crowds on Bourbon and staring down at this old, beat-up bar across the street on Conti. The sign outside said "Absinthe House." When Eddy looked back, Jimmy had disappeared inside the room. The curtains were shut on the Bourbon side. Jimmy was after something in that bar. Maybe he and Jimmy weren't going for the same targets. Or maybe Jimmy Greaseball just wasn't as sharp. Dumb spic. He cast his eyes over the crowds again. It was getting dark, but lights on Bourbon were bright enough. They had to be coming out of that hotel pretty soon.

He swept the street to make sure he hadn't missed them, focused on the hotel's side door.

But he kept glancing back to that bar. What could Jimmy Greaseball want with that fucking bar? Wait! Shit! That was them! The hits! Crossing diagonally to that bar, not out of the hotel at all! The guy broke into a trot, tugging the woman. Fucking-A!

He raised the rifle into the window sill and put his eye to the infrared sight as big as a soup can. But they were already pushing through the swinging door. Too late!

He stilled his breathing, pushed down the rage. He glanced to the third-floor window across the street. At least Jimmy hadn't gotten them, either. He'd had a much better shot. Why weren't they dead?

If Jimmy wasn't after them, then who?

Or maybe Jimmy was just in the can.

Eddy settled down to a long wait and took a pull on his Styrofoam cup. The coffee was dead cold. But it could keep

him alert. He was going to get the shot when they came out,
before Jimmy Greaseball got the hit and the money, too.

The Absinthe House was dark, its dim recesses packed
even so early in the night. Jeff was glad to see it again.
When it had been cleaned out and replaced by one of
those disinfected-looking daiquiri bars, all steel drums with
glass faces, twirling their pastel ices for the drunken tourists, the Quarter lost a piece of its heritage. Blues fans
across the city had mourned.

But here it was again, recreated down to the bare light
bulbs swinging their dim glow from the ends of tattered
wires, and the grimy-looking business cards tacked all over
the wall. If you looked really close, you could tell that the
wiring wasn't actually old and worn anymore—which was
probably a good thing, since a fire had started the work
of the daiquiri mavens the first time around. But the tables
were just as scarred as before, the stage just as tiny. It was
right that the Absinthe House was back. It felt like a haven—except, of course for the voices.

The place was packed. If Jeff and Holland touched, they
could hear all the guys in the room trying to get inside
their dates' pants, and all the women bored or thinking
sentimental thoughts. Every voice was woozy with alcohol.
But if they didn't touch, the Senator would surely recognize where they were.

He led Holland to a table at the back. The band was on
break or something, but the music system was pumping
out classic Robert Johnson at a decibel level just under
earsplitting. The physical noise of the crowd was super-
charged as people shouted to be heard over the din. Just
like it used to be, Jeff thought. Holland looked nonplussed
as he sat her with her back to a wall. He stopped a waitress
and ordered two Dixies.

Holland didn't bother to shout at him. *Why on earth*
would they pick here to meet to talk about how to control
the din in our heads?

Maybe it's perfect. Lots of opportunity to practice. He sat beside her, glancing around nervously. There were lots of cops in the streets as they walked down from Rampart. There were always a lot of cops in the Quarter, what with all the rowdy tourists and attendant pickpockets. But tonight they had seemed ominous.

The waitress slid two sweating, long-necked bottles onto their table. "Ten bucks," she shouted. Jeff took a wad of bills out of his shirt pocket and peeled off a couple.

Just then the band came back. Felipe exuded calm. Lemon and Rusty looked like they'd been doing H, they were so laid back. Felipe scanned the crowd and saluted as the band took the stage. *You made it,* he thought at them.

The band didn't need to count. They didn't bother with introductions. They just launched into free-form blues. Felipe made his guitar wail in grief. Rusty sat his drum set like he was the captain on the quarter deck of a ship, his eyes closed. And Lemon stood at a keyboard, shaking his head and staring at his hands as though they belonged to someone else. Their auras turned the most pure blue Jeff had ever seen and grew into thick, glowing coronas around their whole bodies in the three harsh spotlights on the stage.

Jeff could feel the men drift farther into their own marvelous music. They rode the notes Felipe bent to impossible lengths. They throbbed to the pounding of Rusty's drums, their anchor; and they shivered with the emotion in Lemon's black-and-white virtuosity. The band favored the spare style of mature blues, the kind that valued the space between the notes as much or more than the notes themselves. Music flowed over Jeff. He glanced to Holland. She felt it too, of course. This was how their new acquaintances got their peace. They dove inside their music, and because they dove together, they joined. As Holland and Jeff watched, the band's blue auras expanded until each touched the other and the entire stage glowed with otherworldly light only Jeff and Holland could see.

How long the set lasted, Jeff couldn't say. Lemon rumbled into a microphone that they'd be back. He and Rusty wandered out a side door. Felipe made his way through the swelling Robert Johnson blues and the cigarette smoke toward Holland and Jeff. Jeff realized he hadn't been troubled by voices around him during the set, even though he was still sidled up to Holland.

Jeff just nodded at Felipe. He knew his respect would be evident.

Felipe grinned, his teeth perfect and white in the dim room. The two men felt each other's power for a minute, both magnified since this afternoon.

"So, can you do that with just anybody?" Holland asked, beside him. She didn't bother to shout; the people she was talking to would hear her even if she whispered.

"No," Felipe said, his puzzlement evident. "Just these guys. Sorta like you two. Guess you got to be on the right wavelength."

Jeff nodded. *Or be soul mates.*

He heard Holland's shock at that word. Well, she was shocked that he would use it. They'd both thought about it—two halves joining—they'd just never called it that. But that's what they were; different from each other, they were nevertheless a single puzzle where each owned half the pieces. Maybe someday they'd even know what picture that puzzle made. If they got out alive with everybody in the civilized world after them.

"So," Jeff said. "We need to know how you survive day to day, between the music. We started hearing everybody around us when we touch, whether we want to or not. Since we hear everybody like us when we don't touch, our comfort zone has just about disappeared. You got any hints?"

"You hear normal people?" Felipe asked sharply. "Without tryin'?"

Jeff and Holland both nodded, and they knew he could feel their dismay.

"Whoa. You rampin' up quick." He shot them both a look. Jeff could feel him wondering about what happened to mutants who got their peace by touching when they touched in more intimate ways.

"Yeah," Jeff said. "That seems to be an issue." He could hear Holland's embarrassed protestations, then feel her resignation at not being able to keep secrets anymore.

Felipe grew thoughtful. "I ain't got that far yet. Must be bad. You need it."

"Need *what?*" Holland's voice was soft. Her thoughts were shouting, though. "What do you do to control it? You can. I feel it. Even now, you hear all the other voices, but you're not . . . not jumbled like I am. Is it just because you were playing a minute ago?"

Felipe paused.

Your partners don't want you to tell us? Jeff tried not to accuse them of being prejudiced, but his thoughts leaked through.

It ain't that. We agreed to tell you. It's just . . .

Felipe shook his head. "You ain't gonna like this. It's kinda Zen."

Great, Jeff thought. *You're going to recommend twenty years in a monastery, meditating.*

"Not that bad. You just got to muster some focus, dude. I think you do it now, a little. You found me. That means you filtered out some voices and let mine come through. Right?"

Jeff nodded cautiously, unsure. Was that what he had done?

"That's it?" Holland was incredulous, disappointed, even angry. Jeff couldn't see very much of her aura in this dim light, but there were definite flashes of red in it. "You focus?"

"Yeah," Felipe said simply. "When you practice, you can do it more and more. Pretty soon, you can cut out the noise, or listen to specific ones whenever you want. Try it on the voices like us."

Jeff looked at Holland, released her hand and tried to really focus on her through the cacophony in his head.

"Just let the other voices go," Felipe was saying. "Kinda picture them drifting away."

Jeff started with the screamers. Those were the ones that bothered him most. They drifted into silence. Then the ones he couldn't understand. That was frustrating. The ones that made up the tangled crowd around them like mango roots in a swamp—they quieted. The senator . . . *Don't listen,* he admonished himself. *Just put it away.* Finally, all that was left was Holland and Felipe. Felipe was calm. He heard Holland and Jeff because he wanted to hear them. Holland was trying it, too, skeptic though she was. There, she'd stopped the screaming. *That's it, darlin',* Jeff thought. *You're gonna be good at this. You've got such an organized mind.*

Don't insult me, or patronize. But she was smiling, with her success and something more.

Wouldn't be an insult coming from your father. He wondered if he'd blundered bringing up her father, but there was nothing he could do to stop the thought.

He wouldn't *say it.* Her thought was rueful. *And you're not my father, thank God.*

He could feel the prickle of sexual tension in her, felt it echoed in himself, and remembered at the same instant that Holland did that Felipe could read their thoughts as clearly as they could.

"*That* good?" he asked, one brow raised.

Jeff tried like hell to be silent.

"Yeah, that good," Holland murmured.

Jeff realized that the noise around him in the bar had diminished as well. He touched Holland's thigh. The thoughts around him pushed into his mind.

I wonder if he loves me?

Gotta get a haircut tomorrow.

Here goes the last of the paycheck.

He looked at Holland's turquoise eyes, felt her dismay. Then he consciously let the voices float away. They were stubborn. At first they wouldn't float. Then they started growing fainter. He didn't need to see the crease between Holland's brows relax to know that she was having some success as well.

"See?" Felipe announced. "What'd I tell y'all?" He slapped both thighs and rose. "See, a good deed done between sets. God, I'm righteous." He stood, looked down at them. "Just sit in this noisy ol' bar and practice, my children, while I go play some blues. . . ."

It was just as the next set was ending that they heard screaming in the streets. It happened at the moment when Felipe and Rusty and Lemon let their last note die away. People in the bar got up. Chairs overturned. "What the hell?" a beefy guy yelled. "What's that?" a woman screamed. You could feel the panic in the air.

Jeff looked at Holland. Whatever it was, it had to do with them.

Felipe and his band mates had started toward the front, consumed with curiosity.

"No," Jeff yelled. "Don't go out there!"

But it was too late; they were through the swinging doors. Jeff ran to the edge of the doorway and pressed himself against the wall. Police lights flashed red and blue, making the world into psychedelic unreality. Camouflaged men strode across the intersection to the zydeco place and pushed people back inside, their army-issue guns causing more shrill female screams. The *thwufts* that came in threes were hardly audible against the screams in the street. Lemon stumbled into a cop, Rusty staggered back against the press of people behind him, and Felipe just slowly sank to his knees as though in reverence.

"Come on!" Jeff shouted, and lunged back through the pressing crowd to where Holland stood frozen. "Out the back." He swung up the hinged part of the bar and dragged Holland through. Storeroom. He heard the bang of the swinging doors up front.

"Stay calm," a rough voice yelled. It was too late for calm. More female screams. Jeff put his weight into a doorway at the back of the storeroom, and then they were out in a little ratty garden. The iron gates to the street were closed. Another door. There had to be another way out of here. His eyes darted around the stone wall to the buildings above it. Too high. Only the iron gate. He pulled Holland toward it. He could feel her thinking. *This is it*.

He didn't disagree.

He could hardly believe it when the cop cars converged on the intersection below. His first impulse was to run. Before he could put that thought to action, though, the camouflaged Hummers pulled up and ringed the cop cars, along with a van that had no windows.

The army? Shit. They started for the bar where his targets had been for the last two hours, not even glancing up to where he and Jimmy Greaseball waited. They must not be after him. He would have relaxed, except that they must be after the targets, and they might be taking the targets away, where neither he nor Jimmy Greaseball could get them. This was his last chance. All that money was on the line right here, as well as the rights to future targets. They had to be coming back out to those Hummers or the police cars. Right into his sights. And Jimmy's sights. He wasn't going to let Jimmy get his targets.

Crowds pushed out of the bar. He trained his sight on the doorway. He didn't see his targets. Searing pain caught the shoulder he had hunched behind his rifle. Shocked, he glanced to the hotel across the street. Jimmy Greaseball was standing on his balcony, grinning. Jimmy got off another shot. Eddy's neck burned. He rocked back from the window. His vision blurred. Jimmy got off three shots at the street below, drifted back through the open French doors. Eddy's gaze dropped to the street as blackness closed in. Three black guys were down. Black guys? Jimmy Greaseball had hit three black guys. Where were his hits? But it was too late for that. Eddy felt a strange emptiness and sense of loss. Shit. It was going to end here. Eddy's vision faded altogether. He collapsed away from the window, and black was all that was left to him.

Chapter Twenty-eight

The four military guys dressed in camouflage and heavy, laced boots heaved Jeff's unconscious body into the back of the square van that looked like a spotted green-and-gold bakery truck. He slid a little way across the floor and came to rest in a crumpled heap.

"Ma'am," the one who gripped Holland's elbow said, in apology or command, she couldn't tell, as he urged her up into the back. To her horror, they heaved in three black plastic bags, oblong, with zippers up the front. She had seen enough body bags on television to know what they were. *Felipe!* The shock of those bags hit her like a blow. No more blues music. No more peace. Then the doors swung shut, a bolt was shot home, and she was left in blackness. She scrambled over to Jeff. The engine ground awake.

"Jeff," she whispered frantically. She rolled him onto his back. But for once the constant dialogue between them was silenced. Tears filled her eyes as she sat up and dragged him into her lap. "Don't be dead," she commanded.

Of course he wasn't dead. The doctor in her knew that. But the three blues guys were. And the memory of the troops closing in around them in the garden of the Absinthe House made her shudder. Jeff had pushed her behind him, and he'd gone out fighting. It made her want to cry in admiration, in frustration. The ferocity she'd felt in him wasn't frightening, but exhilarating, triumphant. He'd kicked two Marines, or whatever they were, in their groins, and swung a fist into the jaw of another. But the triumph was short-lived. One Marine buried a rifle-butt in Jeff's gut and another had brought the base of his gunstock down on Jeff's head. When his thoughts blinked out and he crumpled to the flagstone patio, Holland was left staring at a ring of impassive faces. They hadn't made a move for some moments. Were they appalled, somewhere under the stony stares, that their military prowess was directed against an unarmed civilian man and a frightened woman? But orders barked from the rear had mobilized them. They'd dragged Jeff up and gripped Holland's arms.

The van lurched into gear. She and Jeff had lost the battle for freedom. They were in the power of . . . who? The senator? And who was behind the senator? She had no idea where they were being taken, or what would become of them. Someone *did* want them alive. Her father? That should be a comfort, but she wasn't sure it was. The van staggered through its gears as it made its way out of the Quarter. The voices in her head were from those of her kind, even though she held Jeff in her lap. They seemed to reflect her agitation, stuttering and moaning with her dismay. Had they felt the horror that had happened here? Felipe and his friends couldn't help her now. Holland was alone with the thousands of voices. She chewed her lip as she tried to remember Felipe's lessons. Sort the voices. She shook her head as if that would lend her concentration. Slowly, she rid herself of all but the loudest of the voices in her head. One was the senator. He was feeling triumphant. He was getting into a limousine and ordering Brad to get some payment ready. Had he paid for this atrocity? She shuddered and looked for voices that might be able to comfort her. One was thinking about how his horses soothed him. Another wondered whether her new baby had inherited her malady. But there was no comfort.

She was alone, in spite of all the voices in her head.

The jolting didn't seem as though it would ever end. But it did. The van slowed. When the door opened on bright lights, Holland covered her eyes.

"Out!" someone shouted, and hands dragged her to the edge of the van. She stumbled onto asphalt. Many men. Rough voices in the night.

"Get them outta there."

Light stabbed her into blindness. Only slowly did a plane emerge, a small one, maybe an executive jet. They didn't quite push her up the stairs. She crouched to stumble into the cabin, looking back. Two soldiers dragged Jeff out onto the tarmac. He was regaining consciousness. She could tell because he vomited all over one soldier's boots. They pulled him up the stairs and dropped him into a seat before they strapped him in. Then came the parade of black bags, loaded on the floor at the rear of the plane. Tears slid down Holland's cheeks.

"Seatbelt, ma'am," one soldier said. Hysteria lurked in Holland's throat somewhere. What did it matter if she buckled her damned seatbelt? Two Marines sat behind her and two in front. The captain of this pirate vessel, dressed in a short-sleeved white shirt and an oh-so-business-like tie, glanced back and picked up the radio. His compatriot was flipping switches.

"Flight plan filed. Request permission to taxi."

Jeff slumped beside her. The engines whined up some scale to a tone Holland couldn't hear.

"Clearance, registered."

The plane rolled ahead, following the little blue lights onto the taxiway. The tarmac stretched out as far as Holland could see on either side. She slumped back in her seat. It was over.

"They're airborne," Doug reported.

"I'm on my way," Leland answered shortly. He sat in his office at home, unable to sleep.

"Our legislative friend had two snipers after them, in spite of our instructions."

That figured. "Did he? The arrogance of office—" He'd pay for his disobedience.

"I've got everything ready. At no little expense, I might add."

"Think of it as an investment. I'm on a red-eye. I'll be there by noon tomorrow."

"We have a lot to talk about."

Leland heard the accusation in Doug's tone. Doug had been on the verge of realization for days. Now it was a matter of controlling the reaction. "I know."

"We've totally lost control, Banks. It may infect an entire generation. What the hell are we going to do?"

"It *is* accelerating. But it won't affect a whole generation." Like hell it wouldn't. "Remember, most of them take care of themselves—a mysterious rash of suicides—that's all anyone will be able to call it. There will be symposiums from now until mid-century, attended by sincere duffle heads of pseudoscience, about the possible causes. They'll never guess the truth." He spoke soothingly. "And those few that are left, the thrivers, will be useful. Remember that. Isn't that why you got involved in the first place? If they're discovered, we'll publish the studies. I've already laid the groundwork for it."

"We'd better hope there are only a few." It was Doug's tacit agreement that he wanted mind readers for the government enough to see a lot of people die to get them. "I've alerted the appropriate organizations in Amsterdam, Tokyo, Beijing, Singapore, Moscow, Calcutta. The phenomenon is occurring worldwide at this point. I'm not mentioning the DNA changes, or these 'thrivers' you've identified. All we can hope is that our competitors write off everyone who's got it as insane and don't try to save an elite corps of perfect spies. Or that they don't know how to save them. We're starting the round of secondary states. I've written off most of Africa, since pretty much everyone there between twenty-five and fifty has AIDS."

"Get a conference call together. Let's see how much they know." Not much, probably. Even Doug didn't know the consequences of that infection men got after the flu. Nor did he know that naturals could breed and pass the genes along.

"Tomorrow at four Eastern. You sure you can be here by then?"

"Absolutely."

"Get some sleep on the plane, Leland. You're going to need it."

"Doug . . . I don't want our legislative mole to go shooting his mouth off to either side of the aisle, or in the executive branch. Are we clear on that?"

"Clear as a bell."

Doug hung up. Annoying habit he had. Leland ripped off the headset and flung it into the seat of his desk chair. He picked up his soft leather computer case and slung the strap over his shoulder. He hoped Doug had booked him at the Washington Ritz.

Jeff had a concussion. Holland crouched beside him and pulled up his eyelids. "Look in my eyes," she murmured. His thoughts were jumbled, his pupils dilated. His aura was a muddy brown, his skin still a little green. The motion of the plane probably didn't help his queasy stomach. She felt the eyes of the four Marines on her, though two had to crane around in their seats. Their guns were gripped as though they thought Jeff might leap to his feet and attack them. No danger of that. She felt the bump on his head gingerly. He winced.

Sorry. Can you hear me?

Through the static . . . sort of, he thought slowly.

"Lie back." She turned around. "Soldier! See if this thing stocks sparkling water."

The Marine looked rebellious. Because she was touching Jeff, and he was conscious, she could hear the man thinking that he was not about to become a stewardess.

"Calling them stewardesses is out of date. They're flight attendants now. And that's what you'll be if you want your cargo to arrive intact. This man has a bad concussion. And I'll bet whoever's calling the shots doesn't want him damaged. He's top-secret material, you know." She raised her eyebrows at the soldier. "He's queasy. If nothing else, I'd think you'd want to save your shoes."

The soldier looked at her, his eyes widening. He practically ripped off his seatbelt and lurched over to a little cabinet. He pulled open the door and surveyed the contents, wondering how she'd known he was thinking about stewardesses.

Holland looked at the other three guards. "You dumb shits," she said quietly. "You don't even know what they've got you doing here. We're your future." She surveyed them, making sure she wasn't touching Jeff, just to test them. No signs of distress, no whispering in her mind from them. Their eyes shifted nervously, but it wasn't because they were mutants—at least not yet. Still, she had to try to convince them. "Are you by any chance between the ages of twenty-five and forty?" Two of the Marines' expressions fell, almost comically. "Just by being here with us, you're scheduled to be where we are in a week, maybe two, maybe three." She was making this up, but they didn't have to know. "No one told you that we're sick, that our mutation is contagious? What an oversight."

The soldiers glanced uneasily between each other.

"Oh, well. You might not get exactly where we are now. *We've* gotten through the worst. Lots of people don't survive the first onslaught. Why do you think the papers are

341

full of suicides? We're two of the lucky ones." Holland turned her attention back to Jeff, and took the club soda offered by the Marine behind her. What she'd just said hadn't done any good.

She gave Jeff the glass of sparkling water, and he took it in shaking hands she steadied with her own. "Slowly," she urged him. He sipped the bubbly water. "Just take it easy. We've got time." She glanced at the pilot, still touching Jeff. "It's probably three hours to Washington."

The Marines jerked erect, wary, not sure how she knew their destination.

"We can hear you thinking." She smiled grimly. Let them consider that. "Okay, so it's only two hours and twenty minutes." She stared at the guy who had been thinking that.

"Miss, take your seat, now," he said nervously. "That's enough of that talk."

Holland sat across from Jeff and jerked her seatbelt tight. She managed a smile. "Whatever you say, soldier." She had to be strong here, because Jeff was rocky. She was all they had between them and the unpredictability of guys who liked guns.

With her adrenaline ebbing. Holland felt drained. What she wanted was to give herself up to sleep. But something more important called. There was nothing for it. She had to go to the bathroom. The only facilities on the plane were a curtain that you could draw around a seat with a cover, back in the rear. Not appealing. She'd have to step over the body bags. She touched the Marine across from her and watched him start. Some guard. "I've got to go," she said, and unbuckled her seatbelt.

The Marine glanced around, then curled his fingers around the grip of his handgun in its holster. He nodded briskly. "All right, Ma'am. I'll go with you."

"I wouldn't be firing a handgun inside a pressurized plane," she remarked, and pushed herself erect. She headed to the rear. The little area around which you pulled the curtain was absurdly small. The Marines would see every gyration as she tried to get her jeans down and sit on the seat as the plane rocked and swayed. Stupid worry, considering the big picture. She swallowed hard and stepped over the stacked black bags. She wouldn't think.

When she was done, she pulled the curtain aside and tried to step back across the body bags. As she touched the top one with her shin, she felt it stir.

"My God!" she yelped.

The Marines swiveled. Two knelt on their seats. Four guns jerked from their holsters and were pointed at her. She raised her hands. "Okay. It's okay." But it wasn't okay. "I felt the body bag move." All eyes, including Jeff's and hers, dropped to the plastic bag. It moved again.

There was an unmistakable groan. *Where am I?*

Holland knelt immediately. "Felipe! Felipe, is that you?" She reached for the zipper.

"I'd leave that alone, Miss, if I were you."

Holland raised her gaze to see two pairs of cold eyes, and two pair of nervous ones, alternately staring at her and glancing to the body bag.

"Well, if he's alive, *somebody's* going to have to open it," she said with some asperity.

"Return to your seat, miss. We'll handle this." It was one of the cold-eyed Marines. The nervous ones looked like they didn't want to handle anything.

There was no facing down guns and men who might love to use them. Holland stepped over the body bags and sat beside Jeff. *He's alive.*

I heard. But Jeff didn't think he'd be alive for long.

The grate of a zipper made Holland crane around her seat. "He's alive, all right," the Marine said. The zipper grated again. "But he's shot bad—maybe nicked an artery." He pulled the bag open. "How'd they think he was dead?" Felipe's head lolled to the left and another groan escaped him. A stream of half-congealed blood pooled on the cabin floor.

343

"Shock probably stopped his pulse for the wrong minute." Holland made her voice as casual as she could. "Anybody know anything about field dressings?"

"I do," one of the nervous Marines murmured.

Okay. There was no way out of it. Guns or no guns, she wasn't going to let Felipe die. She got up out of her seat. "See if this thing's got a first-aid kit," she ordered the soldier beside her. She pushed her way to the back.

"Wait a minute." The guy with the steely eyes blocked her way.

"You think whoever's giving orders wouldn't want this one alive if he could get him? He's just like us, you know. And I may be a shrink, but shrinks train as doctors first. So, if you think carefully, you might want to let me see if I can save him."

"First-aid kit!" came a triumphant shout behind her. "It's a good one."

The guy with steely eyes glanced behind her. She took that as acquiescence and pushed by him.

"Felipe, it's Holland," she said softly as she surveyed the damage. It was bad. He'd been hit in the thigh just below the groin and was bleeding badly. The femoral artery was at least grazed. He was going to die for real if she couldn't control the bleeding. "What's in the kit—a tourniquet?" she yelled. She felt for wetness on Felipe's torso. His patterned, rust-colored dashiki made it hard to tell if there were other wounds. No, it was pretty much only the thigh. The Marine behind her fumbled in the metal box. If she had to use a tourniquet, he'd probably lose the leg. She physically grabbed the Marine closest to her, another of the nervous ones. "Put pressure here," she said, placing his hand on Felipe's groin where the blood oozed alarmingly.

"Got some coagulant spray, Doc!" the Marine crowed.

Excellent! "Hand it over." She grabbed the little can and scanned the fine print. Fibrinogen. This *was* a good first-aid kit. "Okay. Genetically altered clotting protein. Comes from cow's milk." Holland ripped Felipe's pant leg around the hand of the guy who was applying pressure.

"Works in two minutes, Doc," the Marine assured her. "Even better than the coagulant bandages we used in Iraq."

She shook the can. "Okay, release," she commanded. The guy pulled back and she sprayed the welling blood with the foam. It hardened within seconds. She examined the edges of the puffy seal. No leaks.

She sat back and breathed.

"Good work, Doc," the guy beside her said.

"Yeah, Doc. I think you saved him." This from the one who found the spray.

"Just a spray. Any of you could have done it."

"Maybe," the Marine said. "But you did good." Grudging respect from the hard-eyed one. He thought better of her because she'd pushed him around.

Will he make it? she heard Jeff thinking.

"I hope so," she whispered, suddenly trembling. Felipe had lost a lot of blood. There were definitely no guarantees.

Chapter Twenty-nine

From the approach, you couldn't see that it was five-sided; it was simply a monolithic office building of immense proportions, stretching away into the distance. Holland touched Jeff's hand and heard their guards' knowledge: The Pentagon.

The morning air was heavy. Virginia was going to be muggy today, but not where they were going to be. They would be sealed away with guards and air conditioning. Holland looked at the sky, drinking in the blue, not sure when she would see it again. In they went, through the massive doors in the center of the side that faced them. Jeff and Holland were surrounded by the four Marines. Felipe had been rushed off by ambulance direct from the plane. She had no idea where he was. So it was just the two of them again against the entire military establishment of the most powerful country in the world. That didn't feel great.

They were expected. The uniformed guard at the desk gave the Marines instructions and gestured them ahead. Elevators swept everyone down. A long way down. Holland wondered whether the people who worked down here were the important ones, protected by the mass of concrete above. But the halls were filled only with functionaries, like any office building. Young men and women slipped by the burly Marines and their charges. Holland glanced at Jeff. He was trying to put down panic, just as she was.

They stopped to check in with another guard at a reception desk. Then it was down a second set of elevators. Holland, grasping Jeff's arm, found the plaid shirt comforting. He had recovered his senses, though she knew he had one ripping big headache. He looked haggard. His beard was a two-day growth again. He was sweating slightly. He glanced over at her and managed a smile. He didn't feel like smiling. He did it for her. It made her heart break.

The round metal doors that confronted them looked like they were from a gigantic submarine, or maybe a bank vault. Two impassive guards in blue dress uniforms with crisp white hats stood beside it. They pulled a huge lever until it spun loosely and the door opened.

Holland found herself trembling.

"This is where we leave you," the hard-eyed Marine barked.

Holland and Jeff just stood in front of the open door. Holland looked up at the sergeant, or whatever he was. His eyes were less certain now, less cold, since he could see the fear in hers.

"In with you," he said in a low voice.

Jeff took her arm. "Nothin' for it, darlin'." His tone was careless, if his emotions were not.

They stepped across the raised threshold into what did look like a bank vault. There were two couches-cum-bunks, two chairs, medium-comfortable looking, and a table where someone had placed a puzzle and a deck of cards in mock congeniality. A stack of quilts sat in a parody of hominess at the foot of one of the couches. A video screen at ceiling height flipped like the old TV classic, *Outer Limits.* A regular door ajar across the room revealed a toilet and a shower.

Jeff glanced around him, and Holland followed his gaze. *Cameras. Microphones.*

Behind them, the iron vault door clanged shut. Air hissed as it was sealed.

"Jeff," she whispered aloud, unable to suppress the tremble in her voice. He put his arm around her, and immediately the silence comforted her.

"It's okay, darlin'. We're alive, and we're together. Don't borrow trouble."

You think we need to borrow? This looks like trouble enough.

He agreed with her, no matter what he tried to think. The crackle of red fear in his aura was still a little murky. Two lines of pain creased between his brows.

"You'd think we could get some painkillers around here," she said aloud, looking up at the cameras and the microphones. "Since your goons gave Jeff a concussion."

She took his arm and led him to one of the couches. They sat together, his arms around her shoulders. *What are they going to do with us?* She couldn't help the thought.

347

Study us, I guess. Figure out a way to use us. He closed his eyes. The rich fringe of lashes brushed his cheeks. *Things could be worse. They could have killed us like Rusty and Lemon.*

Sorrow washed over Holland. *And maybe Felipe. They'd better be getting Felipe into surgery, pronto. I don't know how he lasted, with all the blood he lost.* They were so alone.

Jeff opened his eyes. *He's one tough mo fo, that's how. So are we. We're not dead yet, either.*

So cocky, she thought. *So vulnerable.*

Jeez, Holly, don't go all gushy on me.

She stiffened at the use of the nickname.

"I know, I know. Your father calls you that," he murmured into her neck. His breath made her shudder. "But I'm not your father. And I like it. Holly is a nice name. Not so much like a stuffy doctor. More like a friend."

"I've always hated the diminutive." She could feel the edge in her voice.

"There are two kinds of diminutive, Holland. One meant to belittle you, one meant to . . ." He thought a moment. "One meant to convey affection. Can't I use the second kind?"

How much her father had ruled her life! Jeff was right. "Maybe we could try it out."

He nodded, his eyes lighting. Magenta glowed around him.

Now who's going gushy? she asked.

He looked around at their sterile cell. *Maybe we need a few hearts and flowers.*

The air in the doorway sighed, just before it opened inward. This was it. Their captors were at hand. Holland leaned away from Jeff. She would need the noise to hear the senator.

It was her father who ducked through the door. Holland started. "Dad?" His aura was that excited, ambitious orange again.

348

Jeff went rigid. Behind her father stooped a man who was balding, with a shiny pate and a fringe of gray, his equally gray eyes opaque behind heavy-framed glasses.

"Holly. Jeff." Her father nodded as he straightened. "I'm glad you made it okay." He put a paper that had several pills on it down on the table with the puzzle. "For your headache, Jeff."

"Made it *okay?*" Holland repeated. She felt her anger rise. "Some rabid military types just about beat Jeff to a pulp," she said, rising. She let her thigh touch Jeff's knee. "And they killed Rusty and Lemon, and maybe Felipe." *And you knew that,* she thought. *You knew all about it.*

Her father looked surprised. He obviously thought he could still conceal things from them. Which he couldn't. Not as long as she and Jeff were touching. "Two different problems, my dear. Your Negro friends succumbed to Senator Lendreaux's ex-military sharpshooters." He smiled apologetically. "The gentleman from Louisiana got a little out of hand. Doug's taken care of it."

"The *senator* set the snipers on the blues guys?" Jeff asked.

"Sorry, but yes." Leland Banks shrugged. "You would have been killed, too, if Doug and I hadn't sent in the cavalry."

Well, at least that was the truth.

"Oh," Jeff said sarcastically. "You were just saving us from the nasty senator?" He glanced around pointedly. "This looks safe."

"It is." Her father looked smug. Holland wanted to scream. "We need you, you know."

"I'll just bet you do," Jeff agreed. "Didn't finish your little experiments?"

"No, in fact," her father answered mildly. She could feel his underlying excitement, hear his self-congratulation.

Still, his thoughts surprised her. "*You* got rid of the senator?" she asked slowly. "You're the power behind all this?"

Her father shrugged. "Doug and I. Right, Doug?"

349

The man with the cold eyes nodded silently. He didn't volunteer more.

"This is Doug Wagner. He works for . . . well, never mind about where he works. Doug has lots of official resources. Or, maybe we should call them un-official."

"I'm your *daughter*. How can you give me up to the government for experimentation?" Holland swayed a little on her feet.

"I wish it could have been me, Holly. You don't know how much." The pain emanating from him she had never felt before. She had touched some core of desire, regret, so powerful as to be almost overwhelming. "To bear the gene of the future?" he asked. "I still don't know why it appears only in your generation. But my generation is left beached on the shore of the old world." He straightened his shoulders. "Since you are the only thriving female we have been able to acquire, you are of paramount importance to our inquiries."

"I may be the only one so far, but there will be others—lots of others." Holland didn't like the defensive sound of her voice.

"I doubt it. The suicide rates are climbing dramatically. That was always an inherent risk in the mutation. Most of you will die. That's one of the reasons we need to protect you." Holland felt his satisfaction that the mutation was widespread. He thought it would affect the whole generation. She looked at Jeff. Her father had spread it deliberately.

That realization shuddered in her brain. Jeff's eyes opened wide.

He was afraid it would disappear again if there were only a few who had it. Jeff was shocked, but not as shocked as she. Holland turned to her father, straining to hear more. Her father's eyes glanced from one to the other of them, suspicious of their exchanged glances. He knew that they could trade thoughts. She glimpsed another of her father's thoughts, so fleeting, suppressed so quickly that she

350

couldn't identify it. But it made her feel uneasy.

"Wait. Why do you need females?" Jeff's voice was hard, incisive.

Her father raised his eyebrows. His companion was only flat-eyed. Holland had no attention for him. "We have to see what the mutation does, not only in this generation, but in future generations. We need a breeding population."

Holland felt her mouth drop open, then shut it abruptly. "Dad?" Her voice was small.

"You'll be the mother of the future, Holly. A controlled future, not the chaos we have beginning now. Your genes—"

"My genes are my own!" She looked around the prison with new eyes, and her glance fell on Jeff. "You're going to breed me to Jeff?"

"He's one likely candidate. If we can save Felipe Laveau, he might do." Again the fleeting thought that was suppressed. She almost reached for Jeff's hand but suddenly, she didn't want to know what her father was thinking. It was too frightening.

"You see," her father continued, "the males pass the anomaly once the virus infects their reproductive organs. But in naturals, the germic chromosomes are already affected in both sexes. The possibility of crossing two naturals is very exciting, even more than crossing one infected by my virus with a natural."

Holland didn't need to wonder what color horror was. She could see that it was flashing purple in a seething black just by looking Jeff's aura. Hers would look the same.

"I won't do it," she said.

Her father chuckled. "Don't worry, Holly. You don't have to embarrass yourself. We only need sperm and an egg. A little incision every month to harvest what we need—an inconvenience, nothing more. Science does the rest."

Holland thought she might explode.

It isn't worth it, Holly. Save the outrage. Jeff tested out a reassuring smile. It wasn't. Not with his aura the color it was. He sensed something more wrong, too. What could be more wrong than using her eggs against her will to create babies from Jeff or Felipe for her father's colony?

She turned on Jeff. Not worth it? He reached to take her arm, but she pulled away and spun again to the silent bureaucrat and her waiting father. "This is one rat that isn't going to cooperate."

"You're upset right now. But when you realize what's at stake, you'll think about your role more seriously." Her father smiled kindly.

"You have something else up your sleeve, Doctor Banks," Jeff said slowly. Holland could feel him focus. "I can't see you waiting around for years for the next generation to see how it turns out."

Her father grimaced. Holland saw his aura go aubergine again. He raised his eyebrows lightly, and gave a small smile. "Since you asked, I might as well prepare you." He glanced at Doug. "It can't do any harm, not now." He turned to face Jeff. "I'm interested in how the DNA strand achieves its object. The new DNA strand must command the RNA to make proteins that in turn from enzymes to construct new tissue. New capabilities must be constructed to 'hear' others' thoughts, and to 'see' auras. Existing organs or capabilities could be enhanced or new ones created. I've been thinking—Holly, you will appreciate this—that I might replicate the structures themselves, using stem cells that emulate the new organs. We skip the intervening steps of replicating DNA entirely."

Even without touching Jeff, Holland got the forced coldness that he was imposing on himself very clearly. It made her shiver. What was under the coldness? "What 'structures,' Dad?"

Her father looked away. "There will no doubt be a part of the brain that receives the signals, perhaps the area that harnesses what we would call psychic abilities. I think the eyeball may have new receptors in addition to the normal cones and rods, which may communicate with another part of the brain to 'see' colors others can't."

He wasn't being entirely forthcoming. What was he hiding? Holland braced herself against whatever she might learn here. "So . . . that means lots of research on cadavers, right?"

Her father stared at her. "We need information about how the organs work while they're alive and functional. And we need to collect live cells from the enhanced organs for the stem cells to emulate. Cadavers are not useful."

The realization of what he meant enveloped her. Holland began to shake with rage. "You're going to vivisect your own daughter—is that it?"

"Never you, Holly." He glanced to Jeff.

"Dad!" she shouted.

Jeff stared at him, his own aura tight with bundled red anger. "Sounds like Nazi experiments in the concentration camps."

"It's necessary. We can't wait for the usual research cycle of cadavers and monkeys before we study the effect in functioning humans. Monkeys wouldn't work, and we need to know now."

Holland felt the desperation well inside her. Her father was capable of . . . *this* in the name of science? "Hey, you can't destroy my partner in the future generations, right?" She felt like a little girl, begging her father to spare punishment for something she'd done.

He glanced to her, kindly. "All we need is his sperm."

Holland wanted to shriek. "So you'd risk blinding him, or damaging his brain? Dad, you can't mean this. It's against every scientific principle."

"I'll use a reputable surgeon," he protested, as if that were enough.

Jeff reached for her. "Holly," he whispered, trying to calm her. "It's no use." But by touching her he was making

353

his own bid for truth. He wanted to hear her father's thoughts. Maybe he wanted her to hear them.

She stared at her father. His anger simmered just beneath the surface, along with incredible anguish. She saw clearly what he wanted. He was devastated that he would be left behind in this new human generation. He felt he'd been cheated, and he was willing to sacrifice all scientific principle, all morality even, to find a way to share his daughter's new gift, or her curse. He was jealous on a level Holland found astounding, intimidating. He would do anything to have what she and Jeff had. Anything. He had a plan. He was going to replicate the new sensory capabilities she and Jeff had developed with stem-cell technology and inject them into his own brain and eyes. In that way he could be like them, even though he couldn't assimilate the genetic structure that created the organs naturally in them. Was the man who stood before her even recognizable as her father?

"Don't worry, Holly," he was saying. "We'll use surrogate mothers. Harvesting the eggs will just leave a little scar. You won't be used for surgery."

What was he saying? He had moved from the creation of new abilities in himself back to the breeding program.

And that was when she felt his love wash over her, his pride that she was one of the chosen for the new generation. The pride she'd always longed for . . . She finally felt it.

"Not this way," she murmured. "Not like this!" He was deranged. As deranged as any psychotic she had ever treated. But he loved her. And in one final way she couldn't help, couldn't even control, she had not disappointed him.

But there was something more. She gripped Jeff's arm as the rest came washing over her.

"After all," her father said, smiling, his pride suffusing his aura in a green glow. "You are the first, the mother of an entire generation of the new order."

Holland's stomach clenched. He thought she was the root of all the spreading mutations. He was proud of that. It couldn't be true! This horror of suicide and madness wasn't her fault!

"You don't believe me, Holly. But it's true. You were the first 'natural' mutation I found. I used your genes to develop the genetic package my vector would carry. It's your DNA that has escaped into the population."

"How?" But he didn't need to speak. She saw it all flickering in his memory. He was the one who had made her sick five years ago. He was so proud of his subterfuge. He'd weakened her immune system with low-grade poison. He'd wanted her to be so sick she'd end up in the hospital, her care under his direction. There, he'd had her DNA tested. And then there were the blood tests, every month, ostensibly to check the levels of immune suppressant. That was how he'd taken her DNA strings to cultivate and attach to his viruses.

"Why?" she whispered. "Why did you want to test my DNA so badly?"

She felt him contract. "I had to know if you were mine. You were so bright, Holly. You *had* to be mine. But your mother . . ."

Fred. She and Jeff thought it at the same time. Her mother had been unfaithful, and when her father had discovered that, he'd become obsessed with knowing.

And then she felt the pain of the outcome. He had taken her DNA because he wanted proof of her paternity. But she wasn't his. She wasn't his daughter. Holland gasped as though she'd been struck.

Her father turned awkwardly away, embarrassed by his own emotion. "I'll get that monitor fixed. You'll want to follow news in the outside world. It's likely to be interesting."

Her father led the way back through the bank vault door. Doug Wagner followed. It clanged shut. A moment later the shush of air said it had been sealed. Holland

355

stood, rigid, in the center of the cell floor, gazing stonily after her father.

Jeff went back to the couch and collapsed on it.

"How could he be so . . . evil?" she whispered after a moment. *And he's not my father. And he knows it, but he still loves me, even though he's evil.* Confused emotions overwhelmed all thought. Her lungs started pulling for air of their own accord, gasping.

Evil? Jeff thought. *Sounds like something my parents would say.*

"Okay." She was angry now. "Sick. Psychotic. That better?" Fear of those ways she was like her father vied with her anger.

"He's so directed he's lost all shades of gray, all other points of view. It's not so uncommon," Jeff muttered.

"Maybe that's what evil is," Holland choked.

"It's just a fact. Don't load up on morality." But Jeff didn't believe that. His truths always carried a load of morality. That's why he investigated frauds and people who took advantage of others. "Come sit with me. You made different choices than he did."

She settled into his arms. She *had* made different choices. She'd sacrificed focus for connection to others. And she may have been dragged by circumstance into connecting with Jeff, but it was her choice now. She'd been at least as afraid of commitment as Jeff was. Yet, when she wondered whether to make that commitment, it had already happened.

Jeff's answering emotion enveloped her in a magenta glow.

"He wants what we have," she said in a small voice.

Jeff chuckled ruefully. "Right now, I'd give it to him if I could." He rubbed her shoulder.

She couldn't cry. She couldn't forgive. But she didn't have to be like him. There was some reassurance in that.

With a jerk, Holland stood and stalked to the table to gather the pills. She held them out.

"You think they're safe?"

She grunted in derision. "Absolutely. He won't endanger his prime specimen until he get what he wants."

Jeff downed the pills without water. *Did you hear what the guy with the glasses was thinking?* He was trying to distract her from her pain. It wouldn't work.

She shook her head. *I was busy being appalled by my father.* A shot of pain coursed through her, and she pushed it down. He wasn't even her father at all.

Yes, he is.

She raised her eyes to his. "He proved he's not. I should be glad of that."

Jeff bit his lip. "Biology isn't the driver here. The one who raised you is the one you have to deal with. Leland Banks is your true father."

Holland laughed bitterly. "That makes me feel just great."

"I don't like mine much, either. It was you who made me hear what his demons were. You just heard some of your father's. He feels left out, abandoned by the very genetics he's spent his life studying."

"You want me to forgive him," she accused. "I mean, he made me sick, sick enough to almost die, just so he'd have an excuse to take my blood for a DNA match." She began to pace, anger fueling her steps. "And he used me, for years, and all the time he must have been watching me for signs that the anomaly was activating. That's why he always called me a late bloomer. And he knew, he *knew*, I'd never knuckle under to his sick experiments and scientific shortcuts, so he tricked me into giving blood once a month to that slimeball Grayson, who gave it right to him. Patient privacy? They stole my genes to further their own ends!"

"Calm, girl," Jeff said, taking her hand and drawing her back down.

"And he tried to trick me into joining him in his studies, knowing I'd see the relationship between my growing symptoms, and yours, and . . . and his other subjects."

"I don't want you to forgive him. Hell, *I* don't forgive him," Jeff said to interrupt the flow of her anger and pain. "But don't give him the victory of tearing up your life."

"You think he hasn't torn up my life?" she practically yelled.

"Okay, okay," Jeff soothed. "How about, you don't let him tear up who you are? Isn't that why you took me to the revival?"

"I guess so."

He raised his brows.

"Yeah. Yeah, it was." She pressed her lips together.

"He made you strong and smart, you know."

Oh, she did not want to hear that. "He's so self-involved he's pathological, Jeff."

"And you're not. Again, you made different choices. Happens all the time." He ran his palm over the denim on her thigh.

He was right. She'd been alone most of her life. That was her father's path. But she wasn't alone anymore. She loved Jeff.

"Great choice," he whispered. "Don't think I don't appreciate it." She could feel him grin as he nibbled on her ear. Anger dissolved in the face of the throb that brought.

She laughed. "Not now, you disreputable rogue." Where was the ice-maiden stuff when she needed it? *Back to business, here. We have a problem or two. What about the guy with the glasses?*

Yeah, well, he doesn't necessarily think your father is running the show. And he's not a happy camper. Jeff looked at her steadily. *Your father* spread *the anomaly.*

"I felt that." Holland's voice trembled. *He wants to make sure it will survive.*

Wagner doesn't know your father planned the spread. He thinks your father bungled the job, and he's angry. Really angry. They both think there's no stopping it.

358

Holland leaned into Jeff's solid body. Quiet settled in. She realized that the buzz of voices hadn't bothered her while she was focused on Jeff even without the touching. She could feel his surprise as well. *Do you think we're getting the hang of this?*

Day late and a dollar short, darlin'.

No question about that. She glanced up as the monitor above their heads flickered into a picture and real sound instead of static.

"And now to return to the story at hand." It was CNN. The black woman with carefully upswept hair and a blue tailored suit was grave. "The wave of world suicides continues. The totals are staggering and growing by the hour. The Center for Disease Control has just issued a statement linking the suicides to the incidence of flu symptoms in people between twenty-five and forty. Very few self-inflicted deaths have been recorded outside that age range, and the victims have all exhibited symptoms of stress and psychosis prior to their suicide attempt."

Jeff and Holland looked at each other, feeling helpless.

"This just in. People are jumping off the Golden Gate Bridge." She glanced to her paper. "The National Guard has been posted at the entrance to that bridge as well as the Brooklyn Bridge, five major bridges across the Mississippi, and even London Bridge in Lake Havasu."

"Turn it off," Holland yelled, jumping up to find a switch. She couldn't reach the controls. Jeff rose, reached above her head, and hit the off button. The screen didn't fade to black. It kept scrolling stock market stats and quoting suicide stats in sepulchral tones.

"I can't stand this," Holland muttered into his shoulder. "I don't think I can stand this."

"I know, darlin', I know."

"It's my genes that are causing all this pain. My father made me into Typhoid Mary."

Chapter Thirty

The lights went out in the isolation chamber. Only the gleam of the monitor that wouldn't stop spewing noise and horrifying images lit the room in flickering light. Then the sound dimmed to a whisper. Someone wanted them to get some sleep. They were probably right. Even though she and Jeff had dozed fitfully all afternoon, limp with exhaustion, Holland wasn't refreshed, and neither was he. She had dreamed again, the awful kind where she was evil—a danger to all mankind. Only, now the dreams were real. She was not human, not the way that humans were constructed yesterday, and how could anyone be anything but evil whose genes had been the cause of all this pain?

Jeff dreamed, too. She could hear his dreams when she wasn't in the grip of her own nightmares. But now he wasn't thinking about being powerful and evil. There were no knives. Now he felt small and vulnerable, a rat in a maze who didn't know the right response to stop the shocks meted out by some unknown experimenter. Holland woke several times, in response to her nightmares or to his. They tried to comfort each other, each knowing how little confidence the other felt. The guards had brought in some cafeteria food for dinner that neither of the captive lab rats felt much like eating.

Holland huddled in Jeff's arms, wondering if tonight would be the last night they had together before her father put Jeff under the knife.

Holland felt Jeff reach out beyond their cell, testing his ability to hear other minds. She joined him, almost unconsciously. One of the guards outside their sealed cell wanted to get home to his wife and kids; one worried about credit card debt. She felt a doctor of some kind, checking... checking on Felipe. Felipe was here? The doctor thought Felipe was alive. Alive! She zeroed in, trying to hear him. Yes... there he was, weak, groggy. They'd repaired the femoral artery, given him enough blood to float a ship. He was close, too.

Felipe's alive, Jeff thought.

That's a big total of one.

Felipe, buddy, hang in there. We know you're there. We won't forget you.

I hope he can hear you. Holland listened.

I hear you—she heard faintly. Then she felt Felipe drift away.

"And tonight," the man with impeccable gray hair was saying on the monitor above, "we have sad news for the people of Louisiana. Senator Emile Lendreaux, who has served them for the last eight years, and was a rising star in national politics, was assassinated while leaving a rally he was holding in New Orleans at the Sheraton Hotel this evening."

Holland turned to Jeff, inquiring. "Guess Doug did take care of it," Jeff murmured.

"His aide, Brad Weller, gave a statement to the press saying that the police have taken a professional hit man— James Bonafacio, known by some as Jimmy Greaseball— into custody for the murder of Senator Lendreaux. Mr. Bonafacio learned his sharpshooting skills in the military when he served in Desert Storm. He has known connections to organized crime. He may also be involved in an incident which resulted in the death of three local musicians and a man, also found with a high caliber rifle, at the intersection of Conti and Bourbon streets in New Orleans last night."

"He must have been the sniper who killed Lemon and Rusty," Holland said.

"Unless he killed the sniper who killed those guys. Shh, let's hear from Brad."

"This tragic end to a promising career of an extraordinary man has saddened us all," Brad was saying.

"But the senator hired the snipers, why would one of them kill him?"

Jeff stared at the screen. *Maybe they didn't know he hired them. He wasn't the one who paid them. How could he? He would have used a go-between, a money man. Like Brad.*

"Geez. So Brad double-crossed him, and paid the sniper to kill him?"

Possibly. *Brad, Brad, Brad. You little devil, working for Doug all the time. And then you betrayed the sniper. Bet he doesn't last long in jail.*

So, how old is Brad, do you think? Holland felt a sudden certainty in her mind.

"Wonder if he's had the flu lately," Jeff mumbled in her ear so his words wouldn't be picked up by the microphones. Or maybe they heard everything.

"Bet he has a great political future."

"Now, back to the story of the suicides sweeping the nation and—"

"I don't think I can bear to listen to this all again, Jeff." Holland clutched his chest and burrowed her face into his shoulder. "I'm the reason they're—"

"You're not. They've got copies of the changed gene you share with me, and with Felipe, and probably with countless others around the world." His lips moved over her hair. "If anything; it's your father's fault. And maybe it would have happened anyway. We can't know. We can't spend time torturing ourselves over it."

She pushed herself up and looked at him, searched his face. His green eyes were serious, the puckered mouth that was too small, too delicate for such a bear of a man was

pressed into a determined line. "The real question, darlin',
is what we are going to do about it."

She glanced up to the monitor. A soldier in some strange
uniform was screaming as he sprayed automatic fire into
a crowd. "And in Thailand—"

"Shut it out!" Jeff commanded. He turned Holland's face
to his. She felt him lead the way. He focused on her and
the words of the announcer faded. "That's it, Holly. We're
not lost yet."

*Oh, yeah? Well, I'm feeling a little lost, okay? We're
sealed inside this prison, about to become fodder for some
unpleasant experiments while the world is self-destructing
outside. And as far as I can see there's nothing we can do
about it.*

She could feel Jeff's panic, see the red of anger and the
brown of fear in his aura. He swallowed. *So, let's think of
something.* She felt him struggling with the muddy brown
by pushing up the red of his anger. That was what he
meant by letting rebellion heal you. *We've been going
about this all wrong.*

Glad to hear you say it, she thought wryly. She actually
managed to be wry. *I'd hate to think this was the right
strategy.*

Suddenly, she felt him lighten. Blue crept into his aura.
We've been thinking of ourselves as victims. She felt his
sureness grow. *All this sound comes washing over us. We're
just the passive receptors. And things happen to us: snipers,
your father, and dear invisible Doug.*

You're not making any sense. She couldn't help her impatience. *Of course we're victims. We're in prison, aren't
we?*

His eyes widened. His mouth opened a little and a smile
tickled the edges of his lips. *Maybe only because we
haven't decided to get out, darlin'.* He searched her face,
his gaze flickering. *Why can't we send, instead of just receiving sound? People can hear us. We know that. We're*

strong and getting stronger. Felipe said that. I feel it. Don't you?

She nodded, slowly. It was as though she'd been blind all her life, only to discover that she'd just been closing her eyes. "We can help them, can't we?"

And when they get something, maybe they can help us.

Her breasts heaved. She held her lungs full as she looked at him, hope mingling with the fear and dread for the first time. She let the air escape slowly and nodded. *Let's do it then.*

He touched her lips with two fingers. They were warm. His aura was a deep, pulsing magenta now, and his eyes roved over her face. The indigo took but a moment to creep into the magenta in bubbling pools. She knew what that meant. She began to throb between her legs. Was it the rush of possibility that let her respond? Was it relief, or fear?

Jeff's thoughts raced. *We need all the power we can get for "broadcast mode." We know what will increase the volume. . . .*

She knew what he meant. She could feel the physicality of him, and she felt his consciousness of his body and its growing sensation. He glanced behind him to the monitor. *Can you do it?*

The throb said maybe she could, but only maybe. She shook her head. *Not in front of cameras.*

Jeff glanced around and reached for one of the quilts stacked neatly on the floor. It was a wedding-ring design. Jeff pulled it over and shook it out. He was grinning now. *Fuck 'em.* Ah, that delightful, protective rebellion of his. It made Holland go soft just to look at the mischievous light in his eyes. Once, the clinical part of her would have said rebellion was adolescent, something to outgrow. Now, all she could think was that it was endearing and contagious.

Why not? Fuck 'em. She kicked off her leather clogs as Jeff flapped the quilt over her shoulders. He was kicking off his boots. They thudded on the metal floor. Then he lay back and pulled the quilt over her head, shutting out the glow of the monitor and casting them in almost-darkness. She could just make out his features. Suddenly, giggles overtook her as she unbuttoned and pulled his shirt out of his jeans. It was like they were teenagers at some sleep-over camp, about to do some very naughty night maneuvers. Jeff's answering chuckles rumbled in his chest. Only he was remembering a real incident in a college dorm with his roommate snoring in the next bed. His partner was a redhead.

Don't you dare be thinking of another woman, Jeff McQueen, Holland thought severely, as she lay along his body and unbuttoned her jeans. He was doing the same. But she couldn't quit giggling as she realized what the quilt would look like from the outside, all moving lumps, as though it were alive. She pulled one arm out of her sweater sleeve and then the other. How could she be giggling when the world was falling apart and they were trapped in this awful place?

Because what else can you do, Holly? Jeff pushed at his jeans and then kicked them off the couch. He wasn't thinking of his college dorm anymore. He was thinking how much he wanted her. He was admitting to himself how much he'd grown to need her. He didn't mean just as a partner in escape. She was startled. Somehow hearing it directly in his mind was so much more intimate than if he had declared his love aloud. She was almost moved to tears.

When had she started needing him? Maybe even before the first time they made love and experienced the joining. She just hadn't admitted it to herself. He had all the rough edges that somehow balanced her smooth, sliding way of coping. His drive to action equalized her preoccupation with motive and emotion. But that was oversimplification. You couldn't reduce what they were to each other to blithe opposites. Unless you called them soul mates. Jeff's words. Maybe that was the only description that fit.

What fit together were their mouths. Holland bent and pressed her lips to Jeff's as he shrugged out of his shirt. The feel of his lips against hers sent shock waves through her. He pushed her slacks and underwear over her hips in one smooth gesture. She wiggled out of them shamelessly, and he shoved them out from under the quilt with one foot. Then he took her face in both hands, and applied himself more assiduously to kissing. The wash of his desire enflamed her. His commitment enveloped her like warm smoke. She straddled his hips and felt his ready length against her most moist parts. He ran his hands along her back and over her buttocks, clenching them lightly. Then he leaned up to suck one nipple. The wet of his tongue, the sweet tug of his lips, made her shudder. She rubbed herself along him. It was all he could do to restrain himself.

Don't, she thought. *Join with me.*

He clutched her to his body and rolled with her until he was on top. She didn't mind. She wanted him inside her, wanted his weight. She spread herself to him and as he pushed against her secret opening, she felt them both pushing themselves toward the joining which had been so fearful and overwhelming the first time. It wasn't fearful now. She wanted all of Jeff inside her, and she had the opportunity for more of him than any woman had ever had of a man. And she would give all of what she was to him in return, whatever fusion might occur.

The suffusion of Jeff as he eased himself inside her made her shudder in completion. *Yes! I want your hurt, your joy, your wisdom, folly. I want your body and your mind. I want your soul.*

She could feel his breath against her face as he thrust inside her. His psyche opened wider to her at each rhythmic push. Their bodies came together in counterpoint even as their minds twined closer. He leaned close to kiss her, and his chest brushed against her nipples. They tightened and ached for more. As she spiraled up toward some feeling which was impossible and inevitable, Holland knew that she was hurtling toward a new level of consciousness. Her most sensitive point screamed for each rub of flesh against it. She felt herself rocking against Jeff in ever more frantic cycles until sensation broke its bonds and washed over her.

The end, when it came, was a point of light, bright without end, that approached and then enveloped Holland in an incandescent glow. She realized she had been grunting in passion. Her breath was heaving in her chest. At this moment, she knew Jeff better than she knew herself.

She looked at him, hanging above her in the dimness underneath the quilt. He held his weight off her by propping himself on his elbows, but his chest brushed her nipples, and his length, laid along her body, meant belly met belly and thigh met thigh. They were panting in the stale air under the quilt. They shared even breath. She had never felt closer to anyone. And it wasn't a bad feeling. Not like the first time. She examined that thought. She'd been scared that first time. So had he. Joining that closely with another didn't seem natural. And sharing thoughts? It was a wonder men and women ever got together at all. But the second time had been easier. And now? Now she had all of Jeff and he had all of her, and it didn't seem unnatural anymore, to either of them. However strange a man's mind felt, Holland knew hers was just as strange to him. But they fit together. Like a puzzle. Into a single whole.

Jeff lifted a corner of the quilt so they could breathe, but he made no move to get off her. They sucked in the recycled air of the cell. "Bet we gave them a show," she murmured.

He grinned the grin she'd learned to treasure. "What, a little movement underneath a blanket, a little grunting? Hardly worth the effort." What he was thinking was that he wanted to be with her, always, because two halves of a whole dare not be separated.

Tears filled her eyes. This was right. They were strong together.

He nodded. *That we are, darlin' Holly. So let's use it.*

The urgency of their situation pushed the satiated contentment into the background again. *How? How do we do it, exactly?*

He bit his lip and finally rolled to the side. He drew her in to him and wiggled his arm under her head. She nestled there, but her thoughts were scattered in panic as she thought of all the people out there, desperate, in pain, and all because her father who was not her father had given them her genes.

Shh, darlin'. Not like that. Let's just think together about what they should do. Maybe first we get their attention, if we can.

He was right. How would anyone hear them through all the noise that must be cascading in their heads? They were wild with wanting to escape it, sick and distracted.

"Come on, you shrinks always know what to say to crazy people," he whispered. "Just like a revival, call and response. One of us calls it, then we think it together." He slid his body away so they were not actually touching. The voices of their kind reverberated in their minds. She didn't try to push them away. Neither did Jeff. Those voices were their purpose here.

She swallowed and nodded. "Okay. We make them feel like they aren't alone. We know what you feel."

We know what you feel.

Holland started. Jeff's eyes were wide, too. That had felt like . . . like a bolt of lightning, a gush of power, something . . . something she'd never felt before. Jeff was nodding his head. "This just might work."

We feel that way too, she thought. *You hear voices. Maybe you see colors around people.*

We feel that way, too. You hear voices. Maybe you see colors around people.

"Great. That's great, Holly," he whispered.

It's okay that you do. You're not alone.
And we can tell you how to control it.

They felt the wash of excitement from a thousand minds, no—more, many more. Excited chattering filled their minds almost to overflowing. Holland began to tremble.

"Focus on me, Holly." He took her head in his hands and turned her face up so that they were staring into each other's eyes. Then he let her go.

Find something you do that takes your mind away from other things ... running, yoga, music, even knitting. Something that puts you in a "zone." That will bring you quiet.

They listened for a minute. *I write poetry,* they heard someone think. *Video games.* There were several of those. *Boxing. Work out.*

Yeah, poetry, or cycling, sex with the one you love, Jeff suggested.

"Sex? Do we want to say that?" Holland protested.

"If it works for us ..."

"How about touching?" she asked, her annoyance half-feigned. "We don't want to scare away the female half of the crowd.

Yes. We hear you suggesting boxing or poetry, cycling or touching the one you love.
Find what will bring the quiet for you.

Let's tell them we'll talk again, Holland suggested. *After they know how to do that, we can tell them about Felipe's Zen art of filtering voices.*

Darlin', we might not be together again when we're still strong enough to do this.

Holland sucked in a breath. She felt as if she'd been slapped. Not together with Jeff? Jeff robbed of who he was, what he was to her by the man who had raised her and made her what she was? It was an abomination, a sin against the rightness of the world. Worse, it was entirely possible. She clasped him to her breast convulsively. "Okay," she whispered. "Let's do it now.

They released each other slowly. They talked about sorting and focus, of isolating groups of the voices and letting them slip away. For those who had nothing they thought might bring the quiet, Holland recommended playing video games. It was something almost everyone had access to, and she remembered a study that said learning a new game took up ninety percent of the brain's normal activity, while once the game was learned, the brain slipped into a "zone" where less energy was used but beta waves were enhanced. They answered questions that were coherent enough to discern. They used their combined energy for more than an hour, until they were both exhausted.

Try it, they ended. ***Help each other. If we can, we'll talk again.***

Holland realized her whole body had been tensed in concentration. She collapsed against Jeff, who drew the quilt up over her shoulders even as he relaxed against her.

"We did it," he whispered. "We used our power."

"Will it help them?"

"I don't know, darlin'. I only know we did the best we could."

Do you think they can help us in return? We didn't really ask for help.

Maybe not in time to do us any good. First they have to be sane. If we're able, and we hear they're sane, maybe we can ask for help later.

The tens or hundreds of stories of concrete above them weighed on Holland. The dry circulation of recycled air pumped through the room. Who could help them in here? The whisper of the news and the flicker of the horrible pictures on the monitor were the only sounds to answer.

Holland would not have believed she could sleep in that atmosphere of fear and dreadful anticipation, but she must have done so, and it had been a dreamless sleep of exhaustion. She knew nothing until the hiss of the airlock warned them they had visitors. Jeff hastily grabbed a second quilt, and let Holland pull the one warm with their shared heat around her naked body. They huddled together.

Four men ducked through the door: a doctor in a white lab coat followed two Marines with gray brush cuts, and last came Leland Banks. The Marines took up defensive positions on each side of the room. More uniforms could be glimpsed outside the door.

"Good morning, Holly. Jeff." Her father smiled with beneficent confidence, just as though they weren't his prisoners. He might have been greeting them at the breakfast table on a long weekend spent at his Palm Springs retreat. His thoughts were eager, anxious to begin. Then he registered that they were naked, and frowned. "I see you got a head start on our reproductive plan. Perhaps I should have monitored you more closely to prevent unwanted accidents."

Was he just an unhappy father? She could hear him hoping she hadn't been impregnated. But wasn't that what he wanted? Still, a father couldn't be expected to approve when confronted with actual fact, could he? "What does it matter?" she asked, puzzled. "I thought you wanted fertilized eggs."

Not by him.

Holland heard him clearly. Then her father pushed those thoughts away. "I hardly like to see my daughter throwing whatever morals she'd been taught to the wind."

"Wait a minute here, *Dad*. Morality is a luxury you can't afford, given what you're about to do."

Her father's face contorted, just for a moment. She felt his love for her. But his love was subordinate to his overwhelming need. He composed his features into a mask of disapproval. It was an expression she knew well. "You talk morality when it comes to science?" he asked. "Morality's

371

the hobgoblin of small minds, Holly. I would have thought better of you." But he didn't stop to mourn her inadequacy as he once would have. And the morality of what she'd done with Jeff was not the issue for him, no matter what he said. It was . . . that he didn't want Jeff to be the one to impregnate her. Why?

He rubbed his hands together briskly. "Enough of that. It's time to start our explorations, Jeff." He turned to the man in the lab coat behind him. "This is Dr. Sylvanic. An excellent surgeon, I assure you."

The doctor nodded without speaking. His eyes were avaricious, his aura gold and orange. When Holland turned her eyes to him, she could hear him thinking that the surgeries he intended to perform on Jeff would surely make his name.

"Mengele made his name with just such surgeries," Holland said in deadly calm.

She could feel Jeff's fear tremble in the air around her.

Her father ignored her barb. The doctor looked stunned for a moment, then angry. "Shall we?" Her father gestured to the doorway. "Your escort is ready, Mr. McQueen."

"You want to let me get my clothes on?" Jeff growled.

"Actually, I don't think so. You won't need them where you're going. Bring your blanket if you want, but you're not getting out of my sight. You're a very important person."

"A very important side of beef, you mean," Jeff muttered. He stood and gathered the quilt around his waist. It dragged on the floor. Holland could feel the carefully dammed emotions behind his voice. But he couldn't hide the red and brown swirls of fear in his aura.

"Dad, don't do this," Holland begged. When had she ever asked her father for anything? She felt like she was five. She wanted to run to him and collapse at his feet and hug his knees until he said he wouldn't do this to Jeff.

"I must, Holly. You know that. None of us has any choices here." The flattening of his countenance was frightening in itself. "Gentlemen. Will you escort our reporter friend?"

The Marines stepped in toward Jeff, but he moved forward before they could touch him. He looked like some Hawaiian king dragging his cape of rare feathered patterns behind him, his torso bare. "I'm coming." It was an act of heroism that his voice was rock-steady.

In a moment they were gone, leaving Holland alone and trembling. She stood, staring at the door for a long time. The volume rose from the monitor behind her. She couldn't hear what the news was saying. Her thoughts were filled with Jeff, and his with her. He was using his thoughts of her to keep his terror at bay. Suddenly, she didn't mind that he was thinking about their night together. She wanted to lose herself in those ecstatic moments as much as he did—male-female differences be damned.

She felt his fear as they stuck a needle in his arm. The slacking off of fear told her it was some kind of relaxant. She experienced the MRI just as he did. The voices of the lab assistants were clear as they marveled over the power their scans had detected in their two subjects last night. She felt Jeff's calm observation that they were going to stick needles in his eyes.

The surface of the eyeball has no pain receptors, she thought to him. *It won't hurt you.* She wished she could refrain from thinking about possible nerve damage while they were poking around in there. Nerve damage could leave him blind, or unable to focus. Pretty much the same thing.

Holland sat carefully on the couch. She knew she would feel everything happening to Jeff. Right now, it was just the needle. But according to her father they would need to cut the eye to look for new cones and rods, or some entirely new receptor. They would scrape the cells . . . fodder for the stem cell imitators. Cutting and scraping would not be painless. A picture of that horrible opening shot in *Andalusian Dogs* with the razor blade and the eyeball flashed through her consciousness. Or was it through Jeff's? Soon her father would have petri dishes full of thousands of new receptors. Enough to give him or anyone else an ability to see auras.

Another shot pricked Jeff's inner arm. *What are you giving me?* he asked someone.

She heard her father. *We want you to answer some questions during the procedure. This will ensure that you do.*

God, they were going to do it! They were going to cut him while he was awake and get his reactions to their probing. And she couldn't stop it! Her mind began to fracture into pieces. One piece felt the fear and revulsion ramping up to unbearable proportions, while another part looked on and wondered just how much emotional stress a person could stand and remain sane; and another part wondered what she should be doing about that, and still another part realized that the very breakup of her points of view signaled that madness was not far away. She jerked her mind away from Jeff forcibly. Her eyes focused on her hands. Her nails had dug four neat half-moons of welling blood in the mound of each thumb. Not good. She had to think about something else. She wouldn't be any good to Jeff if she went mad.

She searched the cacophony in her brain. The news. The news was easy enough to hear. Let that distract her from what was happening to Jeff, if it could, if she would let it.

"Last night's suicide totals dropped by twenty-five percent," the anchorwoman was saying. "That is the first decline in a week. The Center for Disease Control is unwilling to attribute it to the drug distribution program. They are studying the matter and expect to have a report by tomorrow."

What? Holland shook her head. Suicide rate was down. Good. That was good. She sorted through the noise in her head restlessly, clutching at first one voice and another, trying to find something to take her mind off Jeff and what was happening to him. There were more voices who spoke clearly now. Not so many screamers? Maybe.

A woman was giggling to think that an hour at her son's Playstation video game could give her peace. A guy was startled to find that when he brushed against some girl in a bus station, he'd gotten quiet. They were sitting together now, getting to know each other. Holland felt tears come to her eyes. Some people had been helped at least. She sorted more voices. But these were only a drop in the bucket of worldwide suffering. Feeling threatened to overwhelm her, and the voices rushed together into a roar.

That was when she felt Felipe's voice sounding in her mind, like a familiar old shoe. Felipe! He was groggy. He was thinking about some doctor? Or maybe a nurse. Yes, an attendant of some kind. A young man. Felipe was agitated, his thoughts disordered. He knew he'd had surgery, but he didn't know where he was. And then . . .

"Ohhhhh." Holland sighed as two minds joined and shushed through her. The healing effect of that joining touched her mind as well as both of theirs. Felipe felt only wonder at the wholeness and then the wonder was replaced by muddled recognition.

Touch, she heard him think. *Jeff and the doctor said it was touch.*

And then an unfamiliar voice, *What? What is this feeling?*

Felipe was too feeble to tell him. The young man jerked his hand—it was his hand, she was sure—from Felipe's arm. There was no chance to help him if he didn't touch Felipe.

Then she felt it. He had gathered enough courage to try again.

Touch can bring the quiet. Holland thought with as much force as she could. Could they hear her? She and Jeff hadn't been able to hear others at first. But Felipe's mutation was fully developed. If the guy was touching Felipe, and she was near enough physically . . .

Apparently they could hear her. *Who's that?* The unfamiliar voice was fearful.

A friend. She had to give him hope. *Someone like you and Felipe. My name is Holly.* Holly sounded lots less intimidating that Dr. Holland Banks. *One of the things that can bring quiet is the touch of . . .* Of what? What did she think Jeff was to her? *Of your lover. You are two halves of a whole, though you don't realize it yet. Stay with him. Protect him. You are . . . soul mates.* God, it sounded so corny. But wasn't it true?

I . . . I heard you last night. You were way louder than the others for a while, you and another guy. You talked about the quiet then. The thought was tentative, not quite believing.

Yeah. That was me . . . and my soul mate, Jeff McQueen. She felt Felipe turning his gaze on the young man with such longing, such recognition. It almost broke her heart. Felipe knew that he would never be alone again as long as he had the touch of that young man. A soft feeling of fulfillment washed over her, half her own, half Felipe's. He had found his one true love. *What's your name?* she asked.

Richard. Richard Stallworth.

A scream ripped through her mind. Not the kind that was voiced, but the kind that was bottled up in your mind like in dreams. *Jeff!* Her own lover was stuck in the bowels of the Pentagon having surgery performed while he was still conscious. The valium wasn't enough to erase his fear, and it didn't touch his pain. Scalpels and eyelid clamps and needles flashed in Holland's mind. Jeff couldn't scream, the drugs weren't letting him, but she could.

Holland screamed and screamed.

Chapter Thirty-one

"Holly?"

She looked up from the sofa where she had been hugging herself, rocking back and forth. She hadn't heard the door seal open, but now it was closing. Her father stood there, looking concerned. His aura was shot with little jagged yellow lines. She couldn't think, let alone focus or sort, so all the voices inside her head cascaded over her. All she could think about was that Jeff was lying unconscious somewhere, and about all the things she been through with him this afternoon. They'd put him out of his pain only after the surgery.

"Holly, you aren't eating." Her father gestured to her second untouched tray of the day.

"Why?" she asked her father, who was not her father, who could not be her father. Her voice was hoarse from crying. "If you wanted to scrape some rods and cones, why didn't you just put him out to do it? Did you have to torture him?"

"It wasn't torture," her father answered brusquely. "We needed his answers to questions about the effect of the procedures on the auras. We gave him a relaxant."

"You gave him something else, too, Dad. I felt it."

Her father glanced away. "It's a new drug, called Penphenidril."

"Never heard of it, *Dad*." She made the word an accusation. "But I know what it does. It's like truth serum, isn't it? So he had to answer your questions." The roar in her head made speech halting. Feeling Jeff's pain and fear all day had left her without any control of the voices.

"Half the value of the research would have been lost without it, Holly."

Holland stared at her father for a moment. "Forget the research, Dad. You know? Just get your head on straight here. You've lost a little perspective. Anybody outside this situation looks at it, and you look like the Devil himself. *Dad.*"

"This goes beyond right and wrong, Holly. This situation is bigger than that. You understand that." His voice almost pleaded with her. His hands clenched at his side.

She squeezed her eyes shut and rolled her head. "Nothing goes beyond right and wrong, Dad. Nothing."

"I didn't realize this would upset you so much, Holly." Her father's voice was carefully neutral, but his aura's yellow streaks still said he was concerned. "You are a woman of science, even if it's not hard science."

"You are torturing the man I love, the man I need to keep me sane!" Holland shouted. "You expect me not to be upset? I can't even think when he's not here. I'm so worried about him I can't shed enough of the voices to be manageable. I'm going to be a candidate for suicide-watch in about twenty minutes here, and being a woman of science has nothing to do with it."

"I'll have him brought back," her father said brusquely. "You can always have him around if you want, Holly."

"You had better not kill him." Her voice sounded in her own ears like a cornered animal, ready to fight for her life and the life of her mate.

"No, no . . . we don't want to kill him, Holly."

She pressed her hands to her temples, trying to shut out the noise she couldn't control. She couldn't hear what her father was thinking, without Jeff's touch. She didn't even care what he was thinking. She wanted what she wanted— out of here, with Jeff, whole. She wanted to turn back the clock to a time when there was no mutation, no suicides, no assassinations, no betrayal by her father. She wanted life to be simple again, where boy met girl, and girl said yes, and life went on happily ever after.

It was her father who seemed to read her thoughts. His need to explain himself was palpable, even in her shaken state.

"I had to do it, Holly." He came to stand over her, and looked down at her huddled form. "If just a few of you had had the anomaly, it might have died out. A whole new evolution of humankind would have been lost through suicide and murder. But I gave it to most of your generation. I didn't know it was limited to a certain age range, then. I thought I could get it, too. You should see the needle tracks in my arms, Holly. I look like an addict. I must have injected that virus with your genes riding on it a hundred times. But it wouldn't take. The only way I can join the new world, Holly, is to engineer the capabilities you've developed naturally, or . . . or have my own genetic structure live on through my progeny, who have the mutation. I'm going for both, Holly, just to hedge my bets."

She looked up at him, trying to understand what he was saying.

"I'd rather have your abilities myself, of course. But one way or the other, I'm going to be the father of the future, Holly, just as you are the mother of a new kind of human being."

She stared, and the words sunk in. She couldn't speak for a moment as she wondered whether she was imagining what she thought he meant. "So, you don't really want my eggs to be fertilized by Jeff or Felipe. Do you?"

He shook his head.

They stared at each other for a moment, the horror of what he was suggesting seeping up like pools of black oil around her feet.

"In a way, it's a good thing that you aren't really my daughter." The light in his eyes extinguished some inner flame in her soul.

Leland Banks turned on his heel and signaled to the monitors for the door to be unlocked.

It wasn't fifteen minutes before the door opened again. The Marines who brought Jeff back to her on a gurney were hardly an honor guard. They were all older, with graying brush cuts. Two were sergeants by their stripes. Holland was so stunned, she couldn't even hear what they said to her. They said something, but it was obscured by the voices washing over her. She didn't spare them more than a glance. She had eyes only for Jeff.

The straps that held him to the gurney covered a smooth white sheet. A black patch was tied in place over his left eye. Under the patch was a pad of white gauze. He was unconscious.

Holland held herself very still as the Marines loosened the straps and lifted Jeff's limp form onto the opposite couch.

I'm sorry.

Holland jerked her gaze away from Jeff's slack mouth and stark white hospital gown to the face of the Marine standing just inside the door. He was a major, she thought, or at least he thought so, watching his men work. He looked too old to have the mutation.

What did you say?

I'm sorry, ma'am. After what you two tried to do for us, all of us—well, this just isn't right, that's all. His disciplined eyes never left his men, but his focus was on her. *I felt what happened to him today. I think some others did, too.*

How old are you?

Forty-two, ma'am. Prematurely gray. This by way of explanation.

So, you're what my father would call a 'thriver' now. Watch out. Don't let them know.

I won't, ma'am. I was in a bad way yesterday. You and Mr. McQueen here, you helped me.

380

Tears filled Holland's eyes again. God, she seemed to tear up at anything. *What is it?*

Ma'am?

What brings the quiet for you?

Crossword puzzles, ma'am.

She gave a watery chuckle and nodded. *You learned to focus quickly.*

Military discipline, ma'am.

Tell people how to do it. It's the only way some of us will survive. She looked him over critically. Maybe this guy was their chance. *Can you help me get Jeff out of here?*

The Marines collapsed the gurney. The major let his eyes sweep over her. "He'll be all right, ma'am. The doctor gave him some medication, so he should sleep for a few hours, but they say he'll be better tomorrow. The eye heals faster than anyplace else in the body. He keeps quiet for a day or two and he's fine."

"Probably a little less wear and tear on you if they bother to give you an anesthetic," she said caustically. *You won't help us.*

"No, ma'am." He was ashamed. He set a plastic bottle on the table. "He can have two of these when he wakes." There were only four in the bottle, not enough for an overdose. They were being careful.

Why? Why are you helping them?

I'm a soldier, ma'am. I have orders. As if that explained his actions. Then he turned on his heels and was gone. "At least tell them to turn down the lights," she called after him. As the door closed, she heard him bark the order. The lights dimmed, along with her hopes. Doug Wagner was not going to let anyone near them who had the slightest desire to help.

She went and sat on the floor at Jeff's side, leaning against the couch.

It was over. Everything. Her father was going to torture Jeff and maim him. She was going to be mated to her father, if only in a test tube, to give him immortality. The little seed of knowledge they'd given people like them might bear fruit, but she and Jeff would never see it flower. Their world was reduced to this room and the surgery-cum-torture chamber. They had been naive to think anyone could help them, or would.

Behind her, some talking head was saying excitedly, "New developments! This just in . . ." But she never heard more. The monitor went dead. Her father had decided to cut off even their unsatisfying one-way contact with the outside world.

She couldn't cry. She couldn't think. The voices, speaking in a dozen languages now, cascaded through her head uncontrolled and indistinguishable. She was too tired, too dispirited to care. She reached for Jeff's hand. When he woke, at least she could give him quiet.

Leland pointed his PDA at the medical chart at the foot of the bed where Felipe Laveau lay looking up at him accusingly. "You're doing better than we expected, Mr. Laveau. All those transfusions were worth it. Blood pressure is almost normal. Artery graft is taking nicely. You won't be running marathons anytime soon, but you should be ready to participate in our little experiments in a few days."

"The lady doctor is mighty unhappy somewheres, and I cain't get Jeff McQueen at all," Laveau said warily. "Whatchu done?" He was watching the doorway behind Leland. The place was a hive of activity. There was much to do to prepare for Jeff's surgery tomorrow.

"Are you speaking of my daughter, sir?" Leland looked at him with disdain. Why did the only other thriver he had control of have to be a Negro? "I am Doctor Leland Banks."

"Yo daughter, huh? Well, she not doing real well. Might want to be takin' notice of that."

"She'll be fine. She's just getting used to the fact that her life has changed." He turned and called, "Nurse!" A young man in hospital whites stuck his head in through the doorway. Leland noticed his curling blond hair and peaches-

and-cream complexion only to think they made him look too young to be a nurse. "Get me whatever third-line antibiotics we have available. I don't want this man getting a staph infection."

The young man looked to Laveau as though for permission, then back to Leland, ducked his head in acknowledgment and disappeared. What strange behavior, Leland thought.

"I ain't sure I want to play with you and that doctor you got. Looks like Dr. Caligari, if you ask me," Laveau was saying. The nurse returned with a tray bearing a syringe.

There was a clatter in the hall, and Doug shoved his way into the room past the male nurse. His glasses were slightly askew and his face was not its normal pasty neutral. He was flushed with anger. "Get out!" he yelled to the nurse and Laveau, then realized that Laveau couldn't.

"There's nowhere private, Doug—unless you care to go back to your office for a satisfying little scream?" Leland let his eyebrows rise. Well, Doug knew at last. Doug stood, shaking in impotent fury. "No? I didn't think so. All our personnel have top clearance levels. Give the patient the antibiotics, nurse. Don't mind Mr. Wagner. He wants to discuss something with me."

"Banks!" Doug said through clenched teeth, unable to resist. "What were you *thinking?*"

"About what, Doug?" Here it was.

"Did you think I wouldn't find out that you let the virus escape purposely? Hell, you admitted it to your daughter openly! I saw the tape of your interview." Doug's fists clenched and unclenched at his sides. "For Christ's sake, Banks. We were trying to *stop* it. And you were spreading it all along?"

"The mutation would have expired if it weren't present in a broad gene pool."

"I wanted just a few of them, Banks! That was the deal. The mutants would give us an irrefutable advantage. We'd know everything our enemies are doing." Doug mourned the demise of a perfect plan. "We'd untangle all the lies that are common currency in the diplomatic trade. But now the whole world has got the mutation. It isn't an advantage. And we will pay the price of a whole generation committing suicide or going off their rocker. The country will be devastated for no purpose! Think of the economy!"

"The whole world will be devastated, not just America, if that's what's worrying you."

"It'll take decades to recover." Doug was almost whispering now.

"And when it does, it will be a whole new world. My colonies of thrivers will ensure that the mutation survives in a gene pool diverse enough to pass the mutation on to future generations." He began writing orders into his PDA. "I will have given humanity a new self."

"Like you are doing this for anybody but you," Doug spat. "You want to be the creator of that new world, Banks. You can't fool me. I heard you, remember?"

Leland shrugged. Doug was getting very tiresome.

"And in the meantime, there are subcommittees forming in both houses of Congress." Doug ran his hand over his gleaming pate. "The World Health Organization is mobilizing. Half a dozen private think tanks are floating theories on cause and consequences. The White House is having hourly updates on the situation. Someone will trace the funding trail, or they're going to figure out it was a genetic mutation hooked to a virus, and realize that you're the foremost authority on that. It's going to come back to our organization."

"Come now, Douglas," Leland chuckled. "You always said your involvement couldn't be traced. You were so proud of that. What's different now?"

"What's different is the scale, Banks. I thought there were going to be a few mind-reading mutants locked in the basement on a government secret project. We conceal hundreds of little government projects, because no one knows to look for them. This is *very* public, Banks, and getting more public all the time. There'll be no hiding when this shit has hit a fan this big."

"Everyone will be far too busy holding the world together to bother about your minor funding role in this great discovery." Leland put on a damping tone.

"Well, Banks, you're out." Doug's voice was hard-edged. He drew himself up, righted his glasses and tugged at the shirtsleeves underneath his suit jacket to straighten them. "I'll have a guard escort you from the building."

Leland laughed. "Right. You're going to kick *me* out of the project? I don't think so."

"You were working against our stated goal. You're an unreliable partner, Banks."

Leland snorted derisively. "You can't do anything without me, Doug. I'm the only one with the specialized knowledge and the brainpower to understand what's happened to humanity. You'll get your colony. That hasn't changed."

"Who says you're the only one? Herzog might fill the bill just fine."

"Herzog? You make me laugh." How dare this little toad bring up Herzog? "Herzog isn't capable of breeding lab rats, let alone genetically mutated humans."

"I think we'll just find out." Doug's eyes went so flat, Leland felt a little afraid. He was, after all, in a specially constructed laboratory of Doug's creation under the Pentagon. He was in Doug's world. What couldn't Doug do? More important, what *wouldn't* he do?

"Don't you want to share the future, Doug? I could give *you* the ability to read minds. The ultimate power trip. No one will ever get the better of you."

"Looks to me like the road to suicide."

"You forget the thrivers. Before we implant the altered stem cells in ourselves, we'll know exactly how they thrive, so we can thrive, too." He was bestowing an incredible gift on this little bureaucrat, a gift the man didn't deserve. But it would serve to string him along for a while. Long enough for Leland to get what he wanted. After that . . .

"I'd watch my back, Doug," a rich baritone voice said from the bed behind them. "This guy, he don't really want to give you nothin'. Take my word for it."

Leland whirled to find Felipe Laveau's eyebrows raised and a wry smile on his face. The nurse was holding his arm for the shot. "What do you know?" Leland snapped.

"Only what you thinkin'." Laveau chuckled. "No more lies, you know?"

Leland turned to see Doug's eyes widen. "Jesus," was all he said. His look of sly consideration was almost comical. Leland didn't need to read minds to know what was going through Doug's. Laveau had thought to put a spoke in Leland's wheel. Instead, he had given Doug a timely and convincing demonstration of just how powerful a force was within their grasp.

"Are you ready to give that up, Douglas?" Leland looked down at the shorter man. Doug should really consider a hair transplant. Balding men just couldn't look authoritative. "Our interests aren't so differently aligned. And we're the ones in position to direct this force that's going to form the world—"

Doug raised his eyes, speculating. "In my office in half an hour. Staff meeting."

Leland watched him grab the door handle and stride out into the corridor. He turned to Laveau. "Thanks for making my case."

Laveau's eyes radiated hatred and contempt. So did the eyes of the nurse.

Leland chuckled and returned to his notes.

Chapter Thirty-two

Holland knew it wasn't physical pain that kept Jeff awake in the dark. She'd given him the Vicodin a couple of hours ago. He was wondering how he'd manage to endure the brain surgery they were planning. Holland wasn't sure she could come through it, either. The future seemed a blank after about daybreak. In a few hours, her father's minions would be back.

Holland stretched her hand across Jeff's chest. That cut out the voices of their kind, leaving only Jeff and the few normal humans around them at this hour of the night. Her backside was numb, but Holland didn't care. If only all of her could go numb. She stared at her hand, curled her fingers. Funny, it was the hand she'd always thought was evil in her dreams. She'd never stopped to consider why it should be her hand that was the evil part of her in her nightmares. There was always a reason for things in dreams. She knew all about the not-human part of her nightmares. That was some inner realization of the mutation. She understood the evil part, too. Was she not the cause of pain and suffering for the whole world? Her genes were devastating a generation. A premonition? Who knew? Not this psychiatrist. But why was it always her hand? Hands were a symbol of touch. Maybe she dreamed of an evil hand because touch was the driving force of her mutation. Touch brought the quiet. Touch heightened the effect. She spread her fingers, feeling the swell of pectoral muscle, the nipple that made Jeff a mammal beneath the thin cloth of the gown. Touch gave her control of the noise in her head.

People often mistook power for evil in their dreams.

That observation came unbidden from her years of training. She and Jeff were afraid of their own power to be good or bad, or to affect their environment. But the power of self, which must include bad as well as good, wasn't evil in itself. Accepting that wholeness, that responsibility, was frightening but not evil.

Acceptance is pretty hard.

She'd been concentrating so on her musings, she'd forgotten Jeff could hear her. She smiled. *Yeah. I've accepted you, though. And that was* really *tough.*

No harder than my job, darlin'. Sex helped, though.

Yeah, I bet it did. She laid her head against his arm. He knew what she was feeling. She didn't have to come out and say it, or even think the actual words. He felt that way, too. Not that it would do them any good. They had maybe a few hours to feel anything except pain and fear.

No. She couldn't think about that. That way lay madness. She turned to the others she could hear. The cleaning crew was making its way down the hall, focused on the work at hand and some acrimony with their supervisor. The two older guards by the door were talking about the various scrapes their kids were in.

"Yes, sir!" she heard one of the guards outside the door say. But she hadn't heard anyone give an order. That could only mean . . . She jerked upright, breaking contact with Jeff. As she did, the voices of many leaped into her brain. The door began to shush with air from the outside corridor. The ring that sealed it spun. Jeff struggled up on one elbow. It took a moment for her to focus enough to pick out the thoughts just outside.

"Assist the subjects to the elevator." It was the major, sent to collect Jeff. So early? Not fair that they were robbed of what little time was left to them!

"Yes, sir." But that wasn't one of the guards outside the door. He had brought others with the anomaly. They were thinking . . . that they were going to get her and Jeff out of here.

She looked at Jeff and saw hope spring into his unbandaged eye. *Don't be too sure. He was all duty and obedience earlier.*

Two young Marines stepped through the round, vault-like door. They were wearing camouflage uniforms with round-toed laced boots, and they carried guns—severely military-looking, long kinds of guns slung over their shoulders with straps and dreadfully metallic square-handled pistols in holsters at their belts. One of the older guards said, "Sir, Mr. Wagner said they were to be roused at dawn."

"I have my orders, sergeant. And therefore you have yours." The major put all his rank behind his bark, and offered no explanation.

"Ma'am?" one of the young men said, tentatively. "Can I help you up?"

Holland looked up at him. He was thinking that she was the one who had saved him. And now he was going to return the favor or die trying. He stretched out a hand almost reverently.

She let him pull her to her feet. Two more young men in camouflage, not dress uniforms, came through the door. They went to help Jeff.

What changed your mind, Major? They had no choice but to go with these guys. One, at least, thought he was saving her and Jeff. But she wanted the major to take sides.

"Get his clothes," the major ordered.

Holland pointed to the neat pile on the puzzle table, then turned to challenge the major for his answer.

No one could stand another day like we had today, the major thought at her deliberately. Framing his thoughts and sending them felt new to him. *Not when you tried to help us all. We* have *to get you out of here.*

389

Jeff was looking a bit dazedly from one stern young face to another as they each took an elbow. "It's all right, sir," one said tersely. "You come with us."

"You want him to dress, sir?"

"No time. The Doctor wants him right away." The major stood to the side of the door and gestured them through.

Jeff stood, swaying slightly, in bare feet and the flimsy hospital gown that hit him above the knees. He looked so vulnerable with his bandaged eye. He should be lying flat until his eye healed, but there weren't too many choices here. Better blind in one eye than tortured or dead. But the two strapping lads beside him were strong enough to carry him, if it came to that.

Holland glanced to the major. His aura was stolid gray-blue, like a gunship. She guessed that was determination. *Thanks. You think we can get out of here?*

We're going to try. He grimaced, and she felt his need for haste. "Ma'am?"

She nodded and scrambled through the door, her two personal guards on her heels.

"Dr. Banks didn't call ahead about this," the guard who was a sergeant said slowly.

The major just ignored him. "Careful of your head, Mr. McQueen."

Jeff ducked through the door, helped by his brawny assistants. "Ma'am?" one of her rescuers said. "The elevator is this way."

Relief vied with fear that they would be stopped somehow when escape seemed possible for the first time. Holland hurried forward, before she remembered that the guards could still see them. She couldn't look too eager. She slowed and turned to see Jeff being half-dragged forward. That at least looked real. The hope that flickered in her breast seemed so fragile it might be extinguished at any moment. The Marine at her elbow took her arm and led her around the corner, past a desk at the main double door to the laboratory area. The major nodded to the man in dress blues there, and one of the Marines punched the elevator button. The soldier in dress blues handed a paper back to the major.

"Everything seems to be in order here." He watched them gather to wait for the elevator.

The Marines around her were nervous. So was Felipe.

"Felipe!" Holland gasped. She turned to the major. "I hear Felipe. We can't leave without Felipe."

"Do you know where he is?" the major asked.

The elevator chimed that it had arrived. "A hospital room. Back there, most likely." She glanced to the double door.

We can make it, Felipe was thinking.

She felt Richard's panic. *I don't know . . .*

The elevator doors slid apart.

"No time," one of the Marines around her whispered.

"Wait!" Holland pleaded. She listened again. The two Marines supporting Jeff got him into the elevator. Jeff straightened and gathered his strength.

The major shook his head. "We can't wait."

The double doors burst open and Richard, pushing Felipe's long form slumped in a wheelchair, strode through. The dress-blue Marine at the desk was on his feet in a minute.

"It's okay," the major said, pushing Holland and her two guards into the elevator. "This is the last of them."

"I only saw two on the orders," the guard said, putting his hand on the butt of his pistol ominously. He fumbled with the other hand toward something under his desk, a warning signal of some kind, no doubt.

The major strode toward the desk, pulling the folded sheet from his pocket. "No, it was three." As he handed the papers over, the butt of his rifle swung up from under his arm and caught the guard square on the chin. Holland didn't see exactly how the major did it, even though she was looking straight at them. The guard dropped like a stone.

The pink-cheeked blond nurse who had to be Richard wheeled Felipe right into the center of the party in the crowded elevator. Holland was surprised. The major raced toward the closing doors of the elevator and slid through the narrowing gap.

Felipe looked up at Holland from tired eyes. *Who knew my soul mate would be a white boy from an old Baltimore family? Fate's a bitch, ain't it?*

Holland couldn't help but grin. *Hope he likes the blues. But, of course.* Their thoughts were as one.

Richard smiled. *I play sax.* Felipe looked as though he'd seen a miracle by St. Expedite. Holland glanced to Jeff. The elevator snicked shut and eased up. They were almost there. But they had come down on two elevators, and there had been quite a walk between them.

"They can get us between the elevators," the major observed dispassionately. "The guards at the vault may call to confirm the orders, or somebody may find the guy at the desk. If we make the next elevator, they can still stop the sucker between floors."

"Is there a service elevator?" Jeff asked.

The Major turned. *Good job.* His thoughts were tinged with respect. "You served here, Macintosh. Is there a service elevator?"

"Yes, sir. It's farther away than the regular one, though."

"We'll take that chance. You're on point."

Holland half-expected a reception party when the elevators got them to the official basement of the Pentagon. But the doors opened only on pale green walls and scuffed linoleum. There were fewer people roaming the halls, but even in predawn, the place was not deserted.

The Marines moved out in sober formation surrounding their charges, their auras tight with steel-gray, glinting determination. Two held Jeff's elbows, their free hands on their guns.

"I can make it," Jeff murmured. They glanced to him and took their hands away, still hovering near enough to help if he was mistaken. But they made faster time that way.

The corridors skimmed past in frightening monotony. For all Holland knew, they could have been marching in circles. They passed the elevator bank where three employees waited impatiently for rides to the main floors. A door opened and all three stepped in. Holland hoped it wasn't much farther to the service elevator. So did the major.

Behind them, the faint tromp of running boots echoed in the halls.

"Double time," the major ordered. "Our luck just ran out." He shooed them onward and slapped the elevator call button.

Holland hurried forward, running to keep up with the Marines' jog. Two now faced the rear and ran backwards, their hands on their guns. One had taken Jeff's arm, and he broke into an uneven lope. Richard pushed Felipe, who gripped the arms of the wheelchair like the restraint bar on a roller coaster. They careened around a corner.

Then the major turned and put a hand out. They all almost piled into him. He put his finger to his lips. Holland and Jeff were both panting. So was Richard. The crash of boots behind them sounded so close, Holland thought she might faint. The elevator dinged. The boots stopped.

"They must have gotten the last one," a voice growled. "You four get in there. I'll have a welcome wagon waiting for them at the top."

The elevator dinged again as it left. Quiet. The snick of a cell phone. "They're on their way up. They're all yours." Quiet.

The major tapped his finger to his lips again and motioned his party onward, softly this time. They crept away. Holland was grateful that wheelchairs had rubber wheels. The major was thinking that their escape wouldn't be good for long. When they didn't arrive on the main floor, the search would start again. They had just bought time.

Several members of the cleaning crew waited with a cart smelling of disinfectant and bristling with mop handles in front of the one service elevator.

"Priority," the major ordered, and pushed the cart aside as the elevator doors opened.

They crowded into the larger car, lined with padded gray quilting and floored in scarred wood. The major turned to Macintosh. "How far is the west parking lot from the elevator?"

The floor pushed them upward. "We should go out and around. There are loading-dock doors about fifty feet from where this thing dumps out."

The major nodded crisply and looked to his charges. Holland followed his gaze. Felipe was slumped in exhaustion, but Richard had strapped him into the wheelchair, so he was good to go. Jeff was looking drawn and gray, but he said, "Don't worry about me, Major. I'll make it."

The major was worried that Jeff would slow them down, though.

"Leave me if it comes to that," Jeff said. "Get Holland and the others out."

"We don't leave any fallen," the major said through tight lips.

The elevator doors opened on an empty corridor. Two Marines spun out to each side, weapons at the ready. They nodded, and the others scrambled out, following Macintosh. They burst through the double doors to the loading dock to find a hive of activity. Several trucks were being unloaded. Guys in olive drab jump suits were everywhere.

"Evacuation exercise," the major yelled. A dozen pairs of eyes turned to see what all the commotion was about. Since the workers didn't know whether the exercise was supposed to include them, they just watched the five Marines and four civilians, one in a wheelchair and another in a hospital gown, trot down the ramp and around the last truck backed up to the dock.

They were outside! Holland could feel Jeff's breath heaving in his lungs. He was barefoot still and barely covered by his gown. Good thing the night was humid and hot in the nation's capital.

The Pentagon facade to their right stretched for a mile. Miles. How far around the Pentagon was the West parking lot? *Just concentrate on running,* she told herself. They kept on, moving in closer to the building to take advantage of the smoother surface of a wide sidewalk, pacing themselves. Jeff was tiring fast, though. His feet hurt, cut from the pebbles of crumbling asphalt.

The crack of a door bursting open behind them drew their heads around. The sound was followed by shouts and clatter as a dozen men in security uniforms piled through the door.

"Move it!" The major's order was low but clear.

They needed no urging to pick up the pace. But how long they could keep it up was another story. Shots sounded, but no one went down.

"Warnings," the Major panted. "They won't risk killing the cargo."

Holland concentrated on willing whatever strength she had to Jeff. The corner of the building was in sight now. The men behind were gaining. Two Marines peeled off from their group and turned to face their pursuers. More gunshots.

That broke Holland's concentration. Suddenly voices showered over her from all directions. She gasped with the intensity of them. Behind her all was chaos and pain.

I'm hit, goddamn it!

Go! Get them before they hit the corner.

This, this is how I'm gonna die?

Falling. I'm gonna go down.

Ahead, a thousand voices surged, one on top of the other. She could feel a swell of anger, and of . . . support. Confusion cycled up in waves.

Where are they? They're here somewhere.

The Pentagon. I felt it was the Pentagon for sure.
It was awful. I felt them torturing him.
They brought me back. I was so close . . .
Felt like they were torturing me.
What do we do now?
They told me I wasn't alone.
Where's the major? There! Over there!

The voices almost suffocated her. Jeff, behind her, was stunned by the volume. The major took Holland's arm and almost dragged her forward. The two remaining Marines had one each of Jeff's arms, doing the same. Richard pushed Felipe's wheelchair ahead of all of them. The corner was near now. The major was thinking that all they had to do was make the parking lot, though what difference that would make she had no idea.

And then a crowd spilled around the corner ahead. People were running, all kinds of people, in pajamas or suits or sweatshirts. She picked out cop uniforms and firefighters. There were men, women, one woman even holding a child. The crowd swallowed their little party. Hands reached for them. Everyone was shouting as well as thinking.

They were thrivers.

What did that mean? Holland's panic rose. The swell of thoughts turned triumphant.

"Don't worry, we've got you now, folks," a firefighter said.

"No one's going to take you,"—this from a guy who looked like an investment banker with a very expensive suit. He reached to support Jeff as the Marines and the major turned to face their pursuers.

"You helped us. Now it's our turn." The chubby woman in sweatpants didn't seem a likely source of help. Holland turned to the guards, expecting to see them wading into the crowd. There were nearly two dozen of them and they had guns. But they stopped short, fingering their guns nervously. They were frightened.

At their backs, shoving said the crowd was growing. Half a flight of stairs led down to a parking lot, bordered with raised cement flower beds filled with pink flowering *indica.* Holland looked out from her vantage point at the top of the stairs, stunned. The crowd stretched back and out as far as the eye could see, and more thrivers were joining it even now. Cars streamed in through a faraway gate, its gatehouse abandoned, its striped bar raised helplessly. People ran to the edge of the seething mass of the crowd, some holding hands. Television crews were set up along the outside fence, the lights from their cameras throwing cones of brightness outward. Helicopters looped in the sky above, emblazoned with call letters.

She turned to Jeff. "I guess our broadcast *did* have an effect. We never asked them to help us. Why did they come?"

It was the major who answered. "I tried to send out a call. I'm not as strong as you, of course. But I think others heard your pain today—yours and Mr. McQueen's. A man couldn't hear that and sit at home, I guess." He glanced around. "Or a woman."

"You're a good man, major." Jeff was exhausted, and not sure of the outcome here. What could a crowd of civilians do against the government?

As if in answer to his question, sirens wailed in the background. The government was fighting back. Troop transports pulled up to the guard gate and a phalanx of soldiers issued forth, military rifles in hand, cutting off the crowd's retreat, and preventing any more from joining them. More troops could be seen marching in around the far side of the Pentagon. Somebody had called out the National Guard. Two ungainly military helicopters swept in above. The lighter news copters skittered away and circled tentatively at a distance. Triumph turned to fear in the crowd.

"Oh, this could get ugly," Jeff muttered.

The security guards behind them were joined by seasoned-looking soldiers. Doug Wagner and her father pushed their way through the rattled security guards, accompanied by a guy whose uniform had a star on the shoulder. Wagner stopped dead when he saw the size of the crowd stretching out below him. Both Wagner and her father looked devastated.

"*All* thrivers, Holly?" her father choked.

She nodded. "Looks like you won't get a chance to be the father of the future, Dad. You're superfluous now."

"No advantage if they're everywhere," Wagner murmured.

"Look on the bright side," Jeff said. "A generation won't be devastated. No collapsing economy, no morgues overflowing."

"Don't be too sure," her father said. The vindictiveness in his voice was palpable, though it was too dark to see his aura. "You know you're talking generational wars here."

He was right about that. Holly was so pained by what he had done she could hardly breathe or think. "We'll deal with it," Jeff responded. But she could feel he was shaken.

"Got to stop this thing," Wagner murmured. "You were never going to stop it, Banks."

"I thought most of them would suicide," her father hissed.

"You thought wrong." Wagner's voice grew stronger. "General, you have your orders."

The general was an older guy, his face lined as much by strategy-room conniving as by battle. He swallowed hard. "Round them up, men. We're shipping them to Guantánamo."

"The first volley in the generational wars, General?" Jeff asked. "How do you think the public will respond to the news tomorrow morning?" He glanced to the cameras panning the crowd. "How can you lock up a generation?"

"One batch at a time, son." He motioned his troops around the perimeter of the crowd.

"You still don't get it." Jeff let his voice boom out. He squared his shoulders. "You can't keep what you're doing secret. Even if you take the news tapes, suppress the pictures, thousands, millions across the nation, across the world can hear what we're thinking, and what you're doing."

"Won't matter," Wagner said flatly.

Holland looked at the troops fanning out around the crowd. She could feel the crowd beginning to panic behind her. Jeff glanced at the troops, too.

"It's okay," he said. He didn't need to say it loudly. The whole crowd was focused on his thoughts. "General, the rest of your army had better be very young, or very old, because about half of them I can see here are just like us, or soon will be."

Wagner and the general looked around, shocked. They hadn't thought of that. Her father set his mouth.

"Y'all going to round up people just like you and put them away? Pretty soon they'll want to get rid of us for good," Jeff called out. "And you'll be next. All you have to be is between twenty-five and forty-five to be guilty here."

Some of the soldiers stopped fanning out. One nearest to Holland rubbed his neck. He was trying to make the voices go away. Holland grabbed for Jeff's hand. *We can help you.*

Behind her a thousand voices said, *They can help you* or *They helped us,* or *You can't do this.* It was a collective push at the soldiers. She heard guns clatter to the ground, just a few.

"You can't change what you are," Jeff yelled, though they would hear him even if he whispered. "You can't go back. The only way is forward."

The general was on his cell phone, talking furiously. "Anyone who refuses an order will be court-martialed," he was telling his commanders. "Tell your men."

"Court-martialed?" Jeff laughed. "How many people are in the armed forces these days—a million? You think you can do half a million court-martials? At least. All that is gone, General. The order is rapidly changing, as they used to say."

Outward silence fell across the huge parking lot, except for the helicopters above them and the chug of engines. Inside, the thoughts of the thousand people around them were all focused on one thing, wondering what would happen next.

What happened was that soldiers started stepping away from their perimeter lines and joining the crowd. They were welcomed with embraces, kisses and tears from the women, hearty handshakes from the men. "It's okay," echoed across the crowd. "What you are is okay."

The warmth and acceptance flowing across the west parking lot of the Pentagon was something Holland had never felt before. They were one entity, here, a part of something that wanted them, accepted them, *was* them. She looked at Jeff, knowing he felt it, too. Acceptance. Strength. They were strong together as they couldn't be apart. All those feelings of weakness found balance in another. *Can't add two and two—well, that guy over there can. He's a whiz. Got a tin ear? Not anymore—borrow Felipe's love of music.* And brown skin and brown minds would bond with yellow minds and white minds, until there was no difference. They could be more than they had ever been alone.

A thousand and more turned as one to Wagner and the general and her father. They ignored the remaining soldiers, standing shaken in their decimated line. The only ones left were the very young. And very young soldiers were easily shaken. Someday soon the young ones would be hearing voices, too. Holland was willing to bet on it. Their time would come. Her father's viral vector would probably wax and wane through every flu season.

"Now," Jeff said. "It's time to go home." He looked like a pirate in his black eye patch. It was true; he was a dangerous man. More dangerous than any man Doug Wagner or the general had ever faced.

"You are *not* free to leave," the general barked.

"Do you think your troops—I should say your *remaining* troops—will fire on civilians? I don't think so." Jeff turned to Holland's father. "We can't leave you to trap any more of us." A small cordon of District police formed and moved through the crowd. They didn't need orders. They could hear what was needed. They surrounded Wagner and Leland.

"Holly!" her father pleaded. Holland stood there shaking, her thoughts in disarray. Knowing her father's thoughts might break her heart—either because he was sorry for what he'd done to her, to Jeff, to millions of others, or worse that he was still just focused on his need to have the gene and be the father of the future. There were no good choices here.

"I'm sorry, Dad," she choked. "More sorry than you probably are."

"You won't keep me in jail," he called back over his shoulder. His face glowed with faith in himself, annoyance at this inconvenience.

Jeff wanted Holland to understand her father. She *did* understand. She saw the choices he'd made cycling down around his narcissistic personality disorder into this final corner from which there might be no escape. What he had done was beyond acceptability. "You buttered your bread . . ." she whispered.

Jeff's care for her suffused her mind. He didn't touch her. He could hear how afraid she was to hear her father's thoughts. Police led Leland Banks away as he called, "I have friends in high places!"

"Maybe not for long," Jeff said under his breath. He stole a glance at Holland, then straightened and addressed the other man: "General, you've been following orders. But I think now would be a good time to stand down, before you end up doing some things that qualify as war crimes." His voice was steady. His gaze was, too.

The general looked over the crowd. He took a breath and nodded once. "Back to base," he said into his phone. A flurry of activity ensued. The military helicopters pealed away and swooped off. Young soldiers rushed for the transports, their relief palpable. The general strode off.

Then the crowd was alone except for the cameras and the news helicopters buzzing above. Jeff looked at Holly. *Here we go, darlin'. Can't turn back. Major, you want to help out here?*

The major smiled. "Live to serve."

"Maybe you could get some of the soldiers who just joined us together and show them how to put down the noise. Looks like some of them didn't hear last night's broadcast."

The major nodded crisply. He had his orders, and that was a comfort. He moved off through the crowd.

"We got any religious or community leaders here?" Jeff asked the milling thousands.

"I'm a city councilman," one said.

"I'm an Imam at the mosque in D.C."

A man in a priest's collar stepped forward.

"Let's go give an interview," Jeff said.

Holly let her pride in Jeff wash over him. He took her hand, and the love she felt from him didn't need a bended knee attached to it. They were soul mates.

"We've got to do a little reassuring of the establishment," Jeff said.

The penthouse suite at the Ritz Carlton was donated for as long as they needed it by a grateful manager. He had been one of the crowd at the Pentagon. Another shrink had volunteered to see her father. Maybe someone could help him accept what had happened. It was beyond Holly, and she knew it. She'd lost a father. That pain would be dealt with later, and again many times after that, as she strove for some balance against what he'd done and how ashamed she was of that. She'd called her mother, who was flying out to be at his side. Dear Mom. She'd never stop standing by her man, even if he didn't deserve it. Someday her mother would have to forgive herself for Fred and stop atoning. Holly was going to have to look up Fred. But that was for later. A medical doctor, a dapper man no more than five feet four, had appeared without being summoned to look at Jeff's eye.

Now he removed the patch under Holly's watchful stare. The area was swollen and the eye was red and filled with goo. A series of dark threads tracked across it. It looked awful.

"No, no," the doctor said, hearing her concern. "That's just antibiotic salve." He peeled back the lid, and shone his pen light into it. "The man had skill. You've got focus. The stitches in the ball can come out in a few days. Very tidy work."

"Did all that running around detach anything?" Holland asked.

"I don't think so. The surgery did not disturb the retina, and that's the real danger, you know." The Doctor sat back and handed Jeff the patch. "Wear this to keep the eye quiet. In a couple of days we'll check the sight patterns. If they didn't scrape too much from any one area, your sight should be okay. I'll write a prescription for Vicodin, but you shouldn't need it by tomorrow or the next day."

"I feel okay now, Doc. Just a little swollen."

Holly heaved a sigh of relief and thanked the doctor as she showed him out.

"My pleasure. Your advice saved my wife's life as well as my own."

"Do you get the quiet when you touch her?" Holly couldn't help but ask.

His regret was palpable. He shook his head. "And I know what that means. But we're friends for more than twenty years. Maybe that's enough."

Holly nodded and turned back into the room.

In the background, their interview was on the morning news programs. "We're going to need the experience and guidance of the older generation," Jeff was saying.

The cell phone buzzed. Holly picked it up and flipped it open.

"Doctor Banks?" the voice in her ear asked.

"Yes. I'm Holland Banks."

"The president was wondering if you and Mr. McQueen could meet with him."

Jeff chuckled and raised his brows.

"When?"

"The president has cleared his schedule. Whenever you and Mr. McQueen are free."

"We could use some sleep. How about late this afternoon?"

"We'll send a car at four."

Holly buzzed the front desk. "Uh, can you hold calls?"

"Yes, ma'am, Doctor Banks."

On the television screen, the image of Jeff was saying: "A secret program of the Pentagon was responsible for the snipers. They were sent to kill people with this anomaly." She switched it off. It was going to be one of those all-news, all-the-time days, maybe for days to come, as the world sorted all this out.

"Why did the president call us?" Jeff asked. "We're not the ones to lead this thing."

"They're dependent on us now. Savior syndrome. The real leaders will come out of our ranks, and we'll defer to them when they do."

"Good. I want to get back to sniffing out fraud. Should be a little easier now."

"You might be out of a job." She came and sat on his lap, nuzzled his neck.

"That'd be okay too, I guess. But I'm not sure."

"Don't you think this will prevent lying?" Why was Jeff not sure anymore?

"It does when people actually lie. But if people believe what they say—how do you ferret out what's right, then? And there's always the case of people lying to themselves. As a species, we're very good at that."

She saw what he meant. "I lied to myself for days about whether I was in love with you."

"And we kept where we were from the senator by touching," Jeff mused.

"But neither lie lasted very long."

"I guess we'll figure it out as we go along." His eyes crinkled at her. He was enjoying a future that had lots of possibility for a change.

He was back to jeans and plaid shirts again. She liked it that way. She liked the way he smelled, too. She sort of liked everything about him, even the thoughts he was having about her right now.

"*I* like the way you've taken to thinking about yourself as Holly. I think of you that way."

She considered that. "Yeah. Maybe Holland was always the imposter. I was Holly."

"You're not talking all that formal shrink shit either. You actually say 'yeah,' and 'not good.'"

"I always did, inside." She took his head between her hands and looked into his one good green eye. "The future is still a little scary."

"More than a little," he admitted. He must know he couldn't hide behind false bravado anymore. Not with her. "The unknown is always scary. There's already violence between the generations in China. We've got to stave that off, somehow. But . . . I get such a good feeling about the . . . I don't know . . . the wholeness of all of us. It's powerful. If we can just hold on to that . . ."

"We've come so far so fast," Holland reflected. She watched the hand that represented touch moving through his hair. It was her fear that had made it evil. She let the hand feel the wavy strands against her palm. "First it was noise, then voices, then we got the quiet when we touched, then after we had sex, boy, everything cut loose and we could hear regular people around us."

"And then we grew it even further, and we could send . . ." He got a wicked gleam in his eye. "How far do you think we could take that?"

She pursed her lips in mock disgust. "I think we're pretty much maxed."

"You never know," he warned, all innocence on the surface. Indigo streaks shot through the magenta of his aura. "We should experiment, don't you think?"

"Never, *never* say the word experiment again to me, Jeff McQueen."

"What words can I say?" But he didn't seem bent on saying anything at all. His lips made their way from the hollow in her throat to her chin. *Gorgeous? Lovely, sexual creature?*

She bent her head, her own lips finding his. *How about 'joining,' 'complete,' 'soul mates?'*

He pulled her to him and tightened his embrace until her breath came in pants. *Those, too. Are you happy?*

Yes. And it was true. In spite of the uncertainty, in spite of all she'd lost and the difficulty inherent in what she'd gained, it was true. She stood and drew him up with the hand that understood touch and wasn't evil after all, and she dragged him, laughing, to the bedroom of the suite, making sure she kept contact so the other millions couldn't hear them. *I've always wanted to make love to a pirate.*

SUSAN SQUIRES
BODY ELECTRIC

Victoria Barnhardt sets out to create something brilliant; she succeeds beyond her wildest dreams. With one keystroke her program spirals out of control . . . and something is born that defies possibility: a being who calls to her.

He speaks from within a prison—seeking escape, seeking *her*. He is a miracle that Vic never intended. More than a scientific discovery, or a brilliant coup by an infamous hacker, he is life. He is beauty. And he needs to be released. Just as Victoria does. Though the shadows of the past might rise against them, on one starry Los Angeles night, in each other's arms, the pair will find a way to have each other and freedom both.
